"Come on, you bastards. Don't be bashful."

He crouched low and braced his arm so that he could fire on them the moment they entered. A hand touched his shoulder.

He whirled, expecting it to be one of the Enforcers.

It wasn't. Instead, he saw a beautiful angel who had blood and dirt smeared across her dark skin. Her hair was a tangled mess and there was a determination in her eyes that said she wasn't about to be argued with.

"I can't leave you here, Caillen. We got into this together. Together we'll get out of it or die."

He was stunned by Desideria's heartfelt words. "What about your mom?"

"Your friend knows about her and I'd be dead if not for you. Now move it before *I* shoot you."

He scoffed at her order. "You're an idiot."

"Apparently so." She pulled his arm around her shoulders and helped him move through the dark, vacant building. "Any bright ideas for an escape?"

born of shadows

SHERRILYN KENYON

GRAND CENTRAL
PUBLISHING

NEW YORK   BOSTON

This book is a work of fiction. Names, characters, places, and incidents are the product of the author's imagination or are used fictitiously. Any resemblance to actual events, locales, or persons, living or dead, is coincidental.

Copyright © 2011 by Sherrilyn Kenyon
Excerpt from *Born of Silence* copyright © 2012 by Sherrilyn Kenyon
All rights reserved. Except as permitted under the U.S. Copyright Act of 1976, no part of this publication may be reproduced, distributed, or transmitted in any form or by any means, or stored in a database or retrieval system, without the prior written permission of the publisher.

Grand Central Publishing
Hachette Book Group
237 Park Avenue
New York, NY 10017
Visit our website at www.HachetteBookGroup.com

Grand Central Publishing is a division of Hachette Book Group, Inc. The Grand Central Publishing name and logo is a trademark of Hachette Book Group, Inc.

The publisher is not responsible for websites (or their content) that are not owned by the publisher.

Printed in the United States of America

Originally published in hardcover by Hachette Book Group
First mass market edition: January 2012

10 9 8 7 6 5 4 3 2 1

As always for my boys and husband and to you the reader for taking another journey with me into another universe.

PROLOGUE

"Watch out!"

Caillen Dagan barely got out of the way before three blaster shots whizzed past his head. His heart thumped wildly as he realized he and his father were trapped by what they assumed were loaners out to collect money. It wasn't the first time his father's debts had caused them to be chased. The men after them seemed to be everywhere. And they seemed to be multiplying...

Terror made his breathing ragged as tears welled in his young eyes.

What are we going to do?

His dad grabbed him by the front of his shirt and hauled him into the shadows to crouch down behind him.

Caillen looked around, his entire body shaking as he tried to find an escape for them. There didn't seem to be one, but he had faith. No one was better at getting through tough situations than his dad.

His father shook him roughly to get his attention.

"Listen to me, boy. I need you to take care of your sisters. You hear me?"

Even though he was the youngest of the Dagan children and only eight years old, it was something his dad always said to him. "Yeah, I know."

"No, Cai, you don't. You're too young to comprehend what I'm trying to tell you, but you have to try." There was a sadness in his father's eyes that scared him. A resignation that had never been there before and it made him want to cry. But Dagans didn't cry and he wasn't about to let his dad see him act like one of his sisters.

His father cupped his face in his calloused palm. "It'll be years before you understand what's happening—if even then. But I need you to listen to me and trust me. I won't be here to protect you anymore."

Caillen frowned. "What are you talking about?"

"Listen! Don't speak. We only have a few more seconds. What I need is for you to make sure that you never get into any system for any government for any reason. Keep a low profile. Live off-grid. Don't let anyone have a way to track you. Ever. Not your address. Your likeness. Nothing. Especially not your retina, fingerprints or DNA."

His father's insistence scared him almost as much as the men with blasters looking for them. "Why?"

"They'll kill you. You understand? Governments use that to track people and they will hurt you if they find you."

Those words terrified him even more. "Who will hurt me?"

"My enemies. They'll come for you too. It's why I've never treated you like a kid and why I've made you train so hard. I knew this day would come, but I'd hoped it wouldn't be until you were older. Unfortunately they've found me. Just take what I've taught you and use it to stay alive. I need you to live, Cai. For me. I've risked everything to keep you breathing. Don't let it be for nothing. Not after all I sacrificed for you. I know I did the right thing. I know it. Now run home. Let no one follow you and keep your sisters safe. Okay? I know it's a lot of responsibility for a little boy, but I have faith in you."

"Dad—"

"Just do it, Cai." His dad pulled him tightly to his chest and held him close. "I love you, boy. You've been a good son. Better than I ever deserved. Watch over your sisters, especially Shahara. She'd be lost without you. You're the only one she'll have to depend on now." He kissed Caillen on the head before he released him. He pulled out his wallet and handed it to him. "There's enough money in there to bribe the doctors. Tell them to say I died of pneumonia."

"I don't understand."

"I know, son. Just do exactly what I tell you. Okay? If anyone thinks I died of anything other than a natural cause, they'll come for your sisters and hurt them. You can't let that happen. Remember. Pneumonia. You have to keep my face off the news."

Caillen hated the tears that started falling. He wiped them away with the dirty sleeve of his shirt. His father was right, he didn't understand any of this, but he would obey. "Okay."

His father kissed him again. "Now scurry like I showed you."

"But—"

"Don't argue!" His voice shook as tears gathered in his eyes too. "Just stay alive, Caillen."

Caillen nodded before he darted into a hole in the side of the building to their right. He'd just stood up to run when he heard voices that made him stop and listen.

"Dagan...you treacherous bastard. Where's the money?"

"I never got the money."

A blaster shot echoed.

Caillen heard his father cry out. Even though he'd promised not to stay, he crept back toward the hole in the wall to see his father on the ground, cursing the man who'd shot him as he tried to crawl away.

There was a group of men and women behind him who watched with an apathy that was sickening.

The man kicked his father over and held him in place with one foot planted solidly against his father's bleeding chest. He angled the blaster at his heart. "You're a crafty bastard. I'll give you that. Spent six years of my life trying to find you. Now tell me what you did with our package."

"I don't know. It got away from me...It-it vanished. I didn't get the money for it. Someone else took it. I swear to you. Please...I have little girls who—"

The man killed him.

Caillen clapped his hand over his mouth to keep from screaming out as pain racked him.

His father was dead.

Dead.

Just like his mother.

Tears fell down his face as he wished he was big enough to go out there and kill the ones who'd taken his father from him. But he knew he couldn't fight them. He was just a kid. And if he tried, his sisters would be alone without a man to watch over them.

"Protect my girls for me ..."

He'd promised his dad and he wasn't about to let him down.

"That was stupid." A woman moved forward to glare at the man as he holstered his weapon and wiped the blood on his shoes against his father's pants. The others withdrew, leaving just the two of them to spit on his father's remains. "You should have made sure he wasn't lying before you killed him."

"I doubt he has the money. You saw his ship. He doesn't live like someone who stole ten million credits."

She sighed. "That wasn't the most important part of this and you know it. If—"

"Even if the package escaped him, it won't last long on the street. Trust me. We eat our young out here. I doubt it's even around now. Garbage always burns."

A clap of thunder sounded an instant before the rain that had been threatening to fall all day poured down over them. The man and woman ran off toward the street to seek shelter.

Caillen didn't move. Not for a long time as he sat there, staring at his father's lifeless body while the rain pelted it and made the ground run red from his blood.

What were he and his sisters going to do now? They were just kids ...

He tightened his grip on the wallet. *I will do what Dad said.* Even though he didn't understand the reasons behind his orders. It was to protect his sisters. That was good enough for him. He just hoped Shahara never found out that he'd used money to bribe a doctor 'cause she'd be really mad at the waste when they had so little.

He sniffed back his tears. *I'm the man of the house. There was no one else . . .*

"I'll keep them safe, Daddy."

His only question though was who would watch after *him*?

1

"Thank the gods you're here. I've been running arou—"

Without flinching or breaking his stride as he walked down a filthy, dark alley, Caillen jerked his blaster out and fired straight into his sister's shoulder, cutting her words off before she wasted his time.

Not to kill or hurt her. Just to shut her up before she made things worse for both of them.

Right now, he didn't have time to listen to her bullshit. He was here to save her life.

And hopefully his too.

Gasping, she crumpled toward the trash-laden street. In one smooth move that caused his light-armored brown coat to flare out around his feet, he caught her against him and lifted her into his arms. He groaned under her weight. "Damn, Kase, quit working out so much and lay off the frigs. I've carried men who weighed less." Not that he made a habit out of carrying men, but still . . .

Even though she was six inches shorter, she outweighed him by a good twenty pounds and *he* carried less
than two percent body fat on a lean six-foot-four frame.
His muscles screamed out in protest of his heroics as he
heard the Enforcers moving in.

This was getting bad.

He glared down at her unconscious body while her
brown hair spilled over his sleeve. Her plain features
were so peaceful in spite of the hell she'd unleashed that it
really made him want to hurt her.

But he couldn't do that.

Blood was blood.

Sighing, he moved fast to stash her behind a Dump-
ster and to cover her with his coat. On top of that, he
added enough trash to keep the Enforcers from seeing
her. Yeah, she'd bitch-slap him later for the stench...and
the headache his stun blast would leave her with but it
would keep her safe and right now that was all that mattered to him.

Well, there was the urge he had to wring her neck until
she turned blue—that mattered to him too, but that could
wait.

A beep from his wrist alerted him that his hacked
paperwork for her ship and cargo had gone through. Kas-
en's IDs were removed from everything and his were reg-
istered in her place.

I'm a fucking idiot. By doing all of this, he'd just put
his neck in a noose and he knew it.

What the hell? *Who wants to live forever?*

For the record and in case any higher deity was listening and taking notes, *he* did. But he was definitely going
to cut his life short if he kept rescuing his sisters. Or at

the very least cut his freedom down to the size of a ten-square-foot cell.

Yeah well, at least then I'd get three meals a day instead of six a week.

Pushing that thought away, he pulled his blasters out and set them to stun to do what he did best.

Survive and escape.

"Drop your weapon!" an Enforcer shouted from his left.

Yeah, right. Like he'd ever followed orders. Caillen opened fire as he dodged into a vacant alley that was as run down as the one he'd stashed Kasen in. Their return fire and the holes it left in the walls, street and trash around him let him know fast their blasters weren't set for stun.

They were trying to kill him.

He considered resetting his to return the favor, but he didn't want to kill the drones out to make rent. They didn't deserve to die for supporting a corrupt system. Even the mindless needed to eat and it took more guts than most people had to stand and fight against the League and its sycophantic governments. He wouldn't hold their cowardice against them.

Much.

Jerking his head to the right, he felt the heat from a blast that narrowly missed his face. Strangely enough, he was completely calm as he fought. His sister Shahara called him Eritale—a Gondarion term that meant made of ice. And he was. Since the day he'd seen his father killed, he'd never panicked again in a confrontation.

No idea why. It was like the fear inside him had shattered that day and left something freakishly copacetic in its place, something that set in during a fight and left him totally rational.

He shot at three Enforcers before he holstered his right blaster and launched a grappling hook to the roof of a decaying building. The further he could get them from his sister the less likely they were to find her unconscious body and question her.

The hook caught and set.

Caillen pushed the recoil button on the hook's handle and fired at the Enforcers with his left hand as he sped toward the roof. Return blasts came close to him, but none hit the mark as he quickly zigzagged up the chipped brick wall to the top. Thankfully none of the drones were bright enough to shoot his cord—that would have left an ugly stain on the street and ruined his already screwed up day.

At the top, he scrambled over the lip, dislodged the hook, recoiled it completely, then took off running toward the river across the roofs, jumping from one to another with the grace and flexibility of a gymnast—something he trained hard every day to maintain.

The deep whirring of an engine overhead let him know air support was on its way and it was coming in low and fast. From his vantage point, he could see the number of Enforcers after him. And it was impressive. They ran on the streets below and across the rooftops, all trying to get a shot at him.

What? Was it a slow day? Didn't this place have any real criminals?

No, let's go after the smugglers 'cause they were so much more dangerous than, say, a rapist or murderer.

"What the hell was in your ship, Kase?"

He should have checked the manifest because this was looking bad.

Real bad.

More shots rained down as the airlift spotted him and came in as fast as it could fly. Damn the bright daylight of a double sun. It left him totally exposed without a single dark shadow to crawl into.

Ducking the door gunner's shots, he took off at a dead run as he dodged fire.

Caillen jumped to a roof and rolled to his feet an instant before the door opened and six Enforcers spilled through, aiming and firing at him. He turned to go back, but there were more coming in behind. The gunship was on his right and about to pin him into one seriously nasty situation. Dodging left, he sucked his breath in at the distance to the next rooftop. If he missed that, it was going to hurt.

Who wants to live forever?

Ignoring his favorite motto whenever a dose of extreme stupidity was called for, he pulled his javelin off his belt and extended it so that he could use it to pole-vault over. He held his breath as he soared over the street so far below.

Thankfully years of dodging authority and living his life one half step this side of death had left him with enough skill to make it to the other side. As soon as he was safe on the rooftop, he collapsed the javelin and kept going as shots whizzed past him. Several grazed off his armored shirt and backpack, and would have brought him down but for their protection. Still, it stung like hell and a couple burned his arm.

You know, a sane man would be wetting his pants.

Good thing he was crazy as hell.

He ran to the ledge and in a well-practiced move, planted the hook into the wall. Without pausing, he jumped over the side and rappelled down to the street where he'd have some cover. He jerked the hook free and let it recoil back into the case on his forearm.

At least the city was more crowded here.

Yeah, but it's hard to melt into them while your coat's lying on top of your sister.

True. Without its camouflage, his weapons were out and visible. Something that caused the people around him to cringe, scream and flee as they saw his short-sleeved armored shirt that was covered with light bombs, ammunition clips, four blasters (in addition to the one in his hand), his rappelling gear and all the other "just in case" things he carried in addition to his backpack. Leather straps crisscrossed both of his arms from wrist to biceps.

Badass came at a price and today that price just might be his freedom.

Or his life.

He ran with the crowd which panicked the innocent people even more—no doubt because they were afraid he'd take one of them hostage.

As if. The only life he gambled with was his own.

The Enforcers flanked them, trying to get an aim on his head which he kept low. He could hear from the earwig he had tuned to their frequency that they were setting up blockades around the city.

But that wasn't what concerned him...

They had a Trisani tracker with them that they were about to drop in on the chase.

Damn.

Unless it was Nero, he was a dead man. Trisani had psychic powers that pretty much no one except another Trisani could fight. Nero could actually get into someone's head, shut down all brain activity and, if he was really pissed, melt it and leave his vic a vegetable, sucking his thumb on the floor.

Luckily, Nero was one of Caillen's few friends and no matter what they might have paid him, Nero wouldn't bring him in.

He hoped.

Every life has a price...

And he knew that better than most.

Caillen felt the fissure of power as the Trisani stepped out of a transport and eyed the crowd, reading them as he sought Caillen's position.

Yeah it wasn't Nero...He'd never seen this tracker before.

Shit.

Caillen slowed as he saw the dark blond man with sharp features dressed all in black. Curling his lip as he locked gazes with Caillen, the tracker sent a plasma blast at him that barely missed his head. It ignited then exploded the transport behind him.

Hope no one was in that. Otherwise they were having a worse day than he was.

Caillen pulled out another blaster and opened both up all over the tracker. But the bastard threw up a force field to block it.

"I hate the Trisani." No wonder most of them had been hunted down to a small handful. At the moment, he'd like to add one more to their extinction list.

But that was all right—he still had tricks up his

sleeves. Literally. He holstered his right blaster and jerked a light bomb off the chain. He lobbed it at the Trisani and then followed it with a pulse grenade.

The light temporarily blinded the Trisani and the pulse exploded against the force field. Even though it didn't break through it, it was enough to send the Trisani reeling backward.

Yeah, don't screw with someone whose closest friend was an explosives engineer renowned for making the best toys in the universe. Darling lived and breathed for one purpose only. Making shit blow up.

Before the Trisani could recover, Caillen ducked into the next alley.

Which was crawling with Enforcers.

Damn. Damn.

Double damn.

Grinding his teeth in frustration, he turned to head back to the street.

He couldn't. They'd closed in on him and the air transport was directly above with snipers taking positions on the building's roof.

"Surrender!"

Ah now this was just galling.

"Lay down your weapons!"

That was easier said than done. He was covered in them. Took him two hours to get all this gear on...

Only thing that could induce him to take it off fast was a hot naked woman in his bed, clawing at his back. Definitely not one of those here and he had no interest in being defenseless with this much artillery pointed at him.

A warning blast shot over his head.

"The next one will be right between your eyes."

Targeting lasers let him know exactly what they were aiming for. Honestly it wasn't the one at his forehead that gave him pause as much as the one at his crotch.

"Put your hands behind your head!"

Caillen frowned. "If I put my hands behind my head, I can't drop my weapons, people. Someone needs to make up their mind here. What do you want me to do and in what order?"

"Drop the weapon in your hand, then put your hands behind your head!"

He did as instructed.

They moved in closer.

Yeah, come to Papa, baby. Closer... closer...
Don't be shy.

When one of them went to cuff him, Caillen grabbed him and used him as a shield. Three sniper rounds went into the man's chest. Caillen flung the body at the Enforcer coming in at his back. Twisting, he grabbed another man, disarmed him and knocked him flying. His morals on killing drones out the window under this assault, Caillen used his spring loader to pop his fighting knife into his palm and took out five more before the Trisani grabbed him by the neck without touching him and paralyzed him where he stood.

The Trisani tsked at him. "I almost hate to hand someone with your skills over to the drones."

"Fuck you."

The Trisani laughed. "Sorry. In this, the only one getting screwed is you."

Caillen locked gazes with the Trisani. The moment he did, he felt the surge of power that Nero had taught him. It was the only weapon anyone could really use against the

Trisani species—unless this guy was as strong as Nero this would work.

Here's hoping he's not.

He focused it with everything he had. One second the Trisani had him, the next, Caillen was free and slamming the Enforcers into each other. He shot his cord up the wall and started to leave them in his wake...until he heard something in his ear that gave him pause.

"There's an unconscious woman here in the street, under some garbage. Not sure if she's with our perp or not. But she is covered up by what appears to be a man's coat."

Fu-fu-frick.

They'd found Kasen. If he escaped, they'd take her in and she'd never stand up to their questioning. She was the kind who spilled more guts than a butcher.

Of all the flying-ass bad luck.

Caillen sighed as he flicked his wrist to miss the shot and allowed the hook to fall back to the pavement. He let them think they'd done it when the truth burned deep inside him. But for Kasen's discovery, he'd have made it out.

They cuffed his hands, then carefully disarmed him over the next twenty-eight minutes.

"Damn, boy," one of the officers said as they continued to find weapons hidden on him. "It's like disarming an assassin. You sure you ain't in the League?"

He had to force himself not to lash out and escape again. Submission was not in his nature.

Think of Kasen...

Yeah, what he was really thinking about her was how badly he wanted to beat her.

The Enforcer jerked his cuffed hands. "Who's with you?"

Caillen met the Enforcer's gaze without flinching or hesitating. "No one. I fly alone. Check the logs." Thank the gods he was good at what he did. They wouldn't find a trace of anyone except him.

"What about the woman?"

"Nameless vic. I stole her wallet. You check my pocket, you'll find it." He always had a fake ID and wallet for his sisters with aliases.

Just in case.

The Enforcer pulled it out, then lifted his arm to speak into the mic in his cuff. "She's innocent. Get her to a hospital."

"You want me to take a report from her?" the voice asked.

"No. We have a confession and mugging is the least of what we're taking him in for. Just dump her and go."

Caillen met the Trisani's frown. The bastard either suspected he was lying or knew it for a fact, but for whatever reason, he kept it to himself.

End of the day, the Trisani was definitely right about one thing. He was royally screwed and they hadn't even fondled him yet.

That was bad enough.

Worse than bad came as they were hauling him toward the transport and they began reading him his charges.

"...and for smuggling prillion."

He felt his stomach shrink. Shit.

His sister's contraband carried a death sentence...

2

Three Weeks Later

How bad would decapitation hurt?

From the window of his pathetically small, sparse cell that barely accommodated a bunk, sink and toilet, Caillen stared out across the yard teeming with people, at the heavy electronic blade that was being charged and sharpened in preparation for his execution.

Yeah, that was definitely going to leave a mark.

Don't worry, Cai. In just a few more measly minutes your problems will be over.

Forever.

His neck tingled in expectation of the coming blow, which would end a life that really hadn't been all that great. Strange thing though, bad as it was, he wasn't ready for it to be over. Not by a long shot.

I could have been something.

Ah hell, who was he fooling? He was a third-generation

smuggler with a gambling problem his family knew nothing about...

Yeah? So what? He was still the best damned pilot in all the United Systems. There was nothing he couldn't fly and no one he couldn't outmaneuver when he was in a ship.

He never missed a target. Ever.

None of that matters now. Not while he was standing toe to toe with death.

What a way for a warrior to go...

Forget a last meal, what he really wanted before he checked out was a good lay. One last bang to end all others.

He laughed evilly under his breath as he remembered the look of dumbfounded shock on the warden's face when they'd asked him for his last request.

"Any of your daughters horny?"

That had been answered with a vicious head slam to the wall. Not that he wouldn't have done the same, or more to the point, worse, had someone asked *him* that about one of his sisters. But...

He was ever a thorn in the ass of those he hated and that was basically anyone who had any kind of authority.

Yeah well, that's about to end too.

He sighed as he stared through the small open window covered in bars, watching the soldiers outside rush around in last-minute prep. There was a part of him terrified about dying. Okay, there was a lot of him terrified about dying. He'd always hoped it would be when he was really old and in his sleep. But practically speaking, the alternative druther would have been in a brutal fight where he took out as many of his enemies with him as he could.

At least you're not dying alone in the gutter.

He flinched at a memory he always did his best not to

think about. If he lived a thousand years he'd never forget watching his father die alone like he was nothing but trash. And in all the morbid scenarios he'd conjured over the years for his own death never had execution entered his mind.

Even now he could hear his sister's desperate call. "Cai, I'm in the Garvon sector and running from their Enforcers. Can you help me?"

Kasen had omitted the fact she was transporting prillion—an antibiotic so potent it was outlawed by every government that took payoffs from the medical communities who feared the dent it would put into their profit margins. But to smugglers like him and his sister, it was pay dirt. One shipment would leave you flush for at least a year.

And it was a death sentence to carry it through certain systems.

Garvon happened to be one of them.

Even if she'd told him when she called what she had on board, it would have changed nothing. He'd have still taken her place in the noose.

Altruism sucks.

Right now he was thinking he should have learned some self-preservation and been about ten minutes late. But at the end of the day, his sisters were his world and even though he might like to pretend otherwise, he wouldn't have been able to live had he let one of them die.

Even Kasen's crabby ass.

He checked his chronometer and felt sick again. Thirty more minutes and everything was over.

Thirty minutes.

He remembered times in the past when that had seemed like an eternity and now...

He wished he had the power to stop time. To teleport himself out of here and see his rat-infested dive one more time. To have his sister Shahara tell him he was an idiot.

Well, at least he wouldn't have to stare at the drab tan walls and that nasty crusted-over toilet anymore.

Boy, are my creditors going to be pissed. He still owed two years of payments on his ship that had been impounded by the Garvons after his arrest. And face it, he'd dogged the absolute shit out of it and it still had blast marks down both rear stabilizers from his last run-in with the authorities.

He sighed again.

His friends and family had tried everything to negotiate a stay of execution. But the Garvon governor had been adamant that they make an example of him.

"This is to stand as a lesson to any outsider who thinks they can travel through our system and not obey our laws. We might be a small system, but we are big on intolerance."

Caillen shook his head as the governor reiterated those words he was obviously proud of just a few feet away from his window to the news crews surrounding him. What an effing idiot. Whatever aide was supposed to keep the governor on a leash was failing epically.

One of the female reporters panned her camera Caillen's way to catch a shot of his reaction to the governor's speech while he watched from his cell.

Caillen flipped the camera off.

The governor sputtered in indignation, letting Caillen know he'd struck a nerve with his silent defiance.

Big mistake on the governor's part. That was like baiting a wild predator and the little brother in him kicked into overdrive.

Never let me see your underbelly.

Flashing a wicked grin, Caillen couldn't resist shouting to them. "It's not my friends in high places you need to worry about, Gov. It's the low ones who are going to crawl up from the sewers to cut your throat. You know, my brother assassins who'll be honor bound to come after you and the rest of your sycophantic morons while you sleep. Forever Sentella! We're cleaning the gene pool one fatality at a time."

The mention of the phantom rogue agency of assassins out to challenge the corrupt governments that were led by the League and her goons sent the media into a frenzy and made the governor look around as if trying to find an assassin in the crowd. Like he'd be able to ID one. Beautiful thing about Caillen's friends—by the time you saw them coming for you, your head was already rolling across the floor.

But as much as Caillen wanted to pretend otherwise, he knew his friends couldn't help him today. He'd gotten himself into this and for once there was no escape.

I'm dead. Completely. Utterly...

Painfully.

Twenty minutes and counting...

Might as well accept it. It was what it was and he'd volunteered for it.

"*I'm so sorry, Cai.*" Kasen's tear-filled words whispered through his mind from her last visit.

Not half as sorry as I am. Darling always said his sisters would be the death of him. Little bugger had been right.

C'mon. Better you than her. You know that.

Yeah, that thought not really comforting right now. *I should have drowned her when she broke my favorite toy fighter as a kid.* It'd been the only toy he'd had and she'd stomped it into pieces in a fit of anger because he'd stuck his tongue out at her.

It's all right, Cai. Calm down. You've faced worse.

Yeah, but I didn't die *then.*

There was that and he was getting tired of his brain bitching at him over things he couldn't change. He'd kept his promise to his dad. Kasen was safe.

Him, not so much.

Sliding down the wall to crouch in the small space between it and his bunk, Caillen banged his head against the wall, welcoming the distracting pain. Why couldn't the bastards just come and kill him already? The waiting was the worst part. No doubt that was their intention. Make it as miserable as possible.

Closing his eyes, he rubbed his hand over his face. At least he wasn't leaving Shahara in a bind. Now that she was married, she had someone else who could protect and take care of her.

Which was what really pissed him off at Kasen. There'd been no sense in her making that run. Yes, money was good. But it wasn't worth your life and it wasn't like they were in dire straits for it. Not like they'd been in the past. Their freakishly rich brother-in-law would have gladly given her the money had she only asked Syn for it.

Stupid moronic idiot.

Selfish—

"You ready, convict?"

He dropped his hand and opened his eyes to see the warden in front of his cell with six guards. He was flattered they thought he'd be that much trouble. And his spirit was certainly willing to give them a fight and then some. However, they had a neuroinhibitor on him that prevented him from doing anything other than glaring at them. If he tried to attack, the inhibitors would bite down, flood his body with pain, lock his muscles tight and send him straight to the floor.

Worst of all, it'd make him piss his pants.

They would never have *that* satisfaction—not until he was dead and couldn't control his bladder anymore. After all, he was a Dagan and Dagans, no matter the poverty or situation, were proud people.

Show no fear to your enemies. Only contempt. Never let anyone look down on you. You're just as good as any of them. I don't care who they are. Better in fact. In our world, Dagans are royalty and you, my son, are a prince.

His father had trained him on that and he held those words tight as he faced them.

Activating the electromagnets in his cuffs that caused his hands to lock together behind his back, the guards lowered the force field that kept him inside his cell.

Caillen curled his lip as he looked at them. "You could have waited until I stood up, guys. Kind of hard now."

The warden returned his smug glare with one of his own. "We'll wait."

He snorted. Were they really that afraid of him that he couldn't even stand up without them sweating?

Wow, Cai, even a hard-ass assassin like Nykyrian would be impressed with that feat.

Then again, they had good reason to fear. But for the inhibitor, he'd already be free and they'd all be bleeding or dead.

But not today.

Caillen leaned his back against the wall and wiggled his shoulders until he made it to his feet. The guards moved forward with trilassos—a noose attached to the end of a three-foot pole—to put around his neck so that they could drag him forward and keep him six feet away from them.

He laughed at them and their fear. "Bloody wankers."

They tightened the noose around his neck until he was coughing from lack of oxygen.

"Careful, men. We don't want to kill him in here."

The warden might feel that way, but the look on the guards' faces said they'd be more than happy to send him to death fifteen minutes early.

Caillen wheezed and coughed as they dragged him down the lackluster hallway and out into the common ground where spectators, dignitaries and newspeople waited to catch a glimpse of the legendary smuggler who, until now, had been more myth than real. The networks would make a fortune charging for this show.

Ironic really. He'd had to fight every minute of his life to scrape together two credits, but his death would make some asshole a nice rent payment for a few months.

I should have taken them up on the offer for a tranq. 'Cause right now as he walked up the platform and neared that gleaming blade, his panic was seriously setting in.

Ignore it.

How? Look around you, moron. You're about to die. And there was at least a hundred people here to witness and gloat. Damn them all for their sadistic entertainment.

Don't think about it.

Something hard to do since he was being forced to kneel under a ten-foot blade that was shining with metallic bloodlust over his head.

You can do this . . .

I don't want to die. I don't. I need to live. I got plans.

Well, not really, but I could make some. Some that don't include my head rolling into a plastic bucket that still bears stains from the last execution.

He ground his teeth together to keep from begging for his life. He wouldn't give them that satisfaction either.

"Any last words?"

Caillen glared at the warden. "Yeah…See you in hell." He looked over to the group of three giggling young women standing in the dignitary section. One of them bore a striking resemblance to the warden. "And for the record…your daughter has a hot ass."

She let out an excited shriek.

The warden's face flushed with rage.

The guards tightened the noose again, choking off the rest of his words.

Caillen's sight dimmed as his ears buzzed. Oh yeah, much better to strangle to death.

Not.

They forced him to his knees, then bent his head down on the arc that had been designed to cradle necks and hold them in place until the blade fell. Still, he choked as the guards refused to loosen the noose. He heard something loud, like maybe someone shouting, but he couldn't tell what it was or where it came from.

It was almost over.

A few seconds more.

Just let go.

Relax…

He was too much of a fighter for that. He tried to hang on to every gasping, ragged pain-filled breath. But the fight was useless as he heard a loud clattering sound.

In the end, the darkness took him under.

3

Caillen came awake to a vicious pain throbbing in his throat and a worse one pounding in his head. Yeah, he was in hell. He had to be to hurt this badly.

"Is he coming around?"

He didn't recognize the concerned tone that belonged to an older man.

Someone pried open his eyelid and rudely flashed a light in his eye that made his headache pound even harder. Groaning, he flinched, moving his head away.

Gently, the doctor turned his head back and held it in place while he continued to test the dilation of his eye. Good thing Caillen's arms were strapped down or the man would be bleeding over the intrusion and that light would be shining out of an orifice the gods had never meant to hold it.

"He's conscious." The doctor lowered his voice as he stepped back from the bed and gave Caillen a reprieve from that vicious light. "Do you know who you are, son?"

He licked his dry lips and cleared his sore throat

before he answered raggedly. "Caillen. Dagan." Or rather that was who he'd been before they beheaded him.

Did the keepers of hell not know who was sent to them?

"How many fingers am I holding up?"

Caillen had to blink several times before the doctor's pudgy phalanges came into focus. At least he hoped that's what he was seeing...

If not, that man was real popular with women.

"Three."

The doctor turned to his right and bowed low. "He's awake and alert. But he's still weak from the asphyxiation and the subsequent resuscitation."

Resuscitation? From beheading? What the hell had they done to him and why would they bring him back?

More torture?

Gah, what did I do now?

Oh wait, that was too much to count. The point was what had they *caught* him doing now...

Caillen scowled as an older man stepped out of the shadows and approached his bed. Clean-shaven and well-kempt, he had finely boned features and vivid blue eyes. There was an air of refinement that seemed to emanate straight from the man's DNA. Yeah, he was definitely an aristo. A major one at that.

Why would someone so high ranking be here to see a common piece of condemned filth?

The man's lips trembled as his eyes misted—that concerned Caillen more than anything else. Was the man that angry or that upset?

Oh shit, don't tell me I slept with his wife.

Or worse, his daughter.

The other thing Darling always complained about was that one day Caillen's wandering penis was going to get him killed…

Was this the day?

"Do you remember me?" the man asked hesitantly. "Even a little?"

Did he owe him money? Caillen searched his mind, but couldn't think of any time or place he'd have seen this man. "Uh…no. Should I?"

The old man's lips quivered as he took Caillen's hand that was bound in a padded leather cuff to the bed rail and held it in a cold grasp.

Completely weirded out by that, Caillen jerked his hand away from his grasp and balled it into a fist. But because of the restraints, he couldn't move it far.

"You're my son, Radek. Don't you remember?"

Oh yeah. The man was high. He had to be sucking in some kind of serious fumes for that delusion. "I'm Caillen Dagan. My father was a smuggler."

"No." There was no missing the anger underlying his defensive tone. "You are Kaden Radek Aluzahn de Orczy," he carefully enunciated each name as if trying to impress it on Caillen, "and you are *my* son. You were only a toddler when you were kidnapped. I paid the ransom they demanded. All of it. I followed every stipulation they made but they never returned you. My security detail assumed they'd killed you. Even so, I searched relentlessly for some sign of you for years. Nothing was ever found. Not a single trace…Not until now."

Baffled, Caillen turned to the doctor. "Bullshit."

The doctor shook his head. "You're a lucky man. When the prison staff ran your DNA to see if you were a match for any unsolved crimes, it popped up your old kidnapping report and the DNA that was on file from your childhood hairs they'd collected. You are indeed his missing son."

No, no, no, no, no.

"I came as soon as they notified me they'd found you," the man interjected.

The doctor inclined his head respectfully before he continued. "His Majesty arrived right before they issued the order to behead you. One more second and it would have been too late."

Majesty... That title permeated the fog in Caillen's mind. If this guy was an emperor and he was his son...

That would make him a...

Oh yeah, right. They were so screwing with him. This was complete and utter crap. "I'm not a prince." No krikkin way. Fate would not be that bored today.

Nah, this was some shit one of his friends was pulling. "Who put you up to this? Nykyrian or Darling?"

The doctor smiled. "You are indeed a prince, Your Highness. We double-checked your DNA against your father's when you were brought in and there is no doubt whatsoever. You are Emperor Evzen's son. His *only* son."

Caillen's mind reeled. He might not recognize the man, but he knew the name Reginahn Evzen Tyralehn de Orczy. Emperor to both the Garvon and Exeter systems, his name was synonymous with power and wealth.

Was it really possible?

No. No way. His sisters and parents had always said he was family. If he'd been a foundling, wouldn't they have told him? Given how poor they were why would his father take in another mouth to—

"You are the son I always dreamed of. I'm so glad to have you as part of my family…" His father's often uttered words now took on a whole new meaning. All his life he'd assumed his dad was grateful for the additional Y chromosome in their all-female home. But if he'd taken him in…

"I've risked everything to keep you alive. Don't let it be for nothing. Not after all I've given to keep you with us." Was that what his dad had meant when he'd said that one day Caillen would understand?

Was that why his father had been so adamant that he never disclose his DNA? Why his father had been so damn paranoid about everything? When it came to conspiracies, the man was as creative as he was psychotic. But if he'd known who Caillen really was…

It all made sense.

Caillen couldn't breathe as reality assaulted him.

Holy crap. I'm a prince.

Now ain't that a bitch? All the times in his life he'd had to scrape for every credit and here he was related to one of the richest men in the Nine Systems.

Yeah, that would be my luck.

The emperor took his hand again. "Don't you remember anything about your life before you were kidnapped?"

"No. Sorry. Are you sure you have the right person?"

He let go of Caillen's hand to pull out his wallet. He flipped it open to a picture and pressed it.

There was a beautiful woman in royal robes holding a bald baby boy who couldn't even sit up on his own. She was smiling and waving the baby's hand. "Radek… say, 'Hello, Daddy.'" But what held Caillen entranced was how much the woman favored him. They had the same coloring, the same eyes, nose and lips. Same dark hair...

Something he'd never shared with his sisters or parents. His dad had told him he took his coloring from a great-grandparent who'd died before his birth.

Now he knew that had been a major lie too. He saw his real mother's face and there was no denying it.

She was his mother.

And with that came a forgotten memory of his sister Kasen telling him once when they were kids and she'd been angry at him that he'd been found abandoned in a garbage dump. That had garnered her the worst beating of her childhood. He'd written it off as typical sibling harassment and a stressed parent's overreaction.

But if he really had been found in the garbage, that explained why his father had gone ballistic over her taunt.

Weird as it was, a lot of things he'd questioned over the years now made total sense.

Shit...

I am royalty.

Overwhelmed by his new reality, he looked up at the father he'd never met and wondered about the rest of his blood family. "That's my mother?"

His father nodded as sadness darkened his gaze. It was obvious that even after all this time, the event still hurt him. "She died trying to fight off your kidnappers. I found her in your nursery, and..." He clenched his eyes shut as if trying to blot out that memory. "I lost everything that mattered to me that day. And I do mean everything. What good is it to rule the world when you can't even protect the ones you love?"

Caillen turned his attention back to the smiling image

of the mother he'd never known—he'd been just a kid when his adoptive mother had died. Even though he'd lived with her, he barely remembered her either, and he had no memory whatsoever of the woman who'd given him life and then died trying to protect him. He didn't know which one of those scenarios saddened him most.

His father blinked back his tears and swallowed hard. "I loved your mother, Radek. She was beauty incarnate. And I've never remarried. No woman ever came close to her in any way and I didn't want to shame her memory by marrying someone else to fulfill an obligation. Even a royal one. Not when she gave her life for us." He closed the wallet and held it over his heart. "I wish she'd lived to see this moment. To see *you*. You favor her so much that it's like I have you both back at once. I can't believe I finally found you after all these years."

What should he say to that?

Thanks?

Yeah, no, that was stupid. For the first time in his life, words failed him.

It was so surreal. Things like this didn't happen to people like him. Kicks in the groin. Imprisonment. Clients turning you in to the authorities. Collectors shooting you dead in the street...that was what happened to third-generation smugglers.

They didn't wake up from an execution to become a prince. It just didn't happen.

Caillen tried to reach for the photo wallet and cursed at his bound hands. "Why am I restrained?"

The doctor came forward to free him. "Sorry, Your Highness. It was only a precaution. We didn't want you to wake up and hurt yourself."

Right...more likely they were afraid he'd wake up and attack them.

As soon as his arms were freed, Caillen rubbed his wrists and stared at his father. "This isn't some weird-ass joke or prank one of my friends is pulling on me, right?"

There was no feigning the sincere offense on his father's face or in his stance. "I would never joke about something like this."

No, he guessed not. Still, it was a hard fact to accept. Everything he thought he knew about himself was now brought into question. It was such a strange, lost feeling. Everyone he'd ever trusted had lied to him. His parents. His sisters.

He wasn't who and what he thought. Everything he'd been told about his family and his past was a lie...

Everything.

But for one freak event that'd happened at a point in his life he couldn't remember, his entire childhood and past would have been completely different. *He* would have been completely different. There would have been no poverty. No hiding.

He wouldn't have had any of his teen trauma. He wouldn't have been there to help his sisters...

It was overwhelming to contemplate that he was now someone else.

Someone he didn't know.

I have a father...

Caillen glanced to the doctor before he returned his gaze to his father's. "So what does this mean exactly?"

His father smiled. "This means you're about to have a whole new world, my boy. You're finally going to live the life you were born to."

Caillen wasn't sure that was a good thing. In his experience, change came in with a furry harbinger that usually sprayed crap all over him. Seldom was change for the better.

But at least he wasn't dead.

Yet.

One second more though, according to the doctor, and he would have been.

I'm a prince. That reality kept circling in his head.

You thought you had enemies before? Buddy, you ain't seen enemies yet. This kind of money made people stupid. Most of all, it made them mean. Angry. Jealous and cruel. Everybody wanted to take rather than earn. When they couldn't do that, they just wanted to spew venom and animosity.

Yeah, he was definitely cursed and things were going to get ugly.

Fast.

4

Two Months Later

"Sit up straight in the chair."

What am I?

Five?

Grinding his teeth to keep from lashing out, Caillen did as instructed. A little belligerently, granted, still he did obey as he'd promised his father he would. But it was hard to sit up straight when what he really wanted to do was give the pompous ass in front of him a goblet enema. He felt like he was drowning in nine million layers of heavy fabric. Honestly, how could any aristocrat be fat if they carried this much clothing weight on their bodies all the time? How much food would you have to eat to gain weight? Forget the gym, he felt like he was bench-pressing a ton.

And it wasn't even weight you could use to blow shit up. *That* he could understand hauling around. This? This was ridiculous. He rubbed at his neck where hives were forming from the high starched collar.

At least you still have your head.

Yeah, but that wasn't as appealing right now as it'd been a few months ago. He glanced over to two of his best friends who watched him and the cultural advisor with a stoicism that didn't match the amused gleam in their traitorous eyes. Little bastards were enjoying every minute of his misery.

Eat it up, assholes. My vengeance will come. And you will bleed.

But he knew the truth. He'd never hurt either of them. He'd only imagine the strangulation. They'd been through too much together for him to hold something like this against them.

Lean with dark red hair, Darling Cruel was as reserved and regal as any monarch could be which made sense since he was from one of the oldest aristocratic families. He was immaculately dressed in a black suit trimmed with white that was covered with a lightweight, flowing black dignitary robe. The son of a royal governor and a high prince himself, he was used to crap like this. Yet for all of Darling's breeding, Caillen knew the truth of his renegade friend—a rebellious side no one would ever suspect of him. Darling's shoulder-length hair covered one side of his face and hid a bad scar that Darling never spoke about. Caillen was one of the few who knew how he'd gotten it.

With perfect, unblemished features that would make any woman proud, Maris Sulle was much more flamboyant. His long black hair was tied back and braided with silver beads running through it. He wore a vibrant orange-and-yellow robe that trailed on the ground and pooled in a graceful mess around his red-booted feet. Obviously

Maris wasn't concerned about mobility 'cause he'd never had to run a day in *his* extravagant life. Rather he ordered other people to run for him.

Maris's and Darling's friendship went back to early childhood. Caillen had met Maris about five years ago and had hated him at first because of that spoiled arrogance that bled out of every gesture he made and from every piece of expensive fabric he wore. But Maris was like Gondarion spiderweed—he clung to you and after a while you learned to appreciate the strange beauty that was his quirky sense of humor and his uniquely skewed take on the world around him. Now Caillen treasured his friendship as much as he did Darling's.

The two of them were a vivid contrast to the stone-faced, drab-dressed cultural advisor—Bogimir—who glared at him with open disdain. The man didn't think much of Caillen which was okay by him. He didn't think much of Boggi either.

Bogimir cleared his throat. That sound was really starting to tread Caillen's last nerve into hash meat. "Are you paying attention to me, Your Highness?"

Caillen let out a long breath of annoyance. "Yeah, yeah, Boggi." It was a moral imperative that he use the nickname he knew drove Bogimir insane. "I'm with you."

Bogimir narrowed that beady little gaze that made Caillen want to put his foot in a highly uncomfortable place on Boggi's body. "You mean to say, yes, I see."

Caillen ground his teeth before he corrected his enunciation and words. "Yes, I see." *Asshole*.

Boggi gestured to the table. "Now take a sip of your wine."

His biceps screaming over the weight of his clothes

and his gall begging him to toss the contents into Boggi's contemptuous face, Caillen reached for the cup and picked it up.

Instantly, Boggi started that agitated dance that would only come in handy if walking barefoot on coals or trying to stomp out a nest of fire snakes. "No, no, no. The correct way to hold your goblet is like this." He snatched it from Caillen's hand to demonstrate the proper use.

Caillen rolled his eyes. Damn pathetic when even drinking something was a production. What the hell was wrong with these people? Did it really make a difference how he picked up a krikkin cup and drank out of it? Was that really all they had to worry about in their worthless, overprivileged, overindulged lives?

Boggi set the cup down and glared at him. "Try again."

Caillen curled his lip. "Ah screw this shit." Yanking his blaster out from under his robes, he shot the cup. He laughed as it spun up from the table so that he could shoot it again three more times. On the last round, it shattered and rained fragments all over the floor before the bowl landed upside down at Boggi's feet.

Now *that* was entertaining.

But Boggi didn't think so. He huffed and puffed, then scurried for the door no doubt to tell on him like one of his sisters had done when they were kids.

Whatever. With three older sisters, Caillen was used to being bitched at. And honestly, his father was an amateur compared to his sisters.

Darling didn't make a sound until they were alone with Maris. Once the room was clear, he and Maris burst out laughing. "You are evil to your worthless rotten core."

"Abso-krikkin-lutely." Caillen blew across the hot tip

of his blaster before he bent over and divested himself of the stifling clothes by twisting them off his body to land with a thump on the floor. Bare except for his black pants and boots, he holstered his weapon, then met Darling's amused expression. "How are you people sane? Really? I grieve exponentially for the childhood you must have had. *Don't touch this. Don't do that. Hold the cup like this,*" he said in a high-pitched, mocking tone as he crooked his hand into a claw. Then he dropped his voice to its usual baritone. "Never thought I'd be grateful for poverty. But you know what? I pity the rich. Y'all don't know how to live."

Darling smiled. "There's a reason I hang out with riff-raff like you."

Maris shook his head at both of them. "Your father's going to have conniptions over this."

Leave it to Maris to use a girl word like conniptions.

"Maris is right, Cai. You only have two days to master this before your debut into society. God help us all and especially you." Darling pulled his lightweight robe off and handed it to him. "Trust me, you can't be shooting defenseless goblets at the dinner table in front of emperors and governors. You could cause an interstellar incident."

Caillen snorted. "Didn't realize goblets were a protected class of species. Fine. Can I shoot tableware or is it protected too?"

Darling laughed again, but didn't respond to his sarcasm.

Caillen shrugged the robe on so that Boggi wouldn't call him a savage...again. "This"—he gestured to the ornate palace room that was bigger than most of his former apartment building—"isn't my style. I don't belong here and we all know it." He belonged on his ship, running through blockades and giving cardiac arrests to authorities. Most of all, he belonged in the bed of a woman who was more into keeping rhythm with him than not messing up her hair.

He wanted to leave this place behind and go home so badly he could taste it.

But it wasn't that simple. He actually liked his newfound father.

And worst of all, he'd made a promise to the man that he'd try this for a year before he made up his mind about leaving.

Why did I pick a krikkin year?

Much like that thirty minutes in his cell, it hadn't seemed all that long at the time. Now it stretched out into infinity and he hated it. He barely saw his father and when he did all they talked about was how unacceptable his behavior was.

Suck it up, Cai. You signed on for the mission. And he would see it through.

Even if it killed him.

"I told you, Sire. He's an animal that doesn't belong here. I realize he's your son, but honestly, you need to send him back to the gutter that created him."

Evzen shook his head at Bogimir's condemnation as he watched in front of the monitor bank in his office. Caillen laughed with his friends while he stood with his hand on the grip of his blaster as if ready to defend at a hair's notice. It was a cocky stance that belonged to a rogue outlaw. Not a prince.

But a prince he was . . .

And it was *his* job to make his son realize that destiny.

"He's not an animal, Advisor. And you would do well to remember that he is a prince of this empire and as such deserving of a deferent tone when you refer to him."

While Bogimir blanched from overstepping his position, Evzen glanced at the monitor where Caillen was still grinning with proud satisfaction over the destruction he'd wrought. He, too, was amused by his son's aim. Rude but impressive though it was. "Granted he's a little rough around the edges—"

"Sire, please... He has the manners of a ruffian and the sense—"

"He is my son." One he'd thought dead for these last long years. Dead because he'd failed to keep the boy safe.

To have his son back and alive...

It was a blessed miracle and it was one he didn't take lightly. He didn't care that his son knew nothing of the aristocracy or diplomacy.

Actually that wasn't true and he knew it. "Caillen speaks thirty-eight languages and most of the dialects of each one. Fluently. Not just tutored versions learned through instructional vids and teachers. He knows the idioms and the culture as well as the natives. He understands the intricacies of their politics and laws better than *I* do." He cast a meaningful stare at Bogimir. "Better than most cultural advisors I've known."

More than that, Caillen knew how to fight better than the top ops of his elite forces. The first day Caillen had been in the palace, he'd found twelve holes in their security and had shown them how to shore up their defenses.

His son was brilliant.

"Sire—"

"Don't." He held his hand up to cut off Bogimir's words. "You will train him and you will treat him like the prince that he is. I want no more arguments."

"Yes, Sire." Bowing, Bogimir left him.

Evzen sighed as he turned toward the mic on his desk where he'd been talking to his brother before Bogimir had interrupted them. "Did you hear all of that?"

"I did indeed."

"And what do you think?"

Talian took a minute to consider his words before he spoke. "You want my answer as your top military advisor or as your devoted brother?"

"Both."

"As your brother, I agree with you completely. Even though he's less than diplomatic, Caillen is brilliant at assessing situations and determining how to handle them—if not always at defusing them. You couldn't ask for a better successor."

"And as my advisor?"

"He's impulsive and brash with an overdriven libido that has him chasing anything with breasts. Left unchecked, he'll drag us into war over something completely stupid like shafling someone's daughter and wife, probably at the same time. He has potential, but I think Bogimir is correct. He lived in the gutter too long. Had we found him sooner, he might have been salvaged. Now... he doesn't belong in our world and he isn't adjusting to it at all. Truthfully, I don't think he wants to. Let him go home, Ev. For all our sakes."

Evzen's chest tightened at those words as grief choked him. He couldn't bear the thought of losing Caillen again.

Yes the man was rough around the edges, but he was funny and highly intelligent.

He's my son. Most of all, he had faith in Caillen. In time, he had no doubt his son would adjust.

Yet Evzen was owned by his people. His first priority had to be their safety and welfare. It was a mantle of responsibility he wanted to bequeath to his son. But if Caillen refused...

I have to try.

Evzen met his brother's gaze on the monitor. "Let's see how he does on the *Arimanda*."

Talian heaved a sigh of remorse and disgust that said his brother was nowhere near as thrilled to have Caillen back in the line of succession as he was. "I'll assign an extra detail to him."

"Why?"

"The Qillaqs? Remember them? They're sending an entire quorum for the assembly. And I can see this disaster coming. You know how their women dress... or more to the point, don't. Whatever we do, we have to keep Caillen away from them."

His brother was right. The Qillaqs were a warring race who tolerated no one easily and especially not offworlders or men. One wrong glance and they'd attack.

And so would Caillen.

Evzen frowned. "I thought they had declined the summit."

"They did originally. But I received word this morning that their queen herself will be joining us. Apparently there's something of great import she wishes to declare before the council. Our luck, it's probably an act of war. Let's just hope your son doesn't make it one against us."

Evzen watched while Caillen argued with Bogimir in the room. Maybe he should leave Caillen home while he attended the summit. But he didn't want to be away from his son for two weeks. Not when they were still getting to know each other. Not to mention the fact that Caillen was an expert in negotiating with the Krellins and was even well acquainted with their crowned prince. They desperately needed a trade agreement with them that he'd been working on for three years with no progress. If he didn't get that to go through during the summit and be ratified by the council, it would be three more years before he could attempt it again. By then, their colony, which needed supplies and protection, would be destroyed and all her citizens enslaved. His people couldn't wait six more months, never mind three years.

Caillen was the only hope they had.

Therefore he'd take his son and watch him.

Closely.

He had all faith that everything would turn out just fine.

Until he remembered Caillen's favorite saying. *Never underestimate a Dagan's ability to screw up the best-laid plans.*

And right now, his son still considered himself a Dagan.

Every time Evzen heard that name it enraged him. His son was a de Orczy. One of the oldest and finest of the ruling houses. His was a legacy people had killed for.

But not Caillen. He was the only man who honestly didn't care about wealth and its trappings. While his son was happy to have the finer things, he was just as happy, if not happier, without them.

Baffling.

And that made him want to weep. His son was a complete stranger and he was trying to understand him. He was. But the more time they spent together, the more Evzen had to face the truth.

When all of this was over, he would most likely lose his son all over again...

Caillen breathed a sigh of relief as Boggi took off in a huff again and left him alone with his friends. The moment the door sealed shut, he twisted out of the stifling robes and threw them to the floor. Then he jammed the signal in the room so that neither his father nor his father's security detail could spy on them. He really hated that crap.

Maris tsked at him. "It's just plain cruel the way you flash that hot body of yours at me all the time, Cai. I swear I've never wanted to be a woman more so than I do right now." Biting his lip, he looked at Darling. "Those abs... it's criminal to look that good and be straight. Couldn't you just lick those muscles all night long?"

Darling screwed his face up in distaste. "Uh, no. He's too much like a brother to me. I honestly find that thought repugnant."

Maris snapped his neck and wrist in a purely feminine gesture. "I am yanking your membership card." He returned his attention to Caillen and made a purring growl in the back of his throat. "One night, baby, and I could change your religion."

Caillen gave a good-natured laugh. "You keep saying that, but I know you better. You like to be the pursuer, Maris. The moment someone chases you, you run for the door."

Laughing at the truth, Darling shrugged his outer robe off and tossed it back to Caillen. "You know, Maris is right. You can't keep undressing every two seconds and especially not on a ship during a summit meeting where they'll be monitoring all the rooms. You do that there and it'll end up on the news and you'll be tainted by it forever."

Caillen wasn't worried about that. "I'll jam them."

Darling shook his head. "Take it from the weapons and explosives techspert. It ain't going to happen. You jam anything there and it'll set off all manner of alarms. Not even Syn could break in without getting busted."

Now that gave him pause. His brother-in-law could crack into anything without detection and that told him all he needed to know about his voyage to hell. "So keep it in my pants, huh?"

"Unless you want to be the next viral porno feature. I know it'll be hard—"

Caillen arched a brow at Darling's choice of words.

Darling rolled his eyes. "Your mind is always in the gutter."

"Yeah, well, you know it's got a lot of friends it likes to play with there and I happen to like the view."

Maris made a light "heh" sound. "Give it up, Dar. You have to remember you're talking to the only man I've ever seen who can walk up to a woman he's just met and tell her he needs to have his manhood serviced and instead of getting bitch-slapped or arrested for it, gets to take her home."

Darling crossed his arms over his chest. "That's because most men have more sense than to say that out loud."

Yeah, right. Caillen knew better. "That's 'cause most

men lack my boys and my skills. You may know how to handle explosives, Dar, but I know how to handle women. When it comes to the female population, *I* am the master."

"Please," Darling said with a laugh. "I've seen you with your sisters. You don't handle them at all. You're completely whipped."

"Totally untrue. I just let them think that. That, my friends, is the beauty of it. There's not a woman born I can't manipulate and wrap around my little finger."

Darling shook his head. "And one day you're going to meet a woman who's immune to your charms." There was an odd note in Darling's voice that said he commiserated, but since he knew Darling had never been in a serious relationship he ignored it.

"Never happen. I can even charm a baby out of her rattle *and* milk."

Maris chuckled. "I'm with you, Dar. I'd like to see him get some karmic paycheck, but in this I have to side with Cai. Like he said, I've seen too many women, of all ages, fall at his feet as soon as he gives them that come-here-and-strip-for-me teasing smile."

Darling refused to cede his opinion. "And I'm saying that there's always that one person who will knock you off keel. Always when you least expect it. Trust me, if Nykyrian and Syn can find women to tolerate them and their psychoses, you will too."

Caillen didn't argue because he knew better. He'd spent his entire life having to answer to his sisters for everything and having to watch after them and deal with their drama. Not to mention the one time he'd tried to be serious with a woman...

Yeah, that had taught him and killed any thoughts he

might have ever had about commitment. Women were crazy.

It was why he had no interest in settling on one female. Ever. Or even letting one near him for more than the couple of hours it took to relieve a biological itch. He didn't want the trauma of it. All women wanted to domesticate the male and he was too wild for that. He didn't want kids or a wife. He just wanted to live his life on his own terms and answer to no one but himself.

Freedom. That was what he craved. He lived for the blood-pumping danger of smuggling. Flying fast. Living on the edge, one step away from death. Not even his sisters, who were the toughest females he'd ever met, could keep up with him. If they couldn't he knew there was no one else who could.

Wanting to change the topic, he directed them back to the matter at hand that had caused him to jam the vid surveillance. "Look, you guys know I don't give two shits if I'm a flaming dork in public—which I am most of the time. My philosophy is simple. You want to be my friend, let's take a drink. You want to judge me, duck. But this isn't about me. In spite of the fact that he's an aristo, my dad seems to be a decent man and I don't want to humiliate him in front of his pretentious crew by doing something stupid like thinking the hand-washing bowl is soup and trying to eat it…again. Or breaking some other protocol I don't know about. So can you show me how to be like one of you?" That actually came out easier than he'd thought it would. He'd barely choked on his dignity.

Darling clapped him on the back. "Don't worry, brother. We'll be with you every step of the way."

Maris flashed a devilish grin. "And laughing continuously at your expense. However we do promise to keep it on the inside...most of the time."

Caillen laughed at the way Maris said that. He was lucky to have two friends he could trust. Four if he counted Nykyrian and Syn. He'd had enough people stab him in the back that he knew better than to take their loyalty for granted. There weren't many people who'd lay down their lives for someone else. But any of the four of them would do it for him.

And he'd die for them just as quickly.

Darling wagged his eyebrows at Maris. "I don't know. A flaming dork in public might be highly entertaining."

Caillen shoved at Darling who laughed as he stumbled sideways. "You're both pervs. I don't know why I hang out with you."

Darling snorted. "Probably because we're the only ones who'll hang out with *you*. Not to mention, I was a good innocent child unsullied by depravity until I started running with you and your crew."

Maris nodded. "I can attest to that. You guys seriously corrupted my little buddy."

Darling stiffened. "Little buddy? I sound like your pet."

Maris threw an arm around Darling. "I keep trying for that too, but you're no more game than Caillen is. I swear you should don a monk's cloak."

Caillen clapped his hands together. "And on that note, I'm going to find that cute maid I saw earlier and see if she's single." He made a double-clicking noise with his tongue as he winked at them. "See you guys later."

His thoughts already fantasizing on the maid's charms,

he left them to drift down the hallway toward the conservatory where he'd last seen the petite blonde who'd given him a most salacious smile earlier.

"Come to Papa, baby." He was definitely in the mood to find some alone time with her and that feather duster she'd been using on his father's statues. There was something else hard he wanted her to tease with it.

As he walked past the glass door that let out into the rear gardens, his senses picked up on an ephemeral disturbance. It was a small, subtle smear on one pane. Most people wouldn't pay it any heed, but then most people weren't used to scrounging for survival and having to guard their backs every moment they breathed.

It shouldn't be there.

Caillen frowned. The maids had been in here this morning cleaning everything thoroughly...

He pulled back the curtain to look at the electronic lock. It'd been deactivated and left slightly ajar for a quick exit.

Yeah, someone was in here who shouldn't be.

That calm, dead cold came over him as he went into soldier mode. He knew the perp hadn't gone toward the study where he'd been. The other direction led to his father's private wing.

C'mon, Cai. Don't be ridiculous. There's security all over the place. One of them could have been doing rounds and touched the pane.

Yeah, but when you'd grown up with people who broke into places like this to kill and rob its occupants, you knew just how worthless that security was. Alarms were only for the honest. Professional assassins and thieves picked their teeth with them.

Better safe than sorry...

He followed the wide ornate hallway that was lined with state portraits of ancestors he couldn't keep track of, but didn't see anything out of the ordinary. The white walls and floors glistened to such an extent, he could see his black clothes outlined like a mirror. The scent of the myriad of fresh flowers draping from elaborate bronze vases hung in his nostrils.

You're being stupid. There's nothing here. Just an overactive imagination fueled by gross paranoia.

He was outside his father's bedroom and about to go find his maid after all when he heard something fall.

A second later, his father called out for help.

5

Caillen tried the door.

It was locked. He could hear them fighting on the other side as his father called for security. Grinding his teeth, he kicked the door open. His foot stung from the impact as the door slammed back against the wall with a resounding crash. The force of his strike caused the door to leave its hinges and clatter against the checkered black-and-white marble floor.

Inside, a masked assassin had his father against the wall as they fought.

Without hesitation, Caillen shot across the distance and grabbed the assassin from behind. The assassin turned on him with a curse and slashed out at him with a dagger.

Caillen jumped back and caught his wrist as the assassin tried to stab him. With a quick glance down at their entwined hands, he curled his lip. He knew the black-bladed dagger well. A League weapon, the blade was coated with a toxin so potent one scratch would kill him. Head butting the assassin, he made sure to keep his hand locked on the man's wrist and the blade away from his skin.

The assassin stomped his foot.

"Pansy puss. What kind of girl move is that?" Caillen threw his arm up and punched him in the throat.

The assassin wheezed.

Caillen snapped the assassin's wrist so hard, he felt the bone break in his grip. The knife hit the marble with a thud as the assassin cried out in pain. Kicking it toward his father, he flipped the assassin onto his back and pinned him to the floor. The assassin tried to squirm or punch out of his hold, but it was one Caillen had used many times on Kasen.

No one could break out of it.

Well, maybe Nykyrian. But thankfully this asshole wasn't as lethal.

His father called for security over the intercom.

Caillen grimaced at his father's compassion. "Be easier if you let me kill him."

The assassin continued to struggle against him like a dying fish trying to get back into water. Caillen held him fast.

Coughing to clear his bruised throat, his father shook his head. "I want the pleasure of seeing him executed."

And he'd rather have the pleasure of gutting the bastard on the ground like a pig. "You know if he has a League contract on you, you can't do that. But if I kill him before we find out about it, it's legal. You sure you don't want me to slip and accidentally plunge my knife into him a few dozen times?"

"While I admire your planned accident, son, I'd rather interrogate him."

Caillen heard a muffled pop two seconds before the assassin started convulsing. "Shit!" He shot to his feet and grabbed his father, then pulled him out of the room.

"What's going on?"

Holding his breath, Caillen didn't answer until they were outside and the door was shut tight. "Suicide cap. I don't know if it's airborne or strictly ingested. Either way, he's dead and we don't need to inhale it until someone not us does a hazmat analysis."

Security guards came running down the hall, but Caillen stopped them from entering. "You need a hazmat expert to go in there. The perp just offed himself with a cap."

The captain nodded before he pulled his people back and notified his superior. Then the captain met his father's gaze. "Do I need to call for a medic for you, Your Majesty?"

"I'm fine." His father clapped Caillen on the back. "Thanks to my son. How did you know I was being attacked?"

He didn't answer what to him was a rhetorical question. "My question to you is why didn't your security know about it?"

His father straightened his robes with an imperial tug. "For an obvious reason, I don't have cameras in my bedroom. It's the only dark area of the palace."

Flaky excuse in his book. Better a porn video for the guards than a dark area that left his father open to assassination. But what did he know? "Shouldn't they have seen him in the hallway?"

His father offered him an indulgent smile. "Of all people, I think you know how easy things like this happen. Those who want in will find a way."

Caillen ground his teeth at his father's lackadaisical tone. "You're awfully ambivalent over it."

"Hazard of *my* business. Since the moment I took the

throne, I've had attempt after attempt on my life. You get used to it after a while."

He would argue that, but in his life and business it was so common that like his father he only found it odd when someone wasn't trying to kill him.

His father met his gaze. "You were incredible, by the way. Where did you learn to fight like that?"

"Three older sisters who kept wanting to put dresses on me and paint my nails. Since I couldn't outrun them, I had to learn to outfight them and unfortunately for me, they don't hit like girls. If that's not bad enough, they all fight dirty too."

His father laughed. "Thank you."

He shrugged the gratitude away. "You saved my life, it's only fair I save yours."

Evzen fell silent at those words that cut him deep inside. It wasn't what he wanted to hear from his son. He wanted to hear Caillen say that he'd saved him because he loved him.

Just once.

He's a man and a tough one at that. Men like Caillen didn't admit to tender feelings for anyone. He understood that, but the father in him who remembered holding his son as a newborn was desperate to have his son accept him.

It's a fool's dream. He knew it and yet he couldn't stop the ache inside that yearned for a relationship he feared would never happen. If he could only lay hands on the ones who'd deprived him of seeing his son grow up. Of being there when Caillen had needed him...

He wanted blood over the gulf that separated them.

Caillen still didn't accept him as family. Not really.

His sisters were the only ones he admitted to. *Damn you bastards for taking him from me.*

But at least he had his son now. Though it wasn't the close, tight relationship he desired, Caillen was still here. For the time being, he wasn't running for the door and so he would accept that and hope for a time when Caillen felt like this was his home too.

And that he was his father, not a Dagan smuggler.

Darling and Maris came rushing up to them.

"What happened?" Darling asked as soon as he stopped by Caillen's side.

Caillen's answer was short and clipped. "Assassin." Nothing more than that was needed to explain the commotion.

Darling let out a sound of exasperation. "League?"

Caillen shook his head. "He had on civs, but he carried a League weapon—don't know if it was a trophy or he was a contractor. As soon as they clear the room, I'll have them run the DNA and see if we can find out if he was solo or attached and if there was a contract issued."

Maris scanned Caillen's body with a worried frown. "Are both of you all right?"

Caillen scowled. "I am so offended that you'd even ask that question. I'm sorry but if third-rate shit like that can take me out, I deserve to die."

Maris scoffed at his righteous indignation. "Forgive me for questioning your fighting prowess. However, I do remember having to pull you out—"

"I was drunk."

"And you were bleeding all over my new shoes."

Caillen's scowl melted under a smile he was trying to keep hidden as he remembered the event and didn't want to cop to it entirely. "Yeah well, there was ten of them and one drunk me. Actually now that I think about it, I was so flagged, I thought there was twenty of them. My vision was just that screwed up."

His father sighed heavily. "Oh the stories I overhear. I shudder at how many close calls you've had in your life."

Caillen gave him an arch stare. "I wasn't the one who almost had my head pinned to the wall a minute ago."

He was right about that and while Evzen prided himself on being intelligent with his safety and cautious by nature, he realized how much he lacked when compared to the child he'd fathered. Whatever had caused fate to take his son from his side, it had given his boy life skills that could definitely come in handy for an emperor.

Now if he could only train and hone Caillen's civility to the sharp point of his fighting skills he'd have a legendary leader.

Caillen flagged down the hazmat workers as they came to extract the body. He divested the first one to reach him of her mask and gloves, then went to investigate the assassin's remains.

The man was lying right where they'd left him. A greenish cast to his skin let Caillen know the death had been quick and about as painless as it could be. But that wasn't what concerned him.

Kneeling down, he retrieved the League dagger and searched for the assassin's reader. He found it and rose to his feet.

The worker stopped him from leaving. "That's evidence."

He stared down at the woman's peeved glare. "Indeed it is and I'll hand it over after I look through it." He stepped away from her.

She moved to block him again until her boss cleared his throat and shook his head. Her expression furious, she finally let him pass.

Moving out of their way, Caillen turned the reader on and started scanning the open files. They all confirmed his suspicions. Typical hired hack. Nothing really to differentiate him from any of the other scum-sucking bastards eager to earn a credit at the cost of some poor soul's life. At least not until Caillen bypassed the security on his device and started going through his secure files.

While they searched the body, he isolated himself in a corner to review what their little hemorrhoid had been up to. Typical credit transfers that any butcher would have. Wanted postings where the perp had searched for victims...

Encryption just difficult enough to keep a low-level expert at bay and one interesting nugget he hadn't been expecting.

He stepped out onto the balcony to make a call he didn't want anyone to overhear.

Nykyrian Quiakides picked it up a few seconds later. "I can't imagine what trouble you're in now, Dagan. How many you need for an evac and how covert?"

Caillen snorted at Nyk's dry, thickly accented tone. And for all of his bravado, the last time Caillen had told him he needed an evac, Nyk had told him to suck it up since he'd have started a war to pull him out of the Garvon prison. "Not that kind of trouble."

"Who is she then?"

"That either. Damn, can't I explain before you jump to conclusions?"

Nykyrian let out a dry laugh—something that had

never left the former assassin's lips before he'd married a few years ago. "By all means enlighten me. If this isn't about a woman or your ass in jail, I'm definitely intrigued."

Yeah, okay, Nyk had a point. Caillen glanced inside where they were putting the assassin into a body bag. "What is a tirador?"

"Context."

Obviously the word had a multitude of meanings, so Caillen kept the explanation of his circumstances short and sweet. "I have a hitter on the floor with a League dagger who tried to off my father. His reader has him listed as one."

"Listed by whom?"

Only Nykyrian would revert to formal language in such a hostile situation. "Can't read that part—language unknown and the translator is unable to ID it. I'm forwarding it to you now."

Nykyrian paused to read it. "He's a civ-con under League orders acting as an instigator to cause conflict for your father."

"Meaning?"

"Someone wants a war and they want to start it by assassinating your father. League doesn't want it traced back to them, so they hired your stain to try. Bad thing is, he won't be solo. Another will rise to the greed and take the shot."

"Shit."

"Exactly."

Caillen fell silent as he contemplated how many assassins would want to be a million credits richer... yeah... that was one long list. "So what do I do?"

"Duck."

"Tired of the one-word answers, Nyk. I need a course of action here."

"There's nothing to be done, Dagan. You'd have to know who wants the war and why. I can guarantee you that all the stain might—and I use that word with all due sarcasm—have known was who hired him, and that would be a juiceless flunky who would die before he or she talked."

"So in other words, don't bother looking."

"It would be a waste of time."

Easier said than done. Caillen didn't operate that way. "I can't do nothing."

"Fine," Nykyrian said in a strained tone. "I'll look into it, but I can't make any promises. Just because the League gave me amnesty doesn't mean I have friends there." Nykyrian was the only League assassin who'd ever left the corps and lived. The latter being a testament to the man's incredible fighting skills. To this day, the League wasn't happy about it and if not for the fact that Nykyrian was heir to not one, but two, major empires and married to the daughter for a third, he'd still have a death sentence on his head.

Caillen paused as he saw Darling on the other side of the door. He motioned his friend outside where he was talking, then closed the door so that the others wouldn't overhear his conversation.

Frowning, Darling stood across from him and crossed his arms over his chest.

"What can I do to protect my dad?" Caillen asked Nykyrian.

"Not much. Tiradors are pretty hostile. More than that, they always frame someone for their actions—it's what they're paid to do."

"How do you mean?"

"I meant what I said. He was there to not only kill your father but to pin the crime on an innocent. You search him, you'll probably find evidence he was going to plant."

"I did search him and found nothing."

Nykyrian paused before he responded. "Then that's a good sign. It means whoever hired your assassin is probably close enough that they wanted to plant the evidence themselves and didn't trust him to do it."

"To protect their identity?"

"Exactly."

Which meant the person who wanted his father dead could easily be one of the people standing on the other side of the glass. Caillen narrowed his gaze at his uncle and the other advisors who surrounded his father.

One of them was a traitor . . .

He met Darling's gaze that reiterated his own thoughts. "I need proof."

Nykyrian scoffed. "Of all people, you know how hard that is to come by. These people unfortunately aren't stupid."

He was right about that. And Caillen's mind whirled as he tried to think of how best to protect his father. "What language was that note in?"

"Ancient Pralortorian."

No wonder his translator had been useless. It also made him feel better that he hadn't been able to identify it. "What the hell is that?"

"It's a language the Trisani spoke about four hundred years ago." Only Nykyrian would know something that obscure.

"Why would his orders be in a dead language?"

"League protocol. They use dead languages to communicate so that any mundane who happens on their missives won't be able to understand them." Which was no doubt why Nykyrian had been fluent in it. That assassin training came in handy in so many ways.

Caillen sighed. "So it all goes back to the League."

"Not necessarily. The League might have nothing more to do with it than issuing termination orders. Remember, they're corrupt. Anyone who can afford to bribe them could have gotten this done."

"In other words, guard my back."

"Yeah. 'Cause no offense, this is going to get ugly. If I was the hitter, my next crack at your father would be at the summit."

Caillen arched his brow as he looked at Darling and remembered what Darling had said earlier. "What about their security?"

Nykyrian laughed. "Amateur night."

"Darling told me that it was so tight even Syn would get caught."

"He seriously underestimates our Rit. Trust me. Even *you* could breach it."

Now that was just insulting. "Thanks for that."

"Ah, don't get your feathers knotted. You're one of the best contractors I know. That wasn't meant as a slight. Only saying you could."

Caillen still felt insulted by it. His thoughts went to the summit and how best to protect his father while there. "Are you going to be there?"

"No. Kiara's about to give birth any second. There's nothing this side of hell or the other that could pry me away from being here right now. Sorry."

He couldn't blame Nyk for that either. The man had literally given his life for his wife. "It's all right." He didn't need help when it came to surviving. "Thanks for translating for me. I'll talk to you later."

Nykyrian hung up.

Caillen let out a tired breath as he turned his attention to Darling who'd waited patiently through his call. "What's up?" he asked Darling.

"I found something you missed."

He arched a brow at that. "Pardon? *I* missed something?"

Darling nodded. "He was transmitting right before he attacked. I routed it back and was able to get a twenty-second loop."

"Okay. What did it say?"

Darling pushed the small transmitter in his hand. A deep, accented voice spoke. "Don't worry, Your Highness. I'll kill your father for you and then you'll be emperor."

The blood faded from Caillen's face. "What the krik…"

"You're the one being framed, Cai. I barely got that out before the guards found it." He dropped it on the ground, then crushed it beneath his boot heel. "Someone plans to remove both you and your father from the line of succession."

No shit.

The only question was who.

And when.

6

"Cover your back!"

Circling her sister in the dirt practice ring inside their oversized stadium, Desideria Denarii barely ducked out of the way before her older sister's sword strike separated her head from her shoulders. She countered the blow with one of her own. One that drove her sister back and into a defensive stance.

And that set Narcissa's temper into overdrive. Shrieking, she went at Desideria with everything she had. But with her furious attack, she unbalanced herself and Desideria disarmed her with one stroke which only made her sister madder as her sword was slung ten feet away from them.

It landed in the dust with a loud clatter.

Throwing her head back and spilling her black hair across her shoulders, Narcissa let loose a fierce battle cry, then charged at her. Desideria barely caught herself before she stabbed her own sister through the heart—that was what she'd been trained to do when someone attacked her and they were stupid enough to leave her an opening. Yet even though it was their warrior's code, she refused to kill Narcissa during a practice fight.

Even if it meant days of starvation for her.

They'd already buried two sisters from training mishaps. Desideria had no desire to bury a third.

Instead she allowed Narcissa to shove her to the ground where her sister rained blow after blow on her face. Desideria kicked her back, then flipped up to land on her feet. She moved in to retaliate.

"Enough!"

They froze at the shout from their trainer. At six feet in height, Kara was a well-trained soldier. Her short, slicked-back black hair matched Narcissa's and they all shared the same sharp, exotic features and black eyes. Muscular and curvaceous, Kara and her twin sister had once been members of the High Guard for their queen. A queen who just happened to be Desideria's mother and Kara's older sister. Once Desideria and her four sisters had reached a trainable age, Kara had honorably quit the Guard to be their private instructor.

Kara had been merciless to them ever since.

Kill or be killed—that was her aunt's only motto and it was one she strove to drive home to her nieces.

"Narcissa, hit the showers. We'll talk later about your outburst."

Narcissa curled her lip as she wiped the blood from her nose and glared at Desideria. Without a word, she headed across the ring for the stairs that would take her into the shower rooms.

Her aunt turned that deep, fierce scowl on her. "You..."

Desideria sighed in resignation as she ignored her bleeding lip and swelling eye. "Punishment. I know." Well at least the good news was she'd lose some of the extra weight her mother always complained about her carrying. Not the way she wanted to do it, but...

Kara glowered at her. "Why didn't you strike when you had the chance?"

Because Cissy may get on my nerves to the nth degree, but at the end of the day, she's still my older sister and I love her. I would never really hurt her, never mind kill her. Desideria knew better than to even breathe a hint of that sentiment out loud. Kara would never understand it.

She was Qillaq and they didn't have those weaknesses.

When she didn't answer right away, her aunt grabbed her by the shirt and jerked her until they were nose to nose—an impressive feat since Desideria was a full six inches shorter. The force of her jerk caused Desideria's braid to fall over her shoulder and dangle loosely down her back. "No mercy. Ever. No matter who it is. When you fight, *any* fight, your opponent is your enemy. Do you understand?"

Desideria nodded.

Her aunt shook her. "Do. You. Understand?"

"Yes."

Kara slung her away and she barely caught herself before she went tumbling into the dirt. "Pathetic waste. Just like your worthless mongrel father."

Those words resonated deep inside her and before she could rein herself in, she attacked.

Laughing at her audacity, Kara sidestepped her charge and unsheathed her own sword to engage her.

Desideria hesitated as she realized what she'd done. But it was too late. She couldn't back down. A challenge issued was a challenge met. To withdraw now would be an official and public beating.

True to the nature of her people, her aunt was ruthless as she tried her best to kill her.

But Desideria didn't want to hurt her aunt any more than she'd wanted to kill her sister. *It's your father's blood tainting you.* That accusation had been made by everyone around her. And it was true. Unlike her sisters, she was only half Qillaq which made her less in the eyes of all.

You are my delicate rose—the most precious thing I have. She could still hear her father's last words to her. Delicate rose was what Desideria meant in his language. He'd talked her mother into naming her that even though he'd had to lie about the meaning at her birth in order to get his way. Her mother thought it meant "strong warrior."

The name Desideria was his inside joke on her mother's warring people who'd enslaved him.

And he'd died under questionable circumstances.

Now no one was allowed to even speak his name out loud and she'd been forbidden to mourn him.

To this day, she wanted blood over that too. But right now, as she fought her aunt, she didn't feel like she was part Gondarion. She felt the heat of her mother's people and she wanted to hear Kara cry for the insult she'd given Desideria's beloved father.

Delving deep to tap every bit of her training, she swung her sword and twisted it, catching Kara's blade. In one deft move, she disarmed her. Desideria caught the sword with her left hand and angled both of them at Kara's throat as she circled her.

There was nothing Kara could do without getting her throat sliced.

"Yield?"

Kara narrowed her dark gaze. "Only because this is a training exercise and you're still to be punished."

Of course she was.

But she'd won the fight and that was the most important thing. "You may punish me, but we both know the truth. I'm no longer your pupil." Not after she'd defeated her. Now she was a master and deserving of her aunt's respect.

Mixed blood or not.

Kara inclined her head to her and held her hand out for her sword.

Desideria paused before she handed it over. It wasn't going to be that simple. Not this time. Making sure to keep her expression blank, she broke the blade in half across her thigh before she handed the hilt back to Kara.

Kara's cheeks turned bright pink as her anger no doubt mounted to a murderous level. The sword had been a coming-of-age gift to her from her own mother when she'd advanced from pupil to master. But that was what happened when you lost. The victor chose whether or not to snap the blade or return it intact. Intact was an act of respectful civility. Snapping it was the ultimate act of punishment and a very personal slap. Since her aunt had insulted her father, she would be ruthless in this. Sentimentality be damned.

My father was a good man. And she'd fight to the death for *his* honor.

Sheathing her training sword, Desideria headed for the showers while her aunt went the opposite direction. No doubt planning her demise every step of the way.

Better yet, my punishment. She sighed in resignation of what would be coming to her all too soon.

As she reached the door that led to the dressing rooms, she saw her mother step forward from the shadows of the seating area. That made her suck her breath in sharply. Her mother didn't often attend their training, except to tell them what a massive disappointment they all were and how their skills lagged far behind hers and her sisters' when they'd been their ages.

An older version of Desideria with the same dark hair, deep tawny skin and black eyes, Queen Sarra looked more like Desideria's older sister than her mother. Her body well toned and sleek from her own countless hours of martial practice, her mother could easily pass for a woman in her early thirties.

Fierce and stern, Sarra had no king to co-rule by her side—the law of their people said that no woman could marry a man who couldn't defeat her in battle and no man had ever bested her mother.

No woman either.

But that didn't mean her mother lived without companionship. In fact, her mother's three male consorts stood two feet behind her and each one of them, just like Desideria's father, had been won through battle. In the case of her father, he'd been a slave who had crash-landed here and been stranded. A border patrol had picked him up and he'd been donated as the prize for a competition.

Her mother's other three consorts were Qillaq born and as such had been trained from birth as warriors, the same as the Qillaq women. But because of their perfect beauty, they'd been auctioned off instead of being sent into battle to be scarred. The only time her mother's consorts had been allowed to fight was when her mother had claimed them.

One battle only to see if they were worthy of being a king. All of them had failed. Now they were nothing more than pampered pets who were at the mercy of her mother's whims.

Her mother's eyes glowed with a pride Desideria had never seen in them before. "Kara cherished that sword above everything."

Desideria made sure the regret she felt over those words didn't show in her demeanor or expression. "Then she should have fought harder to keep it."

Her mother laughed. "You continue thinking like that and you may yet be my successor, tainted bloodline and all."

Desideria pressed her lips together to keep from saying something that might get her banished. After all, her mother had chosen to sleep with her father and allowed herself to become pregnant by him. If there was anyone to blame for her faulty bloodline, it was her mother and not her.

But her mother didn't want to hear that.

"You did me proud, Desideria. And since you're no longer a student or a child, I want to offer you Kara's former position in my Guard."

Those words took her by complete surprise. Not hard to do since she was more accustomed to her mother's condemnation than praise. "Pardon?"

"You heard me and you know how much I hate to repeat myself."

Desideria barely caught herself before she hugged her

mother as excitement raced through her. That wouldn't be received well. The only emotions Qillaqs were allowed to show were anger, but never during battle, and occasionally humor. The rest of the time, they were to be stern and serious.

She cleared her throat and inclined her head to her mother. "I accept your offer, My Queen, and am honored that you think enough of me to make it."

Narcissa gasped behind her as she must have come out of the dressing area.

Turning, Desideria saw her sister stalk toward them.

Her sister raked her with a repugnant sneer. "What of me? I'm older. If anyone deserves to stand in your Guard, Mother, surely it is I."

Their mother's eyes were cold and empty. "And you are still a student. You have never defeated your aunt and as such you're unworthy to be in my Guard."

"But—"

Her mother held her hand up fast in a gesture that cut Narcissa off. "You heard me, *child.*" That one word was a slap in the face and a reminder that their mother didn't see Narcissa as an adult yet, but rather as a little girl who needed more instruction and discipline. "Now tend your place."

The look on her sister's face was fierce and it promised Desideria a rematch. Furious at them both, she spun around and left.

Desideria hated the fact that she'd just made a vicious enemy. This was not what she wanted.

But her mother didn't care. If anything, she fostered their resentment toward each other and reveled in it. "Report in the morning for your uniform. I'll make sure that Coryn knows to put you on the summit detail, so prepare to leave with us."

In spite of her sister's anger, that really made her want to jump up and down in excitement. She'd never left their planet before. As a child she'd spent hours listening to her father tell her about all the places he'd visited before being captured and all the incredible things he'd seen and done while there.

Now she'd finally see some of them. She couldn't wait.

Maintaining her exterior calm, she gave her mother a tight-lipped smile. "Thank you, My Queen."

Her mother held her hand out to her.

Desideria bent over and kissed her ring before she bowed low and took her leave. She didn't let her happiness show until she was in her dressing room.

As soon as the door closed, her best friend and servant, Tanith, waylaid her.

"Oh my God! I can't believe what you did! You crushed that bitch and made her eat all her years of insulting you. Congratulations!" Squealing, Tanith grabbed Desideria's arms and jumped up and down.

"Sh, sh, sh," Desideria breathed, refusing to jump with her even though she really wanted to. "Don't let anyone overhear you." They'd both be punished and now that Desideria had earned the rank of adult, it would be much worse than her punishments of the past.

Tanith settled down. "I'm sorry. I'm just so thrilled for you! Narcissa on the other hand... I wouldn't be drinking out of an open cup anytime in the near future if I were you. There's no telling what she might do over this."

"Believe me, I know." Her other sister, Gwenela, would be furious when she found out too. They were still in training and Desideria was the youngest. How dare she be the first to gain adult status...

They would both be out to take her head now.

"I can't believe I won."

Tanith beamed. "I do. In spite of what they say, you are ten times the fighter the inbreds are."

She cringed at an insult that would have Tanith executed should anyone ever hear it. "You shouldn't say that."

"It's true and you know it. Your father was a hero and he was a good man...unlike the others. All they do is sit around and whine, waiting for someone to wipe their butts."

And that was why she loved Tanith. She alone believed what Desideria did. Her father hadn't killed himself like a coward. It wasn't in him any more than it was in her. While it was true that other people were weaker than the Qillaqs, he'd possessed the heart of a warrior and the strength of a cyborg. His fighting spirit flowed through her too.

I will do my mother proud. She would prove her breeding to all of them and she would redeem her father's name. Even if it was the last thing she did.

"What do you mean the assassination failed?"

"The newfound prince has skills we didn't count on. He's unfortunately not incompetent and I can't stress just how well trained he is."

"How is it he survived all these years? He was just an infant when we kidnapped him. I still can't believe he returned after all we did to ensure he wouldn't."

"I know. Both he and Evzen are the luckiest bastards ever born. Every time we think we have them, they escape."

"We cannot fail again. Things here are unraveling fast. After today, we don't have a moment to waste. We cannot allow the line of succession to change."

"I hear you and I will make sure that the next—"

"No. We need to rethink our plan. When next we strike, it must be with purpose. Most of all, it must be fatal.

"And what of our other problem?"

"I have a perfect plan for that as well. Are you sure you can handle your side of the matter?"

"Absolutely. And you?"

"I have it under control. But we must strike during the summit."

"Are you sure you can get past security?"

"Don't insult me with that insipid question. Of course I can. Two weeks and we will live the lives we were meant to and they will be nothing more than bad memories we laugh about having endured."

"And Desideria?"

"Just another casualty. Let her name be banished the same as her father's. Then we will be the only ones left worth remembering."

7

Two Weeks Later

Caillen adjusted the small comlink that was inside his ear so that no one would know Darling and Maris were feeding him instructions on how to behave. *Gah, I really am an effing five year old…*

Just don't drool down my shirt. At least not while he was sober.

Not to mention he still felt like he was drowning inside the heavy layers of fabric. He'd tried his best to talk his father into rearranging five hundred years of royal de Orczy dress code, but his father refused. Apparently it was a mark of honor to look like a ten-ton walking freak of nature.

Boggi kept passing a warning glare toward him.

Oh the urge to make an obscene gesture was so strong that he honestly didn't know how he kept himself from doing it.

But he wouldn't embarrass his father today. Today he was going to look and act royal if it killed him.

And it damn well might. Especially if their assassin decided to make a move while his limbs were weighted down. Then again, all he had to do was throw his clothes at the man. The weight of them alone would crush him.

"Don't worry, Cai. We're with you."

Since he was in public and around so many other dignitaries, he didn't respond to Darling's encouraging words in his ear. His father had taken up an official stance just inside a doorway so that he could greet territorial governors, ambassadors, senators and other representatives from the various planets that made up the highest rank of the Nine Systems—last time he'd seen this many aristos in one place, his head had been under a ten-foot blade that was about to come rattling down and kill him.

Yeah, it felt about the same way today. But at least no one had made a move on his dad. So far the assassin was lying low.

Cowardly bastard.

He stood to his father's right while Boggi remained on the left to introduce the men and women wanting to speak to his father. The lights were turned up so bright that they washed everyone with a halo effect. Most of all, they made the shiny fabrics and jewels glitter. A jewel thief would be in nirvana to see this.

Whereas normal ship walls were most often drab gray, these had been overlaid with gold so that they shimmered. Servants mingled among the elite with gold trays filled with finger foods from numerous worlds and alcohol, which seemed to be a bad idea. Several of the people were imbibing a little too much and speaking way too freely.

Caillen swept the room doing what he always did in a crowd—looking for someone out to kill him or attack.

But there was no visible threat. At least not yet. Well, none other than Darling and Maris off in a far corner, laughing at him as he stood with his feet together and his hands folded stiffly in front of him.

What a stupid gesture. He looked like he should be standing in a box on the shelf of a toy store.

Hello, people, I have no genitalia and I can only repeat three things programmed into my chip.

"It's killing you, isn't it?" Darling let out an evil snicker as he intruded on Caillen's silent tirade.

Maris joined him in the taunt. "I have to say only you could make that garish outfit look sexy." He purred like a contented cat eyeing a piece of meat it was craving.

Caillen made a low "heh" sound before he brushed his hand through his hair and made a subtle obscenity at them.

"Ah, now that's just rude." Darling tsked. "You keep that up and we'll abandon you to this."

Maris scoffed. "Speak for yourself. If that's an invitation, I say sign me up in the backroom, baby. So not fair to tease me like this, Cai, when you know how big a crush I have on you."

"Isn't that right, Caillen?"

His father's question startled him as four pairs of eyes looked at him expectantly. Shit. What had been said and who were the elderly couple in front of him?

Luckily Darling had been paying attention. "They're Ferryns. Ambassador Torren and his wife. Say, yes. Absolutely. And smile like you want her in your bed."

He had no idea why that last bit was thrown in, but he did exactly what Darling said.

The older lady blushed. "You're very kind, Your

Highness. It's such a pleasure to meet you. I've heard only wonderful things about you."

Really? That had to be a first. It definitely hadn't come out of Boggi's mouth.

His uncle's either. In fact, his uncle had done everything he could to make Caillen stay behind. But since he was convinced the assassin would make his attack against his father at the summit, Caillen had insisted he stay by his father's side.

"Kiss her hand," Darling whispered.

Caillen obeyed. She blushed even more before she and her husband left them.

His father frowned. "You seem a bit preoccupied. Are you all right?"

"Not preoccupied. Just not used to having this many aristos around me without them checking their wallets or calling for my arrest."

Darling choked in his ear. "I notice you left out some of the other more choice times."

Caillen gave him a scathing glare.

His father clapped him on the back. "You're doing fine, my boy. Just as I knew you would."

Yeah . . . He hadn't pissed on the rug yet.

But another glass of liquor and he might.

Wishing he were anywhere else, Caillen made himself pay more attention to what was being done even though he felt like a flaming overdressed moron in a tacky suit.

Desideria stood to the far back of her mother's Guard. She had yet to earn a forward spot, but that was okay. She would do so in the next few weeks. Of that she had no doubt. Especially since the other members kept treating her like she was somehow lesser because she was related to their queen. They assumed her appointment came from nepotism.

As if her mother had ever possessed an ounce of that. *Go ahead and sneer at me.* All they did was fuel her anger and make her that much more determined to challenge them once this ended. The only thing that had kept her from issuing a challenge the last two weeks had been her inexperience with social functions. Because she'd been considered a child until two weeks ago, she'd never attended anything like this and she preferred to stand back and get her bearings before she took the lead.

But before the year was out, she would advance to Head Guard and they would all learn that it was respect for her abilities and skills that had landed her where she was and not her blood relationship to their queen.

"Look at them," her mother said in their native language through a fake smile to Pleba—one of her oldest Guard members. "Preening peacocks, all of them and not a cock among them."

Desideria arched a brow at her mother's insult. Unfortunately, it was true. Even her mother's pampered consorts who were extremely womanly by Qillaq standards were far more masculine than anything Desideria had seen since leaving home. While she would have never considered her father effeminate, she now understood why her friends and family were so harsh toward offworlders like him.

They just didn't measure up. It was really scary. Not that she was interested in finding a lover—she'd have to spend a year as an adult before she'd be allowed to even consider one and then only if she earned the right in combat.

Definitely not something that appealed to her at the

moment. She had a lot more things on her mind than anything to do with the male species.

Sex could wait. Men were okay, but nothing...

Her thoughts scattered as she rounded a corner and actually stumbled.

Oh. My. God.

Breathless, all she could do was stare at the last thing she'd expected to find on board this ship.

A full blown masculine god...

He was without a doubt the finest-looking man she'd ever seen and she wasn't the only one to think so. Every woman in the room was throwing covert lust-filled glances at him as he stood oblivious to the gapes. Several groups of women stood apart, making lewd comments about what they'd love to do with and to him.

But it wasn't his looks alone that caught her attention. It was the force of his presence. Even though he was covered by so many heavy robes they obscured whatever shape his body was in, he stood with his weight on one leg, head low, eyes intense...

A soldier's stance.

More than that was the stony look on his handsome face as his gaze swept the crowd. Sharp. Alert.

Predator. It was obvious he was assessing everyone in the room as a potential threat. An aura of lethal killer clung to him, warning all that he would only strike once and it would be fatal when he did.

A chill went down her spine as her heartbeat sped up with a fierce adrenaline rush.

He was absolutely gorgeous. Short dark hair framed a sculpted face that was so delicious it was hard to look at him. It sent a foreign tremor through her.

And when his dark eyes met hers, she felt a shiver of appreciation that caused goose bumps to raise the length of her body.

Oh yeah...For *that,* she'd be willing to fight and then some.

"Caillen! Relax your face. You're scaring the natives."

Caillen blinked as Darling's voice in his ear startled him. His friend was right. He had that deep, intense scowl that he wore like armor around the undesirable crowds that haunted his usual gathering places. It was his basic default whenever he left home or felt uncomfortable with his surroundings. Look tough and no one messed with you.

Look homicidal and they avoided you entirely.

Which wasn't a good thing around the geriatric crew who ran with his father. His luck he'd give one of them a coronary and get sued for it.

"Now you look like you're on massive antidepressants."

Caillen sighed. He couldn't win for losing. At least that was what he thought until he felt that familiar tingle warning him someone was watching him.

A quick sweep honed in on...

Oh yeah. *Now that'll brighten your day.* She was exquisite. Dressed in a tight, and he meant t-i-g-h-t, burgundy leather Armstitch suit that was trimmed with some kind of military designation, her lush curves made his mouth water. Her dark hair was scraped back from her exotic face and coiled into a stern bun at the nape of her neck. It was hard for a woman to look good in a hairstyle so severe, but she wore it well and that made him wonder how much better she'd look naked, with that hair falling loose around her shoulders.

Her skin was a deep tawny color and so smooth it made him ache for a taste of it. But it was her lips that called out to him. A perfect bow, they begged to be swollen from his kisses. Yeah, he could just imagine the sensation of her nails on his flesh, digging in deep, her head thrown back as he—

Darling's voice in his ear was sharp with his reprimand. "Put it in your pants, Cai. She's off limits."

Like hell.

"Seriously, Caillen," Maris inserted. "Down, boy. She's Qillaq."

He grimaced in distaste. Ah damn. That wasn't right. Qills were the worst sort of man-hating, ass-kicking I-have-a-chip-on-my-shoulder women ever bred. From what he'd heard, they'd been normal until about two hundred years ago when a war had depleted a large portion of their population and virtually all of their men. The women who survived had basically bombed their enemies into oblivion and then taken enough of the enemy men as slaves to repopulate their planet. The next generation had purposefully bred men and women so fierce that they'd never again be defeated by another army. In fact, martial arts and law were the backbone of every part of their civilization.

They'd also pulled into themselves and rarely ventured into other planets' politics. While they did have some men in government, it was rare. Their males were reserved to be soldiers and kept breeders.

Yeah well, I wouldn't mind being kept by that for a night or two.

Yet he knew better. As delectable as she was, he hated women who felt the need to order him around. Too many years of living with three older sisters who vacillated from being his mom to his wardens had left him with a bad taste in his mouth where those kind of women were concerned. He wasn't threatened by strong women. He preferred them. But he didn't want them trying to run his life or tie his shoes either. As long as they kept their determination aimed at others, he was fine. When they decided he needed help cutting his food...

He wanted blood.

Damn shame. 'Cause that woman there was a fine piece of ass he wouldn't mind spending a few hours with.

But he wasn't dumb enough to chase after something he knew would only make him crazy. He'd also traveled that road one time too many. So instead, he offered a smile to the elderly cougar who was eyeing him like the last steak in her kennel.

Help me...

Desideria felt a shadow fall over her. Blinking, she focused on her mother's angry stare.

"Are we waiting on you now? Did I miss the memo designating you as queen?"

Heat stung her face as she realized that she'd stopped completely to stare at the handsome man in the corner. *I can't believe I'm so stupid.*

Yet he was compelling and irresistible. As was evidenced by the senator running her hand down his chest while he tried to talk to her.

"Forgive me, My Queen. I thought I saw something."

"You appeared to be daydreaming to me, Desideria. Did I make a mistake by promoting you?"

Those words drove all the desire right out of her and hit her like a blast of ice water. "No, ma'am."

Her mother's glower intensified. "Then you'd best pay attention or you'll find yourself headed home on the next shuttle."

In shame. That would make her sisters and aunt deliriously happy.

Desideria wanted to crawl into a hole as she saw the snide smirks from the other Guard members. To them this just confirmed that she didn't belong here.

And for what? A nameless man? Yes he was sexy and hot, but he wasn't worth her career or her reputation. No man was.

She wanted to die of embarrassment. No matter what, she couldn't let herself be distracted again. She couldn't afford to. Falling in behind her mother, she followed them out of the room, determined not to pay any more attention to anyone, male or female.

Not even if they were on fire and running around calling themselves the devil.

Yet she couldn't resist a quick glance back before she left. At the same time she looked at him, he looked at her and their gazes locked tight.

One corner of his mouth quirked up into the most alluring and yet strangely taunting smile she'd ever seen. It was like he had a secret and he was inviting her to hear it. And damned if she didn't want to go over to him and ask what it was.

I've lost my mind.

If she didn't get her head back where it belonged, she was going to lose her job and what little bit of respect she'd finally managed to carve out of her mother's hard heart.

Nothing was worth that. Nothing.

Breaking that temporary connection with him, she left the room.

Caillen felt a flutter of disappointment that the unknown Qill was gone. He had no idea why. She was not his type. Not by a long shot.

Yeah but at least she wouldn't be boring. Which the pampered women around him were. Yes, they were intelligent and beautiful. But they had no idea what the real world was like, and he found that not only abhorrent and irresponsible for the people who made the laws that governed everyone, he found it naive. They mistook leisurely travel and overpriced education for worldly experience. In his existence, worldliness meant being able to scrape together a handful of beans to make ten meals that fed four people. Being able to repair your home and transportation with minimal parts at a minimum cost.

These people thought they knew what troubles were and yet they were as clueless as a three-year-old babe crying over a petty broken toy because to them *that* was the end of the world. True reality had never once touched them. Not really. Their money isolated them behind a protective wall that kept everything ugly on the outside.

Not having Mummy's and Daddy's love or getting into the right school or having the highest level of a job wasn't a tragedy. He considered it a damn shame their selfish parents couldn't make room in their overindulged hearts for their kids, but it wasn't the catastrophe they made it out to be. Tragedy was watching a loved one die because you couldn't afford one more day of a hospital stay after you'd already gone broke and homeless trying to pay for their treatment, or knowing people who'd sold their bodies just for their biweekly meals. It was having to bury your parents before you were ten and then having to make rent. Having to sell blood to pay for your sister's medicine to treat an incurable illness that would kill her if you didn't. It was going without food for days just so that same sister could have a necessary trip to the doctor that was weeks overdue and then hoping you could talk the doctor into taking a partial payment and not throw your ass out on the street in front of a waiting room full of people.

Those were real horrors. Not being able to buy the painting you "loved" because someone beat you to it wasn't. But to the people around him, the latter was a tragedy of epic proportions.

I don't belong here.

Honestly, he didn't want to.

Feeling sick to his stomach, he cleared his throat to get his father's attention.

His father looked at him expectantly and it hit him like a fist in his abdomen. Even though he'd only known his father a few months, he'd learned to love and respect him in spite of the world he lived in. The man cared about him and he didn't want to disappoint him.

But this...

He just needed a break. "I'm not feeling well—"

"Are you all right?" The concern in his father's eyes tightened his stomach even more.

"I will be. May I be excused?" He hated sounding like that. In his world, the exchange would have been completely different... *"Hey, Dad, think I'm gonna puke. Gonna hit the head and snatch a nap, 'kay?"*

But both his father and Boggi would faint dead if he said that out loud around this group.

His father waved a bodyguard over. "Take your time.

Please let me know if you won't be able to make dinner so that I can inform the others."

"Yes, sir." Caillen turned and headed away from the crowd with that annoying guard behind him. Like he needed anyone's help protecting himself. *Want to wipe my chin while you're at it?*

Darling and Maris met up with him in the hallway.

"You okay?" Darling frowned. "You look like you're about to hurl."

At least Darling used real speak. "How are you so normal having come from this shit?"

Darling gave him a lopsided grin. "My hellbent friends. I owe all my sanity to you guys." Yeah, and what Darling failed to mention was the double life he lived. To everyone here he was royal. To their friends, he was a wanted renegade who protected the innocent victims chosen by the League. One who had a staggering price on his head.

Caillen glanced at Maris. "I know you're not normal."

Maris laughed. "I actually like the pomp and decorum. I find it refreshing to have civility in a universe where people routinely kill each other for profit."

"Yeah, but in case you haven't noticed, all this civility is fake."

Maris arched a haughty brow. "Fake is pretending to deliver flowers to someone and then shooting them in the face when they answer the door. It's smiling at someone while listening sympathetically to their problems and pretending to be their best friend and then doing everything behind their back to ruin them. Taking that gleaned confidential information and turning it against them. Exposing their personal secrets to others for no other reason than sheer meanness and cruelty. Or even worse, lying about them after they've done nothing but try to help you because you're jealous and know you can never accomplish what they have."

Maris indicated the people they'd left with a thumb over his shoulder. "Everyone knows the aristos are out for themselves and are ruthless. They don't pretend to care about you and you know not to tell them anything you don't want made public. We make no bones about it. Yet we still respect each other and all the political machinations that go on. It's honest treachery in my opinion. No one is ever surprised when one senator ruins another. Or one emperor orders the death of his rival. Yet people are always stunned when their best friend talks about them behind their back or tries to ruin them for no real reason other than petty jealousy or just sheer meanness."

Now Caillen was actually scared as he realized that Maris was right. "You know in a fucked up way, that makes sense. Only you could put it all into perspective."

Maris shrugged. "It's all about perspective, my friend. That and the ability to duck fast when life throws excrement at you."

Caillen laughed at his unexpected comeback as he entered his room and his guard remained in the hallway. It was extremely out of character for Maris to talk like that. "I think we've finally corrupted him, Darling."

Before Maris could respond, Darling cut him off. "You want us to stay or do you need some downtime?"

"I need some time."

Darling gave him a sympathetic pat on the shoulder. "It will get easier. I swear."

Caillen didn't believe it for a minute. But he appreciated the kindness. Then again if anyone knew about leading a double life, Darling was it. "Thanks."

He waited until they were gone before he jerked the robes off and let them fall into a heap at his feet. He had a childish urge to kick them. Saddest part? Those damn things cost as much as his ship and would have fed him and his sisters for about six years back in the day.

Raking his hands through his hair, he headed for his closet where he had his backpack stashed. Black and worn, it'd been his security blanket for years. A gadget for every occasion. This was his magic sack that had seen him through many a hairy ordeal.

He smiled as he opened it and rifled through the stuff that belonged to his past. Weapons, dehydrated food, garb...

And finally...

"There you are." He pulled his old link out and cradled it in his palm. This was what he needed...

Exchanging it with the one in his ear, he called his sister. He was still mad at Shahara and the others for never telling him he was adopted, but he understood.

To them he was family. It didn't matter how it'd happened. The moment their father had shown up with him in his arms, the three of them had welcomed him into their hearts and never looked back.

"Cai?" Shahara had a deep, husky voice for a woman, which had been great as a kid 'cause she hadn't been able to scream at him in shrill tones—unlike Kasen and Tess. "Is that you, pook? I've missed you so much! Why haven't you called and updated me on what's going on in your new life?"

He smiled at an endearment only his oldest sister could

get away with. "Hey. I've been busy as hell with all the . . . stuff my dad has been strangling me with. So what's up with you?"

"Nothing." A clipped response that quickly led to her voice dropping two octaves. "Tell me what's wrong."

He licked his dry lips as his gut knotted even more over the sound of her sweet voice in his ear. Gods, how he'd missed her. "Who says anything's wrong?"

"Honey, I know you. I know that tone. You're sad and hurting. What's going on, baby? You need me to come and kill someone for you?"

He smiled at his sister's not-so-empty threat. As a former bounty hunter, she'd probably killed more people than he had. "I don't need you to fight my battles. I just wanted to hear a friendly voice."

It sounded like she was opening something up on her end. "You know we're always here for you."

"Same." It was so wonderful to know that even though she was on the other side of the universe, she would fight to the bitter death for him. He could see a perfect image of what she must look like in his mind. Her long red hair and gold eyes that were always filled with motherly love whenever she looked at him. She most likely would have one side of her hair pulled back from her ear while she talked to him and she'd keep one hand up near her link. No reason for it, just a strange quirk she had. And she was probably wearing a flowing floral dress that would make her appear soft and gentle. A total contradiction for a woman who could take down the nastiest scum the universe had ever spat out of hell.

"Are you going to talk to me or just keep breathing in my ear?" she asked.

"I like breathing in your ear."

"You're a sick man, Cai. I thought I raised you better."

Normally he'd find that humorous, but not at this moment. Right now, those words cut him. "Don't do that."

"Do what?"

"Fault find with me. I know you're joking. I just don't want to hear you bitching at me, okay?"

"That's it. I'm officially worried. Do I need to come get you?"

Would he ever grow up in her eyes? "I'm not a kid, Shay."

"I know you're not. You're the only human being in my life, other than my husband I've ever been able to rely on. And I can't stand to hear you upset. It makes me want to hurt someone for you. I love you, Caillen. I want you to know that."

He held those words like a lifeline. "I love you, too."

Then he heard Syn in the background. "I have his coordinates. I could get us there within two hours. You want me to fuel my ship?"

That succeeded in making him laugh. "Tell your crazy-ass husband that I definitely don't need his help. If I so much as see his shadow, I'll shoot him myself." It was so nice to have a conversation without pretense or worrying about vocabulary, syntax or enunciation. "Here, I won't keep you guys. I only wanted to check in."

"All right." Her tone was reserved and by that he knew she was still concerned about him. "Stay safe and remember I'm only a call away when you need me. And if you change your mind, my crazy-ass husband can get me to you in two hours."

He shook his head as he reached for the shut off button

on the link. "Thanks." He hung up and sighed even while a smile continued to tease the edges of his lips over her last words.

How had his life become so complicated? He'd had many times in the past when he'd wanted to lie down in the gutter and let the universe take his soul back. Times when the crap he had to deal with had rained down on him with a fury so foul it'd left him temporarily bitter.

This was nothing like those times and yet he felt so defeated. Lost.

Hurt.

He couldn't explain the emotions that shredded him. They were there, tearing at his confidence. Making him wish his father had never found him.

Enough whining. Damn, Cai, you are turning into an aristos. Gah. What is wrong with me?

This was absolutely not him. He had money and power. There was nothing wrong with him other than stupidity.

Not wanting to think about it anymore, he closed his backpack, then lay down on the couch so that he could stare out the portal window at the stars that had guided, protected and soothed him every day of his adulthood. What he wouldn't give to be back on his ship, making a deadly run through a hostile sector...

But as he stared at them, his thoughts turning blank, an image jumped into his mind from some place he couldn't even begin to fathom.

It was the sight of a dark-haired Qill with a sassy walk that said she'd rather kick his ass than kiss his lips. Actually he wouldn't mind the former if he could get the latter.

Yeah.

I am a seriously sick bastard. He had no idea why she appealed to him, but in the end, he knew one thing.

He was going to be stupid for her and she was definitely going to get him into a world of hurt.

Some temptations were just more than a mere mortal could deny and she was one of the biggest ones he'd ever come across. Yeah, next time they met, he was definitely going to allow her to lead him astray.

Desideria entered the large suite of rooms to find her mother's migraine meds. A migraine her mother swore was brought on by being surrounded by men who possessed what she called manginas.

She reached the nightstand and searched through several bottles until she found the right one. As she closed the drawer, the small bottle slipped from her hand.

"Great," she breathed. She'd had a bad case of dropsies since she'd awakened. No doubt it was from her nerves and the fact that she was so wary of making even a single mistake for fear of her mother insulting her again in front of the others.

Worse, the bottle rolled beneath the bed to the far side, out of easy reach. She bent down to pick it up, then froze the moment her head was near the vent that ran under the bed. She heard a faint voice saying the most shocking thing she'd ever heard in her life.

"Sarra will be dead before she leaves that ship. If you can get Desideria in the process, all the better. I'm even willing to have her become a state hero who died valiantly while trying to save her mother if you can deliver both their heads to me."

"It's harder than you thought. There are cameras and security everywhere."

"Are you telling me you're too incompetent to bypass them?"

"Never."

"Then I suggest you get started. The sooner this is over with, the better for all of us."

"It will be done."

"Good because if the next transmission isn't a news-feed saying they're dead, there will be one about how a certain someone had a mishap of her own and was flushed out an air lock."

Desideria pulled back, her heart hammering. Someone was going to kill her mother...

Her own life didn't matter to her. Well, not entirely true. She didn't want to die, but her life was insignificant compared to her mother's. As part of the High Guard, she'd taken an oath to lay down her life to protect her queen. Should she fail to keep her mother safe, her own life would be forfeit too.

All members of the Guard would be executed should the queen die by assassination during their watch.

She had to warn her mother before it was too late. Leaning in closer, she tried to hear more of their plotting, but the voices were too faint. Muffled as if they realized someone might be listening.

Desideria moved closer to the vent...

Now the voices were gone entirely.

Damn.

Grabbing the medicine, she quickly made her way back to the ship's forward deck where her mother was talking to Pleba while the other aristos drifted near them. She didn't know why, but the bright clothing reminded her of birds preening around each other.

Except for her mother who was dressed in dark brown and black. The Qillaqs believed the body was a work of art and that it should be displayed and appreciated—why work to perfect something only to hide it beneath layers of fabric? Which was why her mother's dress was made up of leather straps that barely covered the parts of her body other races found vulgar when exposed.

Even so, Desideria was very conservative compared to the rest of her group. While she was proud of her body, she was still shy about flaunting it. She was extremely muscular, but compared to the other women in her family, she was rather heavyset and too many years of her mother and sisters insulting her weight had made her very self-conscious over showing too much of it lest they start in on her again.

Her mother paused as she saw Desideria approach. She held her hand out for the medicine in an imperious gesture that irritated her.

Desideria hesitated. "May I have a word with you, My Queen?"

"Speak."

She swept her gaze over the Guard, making a mental note of who was missing. "Where are Xene and Via?" One or both of them had to be the muffled female voice she'd heard through the vent. No one else would be allowed close enough to her mother to kill her.

"They had to go to the restroom. Would you like to join them?" She held her hand out again. "My medicine."

"Mother—"

Her mother cleared her throat sharply at Desideria's use of a title that was forbidden whenever they were in public.

She clenched her teeth in frustration. "Beg pardon, My Queen, but my news is extremely important."

"Then speak it and give me my medicine to cure my headache instead of adding to it."

"I..." She bit her lip in indecision. What if the killer wasn't working alone? Another member of the Guard could very well be in on it. Right now, she didn't dare trust anyone until she knew where their real loyalties lay. "It's of a private nature."

"There is nothing private from my Guard. You know this."

Why was her mother being so ridiculously stubborn? Was it to keep the others from thinking she had favor toward her daughter? Or was her mother just that stupid?

Desideria debated what to do. Ultimately, she had to speak. The longer she kept silent, the closer the killer could get to striking distance. Taking a deep breath, she handed her mother the bottle and told her what she'd heard. "I have reason to fear for your safety."

Her mother went perfectly still, then cackled. "While we're here? Please. I know you want to prove your worth. But there's no threat here unless they plan to bore me to death."

Several of the Guard laughed.

Desideria was humiliated by her mother's rough dismissal.

Peria, the Head Guard, stepped forward. "Why don't you take a small break, child?"

And Desideria really could have done without that slap. Honestly, she wanted to cry, but she wasn't about to give them the satisfaction.

"I just now overheard a plot to kill you."

That at least got her mother's attention.

Until she burst out laughing again. "Don't be a fool, child. No one here has the balls to come after me. Now go take your break and leave us."

Desideria was mortified as she summoned what tiny bit of dignity she could find and turned away while they laughed at her.

"An attempt at a summit?" Peria's mocking tone sent a wave of nausea through her body. "Really? What was she thinking?"

"Perhaps I was impulsive to appoint her so soon." Her mother sighed. "I had such ambition for her. Oh well. I only hope Narcissa and Gwenela don't turn out to be disappointments too. I should never have bred with her father. So much for thinking of adding to our bloodline with an offworlder. I should have known better."

Those words were like a kick in her gut. *I hate you, you sanctimonious bitch.* But she didn't hate her mother. Not really. She was hurt and lashing out.

It was bad enough when other people mocked her. When her mother did it, it was so much worse. All she wanted was to make her mother proud of her. Why was that such an impossible task?

How will I ever face the others again?

None of them had any respect for her at this point. They thought her inept.

Worse, they thought her weak.

Lost in her thoughts, she didn't pay any attention to where she was going until she collided with a solid wall. At least that was what she thought it was until she realized it was a man.

A huge, powerful man with a body so hard it was like touching granite.

Gasping, she looked up and froze.

Dark brown eyes glowed with warmth as a slow smile spread across the face of the devastating male she'd noticed earlier. And her collision laid to rest any speculation about the body obscured by his voluminous robes. He was as honed as any warrior she'd ever seen.

The teasing light in his eyes faded into a look of deep concern. "Are you all right?"

It was difficult to think of a response when the pleasant masculine scent of him was thick in her head and his eyes captivated her so. Oh, he was gorgeous. "Fine."

His intelligent gaze sharpened. "You don't look fine ... I mean, you do look F-I-N-E, but something's bothering you. Can I do something to help?"

She hated to be that transparent to anyone. *Great. Just great. Now I'm humiliating myself with strangers too.* That was all she needed. "You're right. You are bothering me. Now move out of my way." Her tone was sharper than she meant it to be, but she couldn't control her anger over her own stupidity and embarrassment.

He held his hands up and stepped aside to let her pass. "Pardon me for trying to help."

Desideria took three steps, then turned back to apologize for her rudeness.

He was already gone.

Weird. And fast, not to mention silent. She wouldn't have thought he could move like that, especially while swathed in that much material.

Part of her was bothered that she'd been so curt with him. He didn't deserve it. She hated whenever she took her anger out on the wrong person—like her mother always did. She tried so hard not to do that to others. And here, she'd slapped at someone who was just trying to be nice.

"This is not my day." At this point, she really wanted to crawl under something and die.

Die...

She'd blurted out to her mother what she'd overheard. If whoever the killer was caught wind of that...

Dying was a very real possibility. Drek...What had she done? Her actions might very well have facilitated things. *I've got to find out who it is. Immediately.*

Because if she didn't, both of them would die.

8

Caillen sat with his father in the summit chamber, surrounded by nobles and officials, bored out of his mind. The room was round so that they could all see each other should someone give in to the need to yawn, the sadistic bastards, with dim lighting that seemed to suck all the energy out of the very marrow of his bones. Yeah, there was definitely something being emitted by the bulbs that was dimming his intellect. He could feel his IQ slipping at least one point per minute.

Maybe more.

At this rate, he'd be reduced to a vegetative state within the hour.

It explained much about their current leadership . . . his father notwithstanding.

In the center was a chair that was occupied by the officials and reps who'd come to beg council attention to certain matters regarding their worlds.

Gods what I wouldn't give for one of the senators to go mental and pull out a blaster and kill someone.

Hell, at this point, they could kill him. Anything to get him out of this. But at least he'd helped his father get a treaty with the Krellins. That had pleased the man exponentially.

"We're a small system and the rights to our crops..."

Caillen zoned out again so that he wouldn't have to hear the sharp, nasal whine of a governor wanting more funding for his wardrobe. Oh wait, he wanted funding for his poor people. Yeah...that was what the man was pitching.

He arched a brow at the two million credits' worth of rocks sewn onto the governor's jacket and adorning the man's corpulent hand—wouldn't those help his country's finances just a bit?

And he knew exactly what those stones were worth. Appraising them even at a distance was a talent he'd acquired from a friend of his who was a pirate and jewel thief. After spending years around Chayden and his pirate friends, *he* could price a stone faster and more accurately than most experienced appraisers.

How bored am I that I'm trying to guess carat weight visually?

Shoot me.

The governor finished his plea, then left the senior officials to decide his fate. Unfortunately, the leader of those senior officials was his father, which meant Caillen was stuck in this room until hell froze over.

I feel my life ticking away...C'mon, assassin. Please strike.

Boggi cleared his throat. "Next are the Qillaqs who are here to inform the council of their intentions toward the Trimutians."

Well at least he'd have his hot babe Guard to stare at

for this one. That should help a little even if she'd snapped his head off earlier. So much for his promise to get her into his bed. She'd effectively nipped his erection.

At least for the moment. There was still dinner and if he played his cards right...

Dessert.

Yeah, he could just imagine her spoon-feeding him what he needed most to turn this shitty day around. And if what he suspected about her was right, she'd chisel a smile on his face not even the League could remove.

His father sighed as an apprehensive tremor ran through the room. It was so thick, it was tangible.

Leaning toward his father so that he could whisper, Caillen frowned. "What's up?"

A tic worked in his father's jaw. "It's the way the Qillaqs negotiate. It's embarrassing, really."

He'd opened his mouth to ask him to elaborate when the door opened to show the Qillaq delegation. For one split second, all the blood drained from his brain to one part of his anatomy as the queen and her Guard entered in outfits so skimpy they didn't really cover anything.

Oh yeah, he could see straight to the business end of the queen's body, and her breasts were only covered by a thin gauze that highlighted the fact she'd rouged her nipples to make them more prominent through the material. He knew many places in the universe where going out like that in public would get you arrested.

Or laid.

His tongue thick, he looked past the queen to the woman he'd spoken to earlier in the hallway.

With her hair now braided down her back, she was dressed more sedately in a burgundy halter top and tight pants. Still, that top plunged deep between her breasts making him wish she'd dressed more like her queen.

Yeah, gimme a bite of that...

He'd say that if the other officials had dressed like this it would have kept him awake, but honestly their bodies were best covered. No need in making everyone sick.

These on the other hand made him wish he was a Qill.

Slap my ass and call me yours. She could lock him to her bed and keep him there as long as she wanted.

Baby, what is your name? He wouldn't be able to sleep tonight until he knew it.

He wouldn't be able to focus on anything until he knew her scent.

The men in the room shifted uncomfortably while the women curled their lips in distaste. Yeah, jealousy was a bitch.

Never one to let anything interfere with his decorum, Boggi cleared his throat. "Queen Sarra, please state your case to the council."

She came forward to sit on the chair with a seductive gait that was probably causing the older members to wheeze. When she sat, it was with an open posture that made him want to laugh—poor queen had no idea that he was used to negotiating with women a lot hotter, sexier and more naked than she was at present. If she wanted his mind numb, she should have sent in her little Guard woman dressed like that to speak for her.

He doubted he'd be able to even remember his own name if Ms. Cutie back there were naked. He caught Darling's amused smirk from the other side of the room. There was a challenge in that stare and it was one Caillen planned to meet.

The queen cleared her throat. "Members of the council, I have a dire matter to discuss. The Trimutians are on our borders and are mercilessly pressing into our territory. We have issued restraints and they ignore them. Our next step is to declare war. I'm here today, per League orders, to let all of you know our intentions."

His father scowled. "Why have you waited to tell us this? You should have sought counsel to help police the Trimutians."

"We are a private nation. Proud. We don't seek help when we can deal with the matter on our own."

What that...?

Caillen told himself to keep silent, but as the council began to back her war, he couldn't. He saw through her plan as easily as he saw through her clothes and he couldn't stand by and let an innocent nation be victimized by a profiteering bitch. "The Trimutians are on your borders you say?"

She passed him the most scathing glare of his life—an impressive feat, really, considering how many people he managed to piss off on a daily basis. "I don't like to repeat myself."

"I can respect that. But I am curious, Your Majesty. Can you tell me how long they've been pressing you?"

"Almost a year."

Really? Caillen scowled as he digested that. Seemed odd and off. Then again, she was lying and he knew it. "How many of their armada would you say have been harassing your borders?"

"The majority of it. Every time we turn around, one of them is attacking. They've taken up refuge on one of our colonies and have been holding its inhabitants as hostages, demanding we pay or they'll kill them."

Oh yeah . . . Bull. Shit. It was so thick, they could grow a garden.

Caillen looked around at the faces of the senators whose glares were silently telling him to shut his mouth. But he couldn't. Nothing she said made sense in his world. A colony of Qills would be armed for war and woe to anyone dumb enough to try and take them hostage. It would have been a bloodbath so severe, they'd still be running news segments on it. "For a year?"

"Is that not what I said?"

Nice tone there and if his father wasn't sitting to his left, he'd elevate it up a notch. As it was, he kept his tone level, nice and calm. "It is indeed, Your Majesty. However, I find it odd that they'd be on your borders and occupying a foreign colony when the bulk of their armada is in the Brimen sector for training and has been for the last six months. Their borders are manned by a skeleton fleet that has its hands full dealing with runners and pirates. Therefore, I'm baffled by this phantom group holding your people hostage. Have you considered they're rogues and not backed by the Trimutians?"

Her cheeks flushed as she realized he'd caught her in a lie. "Are you daring to question me?"

The Gondarion governor cleared his throat sharply as he glared at him. "Prince Caillen, we don't speculate here. We only discuss facts."

Caillen took offense at the man's censoring tone that said he thought Caillen was an idiot. He narrowed his gaze and spoke slowly so that the imbecile could follow him. "And I'm giving you facts, Senator. Look it up. The Trimutian territory is the shortest run from Starken to Altaria. Pirates call it the Golden Lightyear because for the last two years, it's been the easiest payday they've seen in decades. It's why the Trimutians have sent their armada in for training. They're trying to come up with some way to catch the pirates and rout them out of their system without losing their entire fleet. The major revenue stream for Trimala has always been shipping and their cargoes are easy pickings. Their colonies are rich in resources, so it doesn't make sense that they'd go after Qillaq territory which only has a pittance of raw materials and open another front to their war while their armada is stretched perilously thin by the thieves plaguing them. However, it makes total sense for the Qillaqs to declare war on them and attack while they're weak and then claim their resources as their own."

The queen shot to her feet. "How dare you!"

Desideria pressed her lips together as the Exeterian prince held his cool against her mother. It wasn't often that anyone got the better of their queen and she was impressed that he'd managed to do so. He was intelligent and courageous to speak his mind when it was obvious the others wanted him to remain silent.

Even with her mother's fury, his eyes held a teasing light in them that said he was used to conflict and found the sparring entertaining. How odd...

"There's no need to be angry, Your Majesty. We all understand profiteering. Me more than the others. I respect your plan. Good luck getting it past the League."

"I already have their backing."

Desideria cringed at her mother tipping her hand. No doubt that was Prince Caillen's intention.

One corner of his mouth turned up into an evil grin. "Then you better attack quick because the minute I leave here, I'm making a call to a friend. I assure you, the League might back you, but the Trimutians won't be as weak as they were before and when my friend hears about this, the League won't be so nice either."

Sarra's gaze left Caillen and went to his father. "You allow a child to speak for you?"

To Desideria's surprise, his father didn't back down. "My son is far from a child and he has more battle experience than the commander of my armada. I always take his advice...as should you."

The look of hell wrath on her mother's face said that they should tighten their borders too. "I'm done here." Her mother stormed from the room.

Desideria stood quickly, but not before she caught a wink from the prince.

Oh what a moron. Had he no idea what he'd just done? Stupid fool. Her mother wouldn't rest until she had him in chains. In the end, it would be her mother laughing, not him.

Once the room was cleared of the Qills, every eye turned on Caillen who suddenly felt like he'd sprouted a second head.

The Gondarion governor curled his lip. "Sarra will want all of our lives after this. None of us are safe. Why couldn't you keep your mouth shut? Better the Trimutians than us."

"What have you done?"

"You idiot! How could you do this?"

"Damn it, Evzen, did you have to bring him here?"

Flabbergasted by their assault, Caillen couldn't hear the rest of the attacks because they all melded together into a cacophonous amalgamation of insults. But it was the disappointed look on his father's face that cut him. His father looked ashamed.

And that set his temper on fire.

That's it. He'd had enough. No more of this shit. How dare they attack *him,* a lying, smuggling thief, for having morals. They were supposed to be the ones who kept the laws. The hypocrisy made him sick.

Rising to his feet, he flung his robes to the ground and glared at them. "Shame on you. *All* of you. I have met some of the lowest life forms in the universe. Beings who would sell their own mothers and children for the right price. And I have to say that I'd rather swap watered-down drinks with them in the back dive of hell than sit here and listen to you whine about the fact that you're all willing to throw an entire system into war because you're all afraid to stand up to one queen from one tiny empire. What kind of cowards are you? If this is your idea of diplomacy, then why have you bothered to sign League treaties? Why not just let the governments go back to the free-for-all they were before the League took power? No wonder the League runs over all of you." He raked them with his own disdainful sneer. "This isn't civilized. It's selfish and it should be criminal. And with all due offense, I'd rather hang with the criminals than any of you. At least they have a moral code, fucked up though it is."

Disgusted, he stormed from the room and left them there to condemn him for it.

If he was going to be judged, it would be for who he was. Not who he was trying to be. And if the Qill queen wanted his head. Let her take a number.

In the meantime, he had places to go, a life to live and a universe to set on fire . . .

9

Desideria watched as the Slexan governor bowed low before her mother. For the last half an hour, he'd apologized profusely for Prince Caillen's actions and had assured her mother that the rest of them did not support the prince's position.

Bloody cowards. She had no respect for them. At least Caillen had spoken his mind and the fact that he stood alone made him even more heroic in her eyes.

The governor had also promised her mother that the prince would be adequately punished for insulting her.

I'd pay money to see that. Prince Caillen didn't seem like the kind of man to bow down before anyone. Never mind coming here to apologize in person like her mother demanded.

It should be entertaining.

After the governor left, her mother rose from her desk to stare angrily at them. She was still seething over her public set down and had ranted nonstop since their return to her office suite. "I'd leave this place, but I refuse to give that bastard the satisfaction of thinking he was the cause of it. I will remain if for no other reason than to be a thorn in his ass." But it was obvious that staying here was the last thing her mother wanted to do. Not that she blamed her.

She didn't want to be here either and a small part of herself that she didn't want to acknowledge had enjoyed seeing her mother receive a little bit of what her mother had been shoveling at her for years.

Go, Caillen, go.

The door opened to admit Pleba back into the room. She'd left right before the governor had shown up to attend some mysterious errand her mother had sent her on.

Pleba bowed low before she spoke words that shredded Desideria's entire world. "As per your orders, I've sent for Desideria's replacement, My Queen. Burna will arrive within the next four hours to relieve her of her post."

Desideria pretended not to hear the words that stung so deeply they might as well be hitting her soul. Worse were the smug and snide looks the others turned in her direction. They were thrilled to see her sent home in disgrace. *I should have stayed in my room.* But she'd thought to prove herself by rejoining them for the earlier meeting and taking her post here.

Big mistake.

Obviously her mother had already made the decision to relieve her.

Fine. No doubt her mother would demote her back to child status as soon as they reached home. And for what? Trying to protect her? Yeah, that did make her feel a childish urge to scream out that it was unfair.

Whatever. There was nothing she could do.

Look on the bright side, if they kill her while you're gone, you won't be executed for it.

True. But she wasn't that petty and as she stood flanking the room with the rest of the Guard, she knew at least one of them was a traitor. One of them was plotting her death and that of her mother. Right now. While that person pretended to do her job, she was one step away from attacking.

The hypocrisy of that churned inside her.

But who?

How?

Most of all, when would the betrayer attack?

Her mother's bedroom would be the most likely place. As per her mother's request there were no cameras there. Only a panic button. But if her mother couldn't get to it...

Or if it was deactivated...

A bad feeling went through her. She needed to check the wiring to make sure no one had messed with it. *Think what you will of me, I won't neglect my duties.* She would protect her mother no matter what. So long as she was on this ship, she would do her due diligence even while they all laughed at her for it.

She cleared her throat to get her mother's attention. "May I be excused, My Queen?"

Her mother didn't even bother answering verbally. She waved at her dismissively. Desideria balled her hands into fists to keep from returning that gesture with an obscene one of her own that would get her into even more trouble.

Without another word, she left the room and headed down the hallway, toward their bed chambers to check her mother's personal quarters. And after that, she needed to pack to return home.

In shame.

Profanity danced in her thoughts as she imagined what she'd like to do to her mother over this latest humiliation. Honestly, she was sick of it. She wasn't a child and she was through being treated like one. Too many years of humiliation and condemnation left a raw bitterness in her heart. She didn't deserve this.

Not when she'd been doing her duty.

Desideria had almost reached her mother's chambers when a door opened behind her. For the tiniest moment her heart skipped a beat as an image of Prince Caillen popped into her head. She could just imagine what he'd look like with his eyes dancing in fury as he stalked toward her with a warrior's lethal grace to apologize to her mother...

Before she could think better, she turned her head, hoping to catch a glimpse of him again.

It wasn't Caillen.

Instead a figure in a hooded dark gray cloak moved past her with quick strides. Not thinking anything about it, she started forward only to find her way blocked as the figure stopped and turned as if heading back toward his or her room.

"Excuse me." She tried to pass the stranger.

The person stepped in front of her, intentionally blocking her way.

A sudden flash of silver caught her attention as a blade came out from under the cloak's folds to dart toward her throat. Her training kicked in. She caught the attack and head butted her assailant. Another knife came up in the other hand, slashing for her arm.

Desideria dodged and went low to sweep at the legs.

But the moment she did, someone came up behind her and caught a garrote around her neck. Gasping, she was jerked back, off her feet, and dragged down the hallway toward her room. She tried to call for help, but the tightness around her throat kept her from making anything more than a hoarse croak.

"We need her dead. Remember, it has to look like she committed suicide in shame."

Her vision dimmed as she kicked her feet, fighting for her freedom and her life. She would not die. Not like this. Not at the hands of a coward who attacked from behind. Desperately, she clutched at the hands holding on to the garrote, but she couldn't get a good grip on them. Rage scorched her. She couldn't stand someone getting the better of her. The fact that they were going to kill her if she didn't win made it all the worse.

Her vision dimmed.

She was losing this fight...

Suddenly her attacker went flying into the wall beside her. The cord dropped from her throat, allowing her to breathe again. The sudden rush of unencumbered air into her lungs left her light-headed and faint. She wheezed and coughed, trying to get her bearings as she turned over on the floor. But all she saw was a dark blur as it attacked her assailants and threw them every which way.

It wasn't until he caught the first attacker and rebounded the masked figure into the wall that she realized it was Caillen who'd saved her.

And just as she suspected, he fought like a seasoned soldier, not an aristos.

She'd barely pushed herself to her feet when she saw Pleba and Tyree rushing down the hallway to assist them.

Now her attackers would pay and her mother would know she wasn't stupid for trying to protect her.

But her relief was cut short as they went for Caillen and not her attackers.

Holy gods...

They were in on the plot!

Caillen saw the assassin's eyes narrow past his shoulder. Since the Qill Guard was in front of him, he knew it meant reinforcements were coming at his back. He turned just in time to catch the first one and launch her into the assassin.

The second one lifted a blaster. He dodged the blast an instant before it would have exploded his head.

The one he'd thrown picked up her link and shouted into it for security. "Help! We're being attacked by the Exeterian prince! He's mad. He's trying to assassinate our princess. We need immediate assistance." She leveled her own blaster at him as she muted the link. "Give my regards to the gods."

He gaped, then dodged her blast as he realized they were setting him up to die. "You harita!" he snarled at the cute Guard he'd thought he was saving when he entered the fray. How could he have been so stupid as to think a Qill would be hurt?

Idiot!

Not only had he embarrassed his father—again—he was about to be charged with a crime he hadn't committed. And all because of *her*.

Nice revenge from their bitch queen.

Desideria was baffled by his insult and the look of hatred blazing in his eyes as he glared at her. But her confusion died as she saw Pleba set her weapon for kill and

open fire on them. She had to do something or they were
both dead.

Reacting on instinct, she launched herself at Caillen
and knocked him into the wall, out of the line of fire. The
moment she did, the wall shimmered and opened, dump-
ing them into an escape pod.

Thank the gods for small favors. She hadn't realized a
portal was there.

Now she had to seal it before Pleba and the others
shot through it. Unable to read the panels which were in a
language she didn't know, she made a guess as to which
button would shut the door and notify security. Red most
likely would launch them, so she hit an orange button in
the center of the console. The door shot down, protecting
them from the others.

Relieved she let out an elongated breath and sat back
to wait for security.

Until she realized the engines were firing and the pod
was launching while they were trapped inside it.

Crap...

10

His head throbbing from being slammed into a hard steel wall by a woman he wanted to throttle, Caillen cursed as he regained his equilibrium and realized what was happening.

They were launching away from the *Arimanda*.

Mobilizing, he climbed over his female annoyance who appeared frozen in horror by her actions, but by the time he reached the console, it was too late.

They were adrift and the ship was leaving them in its wake. *Son of a...*

Would the misery of this day never end? He sat down in the black leather chair next to hers and shook his head as deep aggravation filled him.

There was nothing he could do to stop this. Nothing. He let out a slow, agitated breath and cursed his crappy luck that had betrayed him yet again. Of all the flipping shit...

"Can't we catch up to the ship?"

Oh yeah, there was an award-winning question of the day and it set his temper boiling.

He gave her a withering glare. Not even the vulnerable look on her face that made her extremely attractive could cut through his need to want to launch her out an air lock head first. Still, he forced himself to keep his tone even and his sarcasm at an acceptable level that wouldn't quite motivate her to murder—no need in both of them being pissed in tight quarters. "We have one small thruster that's only strong enough to safely land us on a planet."

Caillen pointed out the window to the ship that was quickly becoming a silver dot in the darkness. "In case you haven't noticed, they're moving a lot faster. I don't know about the laws of physics on your planet, but where I come from an object moving at subclass speed can't catch up to one running at starclass. But if you know something about turbines, thrusters and engines, quantum or classical physics that I've somehow missed, then please enlighten me." Yeah, okay, so he'd never been the best at corralling his sarcasm.

At least he'd tried. That counted for something, right?

She curled her lip. "You don't have to be an asshole."

Now the gloves were off. "Oh, baby, this ain't asshole. Trust me. There's a hole keg of asshole I haven't even begun to tap yet."

The expression on her face was so scalding he felt the burn of her anger even from his seat. Another time and place, they'd be getting naked.

But this wasn't the place and it definitely wasn't the time. All he wanted right now was to finish what her fake attacker had started. Choke her until her eyes bulged out. "Don't even give me that look. Not after what *you* were planning."

She scowled at him as if she were baffled by his words.

It'd be a nice expression if it were real. "What? Protecting my mother?"

What the hell was she talking about? She hadn't appeared to be protecting anyone while she'd lain on the floor being strangled. "Yeah, no. That whole act of setting me up for your queen so that she could get her vengeance on me for calling her crap crap. Nice move. But I'm not *that* stupid." At least not today. And definitely not for her.

"Are you on something?"

She was good. He could almost believe that innocence she was trying to sell. But he'd been around actresses and grifters before who were much more convincing.

"Like you don't know what I'm talking about."

She shook her head. "I have no clue and you're wasting my time." She pointed toward the sector where the *Arimanda* had vanished. "We have to get back to the ship before the assassins go after my mother. It's imperative."

He paused in confusion. Was her mother one of the Guards or someone else? "What are *you* talking about?"

Desideria had never been more frustrated in her life. The man was insane. Did he have some kind of mental problem that he couldn't recall what had happened right before they fell into the pod? How hard had the imbecile struck his head?

"Hello? Remember the fight you broke in on? Me on the floor being choked? The bad guys who attacked you..."

"I didn't break into a fight. You were setting me up by allowing them to choke you."

He really was mentally defective. Did he honestly think she'd allow herself to be choked like that? On purpose? What kind of people did he run with that such an idea would even enter his mind? She pointed to the nasty burn on her throat she was sure was bruised if not bleeding. "Does this *really* look like I was pretending?"

Caillen paused as he focused on the purple welts that belied his accusation. Actually it did look painful and authentic. Not to mention the fact that it would probably scar and most women he knew resisted permanent disfiguration.

Still, there were people who'd maimed themselves before for a lot less reason and Qills weren't normal in any sense of that word. For her queen's pleasure, she just might be insane enough to ruin her neck, scar her face or even eat small babies for breakfast. "You were serving your country well. I'm sure they'll decorate you for it." That was, after all, what her people lived for.

She screwed her face up in disgust. "What do you think was happening when you barged in?"

Barged in? Yeah, she was a piece of work. In his neighborhood it was called helping someone. Which just proved what he knew, she wasn't really in any danger.

"I don't think. I know. I heard your boss lady call security and say that I was trying to kill your princess. That is a cold, hard fact."

"And which of the women in that hallway do you think the princess was?"

Caillen went over the people who'd been there. Two robed figures whose gender was unknown and the three Guards. A princess wouldn't have Guard duty so it left the other two he'd been fighting. "I assume one of the people in the robes or no one at all. The bitch just lied."

She rolled her eyes. "You understand quantum physics and you can't rationalize this? *I* am the princess, nescient."

Yeah, right. Sure she was. That didn't even make the least bit of sense. He'd seen the way the others had looked at her and treated her—like dirt. If she was the daughter of their sadistic queen, they wouldn't have dared such. Not to mention one small other thing..."I wasn't trying to kill *you*." Though he might if she didn't bring that attitude down a notch.

She gave him a duh stare.

And that made him feel like a total fool as he got what she was trying to tell him. "*You're* the princess."

She nodded.

"They were trying to kill *you* and frame me for it... you fice." He wasn't about to let her insult slide without adding one of his own.

By the light in her eyes, he could tell she'd like to beat him into little bloody nuggets. "All right, stop with the high-end insults."

"You started it."

She raked him with a repugnant sneer. "What are we? Four? Please cease before you call me a doodie head. I really don't think in my current mood that I could survive such a juvenile attack. *That* might actually undo me." Curling her lip, she flicked her nails at him—an obscene Qill gesture. "You need to respect the fact that at the moment it's taking every ounce of willpower I have to not hurt you."

He laughed at her threat. While she was muscular, she was tiny in comparison to his size. So long as he kept his cock guarded, there wasn't much she could do to hurt him. "Baby, I'd like to see you try. Believe me, I've had men and women who eat your lunch try to kill me and here I am. Still standing. Still kicking ass."

She scoffed. "Explain to me how is it possible that the three of us actually fit into this pod?"

Now he was the one who was baffled. Did they do math differently on her planet too? "Three of us?"

"You, me and your extremely overdeveloped ego."

He opened his mouth to speak, but she put her hand over his lips.

"Enough," she said in an imperious tone that verified her breeding. "My mother is on that ship and they're going to kill her. Can you understand the written console language enough to help me find some way to let her know what happened? Or at the very least to alert security to guard her?"

Ignoring the fact that her hand was incredibly soft and felt good on his skin, he snatched it away from his lips and returned it to the arm of her chair. "We're in an escape pod, babe. It's not designed for communication of any kind."

"Well that's stupid. How are we to alert them that we're—"

"An emergency pulse is emitted every six seconds. It goes out on the EBF to let the authorities know there are living occupants in the pod who need rescue."

She let out a relieved breath. "Then they'll come back for us."

"No. They won't."

"Why?"

He gestured toward the darkness where the *Arimanda* had vanished. "It's a ship filled with politicians and royalty. They'll notify a League patrol to check on us. But there's no way in hell they'd come near us for fear we're setting a trap for them. For all they know, someone packed this bad boy with enough explosives to disintegrate a sub-class planet with a life form just big enough to register, and the minute they near it..." He ended with the sound of a nasty explosion. "Trust me. They won't chance it."

She raked her hands through her hair as if frustration filled her too. "I can't believe this is happening."

"You? I was planning to leave our little soiree, but not like this." And definitely not with her. This was what he got for changing his mind about leaving and heading back to his rooms to apologize to his father.

Caillen growled as he sat back on the chair and started running over their settings to see where the pod was taking them.

"What are we going to do?"

Like he would tell her that? It wasn't any of her business. Not to mention the small fact that he still wasn't one hundred percent convinced this wasn't a setup on her part. For all he knew, she was still playing him. They might very well be accusing him of kidnapping her right now. Something that also carried a death sentence.

Even for a prince.

Her people were ruthless and he'd insulted their queen. Publicly. There was no telling what they'd do to retaliate. His father had said as much.

"Don't worry about it." He moved his hand over the monitor and brought up the star chart on their main display. He would use his link to call for backup, but without a booster signal it was useless. They wouldn't be able to call anyone until they landed. Damn.

She scowled at the brightly colored chart that showed him every corner of their current sector. "What's that?"

He pointed to a planet on the right and touched it, then

dragged his finger diagonally to enlarge it for her to see. "We're heading there and should reach the surface in a little over an hour."

"An hour?"

He gave her an arch look over her despondent tone. "We're in the middle of space, far away from the gravitational pull of large masses of rock and self-luminous spheres of gas. It makes landing a bitch, but it keeps us from crashing into something uncomfortable. Sorry if that offends you."

"You're what offends me."

He had to stop himself from responding to that imperious tone with something even more juvenile. There was just something about her that got right up under his hack and made him want to hurt her. Gods, if he had to be trapped with a woman couldn't it have been one who would make passing time with her enjoyable?

"Oh well...next time I see someone choking you, I'll leave them to it." Or help them. "Especially now that I understand what it was that motivated them. Too bad I didn't bring the garrote with me."

"You're not funny."

"Really not trying to be." He fell silent as he pulled up information on the planet they were headed toward.

Desideria didn't want to be impressed, but the ease with which he navigated the intricate computer and read the foreign language was something to be envied. It made her wish she'd paid more attention to the classroom portion of her education. "What language is that?"

"Universal. Same as we're speaking. Can't you read it?"

She felt her face heat at a truth that embarrassed her. "If I could, I wouldn't have hit the wrong button."

His eyes widened in surprise. "No one ever taught you to read Universal?"

She glanced away, grateful that it wasn't entirely her fault that she was ignorant of it. "I was to start learning the written part of the language next year. It's not considered a priority to my people. But I am literate in Qillaq."

Caillen backed off criticizing her over that. Since her people were so reclusive that made sense and he could tell by her sudden reservation that she was bothered by the lack of education. Hell, he wouldn't have known it either but for the fact that the more languages a smuggler knew the less likely he was to be caught. "Well be glad you can't read it."

"Why?"

"Because it says we're heading toward an Andarion planet."

She cocked her head. "Is that a bad thing?"

He laughed low in his throat. *Is that a bad thing?* Yeah... "Do you know *anything* about them?"

"No. Not really. My people don't interact with them. Why?"

Lucky them. Then again, the best course of action with Andarions was to keep your head low and put as much distance as possible between you and them. "Simply put, they make your people look like frilly-dressed pansies."

The fire returned to her eyes. "You are shardridden if you think that."

He didn't know why, but he loved the way she looked when she was riled. It made her eyes sparkle and added a becoming blush to her cheeks. "I am so not full of excrement, dearest. It's the truth. They stand around seven feet tall on average, have fangs, night vision and train from birth to kill any and everything that gets in their way. Oh and lest I forget, their favorite delicacy happens to be human meat. Lucky us."

She scoffed at him. "You're just trying to scare me."

He pulled up an encyclopedia in her language and showed it on the monitor. "See for yourself."

Desideria had to force her eyes not to widen as she read words that confirmed his dire prediction. He was right. A warring race in the purest sense of the word, the Andarions did make her people look like pansies. Normally she'd be more than ready to take them on and prove her worth. But the two of them had no weapons that she knew of and suicide didn't appeal to her in the least. "Can we not divert?"

He leaned back in his chair and narrowed that cocky stare at her that she was beginning to loathe. It didn't help that the lights of the console highlighted his arrogant smirk. "See the problem with escape pods . . . they're designed to run even if you're completely incapacitated. Once you're in it and you hit the magic orange button that you so nicely discovered, it takes care of everything for you. It summons help and steers you to the nearest habitable planet that matches whatever breathing mixture is in the pod."

"But it's stupid to not have an override of some sort."

He scratched the side of his mouth while his eyes silently laughed at her. "I suggest you take that up with the designer when next you see him. That is if we survive long enough to be rescued."

"We will be rescued."

"How can you be so sure?"

"Because I won't allow my mother to die. The traitor

happens to be part of the Head Guard. My mother trusts her implicitly. If I don't get to her and warn her about Pleba, she's as good as dead."

Caillen started to point out that he really didn't care about her mother who had intended to subjugate an entire race when his attention was drawn to the display. His stomach hit the floor as he recognized their next obstacle. "Yeah and we have another problem."

"That is?"

He enlarged a portion of the star chart that showed the area where the *Arimanda* had vanished. He pointed to the glowing orb that was quickly getting larger. "I'm really hoping I'm wrong, but judging from the size and speed, that looks like a fighter to me."

Her entire face lit up with hope. "Is it coming to rescue us?"

Wow, he'd sell his soul to be that naive. Without responding to her question, he slid out of his chair and ducked underneath the controls to open a panel so that he could access the wires. "It's a fighter," he repeated.

Desideria was baffled by his single obsession with that one statement. To her, this was a good thing. "Meaning?"

"It can't hold more than two people and it's flying solo." His deep voice was muffled by the metal he was underneath. "They're designed to kill, not rescue. And unless I miss my guess, which I never have yet, I'm pretty sure that one's headed this way to finish what was started in that hallway."

Pah-lease...

There was no reason to think that. It could merely be a scout. Especially if, as he'd said earlier, they thought this might be a trap. It made sense to send a single fighter to see if they were hurt or needing rescue. It might be nothing more than an escort for them. Could the man never be optimistic? Must he always see the worst in every situation even when it didn't warrant it? "You're being paranoid."

Those words had barely left her lips before a blast of color shot across space, straight at them.

They were under attack.

And they were completely defenseless.

11

The blast slammed into the rear of their pod and knocked them spinning. Desideria cursed as she was thrown against the arm of her seat, bruising her ribs. She watched Caillen continue to dig around, underneath the console. He lay on his back with his legs bent and wide apart to keep himself balanced and stable while the pod rocked from its assault. Unused to the motion, she fought down her nausea, then frowned at the sight of his old, scuffed work boots that were tied with laces that had been broken and then knotted back together. Those boots looked like they'd been put through hell—like they were the only pair of boots he owned. She'd never known any prince to deign to touch something so ragged never mind actually wear them. And now that she thought about it, his clothes were the same way. Clean, but worn. His brown jacket even had what appeared to be blaster burn marks on it.

His head and shoulders were completely obscured by the steel panel while he worked in silence. And in his hurry to get under the console, his jacket and shirt had ridden up, exposing his tanned abdomen. With every breath and move he made, his toned muscles contracted, making them all the more pronounced. Yeah, okay, that part of him was totally lickable. And if she didn't miss her guess, his left side seemed to have a tattoo on it that covered a nasty looking scar.

On an aristos? They considered those things vulgar and common...

Why would he have such marks? It didn't make sense. Prince Caillen was definitely a man of complete contradictions.

Another blast hit them hard.

Grimacing in pain, she righted herself in her chair. "Let me guess. No guns on this thing either?"

There was no missing the disgust in that deep baritone. "Which I think is particularly stupid. If you're using an escape pod to...you know, *escape,* nine times out of ten, you're escaping because your ship's under attack and you had to evacuate. What kind of krikkin idiot thought it smart to make an escape device that leaves its occupants defenseless moving targets while they're being attacked? Oh wait, don't answer. I've met too many design engineers whose IQs are smaller than my shoe size"—he tilted his head out from under the console to give her a pointed glance, then added—"which for the record is actually larger than most men's except for Syn who's a mutant sonofabitch"—he returned to working—"but as far as IQs go, it puts them on the same level as protozoa. My number one peeve in life. Think it through, people. Think it through." He paused to curse as one of the wires shocked him. "Just so you know my ship has a gunner pod with enough juice to take down a starcruiser. This one...really sucks."

She couldn't agree more. "You have a bad case of Attention Deficit Disorder, don't you?"

He wiped his hand on his pants leg, then moved it up to hold something she couldn't see. "Just a little. Luckily it's mostly verbal." He hissed sharply as if he'd hurt himself again. "Damn it, I've lost all feeling in my right hand."

"So what do we do?" she asked, trying to keep him focused on the danger.

Another shot rocked them.

Desideria groaned as she slammed into the arm again and it rebruised her ribs. "Besides die painfully." She was trying to stay calm, but it was getting harder and harder. She hated feeling helpless and this situation was really starting to anger her. "I'm about ready to throw my shoes at them," she mumbled under her breath. "I know it won't hurt their fighter, but it would make me feel better." At least if she did, she'd have done something other than sit here and watch.

Caillen laughed as if he admired her spunk. "Cross your fingers."

Desideria was confused by his words as he finally slid out from under the panel. "Why?"

Without answering, he shot into the front seat, then his hands flew over the computer. Schematics and diagrams flashed on the monitor so fast she couldn't even identify what he was looking at or adjusting before he moved on to the next one.

Another blast headed right for them. She sucked her breath in, bracing herself for impact.

It didn't come.

Instead, the pod turned sharply and lurched forward

while the blast shot harmlessly past them by a narrow margin.

Caillen let out a jubilant shout. He kissed his fingers, then smacked them down near the controls. "That's my girl. C'mon, baby, don't be fickle with your love. You know you want to do me right. Stay tight and fly where I tell you." He made more adjustments on the computer and the pod responded.

Desideria was so happy they had some form of control over their craft that she could kiss him. He might be a complete and utter jerk, but, lucky for her, he knew his way around spacecraft.

The fighter changed course and headed straight for them at an accelerated speed.

She cringed as she saw more bright orange flashes in the darkness. "There's another blast coming."

"I know. Hold on in case this doesn't work."

He turned the pod again, but not enough to miss all of it. The force of the shot slammed her back. She struck her head hard against the panel. Wincing in pain, she didn't speak or cry out for fear of distracting him.

To her utter amazement, Caillen dodged the next blast.

"C'mon, baby. Go. You know you want to. Just keep humming and don't stop." Their pod lurched forward again and this time, finally, it made contact with the planet's gravitational pull.

It sped up dramatically as they fell toward the surface.

The fighter opened up more fire, spraying across space in a last-ditch effort to kill them. Luckily Caillen dodged most of it.

But not all. The lights blinked and sparked as the pod

rocked to the point she feared again she might be sick. Or worse that the pod would come apart.

Caillen flipped a switch over his head. "We're going in hot."

"Meaning?"

"The blasts took out our brakes and homing beacon. I'm going to try and find us something soft to land on. However, I make no promises. My control of this thing isn't the best and... well, if you're religious in any way, now would be the time to summon some divine intervention 'cause, no offense, the gods don't think much of me most days. However, they might listen to you."

Desideria started praying. She held her breath as he struggled with short-circuiting electronics. The scent of burning wires was pungent and she hoped the wires were the only thing burning and not their fuel lines.

Caillen appeared completely unshaken by everything that was happening. Other than the occasional mumbled obscenity when their frying electronics shocked or burned him. "I'd kill for one ion cannon. Just one."

She knew the feeling.

Caillen ran over their settings as he assessed their coming situation. The good news? They could breathe on the surface. The bad news? There was no information on this planet at all. No maps, nothing on culture. Nada. Not even the name of the place.

Those were things usually reserved for penal colonies and it explained why the pod hadn't chosen this site for their landing.

Why hadn't he left them on course? At least with the Andarion planet, he'd known what he was getting into.

This one...

An image of them crashing into a prison with giant man-eating aliens went through his mind. Yeah, that'd be his luck. Couple thousand pissed-off superhuman, psychic aliens with an ax to grind against smugglers and royalty...

Why didn't I stay in my room?

He glanced over his shoulder at the princess. Her face was pale and drawn, and she had a death grip on the arms of her chair. But at least she wasn't screaming or having a real girl moment. She was holding it together and he really appreciated that.

Even though she was dressed as a Guard, her posture was that of royalty. She was planning to die with dignity and that caused a wave of respect for her to swell inside him. If he admired anything in life, it was those who could stand brave while terrified.

If I'd stayed put, she'd be dead.

Yeah, okay, he felt better about being here, but not by much. Wouldn't do any good to save her from that only to have her die on impact or from the assassin chasing them.

Or get eaten by giant flesh-craving alien prisoners...

Gods, how do I get myself into this shit? Whatever unlucky constellation he'd been born under had been working overtime lately.

The pod started shaking around them.

"What's that?" Desideria asked with a note of panic in her voice.

Warning lights blinked, letting him know that their engine was failing, meanwhile there was a gash in the back stabilizer that was widening. But only one of them needed to be terrified, so Caillen downplayed the severity of their situation. "Turbulence. Sit tight and brace yourself for the landing." Unless the pod disintegrated before they made it that far.

"Why are you lying to me?"

Her question surprised him. Glancing over his shoulder, he saw her staring straight at his back. "Who says I'm lying?"

"The tone of your voice. It dropped an octave."

Damn, she was good. He returned his attention to the catastrophe at hand. "Fine. The pod is coming apart." He flipped the computer to the external monitor just in time to show her one of their stabilizers being ripped off the right side and with it went the last thing he wanted to see go. "FYI, we needed that. It was the remains of our landing gear. I was trying not to scare you, but since you insist…"

Desideria swallowed. She wished now she hadn't asked. "Would shifting our weight help guide it?"

"You don't weigh enough to affect anything."

"So what do we do?"

"Grab your ass, and hang on like you want to keep it." He was making more mental calculations as the surface of the planet drew rapidly closer.

They were flying so fast Desideria didn't see how they could land and not become a stain on the planet's surface.

Well, her aunt would be happy.

Her, not so much.

She cringed as they started slamming into the upper limbs of trees. It made the pod buck so hard she could barely stay in her seat even with straps. Her heart was pounding as fear held her close and mutilated her hope for living through this.

Suddenly, Caillen turned, unbuckled her belt and

wrapped his body around hers, pulling her onto the floor. The pod slammed down hard. The only cushion she had was Caillen's body. Although honestly, it was almost as hard as the steel walls surrounding them.

Her breath left her as they were thrown against the steel and the pod rolled over and over. They tumbled like a stone in a cylinder and still Caillen held on to her, trying to keep her safe.

For a moment, she thought they'd live through the crash until her head struck something so forcefully it made her sick. Her vision dimmed. She fought the darkness as best as she could, but in the end the blackness took her under.

The ship finally stopped.

Caillen remained still, waiting for more—they'd had such a rough landing that it felt like they were moving even though he could see they weren't.

But they stayed put. The pod snapped and hissed around him. Everything in it had been shaken loose to the point that it looked like the thing had been gutted. Wires, straps and pieces of steel swung and sparked, but at least the fires provided some form of light in the dark interior. The area where their seats had been was completely destroyed. He lay on his back with Desideria draped over him. Her breath tickled his skin, letting him know she was alive even though she was completely motionless. Pain reverberated through his body and head with every heartbeat.

I can't move. But at least by unbuckling them, he'd saved their lives.

The sudden smell of engine fuel hit him...like it was gushing out of something and pooling nearby. It mingled with the harsh odor of burning wires.

Shit. The pod's going to explode.

True to that prediction, he saw flames spread across the floor. They licked at his boots. The heat was searing. Grinding his teeth, he forced his ravaged body to move and move fast. But it was hard. Nothing wanted to work as he stamped out the fire at his feet.

"Princess?"

She was unconscious and bleeding profusely from a head wound. With a loud groan, he pushed her back enough so that he could roll out from under her. On unsteady feet, he picked her up and cradled her close. She really was tiny. Something that was easy to lose sight of when she was awake and bitching at him. Then she seemed larger than life.

His body rebelling against any act that didn't involve him lying down, he carried her out of the craft and took her to a safe distance from the pod before he laid her down on the ground.

He sat back on his heels, grateful to be out of the pod and able to breathe fresh, nonburning air. Brushing his hair back from his forehead, he saw the blood on his hand. Yeah. Just what he needed. A head wound of his own. He took inventory of his condition and hers. Instinctively, he reached for his backpack to get a cloth to stop her bleeding only to realize it was still in the pod.

Shit. He needed that. It would have medical supplies, food and other things they'd need if they planned to survive this.

He looked back at the burning pod. Only a flaming, krikkin idiot would run into something that was about to explode...

Good thing I'm an idiot.

Before his common sense could override his stupidity, he dashed back to the pod. The metal was hot from the flames—which he discovered as his hand accidentally brushed a wall and was burned. Coughing, he covered his mouth with his shirt and held it there with his burned hand while he tried to see into the small compartment. Ah man, everything had been tossed around to the point he couldn't identify anything. Getting down on his hands and knees, he searched the wreckage as fast as he could. He choked and coughed, struggling to breathe. Just as he was about to give up, he saw a black strap on the floor.

His pack was underneath the crushed-in front console. He scooted forward and grabbed it, then paused as he heard something whine.

The roof lining was caving in.

Damn it! Jerking the pack to him, he scurried for the door. Just when he thought he was free, a part of the ceiling fell across his back and slammed him to the ground. He tried his best to crawl out from under it, but he was trapped. Flames blazed higher and brighter. The stench of fuel was making him light-headed. His lungs struggled to find oxygen.

Crap... I'm going to die.

Right here. Right now.

Still he fought even though it was futile. After all, he was a Dagan and Dagans never surrendered to death. Not without a bloody battle.

Desideria came awake just in time to see Caillen running back to their burning pod. What was the moron doing now? Hadn't anyone ever told him that the correct protocol was to run *away* from burning objects?

Her head throbbed so badly that she feared she'd vomit. More than that, her vision was blurry. She reached up to wipe the sweat from her forehead. The moment she touched it, she realized it wasn't sweat. She was bleeding all over the place.

It's a concussion.

Her stomach lurched as more pain pounded through her body. Rolling to her side, she saw Caillen vanish inside the pod. *He's going to kill himself.*

Let him.

Unfortunately, she couldn't. He'd pulled her out twice now and saved her life. She'd still be inside the burning pod but for him.

Get up, soldier. Time to save the heroic idiot.

As she came to her feet, she heard a loud crash from the pod. There was no sign of Caillen. A bad feeling went through her.

He was dead or trapped.

Only a complete imbecile would run into a burning pod...

Bad thing was, she was an imbecile. Especially since she owed Caillen her life and even if it was only a small chance he was still alive, she couldn't leave him there to burn.

Forcing down her nausea, she headed for the pod on unsteady feet.

The smoke was so thick as she neared it that she could barely see. The stench did nothing for her nausea. *You're a Qillaq. Stop whining.*

Over the loud popping and roar of the fire she heard something... A string of obscene profanity.

She couldn't help smiling as she used his angry

tirade against the gods to find him trapped under burning debris. His wrath was palatable as he tried to free himself.

"I hope you melt into oblivion! Stupid, stupid son of a—" His words broke off as he saw her. For an instant, his entire face lit up, then it turned to a dark scowl. "Are you out of your krikkin mind? Run!"

She did, but it was toward him.

Caillen was astounded as she knelt down to help him get free. "There's a tank about to blow. You have to leave. We only have a few seconds. I can smell it."

"Not without you."

"Princess—"

"Not without you," she enunciated each word sharply, letting him know that he was the one wasting their time with a useless argument. She pulled as hard as she could against the hot metal that pinned him to the floor. "I'd already be dead if not for you. I'm not about to leave you after that. Now shut up and help!"

Caillen smiled at her sharp command. Only a sick bastard like him would find that amusing, especially given his circumstances. But they didn't have long.

He growled as she lifted the burning beam where his leg was trapped. He slid his foot free and grabbed the pack. But not before he could hear the tank whine and whistle.

It was about to go. Their time could only be measured in heartbeats now.

Even though his foot felt broken, he grabbed her hand and his pack and ran with her from the pod.

Still they weren't safe. The shrapnel would blow out for yards and could very easily pierce them. Tightening his hand on hers, he pulled her toward a copse of trees that would hopefully offer some protection.

They'd only made it halfway there before the pod blew. The shock wave of the explosion pitched them forward, causing them to tumble. All Caillen could do was try to protect his head as he rolled and fragments rained down all around them.

He came to rest on his stomach.

Desideria lay a few feet away from him, on her back. Unmoving.

A sick feeling of dread constricted his stomach. "Princess? You alive?"

"No," she groaned.

"Me either."

A second explosion sounded. Caillen cursed as he saw more shrapnel heading for them, including a sizable chunk of the door. Grabbing Desideria, he barely made it behind a fallen log before the door impaled itself upright in the ground right where she'd been. Small fires burned all around them.

Her face pale, she looked up at him in awe. "Thank you."

Letting out a long breath in relief, Caillen laid his head on the ground and did his best not to whimper from the pain that was tearing through every single inch of his body. He felt like he'd been run through a compactor. The last thing he wanted was to move, but he needed to check on her and tend the long gash in his leg. His luck it'd turn to gangrene and he'd lose it if he delayed treatment.

"Any time, Princess. But really, we have to do something about these near fatal interactions of ours." Bracing himself for the pain, he sat up.

She glared accusingly as she shoved at his shoulder. "Don't you dare blame me for this. What the hell was so important that you had to go back for it and risk our lives?"

"I only risked *my* life. You're the loon who came back for me."

She rolled her eyes. "I couldn't agree more. Now why would you go back?"

He held his pack up.

She gaped at him, then glared as if she could murder him herself. "You almost killed us for a stupid backpack?"

"Not a backpack, baby. It's a survival pack."

"I would comment on the irony of you almost dying for that, but right now I really ache too much to bother."

He laughed as he rifled through it. Until he heard the soft whir of an engine drawing near. That sobered him fast. "Someone's coming."

Her face lit up with relief. "Oh please, God, let it be a rescue crew...one with a clean bathroom."

He didn't share her optimism. Instead, cold dread weighed heavy in his gut. "C'mon." He pulled her toward the tree line, deeper into the woods.

She dug her heels in and slowed him down. "What are you doing?"

"We don't know where we are or who they are. They could be our friendly assassin or an accomplice. Until we know for sure, let's not be seen."

Desideria wanted to scream in frustration at his paranoia. But not so deep inside she knew he was right and until they discovered the intentions of whoever was coming, they did need to keep a low profile. "I really hate you."

"Hate you too, babe." He gave her a charming grin and a wink that managed to be adorable even though she wanted to kick him someplace that counted. "Now, c'mon."

Desideria groaned as she forced herself to run after him. How could he move on that busted leg of his? Did the man not feel pain? She glanced to the woods and winced. It looked so far to those trees...

Caillen doubled back to try and carry her.

She stopped him. "You're injured too and I can walk. I am *not* helpless or weak. I'm simply pissed," she growled.

He held his hands up in apology. "Fine, but we need to hurry." He jerked his chin to the sky where she could see the craft almost on them.

Run!

They barely made it to the trees before the hovercraft came in. It hesitated over the remains of their pod for several minutes as if the occupants were photographing the area or conducting some kind of test or evaluation.

Caillen scowled as he tried to figure out what they were doing. Normally, they'd be out and scanning the ground on foot. But these...

They had a separate protocol that deviated from the norm, which meant he had no idea what to expect. Damn.

"Can you tell anything about them?" Desideria whispered.

"They're Andarions."

"How do you know?"

He pulled his FVG out of his pack and held it to his eyes so that he could see the pilots in the cockpit who were scanning the ground and talking to each other. "Style of the craft. It's an older Andarion model S10-B60. Most humans are too short to pilot it. And now that I can see them, they're definitely NHL." Non Human Life forms.

"Is that good or bad for us?"

Caillen sighed. "Depends on their intentions."

"You're not funny."

"Not trying to be."

The craft descended until it was on the ground. As the door opened, Caillen motioned for her to be quiet while he shoved an amplifier into his ear so that he could hear their conversation even from this distance. Luckily it only amplified voices and not ambient noises, otherwise his hearing would have been blown out by their hovercraft's engines.

Two officers came out of the back to investigate the crash site while the two pilots remained inside.

Desideria opened her mouth to speak, but he cut her off with a fierce head shake. One thing about the Andarions, those bastards could hear for miles even without an amplifier. They'd be lucky if the soldiers didn't hear them breathing.

And what they were talking about was making his stomach shrink.

No, they hadn't landed on a penal colony. This one was worse.

Much worse.

12

Caillen grabbed Desideria's arm and pulled her back, deeper into the woods. Every time she opened her mouth to speak, he motioned for her to be quiet. Something that was beginning to really annoy her. He made other gestures that she couldn't even begin to identify in a way that said he thought she should understand them too. She only hoped they weren't obscene because if they were, he was going to be limping even worse than he already was.

It wasn't until he found a cave that he allowed her to stop moving. He sent her in deeper before he set the pack on the ground and pulled out two devices she couldn't identify. Frowning, she watched as he attached one to each side of the small opening, then turned them on. A low-frequency hum started and the devices caused the light in the cave to darken even more. She could barely see in front of her.

Without breaking stride, he pulled a light stick from the bag and snapped it, then shook it hard before tossing it on the floor so that it landed not far from her. Everything was bathed in a dull purple glow as he picked up the pack and moved toward the back of the cave where she was waiting beside a monstrous black stalagmite that shimmered from the light.

Only then did he let out an elongated, audible breath.

Can I speak? She mouthed the words.

"Yeah, but keep your tone low," he whispered.

"Why?"

He wiped his chin against the back of his hand in a gesture that was an odd mixture of little boy and all-sexy, rugged male. "Andarions have supersonic hearing and I'm not completely sure my dampeners will work against it, especially if they're using any kind of amp." He gestured with his thumb over his shoulder to the opening of the cave. "Those guys out there…they're not your usual crew. You and I hit the mother lode of bad luck. We didn't just land on an Andarion planet. We landed on one of their colonies." He pulled a small device out of his pocket and put it in his ear.

Call her stupid, but she didn't see what the big deal was. The Andarions were members of the council, subject to the same laws as anyone else. Why was he freaking out? "Meaning what?"

"Their colonists are under martial law. Any offworlders caught without proper papers, visitation passes and authorizations are automatically marked as spies, especially human ones. And prosecuted as such. Standard practice is to lock us up and leave us there to die without ever notifying anyone that we've been taken. In fact, if ever asked, they'll deny all charges. Bastards are good at that."

She lifted her chin at his ridiculous fear. "We're royalty, they can't do—"

"They can do anything they want," he said, interrupting her. "Someone has to prove we were here, and since the only person who knows our whereabouts is an assassin out to kill us, I don't think he or she's going to be real chatty trying to save us should we be captured."

"Can't we explain or even offer them a reward?"

He laughed out loud. "Have you ever been around an Andarion?"

"Well...no."

"Then take my word on this. They can't be bribed. I have several Andarion friends. One of them was born their crowned prince, but because he has some human features, his own biological grandmother sent him to a human work home where he was kept beaten, chained and declawed and raised like an animal. You don't ever want to know what was done to him. Suffice it to say, if they won't protect their own prince, you and I are, pardon the pun, royally screwed. They won't care about us and if it means war? What the hell? Again, they make your people look like pacifists. A war to them is the bonus fun round they live for." He raked his hand through his hair. "This is why you pray to the gods you never get stranded on foreign soil. One wrong battle, one foul landing and your entire life is forever screwed up or ended."

Like her father.

He'd been a pilot who'd crash-landed on Qilla. Taken as a war prize, he'd never been allowed to contact his people or family. His only shot at freedom had been one battle, which he'd been forced to fight while wounded. After that, her mother had never allowed him another chance to let his family know what had happened to him.

For the first time in her life, she understood the real horror that had been her father's existence.

"There's a whole universe out there, Daria, where your mother doesn't rule. A universe of diverse people and experiences. Promise me when you grow up, you'll take time to visit them and learn that though we might be different on the outside, inside we all want the same things. Safety. Love. Family. And peace."

As a child, she'd thought the peace part made him weak. But now she understood what he meant. He wasn't talking about peace from war. He was talking about the inner calm that she'd never known. That comfort that came with understanding who and what you were, accepting your limitations. With being comfortable in your own skin.

Instead all she heard internally was the constant criticisms of her mother, aunt and sisters. If there was one thing in life she knew, it was every shortcoming she possessed.

What was strange to her was that Caillen had the same inner peace her father had always held. That ability to be calm under duress and chaos.

Not wanting to think about those uncomfortable comparisons, she turned her attention back to their current situation. "So what do we do?"

Caillen paused as he considered his options. None of them were stellar.

They couldn't stay here too long or they'd be found. Since there weren't any bodies in the wreckage, the Andarions would comb this area until they found them. Andarions were, unfortunately, a tenacious species who would be itching for a fight.

Not to mention, they had to get off this rock and let his father know what was going on. And as much as he hated to admit it, the Qill queen needed to know too.

Maniacal bitch.

Desideria's dark eyes burned into him. Thank the gods she didn't look anything like her mother. Her features were much softer and kinder. Far more attractive. If she'd been a ringer for her mother, he might have left her in the pod to burn.

"We have to get out of here. Now," Desideria insisted.

"I know, Princess. I know." But first, he had to get them out of the cross hairs. "We have to find whatever civilization they have."

She scowled at him. "You said we couldn't do that."

He dropped his pack on the ground beside her. "I said we couldn't do it as humans."

Desideria was now completely confused. Had he inhaled too many fumes before she rescued him? "Apparently I'm missing something. How do we not look human when, last time I checked, we're humans?" Grubby, bloody and beat up, but still undeniable in their species. "You have a secret you need to impart to me?"

Caillen dug through his pack and pulled out several items.

Bemused, she watched him open a bottle of water and a foil packet. The packet contained a small pink tablet.

I knew it!

He *was* on drugs.

"What's that?" she asked suspiciously.

He popped the pill into his mouth and used the water to wash it down. "In about twenty hours, it'll grow my hair to my shoulders and turn it black."

They had such things? Her father had told her of many marvels, but this was a new one on her. "Is that safe?"

He wiped his mouth with the back of his hand before he

secured the top on the bottle. "God, I hope so. I've never had to use it before, but unfortunately I don't have a wig in my magic bag. Not that I'd use one even if I did. Learned the hard way a long time ago that those things have a nasty tendency to come off at the worst possible moment." He opened a small vial that contained two contact lenses.

Intrigued and confused, she watched as he put them in. Oh yeah, they were odd. It made his pupils red and his irises white with a red rim. "Can you see with those?"

He blinked three times, then widened his eyes as if allowing them to settle into place. "Not as well as I can normally, but enough to get by. So long as no one gets too frisky from my peripheral I'll be fine." Next, he pulled out a small round case and opened it to show what appeared to be two elongated teeth. He took them out and covered his canines with them to give him a fanged smile.

She hated to admit it, but he was actually attractive in a freakish sort of way. "What are you supposed to be?"

He unzipped an outside pocket to reveal a mirror he used to examine his handiwork. "An Andarion. Once my hair grows and darkens, I'll be able to pass as a native. The shorter hair will be a bitch since their males wear theirs longer than yours, but I can make something up as to why I had to cut it. Hopefully they'll buy it without bloodshed." He gave her a thorough once-over. "You on the other hand..."

She held her hands up and backed away in fear of what that look on his face meant for her. "I'm not taking that pill and sprouting another arm."

"I doubt you'd grow another arm...Might lose one though." He flashed an evil grin at her that was even more sinister given his fangs. "Don't worry. I'm not going to offer you one. You're too short and your features are wrong. No one would ever believe you're one of them. Not to mention I don't have another pair of fangs or contacts." He jerked a hooded cloak out of his pack and tossed it to her. "We'll keep you covered and I'll tell them you're my daughter. Just make sure no one sees you uncovered."

"If they do?"

"Then we should have just laid down and let the assassins on the ship have our throats. Believe me, that would have been a lot less painful."

Desideria grimaced at the cloak. "Well, I'll say one thing. Hanging around you isn't boring."

He laughed. "Don't I know it. My first name should have been Catastrophe and I swear in some language, somewhere, that is what Caillen means. Now come over here and let me check out your head wound. Last thing we need is for you to have brain damage."

"I already have brain damage. Why else would I be here?"

He snorted. "Yeah, I resemble that remark."

Desideria sat down beside him while he rooted through his pack. She half expected him to pull a ship out of it. He hadn't been joking when he called it a survival pack. He appeared to have some of everything in it.

Except for a black wig...

As he dug, his hair fell forward over his bruised forehead. His leg looked bloodied and painful through the torn fabric, but he ignored the pain as if he were one of her people. Right now, dressed in those worn-out boots and leather jacket, there was nothing about him that reminded her of royalty. He was more like one of the rogue pirates her mother hired to cause trouble for her enemies.

And a part of her that scared her was actually attracted to that darker side of his personality. More than that, it reminded her of how yummy his stomach had been while exposed and that led her to wonder at the rest of him...

What would he look like naked?

Don't be stupid. Men are not on your menu. At least not for a year, until the anniversary of her adulthood.

But she couldn't help it. He was compelling. Resourceful. Strong. Intelligent.

Insane.

A heady concoction no matter how hard she tried to not think about it.

He returned to her side, carrying medical supplies that he set down next to her before he handed her a bottle of water and knelt. Resting on his good knee, he gently pulled the hair back from her face to examine her injury. His nearness disturbed her and made her heartbeat quicken. More than that, the scent of his skin filled her head with the most pleasant masculine scent. She'd never been this close to a man before except for her father and her mother's consorts. While those consorts were attractive, they'd never enticed her.

Not like this.

Was this the hunger she'd overheard her sisters talking about? While she'd studied and done as she was told, they'd snuck online and collected photos of naked men during their study hours. Late at night, once everyone else had gone to bed, they'd get together and giggle about what they would do once they were able to have consorts of their own.

That had never been her dream. She didn't want a kept pet enslaved to her. Her father had told her stories of how men and women were a team on his world. How they worked together as equals. She didn't know why that appealed to her, but it did. She wanted a partner at her back not someone who resented her power over them and who would have sullen fits like her mother's consorts. They'd always seemed more like children to her than men she'd want to father her offspring.

Caillen looked up and caught her gaze. He arched a brow as a sly, knowing half smile curled his lips. "You imagining me naked, Princess?"

Heat scalded her cheeks at his teasing arrogance—and the fact that he had caught her doing just that. Caillen was definitely not the kind of man a woman with a brain would put at her back or anywhere else in a five-thousand-mile radius. "Hardly. You look really creepy like that."

He laughed good-naturedly. "I've been called worse and that by people who claim they love me."

"You have people who actually love you?"

His smile widened. "Hard to believe, ain't it? But yeah, I do. At least that's what they say when I'm in the room."

She couldn't understand how he took an insult with such grace and humor. In her world, people had killed over less. "Do you ever get angry?"

"Of course I do."

She winced as he wiped the disinfectant along the marks on her neck. "Over what?"

He lowered the linen pad to redampen it. "My sisters and cruelty. And cruelty to my sisters is a double-ass beating to anyone dumb enough to try it."

She pulled back to look at him. "I thought Emperor Evzen only had one child. You."

"He does."

When he didn't elaborate, she prodded him. "Are they from your mother, then?"

"Why do you care?"

Her temper ignited, but she held it back. There was no need to get angry over a simple question. That was something her mother would do. His tone had been inquisitive, not confrontational. So when she spoke, she forced herself to be pleasant. "I'm just curious. When you mentioned them, there was so much emotion in that one word that I can tell they mean a lot to you. In my experience it's unusual for someone to feel that way toward half siblings."

He licked his lips before he continued treating her neck. "Where I come from, family's defined as those who don't screw you over a paycheck. Blood makes no difference. If you can trust them with your life and know that they'll be there come whatever hell rains down, then they're your family."

In her world, family meant they had the good grace to stab you while looking you in the eyes. She couldn't imagine her sisters standing by her side for any reason.

Unwilling to go there, she changed the subject to something a little less painful. "You really think you can fool the Andarions into believing you're one of them?"

"I know I can. Like I said, I have friends who are Andarion."

And that meant nothing. She had a father who was Gondarion and she knew nothing about his people or their culture. "You speak their language fluently?"

"All nineteen dialects."

That was unexpected. While most princes were well educated, most relied on their advisors or electronics for translations. "Impressive."

"Not really. I've spent a lot of time making runs through their system. Since they don't like outsiders, I've learned to fake it, hence the fangs and contacts in my bag. When I was making heavy runs, I even grew my hair out and dyed it to blend in with them. But I'm not a fan of long hair on me."

"Why not?"

"Gets in the way when I'm having sex."

That unexpected answer actually made her laugh out loud.

Caillen paused at the sound of the first real laugh he'd heard from her. It was a pure, light sound that made his cock twitch. Combine that with the way her eyes sparkled and he wished he could keep her laughing. It relaxed her features and made her absolutely irresistible. Damn, she was attractive and he hated that most of all. He didn't want to feel anything for a woman. Especially not one from a world where men were considered beneath them and whose mother wanted him horsewhipped in the worst sort of way.

She wiped at her eyes. "I'm sure that's not the real reason."

"I promise you, it is."

She shook her head. "You're terrible."

"Again, I've been called worse." He brushed his hand over her head, checking for swelling. She winced as he touched the lump where she was bleeding. "Sorry." He reached into his bag and dug out a chemical ice pack. He broke the seal, shook it and then handed it to her to put on the swelling. "The cut doesn't appear to need stitches. Let's get the swelling down and then I'll put a coagulant on it."

Desideria cocked a brow at his authoritative tone. "You're a doctor too?"

He didn't respond. By the look on his face, she could tell she'd inadvertently hit a nerve, though she had no idea how.

Ignoring her, he pulled back the leg of his pants to tend his own wound.

She watched in silent awe as he stopped the bleeding, cleaned and then wrapped it like a pro.

"How is it a prince knows so much about field dressing and medicine? You said you'd made runs into the Andarions' territory. Were they mercy missions?"

He scowled at her. "I thought you knew."

"Knew what?"

Scratching at the whiskers on his face, he snorted. "You must live under a rock on the most back-ass planet in the universe to have missed the news."

She ignored his insult—it was so mild compared to what her family gave her that it didn't even register. And for once, she actually agreed with his summation. Qillaq was rather backward compared to other worlds. "What news?"

"I was kidnapped when I was still a baby and raised as a pleb. I didn't know I was a prince until a few months ago when a DNA test identified me."

That stunned her. "Really?"

"Yeah, really."

That explained the dichotomies she'd noticed. Why he held that feral quality to everything he did. His worn-out clothes and his ever changing syntax that went from royal dialect to street slang. "Were you shocked when they told you?"

"Still am. Not exactly something you expect to learn about yourself. Hey, kid, your parents weren't your parents and by the way, did you know you're a prince and heir to a major empire?"

Very true. And it also explained about his sisters. "Your sisters belonged to your adoptive parents?"

He fell silent as he returned to putting things back in the pack. After a few seconds he spoke again. "Don't worry. I am housebroken. I might not be as refined as the rest of the aristocracy, but I won't crap on the floor either." His tone was dry and even. Still, she understood the pain those words betrayed and knew why he'd said them.

Like her, others had been judging him.

"My people aren't like the other aristos. Hence why I'm in the Guard. Nothing in my world is given to anyone. Everything is earned. It's not how you start in life that matters. It's how you finish."

The look he passed to her was cold enough to make her shiver. "No, your people just accuse others of crimes they don't commit."

"I had nothing to do with that."

He scoffed. "I'd like to believe you, but I don't know you well enough for that. I've had people I trusted implicitly come at me. So you'll have to forgive my mistrust."

"Again, I understand. Trust, like everything else, has to be earned and I have yet to gain it. I get it."

Caillen hesitated. He wanted to believe her. Yet he didn't dare. Too many memories surged inside him. Partners who'd turned on him when he least expected it. "Friends" he'd put at his back who'd knifed him so hard he still felt the burn of it. Most of all was the bitch who continued to come at him for no good reason at all.

People were treacherous by nature. And Desideria was a stranger—one he was attracted to.

That made her deadlier than most.

He moved away from her. "I've got minimal food and water. Enough to hold us today. Tomorrow we'll have to scavenge."

Agitation creased her brow. "We have no time to dawdle with inconsequentials. Every minute that ticks by is one my mother could be slaughtered."

His father too. But that knowledge didn't change their circumstances. "Let me lay this out for you, Princess. We are on a hostile planet with natives who will *eat* us if they catch us. Our pod is no longer transmitting a homing beacon which while it keeps the natives from identifying our origins and the assassin after us from finding our exact location, also keeps our allies from rescuing us. And while your mother's life really doesn't matter much to me, my father's does, so don't think for one minute that you're even an edge more motivated than I am. Because you're not. However, if we die, it's over for all of us and believe it or not, I'm doing my best to make sure we all survive. Body parts intact."

She narrowed her gaze on him. There was no missing the shadow that hung heavy there in those dark eyes. "What aren't you telling me?"

Her questions caught him off guard. "What do you mean?"

"You're holding something back. I can tell by the look in your eyes. What is it?"

Caillen hesitated. Damn, she was perceptive—like his sister Shahara. She'd always had an uncanny ability to read him too.

He started to tell her nothing, but why lie? She needed to know and if she betrayed him here, she'd be cutting her own throat. Andarions didn't play and they didn't tolerate offworlders—especially him. "I'm a wanted felon by the Andarions. While it's technically been repealed by their prince and heir, I'm not about to trust a colony not to carry out my death sentence without notifying the capital government before I'm dead—they have a nasty tendency that way."

All the color drained from her face. "What did you do?"

Caillen sighed. Again he started not to tell her. It was so stupid really. But if he didn't answer her question, she'd probably assume him a rapist or something even more vile. "I'm housebroken, okay? But I don't heel well. Prince Jullien grabbed my sister inappropriately and had trouble understanding the *no* word when she said it forcefully, so I busted loose a few of his teeth. Nykyrian repealed my death warrant when he was crowned, but, as I said, I don't trust their government. And while I know Nyk would bail me out, he has to know about it first and since Jullien still has a hard-on for me over my assault, I'm not betting that these colonies have the most current wanted list— Jullien's vindictive that way. My luck, the bounty for killing me's even tripled."

She gaped at him. "Surely Jullien would have something better to do than worry over a fight, especially if they're anything like my people. That's to be expected."

Yeah, right. "Jullien isn't a warrior and given the asswhipping I gave him and his pompous arrogance, he definitely would leave it in place. That slimy bastard is the worst sort of scum."

"Why do you hate him so?"

"Aside from him trying to rape my sister, he traded his own twin brother's pregnant wife to his brother's enemies so that they could kill her. And we, including me, almost lost our lives getting her out. That's nothing compared to what he's done to others. He's a total scabbing bastard. The only reason he hasn't been executed is that he's royal and his grandmother has paid a fortune to the League to keep him breathing."

He could see in her eyes that she was trying to understand Jullien's crimes, but couldn't quite mentally grasp them any more than he could. The man's cruelty was only surpassed by his stupidity. "Their grandmother did nothing to him for betraying his own brother?" she asked.

"No. But believe me, Nyk did and I'm still amazed Nyk's beating didn't kill him. That being said Jullien will limp for eternity. Officially though, Jullien wasn't punished except that he's been removed from the line of succession. Which I guess to him is probably a fate worse than death. But in my opinion, he got off light."

She shook her head. "And I thought my family was screwed up."

"Yeah...Mine have their problems, but the worst thing I can say about my sisters is they're self destructive...or in Kasen's and Tess's case, fatally stupid. The damage they've done to me was never intentional. The pry bar incident notwithstanding."

Desideria paused at that last bit, curious about it. "Pry bar incident?"

He paused putting the things back in his pack and let out a long suffering sigh. "When we were kids, I made Kasen mad enough, she threw a pry bar at me." He pointed to the scar above his left brow. "Eight stitches."

That had to hurt. "What did you do?"

An unexpected blush colored his cheeks. How strangely becoming even in his disguise. "In my defense I was six."

Oh now this had to be good for him to be that embarrassed and to make excuses. "What did you do?"

He was actually bashful about it. "She refused to play court ball with me, so I burned down her dollhouse."

She gaped at his disclosure. No he didn't… "You burned down her dollhouse?"

He pointed to his scar. "I was adequately punished."

"But you burned down her dollhouse? That's *so* cold."

"So's bashing your little brother in the head with a pry bar. I could have lost an eye that day and I think my recent death warrant while protecting her from her latest bout of supreme stupidity more than makes up for it."

She scoffed at his indignation. "It was a flesh wound, you big baby."

Caillen started to respond, then caught himself as he realized he enjoyed her teasing.

She was charming him…

Crap. That he couldn't allow. Not until he knew what her real loyalties were. She was her mother's daughter.

And they were framing him.

Desideria saw the veil come down on his face, changing it to a mask of seriousness. For some reason, it felt like a blow to her sternum. *Don't be ridiculous.* Yet there was no denying what she felt.

It hurt.

She liked the teasing, fun Caillen a lot more than the serious prince who was guarded.

I've lost my mind. He was all kinds of irritating.

He's all kinds of sexy.

And when he teased and his eyes sparkled, he was all the hotter. Licking her lips, she watched as he returned to the backpack to pull out another item.

This one made her gasp.

It was a subspace link.

Joy exploded through her. "We can call someone?"

"Let's hope. But if we can, we can't talk for more than thirty seconds. Any longer and it'll be traceable. I don't know how high tech this place is. So for now, I'm erring on the side of not getting disemboweled." He tried to hail his sister.

Nothing. The call wouldn't go through.

Growling in irritation, he looked at Desideria. "Either we're too far inside or it's jammed. I'll try again in the morning."

"What if they kill my mother tonight?"

"What if they kill my father? You're not the only one taking a risk here. This shit bites both ways."

She ground her teeth as more frustration burned through her. "I can't believe there's nothing we can do."

"Well we can go out there and let them find us. That is if they don't already have something that can read through my mirrors. If they have that, we're screwed."

She cocked her head at his use of a word that didn't belong in that sentence. Mirrors. "Is that what you placed at the opening?"

"Yeah. It emits a pulse to anything that scans us saying there's nothing inside. No heat signature, no signs of life. To my knowledge nothing can breach it. But technology changes faster than the skin on a rodalyn lizard. So the colonists might be able to find us here." He winked at her. "Let's hope not, shall we?"

Desideria rubbed her head that was starting to ache as she ran over everything that had happened to them and how much danger they were in. "What a day."

"Yeah. I have an assassin running loose after my dad and you now have one after your mom. The only reason I agreed to attend that sanctimonious stratiotes was that I'd hoped the assassin would make a move on my father and I'd be able to capture him on the ship where the escape routes would be limited."

"Strat... what was that word you used?"

"Stratiotes. It means a collection of morons. Is that really all you got out of my tirade?"

"No, it wasn't. It was just the part I didn't understand. Just like I don't understand who's trying to kill my mother."

He snorted. "Motive, baby. It's all motive and that usually leads back to cash flow... Personally, I think it's my uncle after my father. My father thinks I'm insane. But my uncle is the only one who makes sense."

"Why would your uncle want your father dead?"

"Only one who has something to gain if both my father and I die. First blood law: follow the money. It always leads you home."

She considered his words as she remembered meeting his uncle many times since her birth. The man had seemed extremely mild and unassuming. "You don't really believe that, do you?"

"Yes, I do." There was no missing the sincerity in that gaze. "So what about your mom? Who stands to inherit the most with you and her out of the way?"

"My sisters." Her stomach heaved as she rose to her feet. "Oh my God. It's Narcissa. She's the one who killed my other two sisters in training accidents."

And she'd tried to kill *her* just two weeks ago. She'd even made threats against her...

Narcissa had always been ambitious. *When I'm queen, you'll all bow down to me. But don't worry. You can both serve in my Guard like Kara used to for Mother.*

How many times had her sister said that? Yet Desideria had always assumed she was joking or wishing.

What if she hadn't been?

Dear gods, how could she have been so stupid as to miss that? Of all the people she'd suspected of being behind this, the most obvious had eluded her until now. Panic consumed her at the thought.

Unable to stand it, she started pacing as the horror of it all raced through her mind. That was why the Guard was backing her sister and helping to assassinate her mother. If her mother was murdered, Narcissa, as their next queen, would have the power to pardon them and spare their lives.

Suddenly, it all made sense. It was insidious and cold, and it came hard on the heels of her being promoted to adult status. That made her the heir apparent over her older sister. Yes, she'd have to fight for it, but she would be the one challenged. If she survived the fight, she'd be queen.

Narcissa wouldn't even be eligible to try for the crown. But if both Desideria and her mother died, Narcissa would rise to heir status even as a minor and could fight to be queen...

And why was her mother's Guard backing her sister? Because they all thought Desideria was the dirt under their feet. A crossbred mongrel that the Guard resented breathing their air. Of course they'd back her purebred sister over her.

And cheer when she died.

Suddenly, Caillen was beside her, pulling her into his arms. "Shh...it's all right. I know it's a shock. You'll get used to it."

She would push him away, but honestly it felt good to be held while her world unraveled itself and she was faced with a harsh reality she didn't even want to contemplate. She was alone in the universe with no one to rely on. No one to turn to.

Her own family was trying to end her life. And no one knew the truth except her.

"How can you cope with the thought of your uncle trying to kill you?"

He shrugged. "I'm only surprised when people don't try to kill me."

"Well, I can understand that. You *are* annoying."

He smiled at her and that expression made her feel a little better for reasons she couldn't even guess at. "If you don't like the thought of your sister coming for you, is there anyone else you can think of?"

"No."

"Are you sure?"

She nodded. No one else made any sense. "My mother has two sisters, but one married an offworlder, so she can't rule so long as she has a foreign husband, and my other aunt was removed from succession when my mother defeated her in combat for the throne. Kara could rule as a regent, but never as a full queen and she would be replaced as soon as one of us was skilled enough to challenge her."

"Then it is what it is. Your sister's a self-serving bitch out to collect your heads—sorry. My father keeps telling me it's an enemy after him, but I don't believe it. An enemy would gain nothing other than personal satisfaction. And while I can understand that motivation, it wouldn't lead them to me. If both my father and I die, his brother takes the throne and right now, his brother is his chief advisor which means none of the laws would be changed. If it is one of his enemies after him, no reason to risk prison or execution for something that wouldn't affect them at all. They'd be trying to take out his brother too so that they could change things. I've run through a thousand scenarios, but all of them lead straight back to my uncle with no side roads."

Just like all of hers led back to Narcissa... "My mother will *never* believe me."

No one would believe them.

"I know. We have to find evidence. It's the only way to save their lives."

She opened her mouth to speak, but Caillen motioned her to be silent. He stepped back and drifted toward the front of the cave while hugging the wall.

At first she thought it was more of his paranoia until she heard the soft whir of a motor. Her heart stopped beating as a shadow fell over the entrance.

It was a military prober and it was scanning for life forms...

13

Probers were small, electronic scanning devices that checked for living organisms and reported back to a search force. Desideria had no doubt that she and Caillen were the target of this one. If that thing picked up even the smallest trace of their presence, the Andarions would swarm all over them.

Move slowly, Caillen mouthed to her. *Get against the wall.*

She did exactly what he told her to. She focused on her heartbeats to keep from panicking. Any little sound might be detected...

Even her breathing.

Time stretched out like an arthritic snail before the prober finally pulled back.

She started to move, but Caillen motioned subtly for her not to.

Sure enough, another prober popped up from the ground and scanned for several minutes more. Only after it left did Caillen inch his way back to her. He stood between her and the door, shielding her. He was so close that she could feel his body heat.

"Are we safe?" she whispered in his ear.

"We'll know in a few minutes." His breath tickled the skin of her cheek and his warmth went a long way in soothing her ragged nerves.

They stood right beside each other, waiting. And she didn't miss the fact that he was protecting her with his body. Though whether he did it out of habit or on purpose, she couldn't tell. Yes, she could take care of herself, but she found his actions sweet and unexpected.

Most of all, she found them strangely endearing.

Caillen glanced down at Desideria to make sure she wasn't panicking.

She definitely wasn't. Her lips were parted while she stared past him, toward the entrance. But that wasn't what held his interest. It was the deep cleft between her breasts. Her top was so tight, it pushed them up to the point it appeared that even the slightest breath would spill them out.

Sneeze, baby, sneeze.

Unfortunately, she didn't. Damn. He'd like to have some good come to him after the freight load of crap that'd assaulted him today. Even if it did mean the Andarions would find them and he'd have to battle his way out.

Some things were just worth it.

And he had a gut feeling seeing her naked was definitely one of those things.

Just a tiny taste . . .

Desideria went rigid as she realized Caillen had his head practically buried in her hair. "Are you sniffing me?"

His warm, low laugh sent chills over her. "I prefer to say I'm admiring your scent, but yeah, I guess you could say I'm sniffing you and you smell really good."

Normally that would creep her out. Instead, she was actually aroused by the gesture. Or maybe it would be more accurate to say she was aroused by his presence. Even dressed like some phantom creature, he was sexy. Only Caillen could pull off that look. And she had a strange curiosity about what his fangs would feel like grazing her skin.

As if he could hear her thoughts, he dipped his head closer to hers. But before he could make contact with her lips, a loud voice sounded outside.

Desideria listened intently. Nothing was remotely familiar to her. Not a single syllable. "What are they saying?" she whispered in Caillen's ear.

He placed a gentle finger against her lips as he listened. That sensation sent a chill over her and made her wonder what it would have been like to kiss him. *I shouldn't be attracted to him.*

Yet she was...

He didn't move until the voice had drifted out of her hearing range. When he spoke, he whispered low in her ear, raising even more chills along her body. "They're calling in search animals that will be able to sense past the mirrors. We'll have to get out of here."

"And go where?"

"Wherever there's something that can mask our scent." He moved away from her to retrieve his backpack. "We'll need a cover story should we cross paths with the natives. I'll be using the alias Dancer Hauk. Call me Hauk around other people."

She curled her lip at his choice of alias. What a stupid name. Surely that would get them caught faster than her appearance. "Dancer Hauk?"

He held his hands up in surrender. "Believe me, I know the name's a freakfest. But he's actually a real person and he's Andarion. With any luck, they'll know his name and not his face. If we're really lucky, they'll have heard about his fearsome reputation—which will definitely buy us some prestige." He slung the pack over his shoulder. "If they know his face, well...we'll deal with it. Let's just hope we catch a break at some point today."

Her jaw went slack at the way he moved through the darkness. Light of foot, with the fluid moves of a trained dancer, he picked the light stick up and extinguished it before sliding it into his pocket. It was obvious this was his natural habitat—hiding from enemies...not cruising on board a ship full of aristocrats.

In a few heartbeats, he eliminated all traces of their presence, then sprayed something she assumed would mask their scent from the animals. He crooked his finger for her to follow him. At the opening, he removed his mirrors, returned them to the pack and led her back into the woods. He sprayed more of his bottle's contents, but she couldn't detect anything at all coming out of it.

"What is that?" she asked.

"Aquibrade."

He said that like she should know what he was talking about. It was gibberish to her. "And it does...?"

"It's erackle pheromones."

Her head was starting to ache from his unfamiliar vocabulary. "What's an erackle?"

"One of the ugliest-looking animals you'll ever meet.

But they secrete a scent that if inhaled by another animal screws up their olfactory glands for days. One whiff and they won't be able to find us."

"Should we bathe in it?"

He gave her a charming grin. "We could, but if we happen upon an erackle, it would try to mate with us. Trust me, that would get ugly fast."

Yeah, but that might not be a concern for them. "Do they have those here?"

"No idea." He handed her the bottle. "If you're willing to risk it, I'm willing to film it and make a lot of money from it online."

She glared at him. "You're not funny."

"Not trying to be. Simply an opportunistic entrepreneur in the purest sense of the word."

She scoffed at his light tone as she made sure to keep her voice to a whisper like him. "How many sisters did you say you have?"

"Three. Why?"

"Tell me how it is they let you live this long?"

He pointed to the scar on his head. "I assure you, there was no lack of trying to kill me. I'm just really resilient."

She followed him over a fallen tree. "Apparently."

He slid something into his ear as he led her through the thick overgrown weeds, deeper into the forest.

She gestured toward his ear. "What is that?"

"An amp for sound, so please don't scream or shout. It'd take out my eardrum."

Which would be bad. Last thing she needed was for him to go down since she couldn't show her face on this planet without being imprisoned or eaten. That thought made her draw her cloak tighter as she rushed to keep up with his long strides. "Is that what you were trying to tell me with all the earlier hand gesturing?"

Holding back a low-hanging limb, he paused to let her pass in front of him. "You don't know League sign language?"

"Never heard of it."

He shook his head as he retook the lead. "It's a hand language soldiers and assassins use to communicate with each other when they're on missions."

That explained why she'd never seen it before, but not how he knew it. "Were you in the League?"

He laughed out loud, then instantly lowered his voice. "No. I learned it so that I could tell what they were saying while trying to capture me."

Now that was interesting. What kind of criminal was he? "What exactly did you do before your father found you?"

"I survived, Princess. Most days only by the skin of my eyeteeth."

She opened her mouth to ask him to elaborate, but before she could, he pointed up. She followed the line to see the hovercraft coming in.

Why wouldn't they give up?

But that wasn't what concerned her. The fact that a blast of orange shot through the clouds and into the ship did. She watched in horror as the ship disintegrated and then rained down burning debris all around them.

Oh dear Lord. The assassin had found their crash site and was coming in for a rematch.

Caillen took her arm and led her toward a small cut-out growth in a large tree. He pressed himself against her as the area around them was salted liberally with fire. "Looks like our friend decided to join the party."

Desideria grimaced as a part of the bark cut into her back. "How offended do you think he or she would be if we rescinded the invitation?"

"Well since their home-warming gift for us was an exploding Andarion hovercraft, I'd say they'd be real upset. They'd probably want to hurt us."

She rolled her eyes at his sarcasm. "Do you have any weapons in your pack?"

"Not a one."

She was stunned by that. He'd been so prepared for everything else. What kind of lunatic wouldn't have at least one weapon at hand?

He winked at her, then unzipped his jacket to show her an arsenal strapped to his body.

Now that amazed her, especially given the close proximity she'd had to his body over the last few hours. "How have I not felt those?"

"I'm used to wearing them. And it wouldn't do much good if a frotteur or pickpocket could feel them on me."

Yet another word she didn't know. "Frotteur?"

"Someone who takes sexual pleasure from rubbing their body up against another." He clicked his tongue at her. "Frottisse is the female version. Feel free to partake of it with me anytime you so choose. I promise you I won't mind in the least."

How could he even contemplate sex while they were being fired on? The man was completely insane. And still, she was impressed with him. "To have been raised on the streets, you have an amazing vocabulary."

"I have my sister Tessa to thank. Unlike me and my other two sisters, she liked to insult people so that they didn't realize she was being cruel. Hence Kasen's favorite phrase, 'I'm gonna break Tess on your ass and call you names you'll have to look up in order to be offended.' "

She laughed in spite of the danger. "Your sisters sound...interesting."

"That's a polite way of saying they're all effing nuts. But it's okay. Sanity waved good-bye to me a long time ago too."

The fighter flew back over them. The sound of the engine was so loud Caillen jerked the amp out of his ear. He sucked his breath in sharply.

So much for not being able to pick up ambient sounds. Damn.

Desideria glared up at the fighter that opened fire on the ground again as if the pilot knew they were here. "You wouldn't happen to have anything to shoot that down, would you?"

"I could try your shoe theory, but I doubt it would do anything more than land on our heads and give us a concussion. And I think we've both had enough head injuries for one day. What I carry isn't quite that strong. However, I can poke out his eye should he come near us."

"What is it with you and this eye-poking business?"

"Another thing I picked up from my sisters. They never fought fair, especially not Tess." He held his hand up to midchest. "And she's only this tall. Vicious little thing. Reminds me of you."

"I think I'm insulted."

"Don't be. I admire strong women...most days." He cursed as the fighter went over and dropped a smoke bomb on the ground. "Hold your breath."

She did so without question while he pulled out two small masks from the pack and handed her one. Coughing, she covered her face. Still her eyes burned. "How do they know we're here?"

"I don't think they do. The pilot's flying too wide a radius. Bastard's just hoping to get lucky." He made an adjustment on the GPS on his wrist. "We need to get out of here before he locates us."

"How far do we have to go?"

Caillen coughed twice before he answered. "The nearest town's a haul. But there are outlying burbs and he won't be able to fly over them. Sooner or later another Andarion patrol is bound to get here and take him on." He held his arm out so that she could see the satellite photos on his chronometer of the nearest town.

Lightly settled, the houses were rather advanced for a colony. "Are you sure about where we are?"

"Yeah. I think the town we're looking at must be where the local governors and politicians live. Which is not a good thing if we get caught, but if we can get there and snag some sleep, everything should be all right come morning."

Now he decided to turn optimistic? That was almost more frightening to her than the assassin bombing the forest around them. She pointed up at the ship as it zoomed past again. "What about our friend?"

"Once we hit town, he'll have to land, and then he'll have the same problem with the authorities that we will."

"I hope you're right."

"Me too. And if I am wrong...It's all right. There's only one assassin I think I might not be able to defeat and Nyk's not here. The rest are just target practice."

She rolled her eyes again at the ego in those words. "You are so arrogant."

"Not really. I know I'm the best in a fight. It's a fact. Plain and simple."

Yeah, right. "I'm sure you've lost a few rounds."

"Only when I wasn't trying to win. I've never once lost a fight or a battle against an enemy when it counted. Ever." With those words spoken, he stepped back from their cover as if daring the fighter to shoot him.

She watched in stunned silence while he tested their safety. Once he was sure the fighter couldn't see him, he motioned for her to join him. She'd only taken four steps when she heard a new set of engines barreling down on them. Looking up, she realized more Andarion craft were moving in to pursue their "friend."

Never had she seen a more welcome sight. But that caused Caillen to pick up his pace.

"We need to put as much distance between them and us as we can while they're distracted."

She couldn't agree more.

The two of them ran for so long that she couldn't even begin to keep up with how much distance they'd gone. Her lungs ached and her legs were starting to protest. Still Caillen ran with an endurance that was as frustrating as it was impressive.

I can't believe I can't keep up.

But her pride wouldn't let her slow down. By the gods, she'd keep running until she died. And at the moment, it really, really felt like she would.

How could he keep running on his wounded leg? How? Her injuries were throbbing and aching to the point she feared she'd be sick from it. All she wanted was to lie down. Just for a minute.

Still he ran... *Gah, I could kill him.* It was tempting to shoot him just to make him stop.

Caillen ground his teeth as every step sent a fierce wave of pain through him. Damn his leg. He wanted to scream it hurt so badly, but he was used to pain. He'd been hurt worse. Although at the moment, he was hard pressed to remember a time in his life when he'd ached more. But he was sure that he had.

The only thing that kept him going was the knowledge that his father and Desideria would die if he failed them.

He glanced back over his shoulder to check on her.

She was keeping pace with him at a small distance, but her face was pale. Her features drawn tight. Shit. She looked like she was about to hurl. Slowing down, he allowed her to catch up to him. "You all right?"

Her eyes sparked with pride as she gasped for air. "Of course."

The indignation and challenge in those words made him smile. He fell back under cover so that the ships wouldn't see them should they happen by. "Let's take a second to catch our breath."

"If *you* need to..."

He grimaced as the male pride in him reared up and demanded he make her pay for that. Yeah... the little brother in him was desperate to run her until she puked from it. But he wouldn't be that cruel.

Not at the moment.

He pulled out a bottle of water and handed it to her. There was no missing the gratitude in her eyes or the relief that danced across her features. For the merest instance, she looked at him like he was a hero and something about that made his cock and stomach jerk. Never had a woman, other than his sisters, made him feel that way.

"Thank you," she said, taking it from him. Her hands shook as she tried to open it.

"Here." He held his hand out for her to return it to him.

She hesitated before she complied. He could tell it wasn't often she allowed anyone to help her.

He popped the top and this time when she took it her hand brushed against his in the tenderest of caresses. For the merest slip of a heartbeat, he wanted to take her hand into his and kiss those soft knuckles, and tell her it was all going to be okay.

I am insane. He was in excruciating pain. They were in the middle of a chase and all he could focus on was how adorable she looked with her skin glistening from sweat. How cute the dirty streaks and windblown hair were on her.

Yeah, he must have hit his head harder than he thought. Women had never caused him anything except trouble.

Pushing those thoughts aside, he pulled out the bottle he'd opened earlier and finished it off.

Desideria sipped her water slowly while Caillen guzzled his so fast she was amazed it didn't make him ill. He pulled a cloth out of his pack and wiped the sweat from his brow. She didn't know why, but she had a sudden urge to want to do it for him.

"How much further do you think?" she asked, trying to distract herself.

"Couple of miles."

She had to force herself not to whine in protest. *You can make it.* At least that's what she hoped.

"You think the Andarions caught our assassin?"

Caillen shrugged. "I hope so, but my luck says the bastard will be back to hound us when we least expect it."

She took another drink of water. "Is your luck really that bad?"

He gave a sarcastic laugh. "My luck is the stuff of legends. The badness of it is such that if you were to do an analysis of its regularity, they'd say that it is impossible to have it. And yet, it craps on my head every chance it gets. Statistical anomaly and all."

She shook her head as he started forward again at a much slower pace. He continued to lead her through a rough patch of the woods. They didn't speak much for the next few hours as they made their way to the upscale neighborhood he'd charted.

By the time they neared the houses, it was almost dark. She was aching all the more, exhausted and hungry. Given the injuries on his leg, Caillen had to be hurting even worse, but he said nothing about it.

He stopped just outside the yard of a house whose back end was hidden from the road and from its neighbors by a giant hedge. Completely dark inside, it looked to be unoccupied. But of course, there was only one way to know for sure.

One of them would have to break in and see.

Caillen winked at her. "Chin up, Princess. We're almost able to lie down. I'm going in first. If I make it in and don't get caught, I'll motion you over."

She nodded even though she didn't like the idea of breaking into anything. Any other time, she'd decline. But this was a special circumstance and sometimes you had to do things you didn't want to to protect the ones you loved. Her mother better appreciate this.

Caillen paused by the hedge and had a moment of

doubt as he saw the exhaustion in Desideria's eyes. For the last hour, he'd expected her to keel over and leave him to carry her. It was a testament to her strength that she not only kept going, but that she kept up with him and didn't bitch while she did it. If ever there was a woman he could see at his back, she was it. But he knew better than to make that mistake. On her world, men were property and no one would *ever* own him.

He handed her another bottle of water and squeezed her hand comfortingly before he skimmed his way around the hedge in the yard to come out near the house's outbuilding. About four hundred square feet, it looked like a typical storage unit. While the house appeared unoccupied, he wasn't willing to chance it. Even vacant, it could have all manner of security and right now he was too tired to screw with trying to disarm any system. He just wanted to lie down for a few and relax.

Hoping the outer building didn't have a camera pointed at it or was wired, he left the cover of the hedge to reach the rear door. He jimmied the electronic lock, then slid inside.

Luckily it was empty except for a few tools and a pile of grass seed bags. Unfortunately, it was so bare that it offered them no cover whatsoever should anyone come in. Damn. Glancing around, he finally saw a small loft area over his head that would give them a tiny bit of cover.

Grateful for small favors, he went to the door and motioned Desideria forward.

She'd just left the cover of the trees when a light danced across the yard.

Caillen cursed.

Desideria hit the deck and flattened herself against

the ground. For several seconds neither of them moved as they waited for discovery.

But the light didn't return.

He listened with his amp and heard nothing. Assuming it was safe, he waved her toward him again.

She sprang to her feet and ran so fast that he barely saw her before she launched herself at him. The impact of her body sent them both tumbling into the building. It gave him a new appreciation for what it would take to defeat her in battle. She might be short, but she was strong and sturdy.

He lay on his back, staring up at her. "You know this would be infinitely better if we were both naked."

She screwed her nose up at him. "You're a pig."

"Not really, Princess. Just a man. If you'd ever been around a real one and not the whelps who dote on your women, you'd understand that better. See what you've missed by drowning in the estrogen pool?"

She scoffed at him. "I happen to like the way the water there feels."

He arched a taunting brow. "Is that why you have yet to climb off me?"

Desideria was horrified as she realized she hadn't moved. Every bit of her body was lying against his hard, muscled one. And honestly, it felt good. *Real* good. Her face heating, she practically jumped away.

"Ah now that's just rude," he groused. "You know I did take a bath and everything. Several hours ago, but still." He flipped to his feet, then grimaced as if he'd struck his leg the wrong way before he limped over to secure the door.

Even though she felt bad for his new ache, she didn't respond as she looked around the stark interior of their new shelter. "How safe do you think this is?"

"Not very since the owners could walk in on us at any second." He pointed up to the loft. "That shouldn't be too bad though. It ought to keep us hidden until morning."

"Do you really think the house is occupied?"

He gestured to a stack of boxes in the corner of the shed. "Yeah, it looks like someone's been using it. Not to mention there's no rodents or spiderwebs. Someone's been keeping it clean."

Figured.

He indicated the loft with a jerk of his chin. "I'll help you up."

Part of her was thrilled by his offer, but her pride wouldn't let him think her weak. If he could move and act like he wasn't in pain, so could she. "Thanks, but I don't need help."

Caillen watched her jump up, grab the rope and lift herself to the small opening, then climb through so that he couldn't see her. Not one to be shown up for anything, he shot his grappling hook into the top crossbeam and let it jerk him from the ground to the loft, where he swung in next to her.

She tsked at him. "Show-off."

He laughed as he recoiled his hook. "When you got it, baby. Flaunt it."

Desideria pressed her lips together to keep from smiling at him. The last thing he needed was encouragement. But she had to admit he was adorable when he was being aggravating.

I must be high on pain. Only that would explain the bizarreness of her last thought.

Shrugging the backpack from his shoulder, he set it

down and pulled out a small metal envelope of dehydrated food. "It's not the best tasting, but it'll keep us going."

"I'm too hungry to even taste it."

"Good. That'll help." He handed her a small foil pack of wine. "Save this to the end and then use it to kill the taste of the other."

She arched a brow at his serious tone. "Done this a lot, have you?"

When he didn't respond, she realized he had a habit of that whenever she brought up his past. Something about it really bothered him. He'd talk about his sisters, but not anything else.

What was back there that he was hiding?

She'd ask, but she knew it wouldn't do her any good. So she tore into the foil and took a hesitant bite. Before she could stop herself, she shuddered.

"Yeah," he breathed. "Soldiers affectionately call this S.S."

"S.S.?"

"Shit shingles. And for more entertainment, they then try to say it three times fast."

She laughed. "I would accuse you of lying, but I doubt that you are."

"I'm not creative enough to make that up." He took a bite and swallowed without the grimace she couldn't help making at the mere thought of tasting it again.

All of a sudden, his comlink buzzed.

They exchanged a happy, stunned stare.

Caillen quickly jerked it out of his pack, put it in his ear and answered it. "Dagan here."

"Thank the gods, boy. Where have you been?"

Caillen smiled as he heard Darling's sharp castigation.

"I'd say you wouldn't believe me, but yeah, you would. We're on an Andarion outpost."

"We?"

"Me and the Qillaq princess. We were attacked and—"

"Don't say anything more. We've only got a few words before this is traced. Her people think you kidnapped her. Right now all authorities are being told to shoot to kill if they see you."

Caillen clenched his teeth as his fury settled deep in his stomach. Oh yeah, her mother was a major bitch. "Guard my father and her mother. The assassins after us are after them. Her mother's Guard are traitors."

"You sure?"

"Absolutely."

Darling cursed. "No one will believe that."

"I know. Guard her until we have proof."

"Will do. Smooth journeys, brother." Darling hung up on him.

He'd be offended by the abruptness except he knew it was to protect them.

Desideria held an expectant glint in her dark eyes. "What did he say?"

"Your mother has put a call out for my head. Shoot to kill. Apparently I've kidnapped you."

She scowled. "Why would they—"

"Her traitors can kill us both now and say that I killed you and that they killed me while I was being apprehended. It's the perfect way to silence us both at once and leave them free to murder your mom."

Desideria let out a sound of deep frustration as he stowed his comlink. "What are you doing? Why did you turn your link off?"

"If it's on and they find my UIN, they can track me. I don't want any surprises, so until I need it, it's off."

That made sense and she was grateful he knew about such things. Funny, she'd always counted herself as being extremely educated, but as her father had pointed out, there were a lot of things her people didn't know. Luckily Caillen's experience made up for her lack of knowledge. "Thank you, by the way."

"For what?"

"Telling whoever you were talking to to protect my mother. You have every reason to hate her and want her dead. But what you did was decent and I appreciate it."

He scoffed at her praise. "Oh don't worry, Princess. My reasons are purely selfish. I want her to live. I don't want anything to happen to her—not even a hangnail—until I have the chance to choke the life out of her personally."

"You know I can't let you do that."

He raked a measuring gaze down her body. "Then you better start practicing 'cause, honey, you ain't big enough to stop me."

That went down her spine like a razor and made her hackles rise. "I assure you, I'm more than capable of handling *you*."

Still his eerie eyes mocked her. "Whatever lie feeds your ego, babe."

She curled her lip at his derisive tone. At the moment she wanted to slap that arrogant look off his face. Gah, if he was one tenth the soldier his ego thought he was, they wouldn't have been caught in this situation. After all, he'd have been killed by her mother's Guard had *she* not shoved him into the pod.

Come to think of it, he had yet to thank her for *that*.

Yeah... and that made her even angrier at him.

"You are so insufferable."

"At least I wasn't spawned by the she-bitch."

She clenched her fist to keep from punching him in their tight quarters. Oh, how she wished she could get away from him or give him the beating he deserved. But that might get them taken and knocking that smug look off his face wasn't worth her life or her freedom—though it was hard to keep that in mind while he ate his crappy food in a way that really annoyed her. *I hope you choke on it, you arrogant prick.* Why had she thought for even a nanosecond that he was decent or handsome or anything other than a repugnant oaf?

Unable to stand it, she lay down and turned her back to him so that she wouldn't have to look at him for even a trifle of a moment longer.

Caillen was strangely amused by her angry response to his insulting her mother. Surely she had to know the woman was a bitch. How could she not want to choke her herself?

She's her mother. No matter what, people tended to be forgiving of those who birthed them. He probably would have been that way too had he ever had one.

And as he chewed, he tried his best to remember his adoptive mother's face. But all he could remember was Shahara looking so tired as she took care of him, Kasen, Tess and their mother. Of his sister holding him in her arms and weeping the night her mother died. He'd been too young to really understand it. Their dad had gone out on a drinking spree that had lasted for days. Meanwhile Shahara, just a child herself, had been left to make all the arrangements for burying her mother.

If he lived to be a thousand years old, he'd never forget

the sight of her young face and the sad bravery in her eyes as she picked out the clothes their mother would be buried in. *"I wish we had something nice for her. She deserves something pretty. Just once."*

Life had been so brutal to all of them. But for Shahara, it'd been far more cruel.

Because I failed to protect her. The pain of that one night when he'd let her go to the market alone still haunted him. Yeah, he'd only been a kid and had worked all day at the hangar repairing heavy equipment—all he'd wanted was to sit for a single minute without someone yelling at him that he was stupid and slow.

Had he just found the strength to walk down the street with her...

I'm such an asshole. And he would never forgive himself for what had been done to the one person in his life he'd always been able to depend on. The only person who'd ever told him that he was worth something.

He'd failed her so badly.

His gaze went to Desideria's stiff back. Another woman whose safety was dependent on him. The Andarions wouldn't be a bit kinder to her than Shahara's attacker had been. Desideria had no idea just how brutal life could be. She thought she knew, but she'd never seen someone strong broken by brutality. That look of haunted misery and shame that never went away. The fear that lingered forever afterward. Shahara had never fully recovered from her attack. At least not until Syn. He didn't know what his brother-in-law had done, but somehow Syn had finally taken away the ghost in his sister's eyes.

It was why he'd die for the man even though he still didn't like the idea of Syn being married to his sister.

Mostly because he lived in fear of Syn hurting her either accidentally or intentionally. He never again wanted to see Shahara look the way she had those first two years after her rape. Defeated and afraid of everyone and everything, she'd leaned on him so heavily at a time when he'd been nothing more than a gangly kid who needed someone to take care of him. It'd been at a time when Kase had been her sickest and Tess, rather than help, had drawn tight into herself and acted as if she'd been the one who'd been brutalized.

No, Caillen, I can't do anything on my own. Someone might grab me. Help me, Cai! I don't want to get hurt.

Tess had always been an attention whore and she'd refused to do anything for herself. Those years had been so fucking hard on him. The three of them had relied on him so much, he still wasn't sure how he'd managed to hold it together for them.

Yet here he was...

Still screwing up.

And before he realized what he was doing, he reached out to touch a lock of Desideria's hair that was spilled on the boards between them. The dark silken strands teased at his flesh. It was ever his curse to be attracted to women. He loved the way they smelled and the sensation of being held by someone. His mother had been too sick to hold him when he was young and Shahara had ceased to touch him after her attack. The worst part of that had been the way she'd looked at him for the next few years—as if she was afraid he'd attack her too. That had killed him most of all.

As for Tess and Kase, they'd never been affectionate that way. So he'd been forced to find affection with strangers who really couldn't care less about him. People were cruel by nature and he'd seen the ugliest side of them more times than he'd wanted to.

He had no doubt whatsoever that Desideria would hand him over to save her own ass. All lives had a price tag and his was pretty low most days.

Still there was a part of him that he didn't want to acknowledge that wanted what Shahara and Syn shared. That one person who would stand at his back and protect it no matter what. It was a part of him he hated and yet it was still there, needing. Aching. Wanting.

Why are you whining? You're scarred. So what? Everyone's a veteran of a fucked-up universe.

He was no different from anyone else. And as he lay there, twirling her hair around his finger while she held herself rigid, he wondered what scars she carried. Who had screwed her over and hurt her?

After all, her mother was a grand bitch who appeared to be lacking any kind of human decency. The fact that Desideria was serving in her Guard where others looked down their noses at her said that her mother treated her like crap. What kind of parent would needlessly put their child in harm's way like that?

Honestly, her loyalty to the viper was admirable. And before he realized what he was doing a single word slipped out of his lips. "Sorry." Wow, there was something he never did. To him an apology meant weakness, and he was anything but weak.

He wouldn't have thought it possible, but somehow she managed to stiffen even more. "No, you're not. You meant every word."

"Yeah, but I'm sorry I offended you."

"Why?" Her tone was brittle.

He answered her question with the simple truth. "Have no idea."

"I'm still not speaking to you."

He smiled at the ridiculousness of that comment. Whatever. He could probably charm her into forgiving him, but he wasn't really in the mood. He ached too much to try.

This day had sucked in so many ways he couldn't even begin to catalog all of them. Right now he was too tired to care about anything other than catching some sleep.

Rubbing his eyes, he stretched out on the cold floor and tried not to think about her. Unfortunately, the sweet scent of her skin hung in his nostrils and made him so hard he couldn't concentrate on anything except how close she lay beside him and how easy it would be to slide his hand down her warm cleavage and touch skin he knew would be incredibly soft and tasty. If she rode him with even half the passion she put into everything else, she'd be one incredible lover.

I'm in hell.

Not really true. He'd been in real hell and this wasn't it. But this was close.

Think about tomorrow. They had a lot to do to get off this rock and back to the *Arimanda*. At least he knew Darling would take care of his father even if he had to out his Sentella identity to do it. So long as his friend was on board, no one would be able to get near Evzen.

And as he ran over all the technical difficulties of what they'd have to do in the morning, he fell asleep.

Desideria came awake to a light gentle snore in her ear and a warm, heavy weight completely surrounding her. It was like being wrapped in a hard, heavy blanket. At first she had no idea what it was until the scent of Caillen hit her forcefully and she realized her pillow was his left biceps. For the merest instant, she allowed herself to enjoy the novelty of waking up in someone's arms. He smelled so good and the sensation of his body surrounding hers...

Until she felt something strange pressing against her hip. Was that...?

Oh my gods...

Horrified by the intimacy of what it was, she jumped away from him with a mortified squeak. He woke up ready to fight. Out of nowhere a knife appeared in his hand as he looked about for an enemy.

His gaze focused on her before he gave her a fierce scowl.

A shiver went down her spine at his new, sinister appearance. True to his words, his hair fell just past his shoulders. Jet black, it made his Andarion eyes all the eerier. He looked nothing like the rogue she'd come to know...

Until he grinned.

Yeah, she'd know that cocky twist of the lips anywhere. "You are a total freak of nature. You know that?"

His laugh was as dark as his aura. "Yes, but you're going to be grateful I look like this when we run into the natives."

She wasn't so sure about that.

Yawning, he stretched, then scratched at the whiskers on his chin in that familiar gesture she was coming to know a little too well.

She jerked her chin toward his hand. "You always come awake with a knife?"

"No. Usually it's my blaster and normally I'm shooting. Be glad I'm still tired."

She scoffed at his bravado. "You expect me to believe that?"

"Believe it or not, it's the truth." He slid the knife back into a sheath that was hidden in his sleeve.

If he had any memory of cuddling her while they slept, he showed no sign of it as he stretched his body and went through a series of graceful movements that showed her just how flexible he was for a man.

Once he was done, he pulled his backpack up. "You hungry?"

"Not for another round of ick. Sorry."

"I understand." He took a small band from the pack and pulled his hair back from his face to secure it into a becoming ponytail. "Now that I look semi passable, let's get off this rock and find something decent to eat."

Her stomach grumbled a reminder that she hadn't really eaten the day before. "Don't they have edible food here?"

"Probably, but the first rule of survival. Don't stop to eat or get laid. I've known more people to get killed because they let their stomach or hormones dictate evac. I don't know about you, but I don't want to be a cautionary tale for anybody."

He had a point.

Caillen handed her the cloak. "Remember to stay covered no matter what."

Desideria pulled her hair back and coiled it into a bun before she raised the cowl. "How's this?"

"Perfect." He slung his pack over his shoulder, then led her down to the ground level.

They crept out of the shed and back toward the woods where they had cover from any stray glance. Moving quickly and gracefully, Caillen skimmed the yards, heading toward a more densely populated area.

Desideria was surprised at the difference between this town and her native Qilla. The houses here were narrow and long, their roof lines cut at sharp angles. Qillaqs used mostly untinted glass and windows with a lot of circular designs. The Andarion homes had small windows that were kept covered up.

"Do they have an aversion to daylight?" she asked, wondering about the custom.

"Their eyes are more sensitive to it than ours."

Even their transports were radically different. Her people traveled in groups, but the Andarion vehicles seemed designed for speed and few occupants. Yet what struck her most was the lack of toys and children on the street.

"Where are all the kids?"

Caillen stepped over a fallen limb. "Probably in training."

"You mean school?"

"No, training. School is attended at night and usually online. They spend the daylight hours in physical and martial training. I cannot emphasize the point that they make your people look like wimps enough. While you're a warrior culture, you're female dominated. Andarions are male dominated and vicious to an unfathomable level."

"They subjugate their women?"

"No. The only thing more dangerous than an Andarion male is an Andarion female. Their women, as a rule, aren't very feminine in anything they do. There are exceptions to this, but very rare ones. All of them are tough sons of bitches."

She didn't know what he meant until they left their

cover and started walking down the street, toward an intersection.

Caillen cleared his throat before he spoke. "Don't meet anyone's gaze. Keep your head down at all times."

He, however, didn't follow that advice. In fact, he stared down every person they passed as if daring them to speak. It was like every passerby was sizing him up for an opponent and he was begging them to try something.

At the biggest intersection they found, Caillen paused next to a red-marked pole and hailed an autotran for them. He allowed her to enter the small egg-shaped vehicle first, then he got in and closed the door. She started to lower her cowl, but the fierce look he gave her made her pause. He cut a sharp glare to the corner. She followed his line of sight to see a camera there.

So she pretended she was only adjusting it while he swiped his card and entered their destination on the electronic keypad. When he didn't explain the language or his actions, she took that to mean that they also had a mic in the car that was monitoring them.

True to her suspicion, a deep voice spoke to them in what must be the Andarion language. Caillen responded, his tone calm and even. They talked back and forth for several seconds until Caillen, his tone never showing any stress, jerked his blaster out and shot the camera in the car and the one on the street.

He moved so fast and unexpectedly that she gaped. "What's going on?"

"We've been made."

14

Caillen growled in the back of his throat. "I seriously underestimated their tech. Bastards have a face and retinal scanner that notified them that I wasn't who I claimed."

Terror filled her. "What do we do?"

He answered by kicking the electronics panel in front of them so hard that it broke open and exposed the wires. Desideria was dying to know what he was doing, but didn't want to distract him while they were in a crisis situation. The most important thing was for them to get out of here as quickly as possible.

Caillen cursed in a language she couldn't identify as if everything was hopeless.

She started to open the door to run for it, but he caught her arm and held her inside.

"On foot, we're dead. If you want to escape, stay with me."

But did she trust him enough for that? He hated her mother and he didn't seem to think all that much of her.

What if he was lying?

For all she knew, he might be. All of this fiasco and drama could be caused by his fear of them killing *him*. Maybe the Andarions wouldn't do anything more than set her free and let her go home. They might honor her diplomatic immunity.

But what if he wasn't lying? What if they did imprison her like her mother had done her father? Then she'd be trapped here forever. Or eaten alive.

That would be bad and her mother would be dead.

At the end of the day, she didn't know Caillen at all. Didn't know his moral code or really much of anything about him other than he'd been raised as a commoner who had some impressive thief-like skills...

And he was a wanted felon to the Andarion government.

None of that gave her a reason to trust him even the slightest bit.

But if she had to choose between devils, she'd rather choose the one known than the one not. She was too ignorant of other races and cultures to even begin to argue against Caillen about the Andarions and their customs. They could have fat flying spiders who lived on cake trained to capture her for all she knew.

Hoping she wasn't being stupid or fooled, she grabbed his blaster and readied herself for the fight.

Sirens blared and drew nearer as he rifled through the wires and tore out connections only to make new ones. He glanced at the blaster in her hand. "FYI, don't shoot the Andarions with that. It'll only piss them off."

Great. What were they supposed to do if they couldn't fire on them? "Then what..."

The transport shot forward at three times its normal

cruising speed. The unexpected lurch sent her flying back into the seat and caused her to drop her weapon as Caillen took control of their vehicle and sent it careening through traffic at a pace that was horrifying and disorienting.

That being said, he was good at controlling it as he narrowly missed hitting bystanders, obstacles and other vehicles. He might lack all manners and social graces, but when it came to communicating with electronics, she doubted if anyone could be better.

Two Enforcer transports stopped in front of them, cutting off their escape route.

Without slowing down the least bit, Caillen skidded their transport sideways and somehow managed to wedge it through the Enforcers who opened fire on them. He righted their transport and kept moving forward. The back window shattered under the heavy shots, spraying glass fragments all over them.

He started to push her toward the floor out of harm's way, but she stopped him.

"I know how to fight."

She saw the respect in his dark eyes before he nodded. He went back to driving while she shot out the remaining pieces of the back window, then laid down cover fire for them. The transport skidded as he narrowly avoided slamming into a large fuel hauler, then straightened and lurched forward again.

"Air support's coming in," he warned as he did something with the wires that made the transport speed up even more. Now they were flying.

Desideria crawled out of the back window before she fired up at the hovercraft that was tailing them. Her shots glanced off the craft and did nothing more than burn their paint. It didn't even cause them to swerve to miss her blasts. Cursing her weapon, she slid back into the transport. "You got anything with more kick?"

He pulled a smaller blaster out of his boot and handed it to her.

Was he serious? It looked like a child's weapon.

He grinned at her. "It has a plasma recoil. Be careful."

Yeah, it'd hurt her to fire it, but with the right hit, it should bring the craft down. She leaned out the side window only to have Caillen jerk her back in before she could shoot. She started to yell at him for his actions, until she realized that he'd kept her from being flattened by a cargo transport that roared past them.

Had he delayed even a nanosecond, she'd have been cut in half. The thought made her stomach shrink.

"Thanks."

He inclined his head as the air support opened fire on them again. She ducked down as blasts narrowly missed her and cut through their transport. Now her anger was forefront and the taste of bloodlust was heavy in her mouth. Determined to pay them back for the assault, she leaned out the window and braced herself. Then she opened fire. The shots sizzled up, shattering the hovercraft's glass and taking out their upper rotor blade. But instead of falling back, they fell toward them, heading at them so fast all she could see was her death.

"Heads up!" she shouted as she returned to the transport's seat and ducked for cover.

But it was too late. The hovercraft hit the ground right beside them, slinging sideways and catching the transport with its tail section. It sent them careening down the street before they rolled over and over again. Her stomach pitched as dizziness consumed her. Pain slammed into every part of her while she tumbled around the transport, banging into Caillen and everything else in the vehicle.

I'm going to die. She knew it. There was no way they could survive a wreck so vicious. She waited for the darkness to take her, but to her amazement she remained conscious.

When they finally stopped rolling and skidded to an abrupt halt, she was completely disoriented. Her stomach was contracting with such ferocity that she waited for the indignity of spilling its contents. Somehow she managed to keep it in as Caillen tried to open the door that had been crushed by their wreck. The transport was so damaged that there was no escape that she could see. It had them cocooned in a twisted metal pod.

"Get down."

She didn't question his order. The moment she ducked, Caillen pulled out a tachyon charge. He set it on the door, then covered her body with his as it blasted a hole in the side of the transport.

He got out first, then pulled her with him.

As she ran away from the transport, she noticed that she was covered in blood. It was on her clothes, her skin and in her hair. Her heart stopped as panic consumed her. Where was she injured? Every part of her body ached so there was no telling.

It took her a full minute to realize she wasn't the one hurt.

Caillen was.

Still he didn't slow down. He led her into an abandoned warehouse and slammed the door shut behind them and locked it, then fried the lock so that no one could enter easily. His hands shaking, he shrugged the pack off and gave it to her. "Keep running. Darling knows where we are. He'll send help as soon as he can. Just stay hidden until they find you."

She frowned at his calm tone and the fatal determination she'd heard in his voice. "What about you?"

He grimaced. "I'm not going to make it." He opened his jacket to show her that the hovercraft's shots hadn't missed him. His entire left side was riddled with blast wounds.

For the first time, she saw fear in his eyes that overrode his pain. His cheeks were smeared with dirt and blood that was streaked by sweat. There was a tic in his jaw and blood ran from the corner of his mouth.

He pulled out his reserve blaster and held it tight in a bloodied grip. "I'll cover you while you run."

She watched the blood flowing from his hand to make small splatters against the dirty concrete floor. "Caillen—"

"Don't argue. You're wasting valuable time you need to get clear of this place."

Even though she hated it, she nodded. He was right, she had to get out of here. Her mother's life depended on it. Kissing him on his bruised cheek, she turned and ran to find a back way out.

Caillen listened to the sound of her retreating footsteps as he limped away from the door and made sure to cover his bloody tracks to find some place where he could hole up and take out a few of their pursuers before they killed him. For some reason he couldn't name, it saddened him that she'd left him to die.

She's a stranger, what do you care?

Yet he couldn't shake the image of his father dying alone in the filthy gutter like he was nothing but trash.

Like he was about to do.

So be it. Unlike his father, he wasn't lying down to be executed. He would die fighting with everything he had, taking as many of the Andarions with him as he could.

Your father died protecting you . . .

The guilt and pain of that ripped through him as it always did when he thought about it. Which was something he tried to avoid. He knew the truth. His father was a fighter and he'd only surrendered to their pursuers to give Caillen enough time to escape and live.

Again like he was doing for Desideria.

I'm such an effing idiot.

He didn't know her and yet here he was laying down his life to keep her safe. Not wanting to think about that either, he turned his attention to the street, where he saw through a dirty window that the Enforcers were gathering their numbers before they came in to search for him.

"Come on, you bastards. Don't be bashful." He crouched low and braced his arm so that he could fire on them the moment they entered.

A hand touched his shoulder.

He whirled, expecting it to be one of the Enforcers.

It wasn't. Instead, he saw a beautiful angel who had blood and dirt smeared across her dark skin. Her hair was a tangled mess and there was a determination in her eyes that said she wasn't about to be argued with.

"I can't leave you here, Caillen. We got into this together. Together we'll get out of it or die."

He was stunned by Desideria's heartfelt words. "What about your mom?"

"Your friend knows about her and I'd be dead if not for you. Now move it before *I* shoot you."

He scoffed at her order. "You're an idiot."

"Apparently so." She pulled his arm around her shoulders and helped him move through the dark, vacant building. "Any bright ideas for an escape?"

"Not really. Every time I try to think of something, the pain asserts itself to the forefront of my attention. Kind of blows everything else out of the way."

She growled low in her throat. "Oh this is irritating. I hate it when someone gets the better of me. I can't stand to lose."

Desideria paused as she saw an opened trapdoor in the floor. It offered very little chance of nondiscovery, but it was the only one they had. "I have an idea."

Caillen hesitated as he saw it too. "It'll never work."

"Do I crap all over your plans even when they're stupid? No. Now unless you have a better idea, get in there."

He mumbled something under his breath that sounded like death to bossy women as he snapped a small light stick and tossed it into the small room so that they could see. Ignoring him, she helped him down, then went to make sure there was no blood trail leading to their hiding place.

The Enforcers were just outside, working on breaking into the rusted-out door he'd locked. Their electronic torch made a loud hiss as they shouted to each other. Any second they'd be inside and shooting...

Please let this work.

Following Caillen into the hole, Desideria closed the trapdoor barely one heartbeat before the Enforcers stormed inside to search for them. The empty room was bathed in a dull blue light from his stick—a much more somber and dim light than the one he'd used in the cave. He must have chosen it for that reason.

She went to Caillen who'd passed out on the dirty floor that was encrusted with spiderwebs and rodent droppings. Probably for the best—not the nasty spiderwebs and other things, but being unconscious given their situation. If they were taken, he'd have no idea.

Unfortunately, she wasn't so lucky.

She heard the Andarions above opening up their equipment and talking to each other in angry tones as they tried to locate them. Damn it, why didn't she have a translator? It was so frustrating to not be able to understand a single word they spoke.

Biting her lip, she glanced at Caillen's backpack and remembered his mirror devices from the cave. Would that work to jam their scanners?

Better than nothing. She searched out the devices until she had them in her hand. Her heart pounding, she carried them to the small trapdoor and placed one piece on each side of it before she turned them on.

Please let that be the right way to position and operate them.

If not...

She didn't want to think about that as she went back to try and stop Caillen's bleeding. In his pack, he had bandages and all kinds of things she couldn't even guess the function of—gadgets, medicines, weapons. They were all marked, but she couldn't read even one character of the highly stylized writing.

Why didn't I learn Universal?

Because her mother had thought it a waste of time. Yet another reason she shouldn't have listened to the woman.

She clenched one of the bottles in her hand and hesitated as she debated whether or not to give a dose to Caillen. Better not guess on what it was or the dose since that might very well kill him.

Fine. She'd stop the bleeding with pressure.

The voices above her head grew louder and angrier. Had they found the door? Were they summoning troops to enter?

She held her breath in nervous fear, waiting for discovery.

Her gaze went to Caillen. His handsome face was so pale and his skin was covered in sweat. *Don't bleed out.* If he died, she had no idea how she'd get out of here.

But it wasn't just that. She owed him and if not for her, he wouldn't be here wounded right now. This was all her fault. He could have been like other nobles and ignored her attack. Or he could have called security.

Instead, he'd risked his life and saved hers without a second thought. Something very few would do. A foreign tenderness filled her until a sound jerked her attention back to their pursuers.

Someone knocked on the trapdoor.

They're coming in.

She grabbed the blaster, ready to fight it out. They weren't going to take Caillen. Not if she could help it.

Above her head, it sounded like two people were arguing. After a few minutes, the voices drifted away out of her hearing range.

Were they gone?

Or was it the same trick they'd used at the cave with the probers?

She looked back at Caillen who would have probably known the answer.

Either way, she needed to tend him before he lost any more blood. Setting the blaster aside, she peeled his coat back, then raised his shirt. Her lip curled involuntarily at the sight of his mutilated chest. She'd never seen anything more gruesome and it amazed her that he was still alive.

How could anyone survive something so brutal? It said a lot about his will to live and his ability to handle pain. What had he been through that he was able to remain so calm in a fight? The skills he had weren't innate. They were the kind that had to be honed by years of experience and she should know since she'd studied her whole life and hers were nowhere near as sharp.

As gently as she could, she took a bandage from his worn-out pack and pressed it against the worst-looking wound that was in the middle of the ornate tattoo he had running the length of his left side. It appeared to be a foreign bird whose face was painted on his shoulder.

Caillen's eyes flew open as he let out a fierce breath. He grabbed her wrist so hard that she was sure it'd leave a bruise. But as soon as his gaze focused on her, his hold turned gentle.

He dropped his hand away from hers. *Are they still here?* he mouthed the words to her.

She nodded.

He pointed to his pack.

She handed it over to him and watched as he removed several items. The first thing he did was pull out a rubber stick that he put between his teeth. She scowled, wondering what it was for. Was it some kind of painkiller?

He grabbed a large foil pack and opened it, then spread the granules over his wounds. He bit the stick so hard, she heard it snap. By the rigidity of his body, she could tell it had to burn and ache. Still, he made no sound at all.

She took the foil pack from him and started applying it to all of his wounds. His muscles contracted every time she touched him. Poor guy.

But he was one hell of a soldier. He took it like a man.

Once she was finished, she handed him a bottle of water before she started bandaging his side. While she worked, he pulled an injector out and took a dose of pain meds.

Caillen sipped the water slowly as he did his best to not scream out from the sheer agony that pulsed through him with every heartbeat. He didn't need to make himself sick, but he had to stay hydrated. Gah, it hurt.

Closing his eyes, he focused on the softness of Desideria's hands as she bandaged him and let that soothe him as much as it could. He still couldn't believe that she'd come back for him. Most people lacked that honor and decency.

Hell, most of the "friends" he'd had in his life would have tied him up while he was wounded and stolen his wallet before they left him for the Enforcers to find.

But she'd come back...

Like an angel.

She took the water from him long enough to wet a cloth that she then used to clean his face. Her hand was so cool and soft against his skin that before he realized what he was doing, he captured it and kissed her knuckles.

Desideria froze at the sensation of his lips on her flesh. No one had ever been so tender with her. The feathery touch made her stomach contract sharply. Her gaze locked with his and for a moment she forgot everything except for the beauty of his real eyes, the sensation of her hand in his. Without thinking, she touched his soft lips with her fingertip. They were the only part of him that wasn't rock hard. And before she realized what she was doing, she dipped her head down to taste them.

Caillen sucked his breath in sharply at the unexpected kiss. Damn, if he didn't hurt so badly, he'd take advantage of this fire. But right now, he could barely breathe. Still the heat of that kiss seared him. What she lacked in experience, she more than made up for in enthusiasm and it sent a wave of pleasure through him that eased the pain.

At least for a few heartbeats.

Desideria pulled back as she came to her senses and realized what she was doing.

I'm kissing a man. And she wasn't allowed to do that. Not yet...

Her mother would kill her if she learned of this. Worse, she'd have to wait an additional year before she could take a consort. Qillaq beliefs were that if a woman couldn't control her lust, then she wasn't mature enough to handle a lover. What she'd just done would shame her mother and herself.

Heat flooded her face. "Sorry."

His cocky grin was adorable for once. "Don't be," he whispered. "It's the best thing that's happened to me all month. Feel free to fall against my lips anytime you get the urge."

She shook her head at him. "You're awful."

Caillen cupped her cheek in his hand. "Rotten to my core."

He was also charming in a most devastating way. "Just how many women have you seduced anyway?"

He shrugged, then grimaced sharply. "I don't count because it doesn't matter."

Now that offended her. What a callous pig! "How can you say it doesn't matter?"

"Because it was never the right one."

Those words gave her pause. Could he be less piggish than she thought? Was it possible there really was a gentleman hiding under those layers of heartless rogue? "What do you mean?"

"Mmm," he breathed. "Pain meds are kicking in with a vengeance. Yeah, I almost feel semi human again."

She turned his head until he was looking at her. "You didn't answer my question."

"Simple." His words were slurred now. "If there's a selfish bitch to be had, I gravitate straight for her. Women only want to use me, own me or kill me. Not once has a woman ever wanted to keep me." Then he closed his eyes and passed out again.

Those words and the heartfelt emotion she'd heard behind them touched something deep inside her. It made her wonder what the women in his life had done to him to make him feel that way. Of course, her experience with women was similar. The women around her had been petty, judgmental, cutting and jealous. They thought by tearing others down that it elevated them. They were wrong, but it didn't stop them from it.

She had no real experience with men. Except her dad and she'd loved him like no one else. He'd been the only person in her life who'd ever accepted her as she was. He'd never judged her or even criticized her.

Caillen was nothing like her father, but in some ways

he did remind her of her dad. The way he was dependable and caring—willing to sacrifice himself for others.

She frowned at the bloody rag lying beside him. "You are such a mess."

What if he died?

Desideria refused to think about that and the foreign ache it caused. She couldn't afford to. As she began putting things back into the pack, she found a small laptop.

What the...? Why hadn't he used it? Or at least mentioned that he had one?

She opened it to turn it on, then thought better of it. If the Andarions were electronically sweeping the area they'd hone in on the signal. That was probably why Caillen hadn't used it before now. He was too much of a survivalist to allow something like this to go unused unless there was a good reason for it.

You're completely cut off.

She'd never been alone before. Even though she was twenty-six years old, her family had viewed her as a child up until a couple of weeks ago. She'd been surrounded by guards and servants. Her sisters and aunt. It was a lost feeling to not be able to reach out and summon them now. Or anyone else who could lend her a hand. Her mother had never experienced this isolated sensation either.

But her father had. Stranded on a foreign planet with foreign beings who'd seen him as a weaker entity who only deserved their disdain and abuse.

Caillen had assured her that she'd receive the same treatment from the Andarions if they discovered them. They'd be pawns with no way to escape and no hope. She glanced around the bare gray walls as panic set in. How had her father stood being a prisoner for all those years?

It was terrifying. For the first time, she fully understood everything he'd given up.

Suddenly, Caillen's link rang.

Krik! That could get her discovered. Her heart hammering, she picked it up, then froze. Caillen had turned it off. She'd seen him. How could it be ringing?

Was it a trick?

What if it wasn't? It could be help.

Maybe.

Hoping for the best, she answered it before it rang again.

"Who is this?" It was a gruff, accented male voice.

"Desideria," she whispered. "Who are you?"

He hung up.

She quickly did the same as her gut knotted and this time she made sure it was turned completely off.

And then she heard it…the sound of the Andarions returning to the warehouse in force and they were a lot more animated this time.

I've just given our position away.

They were going to come for them and it was all her fault. Damn it! Why had she answered the link?

15

Desideria held her breath as the voices came closer and closer. There were animals with them and it sounded like a lot of them. She could hear them whining and barking as the Andarions searched through the building.

As fast as was possible, she grabbed the spray that Caillen had used earlier out of the bag, and turned it loose on the door and on them. *Please don't have an erackle in that hunting herd.*

According to Caillen, that would be bad. And since he had yet to be wrong about anything to do with their pursuit...

Yeah, a horny erackle would most likely ruin her day.

What she hated most about all of this was her feelings of vulnerability. She'd always prided herself on being self-sufficient—on being able to handle anything thrown at her. And she was.

But this...

This was way out of her realm of experience and expertise. She was in an alien culture with an unconscious stranger. Here, she didn't know the rules or the climate. She didn't even know what foods were safe to eat or how to find them. It now struck her as peculiar that her aunt had taught her to fight to survive, but never how to scrounge and use resources. Not the way Caillen did.

She glanced to him. For some reason she couldn't explain, his presence soothed her. Yeah, it made no sense whatsoever. He was completely out of commission. Would be worthless in a fight or even if they had to run and yet... she could hear his sarcastic voice in her head, giving her tips on what they needed to escape and survive.

What is wrong with me?

Desideria had been taught to trust no one. Not even family. And right now, when she needed to listen to that training, she didn't hear her aunt's careful instruction.

She heard Caillen's.

Without thinking, she took his hand into hers. Even though it was filthy and calloused, it was beautiful—just like the rest of him. He had long, tapered fingers with nails that were clipped but not manicured the way other noblemen's were. Caillen's were rugged work hands. Masculine hands.

And they, too, comforted her...

Something struck the trapdoor. Hard. She bit her lip to keep from making a sound as she tightened her grip on Caillen's hand and her blaster, waiting for them to break through.

They hit it again.

An animal barked, then ran off making unfamiliar noises that sounded like a whine. There was a huge ruckus before the Andarions followed the creature. After a few minutes, everything was quiet again.

Still, she held her breath and kept her grip tight, waiting for them to return and discover their lair.

Hours and hours went by slowly as her heart beat a fearful rhythm. Finally she allowed herself to relax and accept the fact that they were safe.

Even if it was only for a moment.

Sighing, she leaned her head back against the wall and laid the blaster down. The muscles in her arm were tight and strained from having held its weight for so long. She laced her fingers with Caillen's and sat in silence as she let the roughness of his skin soothe her even more. It felt so good to know that she wasn't completely alone in this. Even though he was unconscious.

Thank the gods the Andarions were gone. This one moment of peace was worth a fortune to her.

Please don't let it end.

She'd had enough excitement for one day, or actually fifty thousand. Really, she didn't need any more. Relieved to the point she could almost cry, her gaze fell to Caillen who hadn't moved in so long she became worried about it. When he'd slept earlier, he'd had a faint snore.

Now nothing...

Had he died? Was he breathing? Sudden panic swelled inside her as her mind conjured all manner of bad scenarios.

Please don't be dead. Don't have bled out. Not while she'd been worried about them when she should have been tending him...

She inched forward to place her hand under his nose so that his breath could tickle her skin.

Thank the gods, he was still alive. That was almost as big a relief as the Andarions leaving the building. And as he lay there sleeping, she couldn't help but notice how handsome he really was in the faint blue light. How boyish and relaxed.

How completely out of commission he was and how dependent they were on her for their survival . . .

Yeah, that was a scary prospect.

Caillen, you're so screwed. She'd never taken care of anyone before. Not even a pet. Honestly, she was afraid she might kill the poor man out of ignorance. She knew some field medicine, but not much and all of it was in theory. She'd never had to actually use it. It just hadn't been taught as part of their lessons.

Come on, Desideria, you can do this. Her people prided themselves on their survival abilities. But then survival to them was synonymous with fighting—being able to protect yourself.

Her gaze went to the ragged backpack . . .

A pack that carried everything a person would ever need to live through just about anything. Curious about its contents, she pulled it to her and opened the worn leather. She paused as she caught an unexpected whiff of Caillen's scent. Warm and all masculine, it made her heartbeat speed up. She didn't know why she adored the smell of his skin, but she did. In truth, she'd love nothing better than to bury her face in his neck and just inhale him.

Pushing that disturbing thought aside, she started sorting through the contents of his pack to take inventory in case she needed something before he woke back up. He really did have the most bizarre combination in it. Socks, sunglasses, medicines, dehydrated food and water.

Prophylactics . . .

She didn't even want to think about that one. Well,

not entirely true. For some reason, she did have a strange curiosity about what he'd look like naked. What it would feel like to hold him in her arms and have him kiss her like a hungry lover. To have his hair fall forward in his face as he lay on top of her, looking down with that devilish grin of his...

He probably was great in bed.

Oh, what is wrong with me?

Then again, Narcissa would say there was something wrong with her if she didn't want to have sex with him. That made her feel a *little* better.

Still...

She was in the middle of a chase. Her enemies could find her any second and if that wasn't enough reason to keep her thoughts off his body, there was the small matter of him being a prowling rogue who carried prophylactics in his bag, scamming for an easy lay. Definitely not her type of male at all. Not even a little bit. She wanted someone who could be loyal and sweet. Someone dependable to be there when she needed him who could support but never overshadow her.

Someone like her father.

That thought solidified her conviction as she continued to make her way through the pack's contents which included an obscene amount of small condiment packages.

What in the world? Did one human really need this much sauce or crackers? Really?

All of a sudden, she paused. In the bottom of the pack she found the most amazing thing of all. Something she would have never suspected a man like Caillen to carry.

A small vidframe.

How very strange.

Sitting back on her heels, she turned it on and waited for the photos to load. In the darkness, she flipped through the images that spoke volumes about the man next to her. There was one of a beautiful redheaded woman and a tall dark-haired man standing beside her. They looked so happy and sweet. The love they had for each other as they embraced was more than evident and it was breathtaking.

Both of them were dressed in white for some kind of ceremony she didn't recognize. The man's shoulder-length hair framed his handsome, clean-shaven face. His skin was a much darker tone than Caillen's. more like hers, and his eyes were so black she couldn't tell where the iris ended and his pupil began. He had two small gold hoops in his left earlobe. The woman's dress was strapless and as stunning as she was. It fell in light layers around her skinny body and she had white flowers braided into her long hair.

Desideria pressed the play button.

They immediately kissed.

"Hey, guys, stop. Stop! You're making me sick. Seriously, I'm about to splash shoes here and since Shay splurged to buy hers, I don't want to get hurt." She recognized Caillen's voice, castigating them. Judging from the loudness of the tone, she assumed he was the one holding the camera. "Syn, that's my sister you're tonguing and I'm going to beat your ass again if you don't get away from her. I mean it. I don't care that you're married now. She's still my sister and you're a dead man."

Syn scoffed, his dark eyes sending a challenge. "You didn't beat it the last time, giakon. As I recall, I sent *you* packing."

The camera bounced to show the rapidly shifting ground as Caillen headed for him.

The woman came between them and pushed Caillen back. The camera went swinging around her body until she righted it and forced Caillen to move another step away from Syn. "You touch my husband again, Cai, and I'll paint your rear stabilizer red. Now behave and show Syn that I raised you right." Laughing, she took the camera from Caillen and turned it on him.

Desideria's breath caught as she saw not a rigid aristocrat, but a man so unbelievably handsome that it was hard to even look at him. Dressed in a black formal suit and freshly shaved, Caillen was absolutely stunning even though he was fuming angry. Only he could pull off that amount of hotness and rage at the same time.

"Annoying, isn't it, little brother?" Shahara asked as she moved so close to him that Desideria could almost see up his nostrils.

Recovering his usual good nature, he flashed that charming grin and stepped away from her. "You'll be glad you have these pictures one day."

"Doubt it. I see you act a fool enough. Why would I want to capture it for all eternity?"

Two more women came up and wrapped their arms around Caillen before he could respond.

"Here, Shahara, let me have it." She heard Syn off camera. "Get over there with your brother and sisters and let's get all the Dagans together. It'll be the only still you have of Kasen in a dress."

"Hey!" the heavier of the two sisters snarled. "I'll remember that, Syn. What are you saying about me?"

"He's saying you don't dress like a woman." Caillen

scoffed at her. "And you don't. Worst day of my life was when I caught up to you size wise. You've been stealing my clothes ever since and stretching out all my shirts."

She punched him hard on the biceps. "You better remember I don't hit like a woman either and I know where you sleep. Shay and Tess will weep in agony when they find your bloody remains after I exact my revenge."

"Oh yeah right. Like you'd kill me before I pay off my ship. I know better. You live in fear of that kind of debt and without me you'd get arrested anyway."

"Enough bitching." Shahara held her hand up in an imperious gesture that miraculously kept them from arguing further. Then she moved to the other side and slid in between Caillen and Kasen.

Desideria paused the clip to study Caillen and his three sisters. They looked nothing alike. But there was no missing the love between them. Caillen had his arms wrapped around Shahara and Kasen, and the third, Tessa, held on to Shahara like a lifeline.

All of them smiling. It was such a sweet, tender moment that she felt like she was intruding just to see it. And it made her ache that she'd never once had a moment like that in her own life. Never once had her sisters held her like Caillen held his. They didn't share laughter or gentle teasing. Only caustic, vicious retorts.

She and her sisters would have fought to the death over the words Kasen had said to Caillen or vice versa.

Her heart aching with the cold truth of how little her family cared about each other, she traced the lines of Caillen's smiling face on the screen and wondered if he'd be like her father ... when she'd been a child and on nights when her mother hadn't required his presence, he would sneak out of his chambers to visit her in the wee hours after everyone was asleep. They'd gone on midnight rides, and walks, and had held many a campout under the stars.

Out of sheer jealousy Narcissa would report it anytime she discovered them and her father would be punished severely for it. But it never stopped him from coming. No matter how savage the beating.

"You're worth it, my little rose. No one will ever take you from me and nothing will stop me from seeing you. Not even your mother." She could still feel the warmth of his hug. There were times even now when she was sure he was with her. Times when she liked to pretend that she could feel his gentle presence.

But that wasn't Qillaq.

She glanced over to Caillen and her heart lurched as she saw how badly damaged he was from trying to protect her. Deep inside, she was sure he'd be like that with his own daughter.

That thought brought a foreign tenderness to her. And a part of her, to this day, was still angry at the gods who'd taken her father's life. It was so unfair for him to die and leave her alone, to abandon her to a world where no one would ever again think she was good enough for anything. No matter how hard she tried, she couldn't blot out the memory of her mother and aunt's constant criticisms. If only she could have had a few more years of her father telling her that she wasn't stupid, fat, ugly and worthless...

But there was nothing she could do.

He was gone and she was alone.

Her gaze went back to Caillen, making her wonder what it would be like to laugh with him the way his sisters did. Closing her eyes, she imagined a wedding for them similar to Syn and Shahara's.

A Qillaq marriage ceremony was nothing like theirs. There was no peaceful taking of the hands and telling witnesses how much they meant to each other. On her world, the woman claimed the man by battle. If he defeated her, they were equal. If not, she ruled him and he was forced to obey her orders. In theory, the man had an advantage, but Desideria had a bad suspicion that the men were drugged. No one had ever told her that. Yet she remembered her father once talking about how sick he'd been when he'd fought her mother. It was cruel and unfair.

I would never do that to someone.

If she couldn't defeat the man honestly, she didn't want to rule him.

And that's why you're such a disappointment to your mother.

That thought brought back all her self-doubts and the angry voices in her head that she tried so hard to squelch.

Needing a reprieve from it, she flipped through more pictures of Caillen's family. She only saw a handful of other people. His sisters were in there repeatedly in all manner of candid shots. Along with Syn, two Andarions— one of whom was blond and never smiled—Darling Cruel, and the next to the last was a beautiful lady holding an infant in her arms. The woman looked so much like Caillen that Desideria realized this must be his real mother. Odd that he didn't have a single picture of his adoptive parents or Emperor Evzen.

Just his mother holding him as a baby.

Very strange.

The final photo was one of a beautiful woman who

didn't appear related to anyone else. Though she was smiling, her eyes were cold. Calculating. Something about her sent a shiver over her.

Desideria put the frame aside and continued to take inventory of what they had. She found a small shaving kit, toothbrush and other personal hygiene items, but nothing that said anything more about him.

She wondered why.

Obviously, there'd be no answer while he was unconscious. Only more questions.

Her stomach growled as she put the small frame away. She ignored it. Besides the crackers, the pack contained two more packages of food and she didn't want to eat it while Caillen was down. He'd need it to keep his strength up.

Leaning her head back against the wall, she closed her eyes and said a small prayer that her mother would be safe and that they'd both make it off this planet alive.

Yeah well, if she can't defend herself, she deserves to die.

It was a bloody harsh thought for her mother. One that would probably make her mother proud.

But it shamed her and she didn't know why. Needing comfort, she again took Caillen's hand in hers. It was a minor point of contact and yet it did wonders for her spirit. And as she sat there, she remembered those nights where she'd dreamed of being hugged and held by a man.

Over the years, she'd forced those memories down and banned them. Now they were back and a part of her that scared her craved that kind of warm intimacy.

With Caillen. She wanted him to look at her the way

Syn had looked at Shahara. Like he lived and breathed for her. Like she was his entire universe.

What are you saying? She was tired. Yeah, that was it.

Get me out of here soon. If they didn't...

Maybe being eaten by the Andarions wouldn't be so bad after all.

Caillen woke up slowly to find himself still in the hole they'd crawled into to hide. He was sore and aching, but not as much as he'd been when he passed out. His body was now down to a dull, constant pain, not the violent throbbing he'd had earlier.

It was dark with only the faintest bit of light coming off the blue stick. For the merest instant, he thought he was alone until he heard the sound of a light snore.

That sound quickened his pulse as he saw Desideria lying behind him asleep. She was curled against his spine like a kitten with one hand tangled in his hair. The gesture warmed him and made his body roar to life as he imagined her naked and kissing him. Oh yeah, he'd love nothing better than to bury his nose in the hollow of her throat and breathe her in until he was drunk on her scent while he slid himself deep inside her.

He couldn't remember the last time he'd wanted a woman this badly. It took everything he had not to bend over and kiss her, but that would startle her and he would never, ever touch a woman without her explicit invitation. Her body was her own and he had no right to encroach on it in any way.

Damn it...

He shifted ever so slightly to alleviate some of the pain

of his raging hard-on that now overrode the rest of his body.

Desideria shot to her feet and jerked around as if expecting to be attacked from all directions. Had she not been so terrified, he'd have laughed at her panic.

But he wouldn't be so cruel.

"Sorry." The word came out as a hoarse croak from his parched throat. "Didn't mean to startle you."

She jerked toward him and the relief and tenderness for him on her face stole his breath. No woman not related to him had ever given him a look like that. "You're awake." That one word carried a bucketful of joy. She acted as if she'd expected him to wake up dead.

Which begged one really important question. "How long have I been out?"

She rubbed the sleep from her eyes as she calmed down. "Two days."

Her words stunned him. Was that possible? "Two days?" he repeated in disbelief.

"Yeah. I was beginning to fear you'd never wake up."

He was stuck in a state of complete denial. She had to be wrong about that. She had to be. There was no way he could have stayed unconscious for that long and left her to fend for herself. It amazed him that she was still alive.

More to the point that she was still here.

"How?"

She scowled at him. "How have you been unconscious?"

"No. How did you survive?"

That brought the color into her cheeks as she stiffened, ready to battle. Indignation lit a titanic fire in the dark depth of her eyes. "I'm not helpless."

"I wasn't implying that you were by any stretch of the

imagination, but I know our supplies were almost nonexistent. How did you find more food?"

That seemed to defuse her anger a bit. "I rationed the food between us and you no longer have any crackers or sauce packets in your backpack—they're actually not so bad when you combine them. You didn't really eat, but I gave you most of the water to keep you from dehydrating."

He was floored by her actions. "Why would you do that?"

"Like I told you, we're in this together."

"That's not very Qillaq of you. I thought you guys were all about screw everyone's survival but your own."

Desideria looked away from his piercing gaze as the truth of that seared her. It *was* their code. It'd been preached to her since the hour of her birth.

But it hadn't been her father's. He'd taught her better and she'd much rather subscribe to his loyalty than her mother's treachery.

"I owe you."

Caillen saw a ghost in her gaze. A haunted memory caused by something he'd said, but he had no idea what it was or what had triggered it.

In truth, he was completely stunned by her words and actions. They were so uncharacteristic for her race...

Let it go. It was obvious it bothered her and she didn't want to talk about it. So he switched the topic to something safe. "Have the Andarions been back?"

"A couple of times. I put your mirror devices on the trapdoor and I sprayed your pheromones around. I think they know we're here, but that seems to be keeping them confused as to our exact location."

Caillen grimaced as he moved and pain lacerated his chest and arm. Glancing over to the mirrors, he saw that she'd positioned them correctly, which was impressive. They weren't always the easiest thing to work with.

"Good, the mirrors should hide the opening even from their eyes and block all their scanning equipment—even the most advanced ones."

"Really?"

He nodded. "One of Darling's better toys." Bracing for more pain, he lifted himself up on his uninjured arm.

Suddenly Desideria was there, helping him. An unfamiliar tenderness pierced him through his chest. A foreign sensation he wasn't used to. He leaned against the wall as she reached for the water beside him. The bottle was only half full.

She held it out toward him like a peace offering. "This is the last of it, so you might want to sip slowly."

Caillen hesitated. Yes, he was thirsty, but he wasn't about to slight her. Not after what she'd done for him. "When was the last time you had some?"

"A few hours ago."

Yeah, right. He saw the way she glanced down and left when she spoke—a sure sign that she was lying. "Why don't I believe you?"

" 'Cause it was yesterday?" The expression on her face was adorable. Her smile was impish and her hair tousled. It was all he could do not to kiss her.

But that would probably get him bitch-slapped.

He handed the bottle to her. "Drink."

She shook her head. "You need it more."

"Yeah, no. I'm not being altruistic here. If you collapse,

I can't exactly carry you right now. I need you mobile so that you can carry me when I fall over."

Shaking her head and laughing, she took it from him and drank very slowly as if she was still rationing it.

While she did that, Caillen pulled his pack to him to dig through it. She watched as he pulled out three tablets and held them in his palm.

She swallowed, then lowered the bottle. "What are you doing?"

"One's for the pain and the other two are a healing accelerant I wish I'd taken before I passed out."

She capped the bottle. "I wish you'd shown me a translator so that I could understand labels and people speaking." She gestured with the bottle toward his pack. "A lot of the stuff in there I had to guess at."

He froze as fear went through him. If she...oh crap. "Did you turn my computer on?"

"No. I didn't want them to peg our location."

Good girl. That alone was probably why they were both still breathing. "Yeah, I'm pretty sure they would have too." He let out a deep sigh of resignation before he stood up.

She scowled up at him. "What are you doing?"

Caillen took a minute to catch his breath and to ignore the sharp, shooting pain that begged him to lie down.

But he couldn't do that. He had duties to attend and a small shot of adrenaline would allow him to get it done. *Gah, I hate those shots.*

You gotta do what you gotta do. That had been the whole history of his life.

He offered her a kind smile. "You haven't eaten in days and we're out of food. I'm going to get supplies."

She gaped. "You can't do that. They'll catch you."

That was a quick reminder that she didn't know him all that well. The only way to catch him was when he allowed it. "No, they won't. Trust me, baby. There are three things in this life that I excel at. One, I can pilot anything that can be flown—with or without wings. Two, I'm the best lover you'll ever have, and three, scavenging for supplies even when you think they don't exist. Spent my entire childhood scrambling to help feed my sisters and talking pitiless doctors into helping my sister with her medical problems. When it comes to finesse, no one's better."

She snorted at his braggadocio. "I seem to remember that finesse when we were being chased by the Enforcers. Real smooth there, Sparky. Definitely admirable."

Okay, she had a point, but he wasn't willing to cede it. "We were trapped and I wasn't expecting them. Things are different now."

"Yeah, you can barely stand."

"Not the first time that's happened and at least this time I'm sober."

She gave him a droll stare. "Not amused."

"Wait a few minutes and it'll sink in, then you'll laugh."

"You're not as charming as you think you are."

"Of course I am. If I wasn't, my sisters would have killed me long ago. Now, you wait here and—"

"I'm not about to stay here." There was a hint of fear underlying her determined tone.

But his leaving wasn't what she should be afraid of. The bogeyman was alive and well, and most likely waiting for them just on the other side of that small trapdoor. "You have to. You can't pass for an Andarion and you don't speak their language. I now know what to watch for and how to deal with them." He paused and narrowed his gaze at her. "Don't worry. You didn't abandon me and I won't abandon you."

Still there was reservation in her expression. "You can barely stand. Are you sure you'll be all right?"

He winked at her. "I'm a Dagan, baby. We're street survivors."

"I thought you were a de Orczy."

He screwed his face up at her reminder. "Don't be saying that evil shit to me, hon. You'll jinx me."

At least that succeeded in lightening her doom and gloom.

Resisting another urge to kiss her, Caillen grabbed the injector and a small bottle of adrenaline out of his pack. No need to take that around her. Some things he didn't like sharing. He started to leave.

"Wait."

He turned back to her. "Yeah?"

"I took your contacts and teeth out while you slept. I was afraid they might hurt you."

And that was a really good thought. Though it was also creepy to think about someone handling him like that while he was unconscious. "Where'd you put them?"

She pointed to the outside pocket of his backpack.

Caillen dug them out and put them back on. "Thanks."

She inclined her head to him. "Good luck."

"Don't need it."

He hoped. But no need in stressing her out any more.

Desideria watched as Caillen climbed up and out of their hiding spot. His movements were slow and methodical, and lacked his usual grace but really, if one didn't know how fluidly he normally moved, they'd never be able to tell he was injured. But she knew he was still in pain. She started to tell him he was a lunatic for doing this, but she didn't want to make any sound in case some of the Andarions were around.

"Good luck," she whispered, hoping she'd see him again. Because in the back of her mind was an image of him being hurt and her being killed. God, she really hoped that wasn't a premonition.

Caillen took a moment to wince as he stood up in the warehouse and got his bearings. There was a slight chill in the air that cut through his coat and sent a shiver down his spine. Man, he was in pain. The last thing he wanted was to hunt down supplies, especially given how bad his head throbbed.

You've had worse wounds.

True. Very true. And at least it was night and this outpost only had one moon. Instead of bitching, he needed to be grateful it wasn't worse.

Adjusting his backpack, he started forward, making sure to keep to the shadows.

As he walked along the quiet street, he reprogrammed his debit card for Fain Hauk, Dancer's older brother. The good thing about the last name Hauk, it was so common for Andarions as to be ridiculous and Fain, unlike Dancer, was also a common name for them. While Fain, as a criminal, *was* notorious, the name itself was generic enough to not raise many, if any, questions over it.

And if they did confuse him with Dancer's brother, their fear of Fain's ruthless reputation would be such that none should question or bother him.

He slid the card into his back pocket. If he dared to turn on his computer, he could reprogram his facial recog too, to match the name, but that would be begging for trouble. He'd have to wing it and hope they didn't bother to check his facial recog. If they did…

Please let me have that one more small favor.

With any luck at all, the darkness would continue to cover him enough that he wouldn't have to make a mad dash in his busted body or use the adrenaline shot. But as he crept forward, he saw a shadow mimic his movements.

Yeah, it was definitely following him.

16

Desideria started to follow after Caillen even though he'd told her to stay put. She didn't like being left behind. What if he didn't come back?

Or if the Andarions found her while he was gone?

You turn yourself in and hope they don't eat you. Yeah, getting eaten would definitely stink. And it was strange that while he was unconscious that fear hadn't been as potent as it was now. Now it was palatable.

What is wrong with me?

She could fight the Andarions on her own. It would be easier now since she wouldn't have to cover someone who was unconscious. She tightened her grip on her blaster as she plotted various escape and fighting scenarios in her head. Luck always favored the prepared. One thing her people knew how to do was plan for battle.

Caillen had left her with two weapons, but he'd taken his backpack. She hated that. Over the last few days, she'd come to rely on it as much as he did. There was something weirdly comforting about its contents. No wonder he'd risked his life to go back for it.

I've gone insane.

Who would consider a backpack worth their life?

Besides Caillen.

And with every second that passed, she sensed more of her sanity slipping away. In fact, time stretched out to the point she had to get up and pace around the cramped, empty space. Odd how it hadn't bothered her to be here when Caillen had been unconscious. Even passed out, he had such a commanding presence that it'd soothed her and kept her patient.

Yeah, okay, I am losing it for real this time.

'Cause all she could focus on was how much she'd enjoyed using his body as a pillow at night and dragging her finger down the line of his whiskered jaw right before she went to sleep. He'd probably kill her if he realized she'd done that. But he'd been irresistible and it'd led her to thoughts that she shouldn't have about any male. Especially since she couldn't mate for at least a year.

That was if her mother didn't fully degrade her back to child status once she was home.

Don't think about it.

She continued to pace the small area as she waited. It seemed like years had come and gone before she heard a sound above.

Her heart stopped. Pulling out the blaster, she braced herself for a fight and aimed it to shoot whoever was about to pounce on her. The rusted lock turned with excruciating slowness as someone fumbled with it.

Finally, the door creaked open to show her Caillen. Unconcerned about the heart palpitations he'd given her, he lowered himself into their space. He ignored the fact she had a blaster aimed at his head, as if it were a normal occurrence for him, then shut the door tight.

Handing her a small bag as she holstered her weapon, he grinned. "You a cannibal?"

She scowled at his peculiar question. "Beg pardon?"

"Do. You. Eat. Humans?" he repeated, carefully enunciating each word.

"Not. That. I. Know. Of." She mimicked his staccato rhythm and dry tone.

"Didn't think so." He dropped his backpack in the corner, then took out a new light stick that he snapped and shook. He dropped it on the floor before he faced her. "Any idea how hard it is to score nonhuman meat in this place? Really, the League would have a shit fit to see the menu items on this rock."

She would have been amused, but for his new appearance. There was a cut above his eye and his clothes were even more rumpled than they'd been before he left.

Had he been in a fight? Surely not and yet…

"Are you bleeding?"

He scratched at his chin in the most adorable sheepish action she'd ever seen. "Flesh wound." Oh yeah, that tone was completely defensive.

"What happened?"

He let out a tired sigh. "Would you believe some psycho dumb ass tried to mug me? Me? At first, I thought it was the authorities with a lucky strike. Nah. Moron. He's having a worse day than we are."

"How so?"

"I switched IDs with him."

She was both horrified and amused by what he'd done.

If they found the ID, they'd know they were here. "Are you out of your mind?"

"Yes. But it gets the Enforcers off our backs for a bit and hopefully our frenemy assassin won't have a brain either. They'll be chasing the mugger every time he tries to use it which will hopefully be a lot—and if he's good at eluding them, he could buy us a lot of time. And best of all, I picked his pocket and got a pretty good wad of cash from him. The idiot didn't even know what I did. What kind of thief can't feel his own wallet being lifted, I ask you? You know, it's time to just surrender the occupation when you suck that much." Laughing, he pulled a hot sandwich out of the bag and held it out toward her.

She could kiss him for his kindness. The delicious smell made her stomach cramp so hard that for a moment she thought she'd be sick. Forcing it down, she took the sandwich from him with a calmness she didn't feel and unwrapped it even though part of her wanted to start eating it, wrap and all.

"If I start biting on my fingers, don't stop me."

He gave her a knowing grin as he ate his own.

She bit into the sandwich and savored the sweet meat taste. Oh yeah, this was good and she was unbelievably grateful to him for bringing it back. "Thank you."

"No problem." He swallowed his bite before he spoke again. "By the way, just so you know, I'd normally be charging a fee for this service."

"What service?"

"Feeding you."

She didn't know why, but that offended her. "Excuse me?"

His dark eyes glowed with wicked warmth as he raked

his gaze slowly over her body as if savoring every inch. For some reason she couldn't name, it made her stomach flutter. "Oh yeah, baby. A meal for a beautiful woman... at least a kiss for it. It's mandatory. But since I know how hungry you are, I'm letting it slide. Next time...it *will* cost you."

Her anger vanished under the weight of his gentle teasing.

"I don't know. If I were you, I'd hold out for something better."

His eyes widened. "Really?"

"Mmm...yeah, hell to freeze over."

He laughed good-naturedly before he returned to eating his sandwich. "There's more food in the bag and drinks. Just so you know. I got plenty to feed even my sister Kasen, and believe me, she eats like an overweight torna."

Now that *was* impressive. It was said a torna ate three times its two-hundred-pound body weight a day.

Desideria fell silent as she tried to eat in spite of her cramping stomach. She was starving, but at this point her body was so used to being hungry that it wanted to reject her offering. Never had she been more miserable.

It was several minutes before her body calmed down enough that she could focus on anything else. She glanced over at Caillen. He sat in the corner, on the cold ground without so much as a thought about it. The laces on his left boot were untied. He was such a beguiling combination of rogue and gentleman.

His sister had definitely raised him right.

And that thought led her to the memory of the woman in the vidframe she couldn't identify. She didn't even know why, but there was a bitter pain in her every time she thought about why he kept that woman's photo with the rest of his family and friends.

Before her brain could interfere with her mouth, she found the last question she wanted to ask falling out and breaking the silence. "Who's the woman in the last still when you turn on your frame?"

He froze midchew before he leveled a murderous glare at her. That menacing look actually sent a shiver over her body and she saw the killer that resided inside him. For one nanosecond, she half expected him to leap at her throat. "You went through my stuff?"

"It was a long two days."

That only seemed to anger him more. "You went through my stuff?"

She sighed irritably. "Are you going to keep repeating that question?"

His glare intensified and the venom in his voice was chilling. "I *hate* for anyone to search my things without my permission. It gets so far under my skin that it might as well be a DNA marker."

"Sorry," she said honestly. "I didn't realize it was such an issue for you."

He scoffed before he took a drink. "You grow up in a six-hundred-square-foot box and have three older nosy-ass sisters in your business all the time, claiming it's for your own good, then you'll see what a big deal privacy is. I cannot stress enough how much I hate the thought of my belongings being touched without my consent. By anyone but me."

Obviously they'd searched his things a lot and left him very bitter from it. "I said I'm sorry and I really am—I promise I won't do it again now that I know how much it bothers you. Now who is she? I figured out your sisters and your mother. But she doesn't seem to fit." The unknown woman was much taller than his sisters and even more beautiful than Shahara. He'd only had one photo of her standing near a rundown cargo ship Desideria had assumed was his. In spite of her cold eyes, the woman had looked angelic and so sweet that it'd sent a wave of unfounded jealousy through her.

Caillen didn't respond for a few minutes as he glared at the floor as if it, too, had offended him somehow. It was obvious he still had very strong and very ill feelings toward the woman—at least she hoped it was toward the woman and not her for her snooping. "Her name's Teratin."

He used the present tense which meant the woman was still alive—another thing that really annoyed her when it shouldn't. *You can't kill her, Desi.*

The peculiar thing was that she did want to hunt her down and at least punch her.

But she had no intention of letting Caillen know that. "That's a pretty name."

"Yeah well, lots of poisonous things have pretty names." There was no missing the venom that shot daggers toward her as he met her gaze. He hated that woman with a passion that was staggering.

That degree of animosity surprised her and in a part of her that would make her mother proud she was glad he hated her. "If you don't like her why do you keep a picture of her in your frame?"

The heat in his gaze was scorching. "To remind me not to trust anyone. Ever. That no matter what comes out of

someone's mouth—no matter how much they say they'll
never betray you—one tiny, insignificant thing can turn
them against you forever."

Her heart clenched at the pain she heard beneath his
angry tirade. Given the decent, honorable man he'd shown
himself to be, she couldn't imagine someone hurting him.

Had he done something to deserve it?

"What'd she do to you?"

Caillen glanced away as old memories surged. Teratin had seemed like such a decent person when he'd met
her. Unassuming, even sweet. Bashful just enough to be
endearing, but not off-putting. Little had he known at the
time that all of that was well-practiced affectation. Hell,
she'd even been easy to talk to most days.

A snake hidden underneath a pretty cover. Damn him
for being stupid enough to be deceived.

He felt the tic in his jaw as he took a drink of water
and tried to squelch the need he still had to hunt the bitch
down and kill her. "We were together casually for about
three years."

She arched her right eyebrow northward in an expression that would have amused him if they weren't discuss-
ing the Great Evil. "Define casually."

Yeah, that was the crux of it. One word, many defi-
nitions. Too bad his perception of their relationship had
been completely different than her psycho ass.

"We had sex a couple of times, dinner a few more and
hung out from time to time whenever she was in town. I
never sought her out. Not once. But she'd come see me for
no particular reason. Said she just liked hanging out with
me, and I felt sorry for her that she didn't have anyone else
to be with—in retrospect I should have realized anyone

who travels from one planet to another just to spend an afternoon with you is krikkin insane. But I like to give lunatics the benefit of the doubt and if I have one flaw in life it's that I too often take people at face value even when I should know better. I swear, one day I'm going to learn to be jaded with the loons and underdogs too." Something easier said than done. He knew to be jaded around takers and grifters. But he was a sucker for anyone with a sad story. Loners who had no one. People who weren't liked by others. Any underdog could take him.

Most were decent. But a handful...

They were nuts to a level that defied human understanding.

He tightened his grip on the bottle as he took another drink and rode hard herd on his temper. Gods help Teratin if he ever came across her again. Most likely, he'd kill her.

And he'd relish her death rattle.

Probably celebrate it too and that was what scared him the most.

"Let me reiterate, it was nothing serious. Or so *I* thought. One day I get this hostile voice mail from her because I forgot her birthday. Hell, I hadn't thought anything about it—you know, three years and I'd never wished her a happy birthday before. Didn't know three was the magic number and if I failed to acknowledge it on that particular year, Crazy Bitch would rain down hell's wrath on my head. At that time I was being slammed with a massive shitfest every which way I moved. My sister Tessa was being chased by loaners who'd already landed her in the hospital for her debt, Kasen was in the hospital with another round of stop-the-blood-disease-from-killing-her and Shahara was after a target and missing in action—I was terrified she was dead and that we'd find her body somewhere gruesome. One of my regular jobs had just dried up completely and another was pushing me to the wall with regulations and equipment requirements I was struggling to meet. Little preoccupied with family and work at the time which any normal, sane human being would have understood.

"Instead, she goes mental on me and the next thing I know the bitch has called the authorities in an attempt to get me *and* my sister Kasen arrested. She's contacted my business associates trying to ruin my reputation any which way she can. She even called my best friend and tried to get him to turn on me. Never have I seen anything like it. And for what? A fucking birthday wish? Hell, I don't even know when Kasen's birthday is and I was not only raised with her, I love her—anyone who knows me, knows this about me. Failure to acknowledge a birthday doesn't mean I don't love you. I believe in celebrating the life of the people you love every day—not just on one particular day. All it meant was that I was up to my neck in crap to deal with and the last thing I needed was one more pain in my ass. Little Miss Give-Me-Attention-Cause-I-Have-No-Real-Friends needs to be schooled on the fact that the universe doesn't revolve around her and when other people are barely hanging on by their fingernails, a real friend would have helped and not added to the stress."

Desideria let out an elongated breath as he finished his diatribe. Not that she blamed him. He was right. Any human who would hurt another and try to ruin them over something so petty was sorry beyond belief and she hated that he'd been forced to go through that. It made her want to hurt the woman for him.

Like Caillen, she didn't keep track of that sort of thing either.

But it left her with one question. "And you judge all women by her actions?"

He shook his head. "No. I judge *all* people by that. I've seen too many spaz out over absolutely nothing, not quite to her dangerous extent, but enough that it's taught me to be wary of everyone, especially when they're trying to play the victim role. And she's an extreme reminder that no matter how well you think you know someone, they can turn on you for the dumbest reasons imaginable. Male, female, whatever. I mean, shit. Happy Birthday, bitch. Didn't she have anyone else in her life that mattered? I mean really, my sisters and friends don't call me on mine and I'm good with that. Never have I held it against them. I wish my life was so pathetically uneventful that all I had to get torn up over was the fact that some casual friend didn't wish me a Happy Birthday. My own family forgets mine about half the time and none of my friends know when it is and never once have I doubted their loyalty to me. What's the big deal?"

Desideria bit back a smile. Not because it was funny—it was actually very tragic—but because his over-the-top tirade was so out of character that it amused her to see this side of him.

He did indeed have a temper.

However, she didn't want to offend him, especially over something that had left a lasting scar and changed the way he dealt with people. It angered her that anyone would be so needlessly vicious.

"Obviously to her, it was a big deal. But I agree with you. She had no right to do that to you."

"No kidding and do you know to this day, and it's been over four years now since it happened, she's still taking swipes at me? Any chance she can get to try and damage my reputation or interfere with my business, she takes. I've never seen anything like it in my life, and believe me, I've seen some shit."

She was aghast. "Are you serious? Four years later?"

He held his hand up in indignation. "Right hand to the gods and I swear to you I did nothing to her at all. Nothing. I was never anything but nice to her no matter how weird she'd get around me and even while her supposed real friends criticized and mocked her behind her back. I guess I should have done what they did. Then she would have loved me forever."

Desideria actually believed that. He'd been nice to her and that after her mother had tried to harm him and she'd gotten him shot. "I'm so sorry, Caillen."

"Yeah, don't be. It is what it is. I just don't understand people who are cruel without justification. People who try to tear down someone over petty nothings." He leaned his head back as he reached for a small bag of food. There was something boyish in his manner. Something that belied the ferocity and power. The more she was around him, the less threatening he appeared.

Weird. Very weird. She knew he could kill her and yet, she liked being with him.

She licked her suddenly dry lips as a wave of desire ripped through her. "I admire that about you though. I think it's a great thing you can't understand that kind of cruelty."

Caillen paused as he realized what she was saying to him. The tender look she gave him made his heart speed up as a part of his anatomy jerked to life and wanted something a little more intimate than this chat. "You admire me?"

She raked a playful glance over his body that sent chills through him. "Don't let that go to your head. If it grows any bigger, we'll have to find a larger place to hide just to accommodate it."

He laughed and that amazed him most of all. He'd never been able to laugh about Teratin's PMS until now. Not even Shahara had ever been able to cheer him on the topic. Anytime her name came up, he went into a fume for days. Yet Desideria had done the impossible. "So are you another deranged woman out to ruin a man over forgetting your birthday?"

She picked at her food in a dainty way that was incongruous with her tough aura. He didn't know why, but there was something about her right now that was almost vulnerable. Something that called out to him and made him want to brush his hand through her hair and taste those moist lips and sample other, more lush parts of her body.

But she wouldn't welcome that and he would die before he ever pressed himself on any female. He only proceeded when they were jumping on him.

And yet it was hard to sit here and not do anything when she was so close to him that all he had to do was reach out and touch her. Oh to have the ability and right to close the distance between them and kiss those gorgeous lips. Damn. The more he was around her, the more he wanted her. It was slowly driving him crazy.

She glanced at him again, then stared at a space by his side. "Birthdays are unimportant to my people."

"Because you celebrate accomplishments?"

She nodded. "Being born is a state of the natural order. Why should you celebrate something that happens to everyone and everything?"

That was harsh and it made him glad he wasn't a Qill. While he might not care about them as an adult, some of his best memories of childhood had been his sisters decorating their small house with signs they'd made for him. Of Shahara bringing him a small treat whenever she could. It was why he didn't sweat when people ignored it. *Don't stab me in the back and we're all good.* "Your people are seriously screwed up."

She arched a brow at him. "Like yours aren't?"

"Oh, I never said they weren't. We invent other ways to be total assholes to each other."

She laughed, then sobered. "It wasn't all bad though. Unlike my sisters, when I was little, my father would sneak gifts to me on my birthday and he always remembered the date."

He caught the way her voice softened as she spoke about her dad. It was obvious she loved the man. "That was nice of him."

"You have no idea."

Desideria fell silent as a surreal out-of-body experience came over her. She was sharing stories of her past with Caillen like he was an old friend. More than that, she became aware of how much physical pain he had to be in from his injuries and yet he managed to tease and not snap at her. He never took his emotions out on her.

Poor baby. And she appreciated his control. It meant a lot to her that he was being pleasant when he had no reason to.

She leaned forward and wiped at the blood on his

bruised forehead. "Do you ever have a fight where you don't bleed?"

"All the time."

She held her hand so that he could see how much damage he'd done to himself with his latest run-in with the mugger. "Not since I've met you."

He gave her a napkin to wipe her hand on. "Yeah, you're like an unlucky charm for me."

Feigning indignation, she tossed the bloodied cloth at him. "You need to be nicer to me. Remember I'm the one who tends your wounds."

"Uh-huh. And if you're true to your gender, you'll salt it anyway and kick me in the teeth on your way out the door."

She scowled at him as her humor fled. He was serious with that comment. "Why would you say that?"

He cleaned away the remnants of his food. "Simple. Women only want to jump my bones or take my money. Outside of the bedroom, they don't really think that much of me and most of them are only after a quick take."

"Your sisters aren't like that. They love you."

"Yeah, but they think I'm mentally challenged. They still try to cut my meat for me most days."

That surprised her. He was without a doubt the most capable man she'd ever met. Why would they treat him like a child? "Really?"

"Yeah, it's the most screwed-up thing you've ever seen. They really think I'm a kid until one of them gets into trouble, then I'm the first one they call to bail them out. Insanity, right?"

She didn't want to agree, yet he was correct. It would be weird to be treated like a child and then be relied on so heavily by the very people who refused to see her as an adult. "So what do your sisters do for a living?"

He rose to his feet before he stretched. The tightness of his shirt over his chest distracted her from the question as she became fascinated with the way his muscles played.

"Shahara's the oldest. She was a tracer until she married a couple of years ago. Now she runs a charitable organization for her husband. Kasen's my business partner and I use that term with all due hostility and sarcasm. She mostly sucks off my share of our profits by making me feel guilty over her medical condition."

"Which is?"

"Diabetes and a rare blood disorder. She's spent most of her life in and out of hospitals and you have to be really careful with what she comes into contact with or you can kill her—which has occasionally crossed my mind. And lastly there's Tessa." He let out a long breath as if the mere thought of her gave him an ulcer.

"What about her?"

"I love her, don't get me wrong, but she's constantly in trouble with loaners. Not that I can say much. I have a nasty tendency to gamble too. But I stop before I go into debt doing it. She doesn't. Since she was sixteen, we've all had to chip in to save her ass. Over and over again. But she married last year and seems to be doing better now. She works as an admin for the Ritadarion press corps." He came back to help her clean up her food. "What about you? What do your sisters do?"

"I only have the two still living. They either train to fight or plot ways to embarrass me in front of my aunt and mother—usually during training."

Caillen paused at the lackadaisical way she said that.

As if it was so normal for them to attack her that she thought nothing about it. "Seriously?"

She wrinkled her nose. "Sad, isn't it?"

Yes it was. But he refused to say that out loud and hurt her any worse when it was obvious this topic bothered her.

She shook her head. "I don't know why they bother really. My mother practically hates me most days anyway."

"Why?"

Her gaze went back to the floor, but not before he caught a glimpse of how much pain she kept inside herself. "I'm only half Qillaq."

That stunned him. Her people were such isolationists that it was rare they bred with anyone else. There had to be a juicy story behind her conception. "Really?"

"Yes and they don't think much of me because of it. Everyone considers me tainted by my father's inferior blood."

"Which was?"

"Gondarion. He was a pilot who'd been shot down in battle. He crash-landed and was taken prisoner."

Caillen winced at the thought and the irony that Desideria had followed in her father's footsteps by crashing here—while dragging *him* along for the ride. "That's tough for both of you."

"You have no idea. Everyone stares at me like I'm a mutant. Like I don't belong. You have no idea what it's like to be judged for a birth defect you can't help."

"Oh not true," he corrected. "We're all judged for things we can't help. Whether it's our clothes, our birth, our social class or our appearance. I swear sometimes it's like people just look for a reason to hate each other."

"I don't do that."

Caillen snorted in contradiction. "I seem to recall the first time you saw me. There was judgment in those beautiful brown eyes when you looked my way."

Her cheeks turned a becoming shade of bright red. "I should say I *try* not to. But it is hard."

"It is indeed."

Desideria fell silent as she realized that Caillen didn't judge like that. At least he didn't seem to. "How do you not do it?"

He shrugged. "People are people. I've been kicked enough in my life to not want to return the favor to others. Like you said, it's hard and I'm not perfect. When you've been beat down all your life it's a natural inclination to want to strike the first blow. But I learned to fight that instinct. Sometimes I'm more successful than others and in cases like Teratin, I wish I'd been more judgmental. It would have saved me a universe of hurt."

She frowned at his words. It was like he described someone else entirely. "You don't seem like you've ever been beaten by anything." He was too proud and strong for that.

He handed her another drink. "See that's the thing… You can't look at someone and tell what they've been through. The scars that hurt the most are never visible on the surface. You're a princess and everyone would assume you've had a life of luxury with servants doting on your every whim."

"So not true."

"My point exactly. And that's one of the things I really hate about being with my real father. His crew of people have turned me into something I don't want to be."

She was baffled by his words. "A prince?"

"No. That I don't mind. When I'm around them, they make me a judging snob. Sad thing is, it's not the poor I'm judging like they do, it's them."

That she understood more than she wanted to. "It's odd, isn't it? The poor hate the rich for having a life they think is easy and for the fact that they think the rich only got the money by screwing them. The rich think the poor are all rustics lacking manners and grace who are unwilling to work as hard as they do to get the money. Both groups see each other as thieves out to steal everything they've earned."

He nodded. "You're right and what I find most ironic . . . I've never been screwed over by anyone who was rich. Judged, but *never* screwed. It was always the poor or middle-class people I've known who've fucked me over for money. My poor friends have always been the ones who were jealous and petty. If I have two credits more than they do, they start in on the 'it must be nice' and then feel justified to tear me down because they think I'm getting a big head and that they need to bring me down a notch. People with money have too many other things to worry about than what I have or don't have in comparison with them. In fact, it's people like Darling, Nyk, Syn and crew, the ones who are seriously loaded, who've helped me while all my working-class friends have either abandoned me or tried to take what little I've earned."

"People see their own sins in others."

"Yeah, I guess." He returned to sit closer to her.

Desideria tried to remain nonchalant, but his nearness was so distracting that it was hard to focus on anything other than how much she wanted to curl up in his arms. "So what's the worst thing that's happened to you?"

He pulled away.

"Caillen?"

She saw the veil that came down over him, shielding him from what he obviously thought was a probing question. "I have many to choose from and really don't want to talk about any of them."

"I'm sorry."

He scoffed. "Don't be. As my bud Nyk says, life makes victims of us all." He took another drink. "So what about your father? Is he on the ship with your mom?"

"No. He died a long time ago."

To her shock, he put his arm around her and gave her a tender squeeze. "I feel your pain. It sucks to lose someone you love when you're too little to really understand why they're gone."

"Do you ever really understand?"

Caillen paused as he considered that. "No. Death sucks always."

Yes, it did. And she really didn't want to think about that right now either. Instead, she went back to something he'd said earlier. "Do you really think my eyes are pretty?"

He flashed her a wicked grin. "Baby, if it wasn't for the fact you'd slap me, I'd show you exactly how beautiful I think all of you is."

She blushed. "I am so not used to being around someone as outspoken as you." Or anyone who complimented her on anything.

"Yeah. I'm told I'm unique unto myself."

"That you are."

He pulled his arm back to his body. They sat on the floor, their hips barely touching. Her legs were stretched out before her while his were bent at the knees and he kept one arm braced on his leg. It was a decidedly masculine pose.

His eyes flashed as he offered her an odd half smile. "You are not what I expected the first time I saw you."

She gave him an arch stare. "I think I'm closer to what I appear to be than you are."

He laughed. "True. I'm not much of a prince."

There he was wrong. He was closer to one than anyone she'd ever met before. And that turned her thoughts back to what they needed to do. "Shouldn't we be leaving and getting—"

"Too much activity right now. I'd wait at least another two hours and then we'll try for it."

That made sense. "What did you find when you went out?"

"A *lot* of Andarions."

And he certainly looked the part. Though to be honest, she was getting used to his long black hair and those creepy weird eyes. Even the fangs were starting to grow on her.

"Does it hurt to eat with the fangs in?"

"Only if I bite my cheek."

She laughed.

His gaze turned suddenly serious as he went back to their earlier topic. "So what's the worst thing that ever happened to you?"

Her heart dropped at the unexpected question. Now she understood his defensiveness. But in her case, she had nothing to hide. She lived with her pain every day. "Watching my sister die in my arms."

The color drained from his face as he let out an audible gasp. "What happened?"

"Training accident." Her throat tightened as the familiar pang of grief choked her. "My aunt had been pushing us on an obstacle course. Shayla went to climb over a spiked barrier while Narcissa was fighting her and the rope broke. I can still hear her scream as she fell in front of me. I tried to grab her, but she weighed too much to hold. She slipped right past me and was impaled before I could stop it. I did my best to save her even after she'd fallen. But the spikes had cut through her femoral artery and she bled out in a matter of minutes."

A muscle worked in his jaw as if he felt her pain too. "I'm so sorry."

She blinked several times, trying to banish the sting in her eyes. She wouldn't weep in front of him. It was forbidden. Still, the pain of losing her sister bit deep and she would give anything if she could have kept her from dying. To have that one moment back and to undo it. Why was life so unfair?

"You know my mother didn't even cry. When we told her about Shayla's fall, she glared at us and said that's what happens when you're incompetent. She said a real warrior would have been able to save herself, and if I'd been stronger and quicker, I might have been able to spare her. She claimed it was the will of the gods that Shayla died for her weakness. But I don't believe that."

"How old was she?" he asked.

"Sixteen."

He let out a low whistle. "And you?"

"Fourteen."

Caillen wanted to beat her mother for the cruelty. Not just in her sister's death, but for the coldness of not comforting Desideria. Telling a kid that it was her fault her sister had died in front of her...What a bitch. That was just so wrong. "What happened to your other sister?"

That too was forever etched into her memory. Even now, it played out in slow motion in her mind. "Narcissa killed her in a practice match. They were sparring and Cissy's sword strike cut her throat when she accidentally tripped over a piece of broken tile in the ring."

Looking back now, she wondered how much of an accident it'd been. If Narcissa was trying to kill their mother to rule, it would make sense that she'd sabotaged the tile and then used it to kill Bethali.

He curled his lip. "How old was she?"

"Seventeen."

His scowl left deep lines in his forehead. "Why were you using real swords for a practice match?"

She didn't comprehend his anger. "You don't use fake ones in battle. Why would you use them in practice?"

"Because it's stupid to use something that could kill the person you're training. They don't even do that in the League at that age, and believe me, those bastards seldom pull punches."

His words offended her. "They're not training Qillaqs."

"Do you really believe what you're saying?"

She wanted to keep her bluster up and defend her people. But the truth was very different. "No. I thought it was ridiculous to kill them over simple mistakes and I hate that they're no longer with me. I like to think that when I have a child, I'll be kinder to her and protect her better." But she lived in fear every day that she'd wake up as heartless as her mother and sister.

As heartless as her aunt.

And that brought out another memory that she did her

best to keep to herself. Yet, sitting here with Caillen, it came tumbling out of her mouth before she could stop it. "You know I had a brother."

His jaw went slack. "Really? What happened to him?"

"I don't know. He was born before I was and sent away. My aunt would use his disappearance to motivate us. She'd say that if we didn't please her or my mother, we'd be sent away too."

Her gaze burned him as all those threats and fear of what had become of her brother poured through her. "I've never told anyone about this before. Talking isn't exactly something we do and shared confidences are the worst sort of suicidal act. Whatever is said will be used against you at the worst possible time."

"Then why tell me?"

She shook her head as she tried to understand that herself. "I don't know. Weird, huh?"

"Not really. We're in a bad situation, stuck in a hole for a few hours alone. People do all kinds of strange things when they're under fire."

The way he said that...it made her wonder what experience of his had prompted it. "So what's the strangest thing you've ever done while being chased?"

"Strangest or stupidest?"

"Is there a difference?"

He paused then smiled. "Not really. My strangest probably was my dumbest move of all time."

"Which was?"

"I shot my sister."

She gaped at his words. "What? Which one? Why?"

He laughed at her stupor. "Relax, sweet. I did it to save Kasen's life so that I could go to jail for her."

It was noble.

Foolish, but noble. "Why would you do that?"

"I told you. Stupidity." He feigned a moment of innocence before he answered. "With her health and crappy personality, I knew she wouldn't be able to survive jail. The inmates there would cut her head off three minutes after incarceration. I, on the other hand, am a little tougher and can take whatever they throw at me."

Still…she couldn't imagine having someone love her so much that they'd put their own life, their freedom, on the line to protect her. "That was a nice thing to do."

He shrugged it off. "Where I come from, it's what family does."

Caillen checked his watch, then stood up. "You ready to get out of here?"

"You think we've passed enough time?"

"God, I hope so. Otherwise this will be a short trip." He winked at her.

She made a "heh" sound at him before she pushed herself to her feet. "What's the plan?"

"While I was out, I found the local bay. It was pretty bustling then, but I'm hoping it's calmed down by now. If it is, we should be able to commandeer a ship."

Commandeer…she adored his word choice. "You're not suggesting we steal something, are you?"

His expression turned impish. "Stealing is such an ugly word."

"Stealing is wrong."

Still those eyes teased her. "Look, Princess, survival has no morals. You do what you have to or you die."

Perhaps, but she'd been raised differently. "I disagree. The depth and strength of our character is defined by our moral code. People only reveal themselves when they're thrown out of the usual conditions of their lives. That's when the truth of who they are is revealed and I am not a thief."

"Neither am I, but I see nothing wrong with borrowing something we need for a bit. If not for the fact they'd eat my head, I would ask. As it is, I'll make sure they get it back once we're safe."

"Sure you will." She didn't mean to be such a bitch, but this *really* offended her.

He stiffened, his humor completely gone. "Now who's judging whom? Fine. Stay here. Give my regards to the Andarions. I'd rather get back to my father and make sure he lives."

Desideria watched as he headed for the trapdoor and removed his mirror devices. Part of her wanted to hold her morality close. But in the end, she knew he was right. She couldn't stay here and let her mother be hurt.

Disgusted with herself and what they were about to do, she got up and followed after him.

He arched a taunting brow as she caught up to his side.

She glared at that smugness. "Not one word or I swear I'll gut you where you stand. If my mother's life wasn't in danger, I would *never* agree to this."

"Love is the greatest corruptor ever known and has been the number one downfall of mankind since the first creation."

She didn't comment as they kept to the shadows while navigating through the empty streets. Lifting her cowl into place around her head, she realized that he was moving a lot easier this time than he'd been when he left earlier. Even so, it was a miracle he could move at all given the severity of his injuries.

She was still sore from the crash, but nowhere near as badly hurt as he'd been.

They kept to the back alleyways, out of the sight of the people on the street or surveillance cameras. Caillen seemed to have an uncanny ability to see them and stay out of their range.

Desideria hesitated as she saw another camera on the street that was too close for comfort. "We're being watched."

"No. I've got a jammer. By the time they realize we were here, we'll be gone. All they see is static."

"Is that why you're avoiding them?"

"Better safe than sorry."

He was probably right about that. And as they drew closer to the bays, the amount of cameras and activity picked up exponentially. But at least it wasn't people bustling about. The bay seemed to be fully automated. Machinery buzzed and whirred as they slipped inside the hangar.

Caillen froze instantly, causing her to run into his back.

She scowled up at him. "What are you doing?"

He didn't speak for several heartbeats as he stared at a black ship in the rear corner. From the style, she knew it to be a fighter class—an older model. The paint was streaked by what appeared to be a blast mark. Other than that, it looked like all the other ones here.

Why would he stare at it?

Unless...

She swallowed as fear gripped her. "Is it the assassin?"

Again, he refused to answer as he skimmed around the wall toward it.

Frustrated, she trailed after him, dying to know what was going on and why he was acting so strangely.

Caillen ducked his head as he slid toward the cockpit entrance. Just as he reached the fighter's ladder that deep, sinister voice she'd heard on his link spoke out of the darkness.

"Move and die."

17

That thick, deeply accented voice was ominous and cold. It sent chills up and down Desideria's spine. She turned her head slowly to see a...

Oh my God. He was huge! A full head taller than Caillen, the Andarion dwarfed them both. But it wasn't just his massive, muscular size that was terrifying. His black hair was liberally laced with white streaks and matted into dreadlocks that fell to the middle of his back. A black cloth mask with some kind of spooky symbol painted in a blood red that matched the rim on his eerie irises covered the lower part of his face so that all you could see were those white demonic eyes that glared in anger. He'd smeared green paint with a black-dotted pattern over his forehead and temples, and down the bridge of his nose to give himself an even more sinister appearance.

Boy did it work.

It sent her stomach straight to her feet and made her instinctively reach for her weapon in trepidation.

Until he clicked back the release of the blaster, letting her know silently that if she moved again, he'd shoot her.

Dressed all in black, he reminded her more of a malevolent phantom than a living, breathing person. An image that was heightened by the sharpened silver claws on both of his hands and the weapons that covered every inch of his body and especially the large blaster that was aimed right at her heart. Any doubt about his intent was laid to rest by the bright orange targeting dot hovering right between her breasts.

We're so dead . . .

Never one to be intimidated, Caillen moved so fast that she hadn't even seen him do it until he had the Andarion's blaster in his hand and aimed at the creature's head.

The Andarion grabbed him and shoved him toward a large shuttle with an open hatch before he disarmed Caillen.

With a gymnastic twist, Caillen came up from below and swept the weapon from his hand again. He angled it at the Andarion's chest. "You better be glad I don't overreact to things, Fain, or you'd be dead right about now."

Fain snorted as he knocked the blaster out of Caillen's hand and slid it gracefully into his holster before he took a step back. "Didn't your sisters ever teach you not to mess with your betters, food?"

"Yes, but there aren't any betters here." He raked a smug look over Fain's body. "Just you, witling."

A twitch started in Fain's eye at the insult. He didn't respond to it. Instead, he crossed his arms over his chest. An action that caused the veins on his arms to bulge as he swept a frown over Caillen's body. "Out of curiosity, why do you look like a cheap Andarion hooker?"

"Spend a lot of time trolling for them, do you?"

Fain made a low growl that conveyed his annoyance. "I have a lot of friends in their community. They're more loyal than most, so don't go there unless you really want to toss down with me. Which is why your garish appearance offends me for them." Yeah, Fain was definitely lacking in tact and manners.

Caillen shrugged his insult aside. "I was trying to blend."

He scoffed at Caillen's answer. "Yeah... okay, that explains a lot about your current predicament. For the record, giakon, you don't blend here—you smack of offworlder—and you're lucky the natives haven't eaten you. I still can't believe you were dumb enough to get made in a transport of all things. What the hell were you thinking?"

"I was hoping they'd think I was you."

Fain sighed. "All I need. A human riding my reputation. Thanks. Appreciate it. Might as well hang a sign around my neck calling myself a wuss. Pisses me off. A lifetime to build my reputation, three seconds for you to destroy." He narrowed his gaze on Desideria. "So who's your trim?"

Caillen stiffened right along with her at the derogatory word that meant she was nothing more than a mindless adornment for his arm. "I seriously object to that term, Fain."

He held his hands up in surrender. "Forgot you're from the all-estrogen nest. No offense meant to your woman or you, but if you are offended, I really don't care. Don't have time to deal with something as petty as human emotions while under fire. So given all that, I'm going to assume this is the princess you're accused of trying to kill."

Caillen made the introduction. "Fain Hauk meet Princess Eternal Pain in my Ass."

Desideria gaped at him. She couldn't believe he'd introduced her that way.

Fain laughed, then nudged her toward the shuttle hatch that was open. "Yeah, well, you and Princess Pain in the Ass need to get on board quickly."

Caillen hesitated. "Why?"

Fain pulled the blaster out again and acted as if he'd captured them. "Move. Now." Then he spoke between clenched teeth. "Get on board the damn ship or I'm leaving you here."

Caillen jerked his hands up as if he was surrendering in the most sarcastic manner imaginable. Last thing he wanted was to feed Fain's ego by having a tape of him being taken into custody. "Bite me, asshole."

"I would, but your greasy ass wouldn't be worth the indigestion."

Caillen snorted before he led her up the ramp. Fain would pay for this, but obviously the Andarion had concerns about them being monitored and wanted this to look authentic if that were indeed the case. So for now, he'd play along.

Once they were inside, Fain followed them in and closed the hatch. Only then did he relax and return his blaster to its holster. He activated the link in his ear. "Got them. You were right. Dagan headed straight for us when he saw Nyk's fighter." He paused to listen. "I've got the scanners running already. See you when you get here."

Caillen ran his thumb along the edge of his lips as Fain's patient tone amused him. A ruthless killer who'd been thrown out of the house by his parents when he was just a kid and forced to grow up hard on the streets, the Andarion had little tolerance for anyone except the younger brother he guarded like treasure. "Only one person I know you'd be that civil with. Dancer?"

"Yeah, and you better be glad you're friends with him. There's no one else who could have called in this favor, especially for a human." Fain sneered the word as he shut the link off and ran over the shuttle's settings. "After your suspicious exodus from the *Arimanda*, Darling deployed Dancer out to look for you and he called me as soon as he realized where you were. You're lucky I happen to live on this hell rock."

"Since when? I thought you lived on Kirovar."

Fain scoffed as he pulled back from the console and moved to make a systems check. "Too many humans wetting themselves whenever I walked down the street. Got tired of the mamas grabbing their kids up like I couldn't control myself and was going to snack on one of those repulsive creatures. Have you seen what human kids eat? Gah, most of them munch their own mucus. Disgusting little parasites." Shivering, he flipped several switches.

Caillen laughed out loud at Fain's uncharacteristic rant—normally he didn't do much more than growl at anyone near him. This was probably only the third time he'd ever said more than a handful of syllables around him.

And it was highly unusual for Fain to show any form of weakness. The Andarion didn't believe in ever exposing his underbelly in any way. "Wow, that's all it takes to make you, Captain Badass, squeamish? I had no idea you were so easily cowed. Forget trying to shoot you. All someone has to do is send a kid into your general direction and you'll run for cover."

Fain slid a threatening grimace at him. "Don't go there. And my habitat and repulsion triggers aren't the daily topic. You two are."

"Yeah, I know. We have an assassin after us."

Fain snorted in derision. "That's the least of *your* problems given what you're accused of."

Those words set his temper on fire as he remembered what else he was facing and he slid an irritated glare at Desideria. He was still livid over the stunt her crew had tried with him. He couldn't wait to get back and set the record straight. "Again, I know. The Qills have accused me of trying to kill Princess Pain."

She gave him a glower that would shrivel a lesser man. "Would you stop calling me that?"

Fain ignored them. "That's still nothing."

Now that got Caillen's attention. That and the deadly look emanating from Fain's eyes. "What do you mean?"

Desideria frowned as a bad feeling went through her. Obviously something had happened that they didn't know about.

Fain pulled the mask down from the lower part of his face so that it lay against his neck. His handsomeness actually caught her off guard. If he would wash the makeup from his face, he'd be every bit as devastating as Caillen...

In a freakish kind of way.

When he spoke, his fangs flashed in the dim light cast by the control panel. "Your father was killed and so was the Qill queen. The entire universe is now after the two of you for their murders."

Desideria couldn't breathe as that news tore through her like a dagger. Her mother was dead?

No...It couldn't be.

It wasn't possible.

And yet she could tell by Fain's expression that he wasn't lying. Her mother was dead.

I'm too late.

She wanted to cry, but Qillaqs didn't weep. Not about death.

They got even.

And still the pain of her mother's loss washed through her entire being. It hurt much worse than she would have ever thought possible. Until this moment, she hadn't realized just how much she'd loved her unlovable parent.

She wanted to see her mother again. To hear the sound of her voice even if it was criticizing her.

I'm an orphan.

It was a stupid thought really, especially given what was going on and what was at stake. She was a grown woman and yet she felt abandoned and alone in a way she wouldn't have thought possible.

What am I going to do?

Her life would be forfeit once they found her.

Over and over, she saw images of her mother boasting about how no one would ever be able to defeat her—how she could take down any assassin who dared to look askance at her. That she was the strongest of warriors. But beneath that was the memory of her mother's happy smile when Desideria had joined the Guard. There for one tiny moment, her mother had been proud of her.

And she'd failed her in the worst sort of way.

Her mother was dead.

This can't be happening.

Her people were without leadership and she was

wanted for her own mother's murder. Her emotions were so tangled. She was angry, hurting and most of all there was a deep, dark hole inside her that felt like it would swallow her up until she lost herself completely.

Her life would never be the same.

If she lived...

The horror of it all washed over her in a tidal wave of pain. She couldn't breathe as panic set in.

What am I going to do? How would she survive?

As if he understood her rising panic, Caillen pulled her against him and held her close. Normally, she'd shove him away for intruding on her personal space, but right now she appreciated the comfort.

No, she needed it. The sound of his heart under her cheek...the sensation of being cocooned by his warmth. He gave her strength even while her entire world was spinning out of control.

Glancing up, she saw the same look of grief-stricken shock on his face that she felt. "What happened?" he asked Fain.

"Your father was executed in his room. They found his body right after you'd left—when they'd gone in to tell him what had happened to you. I don't know what their evidence against you is, but there's a standing League contract out on both of your lives. And we are talking *major* bill-kill."

She winced at a term that meant the bounty on their heads was so steep that most people would sell their own body parts for it.

Never had she felt more lost. How could she prove her innocence? No doubt her mother's Guard would kill her the moment they saw her again. It would be expected.

Yes, she could demand a trial which would pit her in a death match against her aunt or her sister. But she had no doubt her mother's killers would terminate her before she had a chance to clear her name. They wouldn't allow her a chance to prove her innocence.

And even if she was found innocent, it wouldn't change the outcome. As a Guard member on duty at the time of her mother's death, she'd be held accountable. The only person who could pardon her would be the next queen.

Narcissa.

Yeah…

I'm so dead.

Caillen tightened his arms around her as he spoke to Fain. "Darling told me my father was all right when I spoke to him."

Fain leaned back against the seat. "Darling didn't want you to panic. According to him, your father had his throat slit and Princess Pain's mother was left in little bloody chunks all over her bed."

The bile rose in her throat at those unexpected cold, brutal words. A vivid image of her beautiful mother was blotted out by what he'd described.

It was more than she could take.

Before she could stop herself, she ran to the bathroom barely in time and lost what little contents she had in her stomach. Her spasms were violent and loud as her entire body shook.

Suddenly, Caillen moved in behind her while she was sick. Without a single word, he stayed with her until she was finished. Then he silently flushed.

Weak and spent, she wanted to crawl in a hole and die of embarrassment. She was acting like a child, not the warrior she'd been trained to be. Worse, tears glistened in her eyes while she did her best to not give in to emotions she knew she shouldn't have.

I won't cry. I won't.

Her mother would be disappointed in her if she did and the last thing she wanted was to shame her mother any more. But Caillen wasn't looking at her like she was an embarrassment or weak. There was compassion and something that might even be respect. But now?

Caillen handed her a cool, damp towel. "Are you all right?"

She nodded. "I'm so sorry about that."

"Don't be. Believe me, your strength has impressed the hell out of me and that's something that's hard to do where I'm concerned." He brushed a stray strand of her hair back from her forehead. The warmth of his hand on her skin sent a comforting chill through her.

His gaze was kind. His touch gentle. She wanted this moment to last until it drove out all the pain she felt.

Most of all, she wanted *him*.

That thought terrified her.

Yet, he'd been with her through all of this. Strong. Protective. Comforting. Dependable.

Everything a man should be. Things as a Qillaq she shouldn't want. Things as a woman she needed.

She swallowed as she pushed those thoughts away. "Thank you."

He inclined his head to her.

A furious light sparked in his eyes as he returned to where Fain watched them. "You are such an insensitive ass. You know you don't just blurt out someone's parents are dead and then describe it."

Fain wasn't the least bit contrite. "Why? You didn't vomit. Besides, I'd kill to have someone give me news that good." He glanced back to where Desideria was pushing herself to her feet. "By the way, is she going to do that for long? If she is, I say we leave her in the head and flush her out the air lock once we're launched."

Caillen tossed a knife at his head which he caught without hesitation.

"What?" Fain was truly baffled by Caillen's indignation and her sympathy for her mother. "It's not my fault I forget how sensitive you humans are. Our women don't cry."

"Oh trust me, Fain. Any living Andarion female who's forced to bed down with you weeps hysterically at the mere thought of that horror."

Fain threw the knife back at him.

Caillen caught it without blinking.

Desideria had barely pulled herself together when another Andarion male entered the shuttle and quickly closed the door behind him. This one she recognized from Caillen's pictures.

It was Dancer.

Dancer scowled as he felt the tension between them. His gaze went from his brother to her and then to Caillen who still looked like he wanted to shoot Fain. "What'd I miss?"

"Your brother's an idiot," Caillen snarled.

"Yeah, I know."

Fain scoffed at Dancer's calm acceptance. "You don't have to agree with him."

"You don't have to be an idiot either. But I notice that doesn't stop you from it. And I've seen you actually use your brain, so I know you have one." Dancer glanced back to Caillen. "So what'd he do?"

Fain gestured toward them. "I just told them their parents were dead and she threw up."

"Ah, krik, Fain..." He broke off into Andarion and for several seconds the two of them argued back and forth while gesturing wildly.

Caillen whistled to get their attention. "You two can play a round of Insult My Gene Pool later. Right now, we need to focus on getting us out of here."

Fain snorted. "Not so easy, brother. Anyone leaving here will be scanned for hijackers. I don't think you understand that there's a ten-million-credit bounty on each of your heads. For that kind of money, you're lucky I'm not handing you in."

Caillen was stunned by an amount that was usually reserved for traitors, pedophiles and rogue assassins... and now two royal members of the council. "Ten million credits?"

"Each," Fain reiterated.

"Shit. For that, I'm tempted to hand myself in."

Dancer, who normally only went by his last name Hauk, because face it, Dancer sucked, was a smaller version of his older brother. But no less fierce. Aside from their difference in height and build, it would be hard to tell them apart. "Don't be so hasty, Cai. Alive, you're only worth three."

Now that was just cold and wrong. But it also told him that they were being framed by someone who wanted to make damn sure the truth never came out. "Are you kidding?"

Hauk shook his head.

"Who issued the bounty?" Caillen asked.

"The League," Hauk said snidely. "They're forcing each of your planets to cough up the money."

Great. So much for hoping the one leading the investigation would help him find the truth. He should have known it wouldn't be that easy. All the League would want was closure and if they had to kill two innocent people for it, they really couldn't care less. "Did anyone defend us?"

Hauk shook his head again. "Threw you to the wolves." He flipped on a monitor and did a quick search to show Caillen the cold, harsh truth. News article after news article had them convicted. Everyone they'd interviewed said they weren't surprised by either of their actions.

Even Desideria's two sisters.

You have Darling and Maris. No one had interviewed them and they hadn't betrayed him, but then given the severity of the crime they were charging them with that was probably for the best. Had they stepped forward at this point to defend them, they would probably be charged as accessories.

Which meant he might have other allies he didn't know about. He held that thought tight.

Until he watched as his uncle showed up on a vidclip to speak to the news agencies from the *Arimanda*. If he didn't know better, he'd swear the man actually looked grief stricken while he addressed the vultures who'd come to cash in on his pain. "It is with a sad heart that I'm forced to step into a place I never thought I'd occupy. My brother was a great emperor and I know I'm a shallow substitution. We are still reeling from the actions of my nephew. I can't understand how anyone could be so ruthless and unfeeling, especially toward their own father who loved them so much. I tried to tell Evzen that no one can tame a wild animal. True to the generosity of his spirit, he refused to believe it and he let the love of his son guide him to suicide. I don't know what madness infected the prince, but I can assure all of you that he will be held accountable for his actions and I will not rest until he's behind bars where he belongs and is executed for this heinous crime."

Love you too, you old bastard.

Caillen shut the browser off. Last thing he wanted to see was any more allegations directed toward him. "Why do they think I did it?"

Hauk pulled up another clip. This was security footage on board the ship. And there in his father's room, standing over his body, was a man who looked so much like him that even he doubted his innocence.

Holy . . .

Hauk nodded as his expression mirrored the sick horror Caillen felt. "You want to live. We've got to find this asshole and expose him as the killer or whoever doctored the footage. Nyk, Syn, Shahara and Jayne are already on it."

"What about my mother?" Desideria's features were pale from her grief. She was still beautiful, but she looked so tired that all he wanted to do was make this better for her.

If only he could.

"That's where it's really odd," Fain said, directing their attention back to the monitor and a new clip that was filled with static. "There's no footage from your mother's room, Princess. Someone tampered with the camera. But two members of her Guard swear they saw you running out of there right before her body was discovered and that they pursued you only to find you fighting with Caillen. At first, they claim they thought he was attacking you. Then when you two turned on them to fight and then escaped together, they realized you were working as a team to kill your parents."

She gaped at how preposterous that was. "I'm sorry, but that's the dumbest story ever conceived. Are you telling me anyone is stupid enough to believe it?"

Hauk scoffed. "Two words. League bureaucrats. Thinking waved bye-bye to them a long time ago."

He had a point.

"I can't believe this," she said, wanting to hunt down her mother's Guard and carve her initials into their useless brains.

Caillen reviewed some of the data that Fain was still calling up.

Desideria moved to stand so close to him that her breath fell against his skin, tickling his flesh and making him wish he had a spare moment so that she could do that to his entire body. "They can't honestly believe this."

Caillen met her gaze, wishing he could be so naive. But he knew better. "Greed makes people stupid. Always. It stands to reason in their world that we would kill our parents to inherit their positions. Face it, it's a common enough occurrence. Why should anyone doubt it?"

Hauk nodded in agreement. "Darling said that you'd already been suspicious of your uncle."

"I was."

Fain gave him an arch stare. "Was?"

Caillen took over the search as he reviewed the news

reports about his father's death. "Something's not adding up to me." It was too easy a jump to his uncle.

Wasn't it?

But then he'd seen people do far worse for a lot less. He didn't want to believe that the brother his father had loved and trusted would be so cold.

However, that was as cliché as kids killing parents for inheritance. His uncle made sense.

Fain scoffed at his doubt. "What are you? Trisani now? You want to give me the winning lottery numbers while you're on a roll?"

He ignored Fain's sarcasm as he rethought his earlier conviction. "I'm telling you, something's wrong. How did both get killed on a ship with that kind of security? And so close to us leaving? At basically the same time?"

Hauk answered before Fain could. "Obviously the assassination was in place and they sped it up after you guys evaced so that they could frame you."

He just couldn't make himself buy Hauk's explanation. It just didn't fit. There was something more here. Something they didn't know about.

To his amazement, Desideria backed his position. "Caillen's right. It's too convenient and two well executed to be pulled off by two independent parties. Why would they both strike right at that same time? It smacks of collusion."

Caillen pulled the clip where his uncle was being notified of his father's death. The man actually stumbled from the weight of the news and had to be held up by his guards.

Could he be that good an actor?

It was possible and yet...

Why would his uncle want to kill Desideria's mother? Aside from the fact she was a roaring bitch, he had nothing to gain by killing her too.

But who did?

Caillen stepped back. "I need to talk to my uncle."

"Are you insane?" Hauk's jaw went slack. "He'll have you arrested if not executed on sight. The man either thinks you killed his brother, or, and more to the point, he knows for a fact you didn't and doesn't want you to talk and expose him."

Hauk was right, but Caillen refused to listen to reason. Why should he start that bad habit now when he'd never listened to it before? "Work with me, Hauk. Let's say for a minute that my uncle's not behind this... that means his life will be in danger too. The more I think about this, the more it's looking like some kind of coup."

Fain frowned. "But why would the Qills lie about—"

"Would you stop using that term?" Desideria snapped, cutting him off. "We don't like it. We're Qillaqs not Qills."

Caillen admired her temerity, especially against Fain who was known to gut people for glancing at him askance.

Fain passed her an annoyed look, but true to form, refused to apologize. "Why would they lie?"

"I don't know." Caillen sighed. "But why hit both the Qillaqs"—he stressed the word to let Desideria know that he was trying not to insult her—"and the Exeterians? There has to be some connection."

Hauk scratched his chin. "Maybe it has to do with the fact that the queen was about to start a war with your allies?"

Caillen sifted through more data. "There's some vital something here that we're missing."

Fain sighed. "I think you're giving it too much credit. No one says the two have to be connected. Weird shit happens. Trust me. I'm usually its favorite victim."

Desideria narrowed her gaze as if she was still thinking it all through. "When I overheard them plotting to kill my mother, there was no mention of your father or you. Maybe it *is* coincidence."

Caillen shook his head. "I don't believe in coincidences."

Hauk exchanged a wary look with Fain. "You said your uncle's been a total bastard to you since you started living with your father. Maybe he's the one who hired your kidnappers to kill you as a kid to get you out of the way so that he could inherit."

That was just dumb, but he wasn't about to say it to Hauk and start a fight. "Why wait to seize the throne then?" Had his uncle done that, he would have killed his father years ago and seized power.

No. Something else was going on here. He just needed to find out what.

"We're onto something." Caillen breathed. "I just don't have enough pieces to put it together yet."

Hauk let out a low growl as if he was as frustrated as Caillen. "First thing is to find the shooter, then, and question him."

Caillen agreed. "Just don't let Nykyrian interrogate him. We need the hitter capable of speech."

Desideria frowned as she thought more about it too. "Wouldn't it be better to talk to my mother's Guard? They were trying to kill me and set us both up. You think they would know something about all this?"

"Princess Pain has a point," Fain said.

She glared at him. "And could you please stop calling me that? My name's Desideria."

"But I like Princess Pain. It has a nice ring to it."

Desideria barely resisted the urge to choke him. He was so much taller she'd be lucky if she could even get her hands around his throat. "It was bad enough when there was just Caillen. Now I have his friends to irritate me too. Gods save me."

The words were barely out of her mouth before something struck the side of the ship.

Hard.

All of a sudden, a gruff voice rang out. "Open up! We're detecting unauthorized heat signatures and weight in your ship."

Fain let out a foul curse. "Ding-dong, children. The authorities are here."

18

Hauk groaned audibly at the sound of the Enforcers firing on their door hatch, trying to break in. He met Caillen's gaze. "For the record, it's a death sentence to anyone caught helping you guys. Just so you know."

"Appreciate the IFO update, pun'kin." Caillen made that strange clicking noise with his tongue at him. "And that's new for us how?"

Hauk sighed heavily. "I hate you, Dagan. I really do."

"Know you do." Caillen started flipping switches over his head. "Now pucker up, baby, you're about to have to kiss my ass for saving yours."

Fain snorted as he pulled his mask back into place. "I'll get the engines fired. May the gods be with us. This has all the markings of a very short trip."

Caillen smirked with a nonchalance Desideria definitely didn't feel as he took over the controls and did a prelim check. "Who wants to live forever?"

Actually, she wouldn't mind a small dose of immortality. The concept worked well for her.

Fain muttered as the engines roared to life, "Yeah, but no one said I wanted to die today."

In spite of the danger and her racing heart, Desideria laughed at his dry words. Normal men would be terrified, but Caillen, Hauk and Fain seemed to thrive on imminent danger. Their attitudes were infectious and it brought the warrior in her to the forefront and made her ready to fight to the bitter end. "Where are the guns?"

All three men turned to her with curious stares that annoyed her. "I know how to fight, boys. I am Qillaq." She narrowed her gaze at Caillen. "You might be able to fly anything with wings. I can shoot anything with a trigger and if it can be aimed, I can use it to maim."

He did a charming sweep of her body that turned her body strangely hot. It also made her feel very feminine and desirable. "Baby, I never doubted you for a minute."

Fain jerked his chin to Hauk. "Take her up and don't get hurt. I'd have to kill your ass if you did."

She didn't even want to comment on the oddity of that particular threat. Hauk inclined his head to Fain before he pulled Desideria toward the rear of their ship.

. Caillen slid gracefully from the navigator's into the pilot's chair as an ion cannon blast struck the shuttle so hard it caused it to rock. Just like old times for him—it wasn't a launch unless he was under massive local fire. The steel around them squealed in protest, but lucky for them it held. They only had a few seconds before the authorities were in and they were dead.

Really, it would be impossible to fly a shuttle with a giant hole in the door and he ought to know since he'd tried to do it on more than one occasion.

The good news was, he'd actually succeeded in doing it.

Once.

Don't go there. Some memories just needed to be purged.

Fain arched a brow as he took the con. "You going to jerk my guts out?"

"Probably."

Another loud blast rocked the craft.

"Now that's just rude." Caillen flipped another switch over his head which generated a pulse shield. He heard the soldiers curse and whine as it knocked them flying.

Good, you little bastards. I hope it leaves a mark and ruins your sex plans for at least a week.

He did the final sys check and felt the blood pick up its pace in his bloodstream. The ship was ready to launch.

Except for the fact that the hangar bay door was still closed and reinforcements were arriving by the dozens to keep it blocked and them from leaving.

"That don't look promising," Hauk said through the intercom.

All of a sudden, blasts shot from their ship to the Enforcers. The authorities scrambled for cover as the bright color bursts exploded around them and left marks all over the walls of the bay.

Putting the mic in his ear, Caillen grinned at Desideria's precision. She nailed everything she aimed for which wasn't the soldiers. She blasted close enough to keep them down or scatter them away from the exit, but not enough to kill.

Go, baby. He respected her mercy and it said a lot about her that she wasn't gunning them down.

While she did that, Fain hammered the hangar door with their cannons. The hole he created wasn't that big, but Caillen should be able to squeeze through.

Unless he sneezed. The slightest miscalculation would kill them faster than the Enforcers.

Caillen dropped the grav weights and held the throttle wide open as he headed for the opening at full speed—a fool's pace indeed and one he was famed for.

He scowled at the angry voices from the Enforcers' open channel that echoed in his ear. "Is my Andarion rusty or did they just call us the ass of a dung beetle?"

Hauk laughed over the intercom. "You're an idiot. They said they're launching fighters to come at us."

"Ah. I think I like being called a dung beetle's ass better. Guess we better go, huh?"

"Nah, let's sit around and invite them for tea." Fain's voice dripped with sarcasm.

Caillen activated the ship's force field to the max. "Hold tight, kids. We're going out hot and we're staying that way until we either escape or end up as a bright burst of flaming fuel. I hope someone remembered the marshmallows. Just in case. We might as well go into paradise with a sweet taste in our mouths."

"You're a sick bastard, Dagan." Fain took up the navigator's position. "You know we won't be able to jump. They'll have your drive jammed."

Caillen laughed at his dry, dire tone. "Oh ye of little faith. You ain't with some run-of-the-mill pilot, giakon. You're with a Dagan. There's not a wormhole in this sector I'm not dating tight."

"Incoming!" Hauk warned.

Caillen saw the ships hovering right outside the door with their cannons locked on the shuttle. He charged the front shields and headed straight for their pursuers. "Give them everything you got, Desideria. And get ready to toss your shoes in too."

Desideria laughed as if she was as thrilled with the prospect of a fight as he was. She and Hauk sprayed fire all through the bay and on top of the patrols coming in.

The ships tried to block their exit for several heartbeats before they realized just how suicidal Caillen really was. He'd slam into them before he'd yield. In a game of header, he refused to blink or swerve.

Fuck them. If he was going to die, so were they.

Just as he would have hit them, they veered off sharply, out of the way.

Laughing from his adrenaline rush, he flew out and up at such a climb that a lesser pilot would have lost consciousness.

Hauk groaned in his ear as Fain adjusted their fuel levels to give the engines the juice they needed to surpass escape velocity. But it wasn't that easy. The fighters turned to give chase, shooting cannons the whole way after them.

Oh to have his ship or anything that was more maneuverable than this crate. At least that was his thought until he took notice of Desideria's competence.

Damn to have had her as his partner all these years instead of Kasen who'd be screaming by now that they were going to die. Not a peep came out of his little Qill as she reloaded and laid down more fire.

Fain shot a vid to his lower left quadrant for him to see. "Cruiser moving in on port aft."

"Got it." Caillen dropped low and spun out of the line of fire.

"Tractor beam pulse," Fain warned.

He sent a fierce glare at Fain. "You going to give me play by play every time they twitch?"

"Want to make sure you don't miss anything."

He snorted at the Andarion. "Only thing missing here is my sanity."

More ships came in for them. Caillen kept his eye on the scanners as he made numerous calculations in his head and on the con. He needed a few more minutes to get to a wormhole.

C'mon, baby, don't fail me now...

Desideria backed off as she saw their cannons overheating. Designed to be a passenger transport, the shuttle didn't want her using so much fire power and it was straining with her efforts. The guns were merely a precaution and not meant to defend for any longer than it would take for a backup patrol to come save them.

Oh to have that backup right now...

She leaned to the side so that she could check Hauk's status in order to verify her dread. Unfortunately, she'd been right. Hauk's cannon was already out of commission.

The Andarions were still coming after them.

She tapped the link in her ear. "Caillen, we're in an overheat situation."

"I need a couple of minutes."

She squeezed the trigger.

Nothing happened.

Cringing, she exchanged a concerned look with Hauk. "We don't have a couple of minutes, dearest."

"Then you better start kicking off those shoes, sweetling."

He wasn't funny in the least. Especially as she watched

the Andarions gathering a force that stunned her. But it was the one fighter that concerned her most...

One she'd hoped to not see again.

"Our assassin's back and he looks determined."

"I'm on it."

Desideria held her breath as they dropped low and spun away from their pursuers. Even the assassin.

Hauk tapped her shoulder and pointed to a dark cloud they were headed toward. "Wormhole."

Relief poured through her. If they could make it to that, then it would propel them out of the sector and leave them a ghost to the Andarions and assassin. There would be no way for them to track them at all.

Just a little ways to it...

Almost.

There.

Holding her breath, she wished she could get out and push. But all she could do was imagine herself there with everything she had.

Caillen let out a whoop as they approached it.

Just as she thought they were safe, a net shot out in front of them, cutting them off. The force of impact brought them to an abrupt halt and sent her flying against the straps of her seat. The leather dug into her, bruising her hips and shoulders.

They were caught.

"Surrender!"

She didn't need a translator for that word.

Worse, the assassin flew in and took advantage of their disabled craft to fire torpedoes at them. The Andarions opened fire on the assassin, but it was too late.

She saw the light bomb coming straight at them.

We're dead...

Not even Caillen or his magic backpack could work a miracle great enough to save them now. Sucking her breath in, she waited for the fatal impact.

Caillen cursed in her ear. "No one move. We're pulling a Nykyrian."

"What's a—" She paused midsentence as the shuttle went completely dark.

One second she was strapped into her chair. In the next, she was standing in the center of an unfamiliar bridge. The explosion from the shuttle was so bright through the main bridge portal that it temporarily blinded her.

Until a cry rang out from the engineer on her right, alerting the crew that they had intruders.

Caillen, Hauk and Fain leapt into action. Desideria spun and tried to disarm the first crew member who reached her. But disarming an Andarion was something easier said than done. He didn't react to pain at all.

Did they not have the same nervous system?

He picked her up, literally, and threw her against the wall. The impact knocked the wind out of her as pain exploded through her entire being. In all the fights she'd had in her life, none of them had prepared her for this amount of damage. While she'd been bludgeoned and punched, no one had ever thrown her across the room before.

She tried to push herself to her feet, but she couldn't. *Oh my God, I'm helpless.* That feeling horrified her.

Dazed, she felt the Andarion grab her from behind. He wrapped his arm around her throat and choked her until her ears rang and her vision dimmed.

Suddenly, she was free. She turned to see Caillen

beating the Andarion so hard she wasn't sure how he kept standing. It was fierce and impressive.

Fain whistled to get Caillen's attention. "Enough! We have control of the ship. Focus, drey, focus."

Caillen appeared to calm down, except for the wild look in his eyes. It was obvious he was more than ready to continue the fight. But somehow he maintained control of himself.

Hauk and Fain directed the four-man crew toward the escape pods with their blasters. "Take the controls, Cai, while we toss out the trash."

Caillen held his hand out to her to help her to her feet. "You dead?" The humor in his voice undercut the dead seriousness of his gaze. If she didn't know better, she'd think he was worried about her.

"Close, but not yet. Thanks for the assist."

There was a softening in his gaze that made her stomach flutter. She didn't know why, but she had a feeling that his anger was actually over the Andarion attacking her...

"Anytime." With an adorable and sheepish dip of his head that was completely out of character, he turned and went to the controls. It was only then she realized that at some point over the last hour, he'd removed his contacts and had his normal dark eyes. Most likely because it limited his peripheral vision in a fight and while flying.

But when had he removed them?

And why did the sight of his real eyes do such peculiar things to her body? She was both hot and cold. Shivery. Not wanting to think about that, she took a moment to push her pain into submission and to watch as Caillen slid into the chair to begin working the controls as if he'd been born to them. As much as she hated to feed his overbloated ego, he really was a great pilot. Every bit as skilled as he'd claimed and the fact he was piloting a ship with controls and monitors that weren't his native tongue or Universal was even more impressive.

Before she even realized she'd moved, she was standing behind him, watching his hands fly over the controls and computer in a way that brought chills to her. How could he process an alien language so easily?

And that turned her thoughts to the last few days. So much had happened to her since she'd met him.

Almost all of it horrendously bad.

And yet somehow he'd managed to be a bright spot through the hell that had been this trip. How strange was that?

Right now, his presence was the only thing that kept her holding on to a life that had become a nightmare. Panic swelled inside her as she tried to come to terms with what was happening to her and the speed with which her life had unraveled.

Her mother was dead and she was being blamed for it. Every known government was looking to arrest and then execute them. Public humiliation and death.

My life is over and I'm innocent...

Caillen froze as he felt a hesitant hand brush through his hair. He turned his head to see Desideria staring at him with a look in her eyes that was both vulnerable and sexy.

He let out a relieved breath. "Oh thank the gods it's you. It would have seriously messed up my day to have Hauk or Fain start coming on to me in the middle of all this shit."

She laughed. "You are not right."

"So they tell me. Often." He jerked his chin to the seat beside him. "Lend us a hand?"

"I'm not a pilot."

"I just need you to key in a sequence with me to unlock the controls so that I can get us out of here."

"I can't read Andarion," she reminded him.

"You won't need to. It's a simple sequence. You move your hands with mine to the same place on your panel and we'll be fine. Or we'll explode, but I'm hoping you have more rhythm than Hauk."

Cringing over what she hoped was more humor and not a true prognosis, she sat down and ran through it with him. She had no idea what she was doing, but his patient, calm voice walked her through every stroke and made it as simple as he'd promised.

Luckily they didn't blow up.

Just as she finished, Hauk and Fain returned. There was a satisfied gleam in Fain's eerie eyes that said he'd thoroughly enjoyed tossing the other Andarions off the ship.

Hauk moved to stand behind her chair as he went over her settings. Then he looked at Caillen. "We'll have about two more minutes until the Andarions realize we're alive and on this ship."

Caillen nodded, punching in coordinates. "You know the drill. Strap tight what you don't want to lose."

As soon as they did, Caillen banked the ship and spun it straight toward the wormhole. That alerted the Enforcers who instantly gave chase.

Fain cursed as the Enforcers opened fire on them again. "You could learn a little subtlety, Dagan."

Caillen scoffed. "Subtlety is for those who lack the skills and the balls to be bold."

Fain's glare was murderous. "Subtlety is for those with the brains to not get a fleet chasing after them."

Caillen snorted a denial. "I'm in a real ship now, boy. You forget that this is what I do for fun. There's no danger here."

Desideria would argue that, but instead she gripped the arms of her chair as Caillen narrowly flew between two fighters, shooting the whole way.

A warning light flashed.

Fain cursed. "Ah now you've gone and broke the damn ship, Dagan. Can't we let you do anything?"

Caillen made an obscene gesture at him.

Just as she was sure they'd be caught again, Caillen did a hard right and dip that slid them straight and smoothly into the wormhole. For a merest slip of time everything went dark. All power vanished before it came back on and they shot forward with a force so strong, it plastered her against the seat.

As they leveled out, Caillen turned a smug smirk at all of them. "And you actually doubted me." He tsked chidingly.

"Every minute you live and breathe," Fain muttered. He took the controls by slapping Caillen's hands away. "Now get away from there before you do any more damage to my limited sanity."

Caillen started to protest, but Hauk stopped him. "We have a couple of hours before we make it to Sentella VII. Why don't you two take a breather?"

Fain agreed. "And a bath while you're at it."

"I don't stink." Caillen's tone was completely offended.

Fain raked a contradictory grimace over Caillen's scuffed appearance. "Trust me, human, you reek. When was the last time you washed anyway?"

Caillen tucked his hands into his back pockets before he recovered his usual good humor. "Yeah, all right. So I *might* resemble that remark. You still don't have to be so rude about it."

"You think this is rude—"

."People!" Hauk said, breaking up their argument. "Let's stow the attitudes and take a moment to be grateful we're alive and intact which given Caillen's suicidal tendencies and limited piloting abilities is amazing. You know, we did just live through a miracle."

Caillen would argue that it was a testament to his skills and not an esoteric being, but as he caught the grief that hung heavy in Desideria's eyes, he decided to heed Hauk's words. She could use a break and honestly, so could he. "Fine. We'll be in the crew quarters if you need us."

Hauk took over his chair the minute he left it. Relinquishing the controls—which was a really hard thing for him to do—Caillen led Desideria down the narrow hallway, so designed to keep any outside attackers in single file and to limit their movements, to the small bunk room where the normal crew could take their breaks should they be on a long patrol. There wouldn't be much of a shower there, but it would be enough for a quick rinse and hopefully one of the original Andarion crew members would have had a penchant for soap. Maybe even shampoo.

He opened the door to the room and let Desideria enter first. The lights came on automatically as she headed to the corner where a small round table and two padded chairs were set next to a cooling unit and food cabinet. Three narrow, stacked bunks lined the opposite wall next to the small shower stall. "You okay?"

Her eyes were haunted. "Not really. I'm…weirdly numb."

"Yeah. Me too. It's a lot to take in and we've been hammered with it over a very short period of time. The mind tends to shut down so that we can cope." Unfortunately, it would hit them both later and be even harder to deal with.

Like when his adoptive father had died when he was a kid.

He'd been completely normal for three days as he bribed the doctors and helped his sisters cope, then after the funeral when he'd been on his way to school, something inside him had snapped. In a back alley alone, he'd cried until he made himself sick.

No one knew about that and they never would. It'd taken him hours to pull himself back together.

"Don't worry, Princess. I'm here if you want to talk about it."

Desideria didn't respond as the reality of her predicament hit her all over again. There was no escape for them. No hope. All of her dreams of a future were gone. This could very well be the last day she'd live…

Fear and grief choked her. "I'm not ready to die yet."

"You won't."

How easy he made that sound. But not even his conviction could sell that lie to her. The truth was cold and harsh.

And it was in her face.

I'm the walking dead. They would condemn her for this and there was nothing she could do.

He held his hand out to her. "C'mon. Take a shower and you'll feel better."

She scoffed at his useless optimism. "A shower won't cure my problems."

"No, but it'll help your mood. I promise."

"Yeah, right. It won't—"

He silenced her words with a kiss so hot it set fire to her blood. Her head spun at the warmth of his hard body pressing against hers. Of the sensation of his arms wrapped around her waist. Her raw and ragged emotions were so overwhelming and confusing.

No one had ever held her like this before.

Like she was precious. Like she mattered.

Like she was loved...

In that moment, something inside her burst. All her repressed emotions flooded through her with a ferocity so intense that it left her as breathless as his kiss.

But the one thing that held her grounded fast and kept her sane during this insanity was the taste of his lips. The scent of a man who had walked her through hell and had stood by her every step of the way.

A man who had protected her even when they'd been fighting against each other. No one had ever shown her that kindness or consideration.

One way or another, her life would be forfeit. Even though she'd lived her entire existence with her singular purpose to be dutiful and to make her mother proud—all of that was for nothing now.

Absolutely nothing.

But if she had to die, she wanted something for herself. Something uniquely hers.

She wanted Caillen. She wanted to go to her grave with the memory of his touch forever branded on her skin. To know what it was like to be with him, just the two of them with no pretense or regrets.

For the first time in her life, she felt like she was making a choice not out of duty or obligation. She was making a choice for her because it was something she wanted.

You're Qillaq, bound by the laws of your people.

Yes, and part of that was knowing herself. Deciding her own fate and not allowing anyone to rule her. Ever. Her mother was dead. It was up to her to find the killers and bring them to justice. Only she could do that. But until they landed, there was no way to pursue her traitors. Nothing to do except claim the only man who'd ever made her feel like she was human.

A man who touched a part of her no one ever had before.

Caillen growled as he felt the change in Desideria's kiss and in her mood. She clutched him against her, taking control of the situation in a way he'd only dreamed about. His senses spun as she explored his mouth and teased his lips with her teeth.

Oh yeah, baby . . .

This was what he'd been craving since the moment he first saw her. Every hormone inside him was salivating, dying for a taste of her body. When she pulled back to stare up at him, he felt his cock harden even more. He waited for her to speak, but she didn't. Instead, she opened his shirt and splayed her hands over his chest, brushing against his bruised flesh. Her caress sent chills down the entire length of his body.

In that moment he was undone and he knew there was no going back.

"Don't start this fire, Desideria. Not unless you intend to see it through."

She leaned in to nip his chin. "I'm willing to see it through."

He kissed her quickly, then moved toward the shower so that he could start the water.

She frowned at him. "What are you doing?"

"In the event Fain is right for the first time in his life, I don't want to offend you with my body odor."

Laughing, she shook her head. "As you would say, I think I resemble that remark. It's been a few days for me too."

"Yes, but you smell a lot better than I do. Believe me, my sisters tutored me well on the fact that men stink more than women."

"I don't know. I'd run my sisters up against the smelliest beasts in the universe. In fact, Cissy is always complaining that if we could bottle Gwen's sweat we'd have an entirely new biological weapon capable of dropping entire armies after one sniff. And I have to say, it's pretty potent."

Desideria sobered as Caillen undressed and he exposed more and more of that delectable flesh for her hungry gaze. Okay, her sisters weren't crazy. There was definitely something to be said for a man's naked body and Caillen's was exquisite. From his broad, muscled shoulders to the flat, tight stomach she could do laundry on, down his long, hairy legs all the way to his feet. Yes, he was bruised and wounded, but it didn't detract from the beauty of him at all.

She reversed her gaze and heat exploded across her face as she saw the part of him that was uniquely male. God love him, he was totally unabashed by his nudity. What she wouldn't give to be so secure in her own looks. And she was both fascinated and terrified by that stiff male part of him. It was alien and strange, and at the same time beautiful and beguiling.

His gentle laughter teased her as he reached out and pulled her closer to him. "It won't bite you, sweet, and neither will I...at least not without an invitation."

She shivered as he started opening her shirt and her old insecurities slammed into her. Would he find her unappealing? "You know I've never been with a man before."

He froze before those sharp eyes narrowed on her. "How is that possible?"

"I haven't earned the right yet."

He scowled at her. "Then why would you—"

She cut his words off by placing the tip of her finger against his lips. "We're not on Qilla now. I think I want to try your customs for a while."

He nibbled her fingertip, savoring the salty taste of her skin. "Are you sure about this? Sex is the one thing you can't undo. The last thing I want to be is a mistake that eats on your conscience."

She stared at him in awe. "Are you always so concerned about your lovers and their feelings?"

Caillen swallowed as those words took him back to the day he'd found his sister after her rape. She'd been so shattered and hurt. So damaged both mentally and physically. That one moment in time was forever branded into his heart and mind. The way Shahara had clung to him, then cursed him for being male. The way she'd cut her hair and then refused to be touched by anyone for years afterward. All the times she'd been afraid to leave their apartment. Even now, after all this time and her extensive combat training, she'd cringe if he came up behind her when she wasn't paying attention. And she still rarely hugged or touched him.

He would never do that to another human being. Never

tear a woman down to that level, especially not one who meant as much to him as Desideria did. "I don't want to be something you regret. Ever."

Desideria's eyes teared up. In that moment, she made a horrifying discovery.

She was falling in love with a lunatic rogue who lived with a death wish. One who had an amazing smile and an irritating ego. That realization floored her.

Love. Such a stupid emotion. She'd never understood it. Not until right now as she stared into the dark eyes of the only person she'd ever trusted with her safety. The only person she'd ever taken care of even though she didn't know how. This man who was grating, arrogant and annoying.

And perfectly wonderful.

She wanted to cry from the fierce emotions that swelled inside her. A part of her wanted to devour him. Another part just wanted to hold him until everything was good again.

Unable to stand it, she pulled him into her arms and just let the sensation of his body soothe hers. It felt so good to be so close to him.

Caillen sensed something different about the way she held him this time. She clung to him with her face buried against his neck. Not moving, just holding on for dear life like she feared he'd shove her away.

Had she snapped a wheel? Had all the bullshit of the last few days finally broken her?

He didn't know why, but that thought actually angered him. He couldn't stand the thought of anything bad happening to her. "Are you all right?"

She nodded, then stepped back to shrug out of her top.

His throat went dry at the sight of her bared breasts. He'd known she was beautiful, but the bounty in front of him was more than he'd expected. Oh yeah, those would overfill his hands and leave him completely satisfied. Growling, he dipped his head down to taste a piece of heaven.

Desideria shivered at the warmth of his breath on her naked flesh. And each stroke of his tongue sent a wave of heat through her. Never in her life had she felt anything like it. Her embarrassment fled under the assault of her desire and her need to please him.

Before she even realized his hands had moved, he had her completely naked. For the merest instant, she was bashful, but Caillen didn't leave her any time for that as he pulled her into the shower. He pressed her up against the wall while the hot water pelted them.

Only he could be that gorgeous with this long black hair plastered against his skin. Biting her lip, she brushed it back from his face and smiled as she remembered what he'd told her when he took the medicine to grow it. "Is this going to get in the way?"

He flashed that playful grin that made her stomach contract and a part of her throb. "Yeah, but you're worth the pain." He caressed her cheek with his, allowing his stubble to raise chills along her body.

She sucked her breath in sharply as she touched the scars on his back and the deeper one on his abdomen. His scrolling bird tattoo blended with them in a way that made her curious. "Did you get the tattoo to cover your scars?"

Caillen froze at an astute question no one had ever asked him before. He started to lie, but he didn't want a relationship with her that was built on that. "Yeah. I've always been self-conscious about them."

"Why?"

He brushed his hand down the worst one on his left side where it appeared someone had carved him open. "Women like perfect bodies and I've been around enough of them to know that the number and depth of scars I have can be a turnoff."

She ran her hand along the one he'd traced. "I don't mind it at all. It just proves you're insane."

The warmth in his eyes scorched her. "That I am."

Biting her lip, she saw the new scar that was forming where he'd been shot. And it made her wonder about the others. "How did you get them?"

"Shahara has always said that I can only learn by screwing up first. Each scar serves as a permanent reminder to me that that which doesn't kill you will just require many stitches."

Caillen tried to keep his tone light, but the truth was, he hated the damage he'd done to himself. The toll his stunts had taken on his body. But that being said, he didn't see even the faintest trace of disgust in her beautiful dark eyes.

A deep frown creased her brow as she touched the scar on his forehead. "I can't believe your sister hit you with a pry bar."

"You said I deserved it."

"I didn't mean it."

Those words warmed him as he kissed the tip of her nose and took her hand into his. With his gaze locked firmly on hers, he led her hand until she cupped him where he was most desperate to feel her touch.

Desideria held her breath as she allowed Caillen to show her how to stroke his body. She was amazed at how soft his skin was over the hardness. But what thrilled her most was the look in his eyes as she explored him. There was so much passion and desire. Such tenderness for her. He traced circles over breasts, teasing them until she feared she'd melt. No one had ever looked at her like he did—like he could devour her. It made her feel powerful and strong in a way nothing ever had.

His murmured sounds of pleasure filled her ears, making her even bolder with her caresses. She reached down and squeezed him tight.

He jumped back with a hiss. "Careful, love. Too hard and we'll both be disappointed."

She clenched her hand into a tight fist. "I'm sorry. I didn't mean to hurt you."

He kissed her hand before he led it back to his cock. "It's all right. You'll just have to rub the pain away. Kiss it and make it better."

"You're devious." She wrinkled her nose at him.

"Absolutely." Cupping her face, he kissed her again while she ran her hand down the length of his shaft. It was so strange to her that she was completely unbodyconscious. All her life, she'd been so careful to stay covered up so that her mother and sisters wouldn't belittle her. But with Caillen, she felt beautiful. He didn't seem to mind the fact that she was muscled and larger than other women. If anything, he enjoyed it.

In fact, he bathed her slowly, his hands sliding over and into her. Every stroke and caress made her tremble. It was like electricity ran through her body. And when he knelt down in front of her and replaced his hand with his mouth she cried out in pleasure. Her senses exploding, she buried her hand in his slick hair as he teased and tasted her.

Rational thought fled her mind. How could anything feel so incredible? In all her fantasies, she'd never considered this. All of a sudden, she felt her body explode into wave after wave of ecstasy. Her eyes widened as she cried out again.

Caillen held her close and continued to taste her until her body finally floated down to a semblance of sanity.

Her breathing still ragged, she stared at him in wonder. "What did you do to me?"

He nipped gently at her thigh. "That, my sweet, is an orgasm."

No wonder people risked death for it. She finally understood why people craved sex. It was incredible.

Caillen's eyes darkened as his expression turned serious as he stood up in front of her. He took her hand into his and lifted one of her legs to wrap around his hip.

Her body was still quivering and pulsing as he slid himself deep inside her. She sucked her breath in sharply at the foreign sensation of him filling her completely. A piercing pain overrode her pleasure for several seconds until he began stroking her with his hand. The pain fled as he pinned her against the wall and kissed her. She wrapped both of her legs around his lean waist, reveling in the sensation of him pressing against her while he filled her body.

"You feel so good," he breathed in her ear.

Her reply ended in a small gasp as he thrust against her hips. More pleasure rippled through her body as he rode her slow and easy. The intimacy of this moment stunned her in a way she'd have never imagined. She was naked with a man inside her. There was no one else in the universe but the two of them. Nothing but the sensation of them sharing their bodies while the hot water showered over them.

He dipped his head down to nibble her breast as he continued to thrust against her. She cupped his head to her as emotions confused her even more. She was now a woman in every sense of the word. And Caillen, a wanted fugitive, was her lover.

That one word whispered through her mind and for a moment she felt like she was outside of her body looking down on them as they stood in the small cubicle. Connected. Not just by a physical act, but by something much deeper. Much more profound.

Caillen buried his head against Desideria's neck as the hot water pelted his back. She raked her nails gently over his skin, raising chills the length of his body. Never in his life had he felt like this. He didn't know what it was about her that had slid past his defenses, but he'd let her into a place where only she could do him harm. It wasn't just that he was her first, there was something more.

The way she made him feel...Not like a loser or a player. She made him feel heroic.

How stupid was that?

She'll betray you. Sooner or later, everyone does. He didn't want to believe that. Not even for an instant. For the first time in his life, he could see past the possibility of a betrayal.

He could see...

A lifetime spent like this—lost in her arms.

Don't be stupid. You're both dead if you're caught. That was a big *if*. And right now, he wanted to make sure nothing happened to spoil this.

To hurt her.

She was the most important thing to him. And with that thought, he felt his body tilting over the edge. Throwing his head back, he let his orgasm take him to the highest level.

Desideria held him close, her breath tickling him as she tightened her legs around his waist. Yeah, he could definitely stay like this for eternity.

Two hours later, Caillen lay naked on the cold floor of the crew members' lounge listening to Desideria's quiet snore as she rested on top of his chest. He was every bit as exhausted as she was and for the first time in months he wasn't completely stressed out even though he should be. Her breath tickled his skin as he tried to plot through everything he'd have to do once they landed. He still had no idea how to get the evidence he needed to clear his name and find his father's killer.

Unless he found the assassin and could get that bastard to talk. That was much easier said than done. The most unfortunate thing—freelance assassins were more common than grains of sand on a beach. Finding any particular one...

That was more luck than skill.

And then there was the matter of Desideria.

The mere thought of her name made his heartbeat race. The scent of her hung heavy around him and all he wanted was to stay like this with her forever.

That fact terrified him. He didn't want to be attached to anyone. It brought too much drama and crap into his already screwed up life.

Yeah, but wouldn't it be great to have a relationship like Shahara's and Syn's? Like Nykyrian's and Kiara's?

He wanted to tell himself that he didn't care about that at all, but deep inside he knew the truth. He'd love to have a woman whose face would light up the way Desideria's did whenever she looked at him.

I wonder if she even knows she does it.

Could I really mean something to her? He was too used to women telling him he was worthless and a waste. Women who wanted to claw his eyes out over unintentional slights. Such as forgetting a birthday while his entire life fell apart.

To have one who might love him and be there when he needed her…

Stop acting like a woman, you moron. You have way too many other things to focus on right now and if you both get killed fat lot of good love will do you when you're dead.

True, very true.

My father's gone. That reality kept coming back to him and kicking him hard in the stomach. He hadn't known his real father any time at all really, but the man had come to mean a lot to him. He still couldn't believe he wouldn't see him again. Wouldn't hear the note of exasperation in his father's voice as he said the dreaded words "I've spoken to Bogimir."

Maybe he should have tried harder to be a prince. To make his father proud. The man had loved him, and in truth, he'd learned to love the old man himself.

I should have told him that.

Of all people, he knew how fleeting and fragile life was. Every time his father had told him he loved him, he'd seen the expectation in his father's eyes, waiting for Caillen to return the sentiment. And he never had.

I'm such an asshole.

Why hadn't he said it to his father? Just once? It would have made the man's day and cost him nothing. *I can't believe I didn't tell him.* Guilt and grief choked him. But there was nothing he could do to rectify it now.

It was too late.

Sighing, there were a lot of things in his life he regretted.

Except for being with Desideria.

Looking down at her on his bare chest, he smiled. Yeah, he'd never regret her.

"Hey, Cai?"

He frowned at Hauk's strained tone that echoed from the intercom. "Yeah?"

"We got a little situation up here. I think you need to come to the bridge. Fast."

"Why?"

It was Fain who answered. "Oh nothing really. We're just about to be attacked, that's all. Thought you might want to see the death blast coming before it turned us into a flaming ball of twisted metal."

19

Caillen was still pulling his jacket on as he rejoined Fain and Hauk on the small bridge. "What's going on?"

Hauk pointed to the monitor. "Look familiar?"

Caillen's jaw went slack as the computer brought up the image and schematics of a black fighter and enhanced it. It was one he'd become a little too acquainted with lately. "What the hell? How could he have followed us through a wormhole?"

Fain shrugged. "Well hell if I know. Why don't you go on out there and ask him? I'm sure he'll be willing to share. We could have a whole group therapy session and talk about all of our negative feelings and deepest-held secrets while we're at it too."

Hauk rolled his eyes at Fain's sarcasm. "Technology is ever evolving, my friend."

"Evolving my ass." Caillen switched to the ship's markings just to be sure. And yes, there was no denying the bastard's identity. It was the same assassin who'd been following them since the beginning. "This is ridiculous.

No one can trace through a wormhole. There's too much distortion."

Hauk shrugged. "Ridiculous or not, he's on our tail and our weapons are still down."

Caillen growled low in his throat as he motioned Hauk out of his seat so that he could take the controls from him. It was time he—

A blast of orange lit up the space in front of him. His blood pumping, he saw the new addition to their party. Small, sleek and blood red, the fighter shot past their nose so close he could feel the vapor trail. It flew in a familiar erratic pattern...

Fain headed for the guns to try and repair them.

Caillen stopped him as he had a gut suspicion about the pilot's identity. *Please let me be right.* If he was, this was a good thing.

Maybe.

God, don't have a long memory. Was it too much to ask for a small concussion to forget just that one little incident...? Opening a channel, he hailed the new fighter. "1-9-8-2-6 is that you, Aniwaya?"

When the answer came in, the deep baritone voice made him smile. If lethal ever had a proper name, it was Chayden Aniwaya. That rogue bastard was many things to many people. Assassin. Self-serving pirate. Thief. Brutal fighter when crossed. But to Caillen he was known by one simple thing.

Friend.

At least some days.

Please gods let this be one of those days.

"Dagan, you worthless bastard, what are you doing in my sector and in the company of an unauthorized fighter no less? Don't you know that's suicide here? You're lucky my boys haven't raked your basement."

"Bleeding mostly," Caillen said, answering his first question before he addressed the latter. "That UF you noted happens to be an unidentified assassin on our tail. Any chance of an assist?"

"Depends. You going to sleep with my girlfriend again while you're in my sector?"

Gah, so much for a concussion. Why did Aniwaya keep bringing *that* up? Make one little mistake and damned if you couldn't ever live it down. It was doubly annoying since Aniwaya basically agreed with him. Any woman who'd snake around when attached wasn't worth grieving over. "How many times do I have to tell you that I had no idea you two were together?"

"Until the day I actually believe your sorry hide."

Caillen scoffed. "Hey now, I only lie about my cargo, *never* my women."

"Sad thing, Dagan, I actually believe that." Chay broke off their conversation as he engaged the fighter.

"Hey, hey, hey," Caillen said in rapid succession as Chay went to the fight like he always did . . . with everything he had. "I don't want him dead. I'd like to haul him in for questioning if you can refrain from execution for a few."

"Lazy krikkin pacifists wanting to save the bunnies when they need to be skinned . . ." Chay grumbled under his breath before he called in for his fellow band of miscreants to help trap the assassin. "We'll let him live, but you owe me, Dagan."

"Bullshit. This is me claiming a debt *you* owe me."

Aniwaya let out an annoyed breath. "Fine . . . asshole."

Hauk arched a brow at Caillen as he closed the channel

between their ships to keep Aniwaya from hearing their conversation. "Who's our new friend?"

"One of the surliest pirate warlords in the business. Chayden Aniwaya." He jerked his chin toward Fain. "Do you know him?"

"Why would I?"

"You're both Tavali. I figured you might have run across him at some point in your travels." The Tavali were an interstellar organization of pirates who flew under one single banner—their symbol was the same one Fain had on the mask he normally wore. A mask that also marked him as Tavali. It was a warning to others that if you messed with one of them, you messed with them all. They might be liars, thieves and riffraff, but they were loyal to each other to the end. No matter who you were or where you came from, if you bore their mark, you were family and they would all fight to protect you whether they knew you or not.

Fain snorted. "In case you've had massive damage to your temporal lobe, there happens to be a lot of us. There's no way to know them all."

"Yeah I know. You breed like rodents."

Hauk cleared his throat to get Caillen's attention back on his inquisition. "His girlfriend? How did you get hooked up with her?"

That was a long story so he shortened it. "She went to school with Kasen back in the day."

"And you slept with her?"

Caillen let out a disgusted breath at his own rank stupidity. If he could only change that... "Four years ago and in my defense she was seriously hot—even you'd have slept with her." Hauk wasn't fond of human women as a rule. "Lethal harita forgot to tell me she was engaged to

Aniwaya who almost had both of my heads for it when he found out." Not that Caillen blamed him. He'd have been pissed too. But really, it wasn't his fault.

"How'd he find out?" Fain asked.

"She told him as soon as she crawled out of my bed. Apparently, I was a tool she wanted to use to strike at him and stupid me, I let her. She thought it'd be funny to betray him with a friend. Lucky me, huh?"

Hauk shook his head. "Yeah, some women will do it to you."

And Hauk would know. It was amazing he'd even go near a woman again after what had happened to him.

Then again, sex was one hell of a motivator and they were dumb enough to let it rule them…"Tell me about it." Caillen turned his attention back on the action outside.

Within seconds, Aniwaya and his band of pirates had the assassin routed and captured in a tractor beam. Damn, the renegade bastard made it look easy, but then when you had five people to move as a team it was a whole lot easier than when you only had yourself and one overemotional sister trying to do it. Aniwaya's team moved like they shared a single mind. They knew each other so well that half the time they finished each other's sentences.

It was the kind of team Caillen would kill for. Unfortunately, he'd never been able to find that many people who wouldn't knife him in the back as soon as he let his guard down. Aniwaya had a rare team and they all knew it.

Chayden opened the link between ships. "Where you want him?"

Dead, but that wasn't an option quite yet. "Sentella VII."

Aniwaya let out a scoffing laugh. "Uh…yeah. Negatory, Captain. We're not exactly welcomed there. So I think I'll keep my head and my distance away from those psychos."

Caillen was surprised by that. Usually the Sentella welcomed any pirate who preyed on the League and her allies which was what Chayden and his crew lived for. There was only one thing he could think of that would have them skittish of the Sentella. "Who'd you kill?"

"No one. We captured one of their extremely loaded and enticing supply ships a few months back and they've been a little cranky with us ever since." .

Yeah, that would do it. The Sentella didn't like to be victimized in any way. "Chay…"

"Don't give me no lip, Dagan. You'd have done it too if you'd seen what they carried and I can still shoot you down and no one would care."

Well, he was right about that at present. In fact, his enemies would reward him mightily for it.

Hauk took over the conversation. "For the record, *I* would care if you shot us down. And don't worry about going to the station. I'm one of the core Sentella members."

"Yeah, right. I've heard that before. How stupid do you think I am?"

Hauk passed an irritated look at Caillen.

Caillen held his hands up in surrender. "I don't control the pirate brigade. Chay's a paranoid sonofabitch—and deservedly so given the people out to slay him—so don't cut those freaky eyes at me, looking for help with him. I got nothing useful."

Sighing, Hauk opened the channel. "On my honor, the soul of Akuma, no harm will come to you or those who fly under your banner."

Aniwaya's voice dripped with suspicion and ridicule. "You telling me you're the infamous Akuma wanted by the League and all the United Systems combined? Flying in that hunk of shit with a lowlife like Dagan? Boy, find another gullible fool. This one isn't taking."

Hauk growled in the back of his throat as frustration must have strangled him. Not that Caillen could fault Aniwaya for his skepticism.

Akuma meant demon. Each one of the five founding members of the Sentella had an alias they used to protect their identities and to keep their families safe from the wrath of the League and her allies.

Nykyrian was known as Nemesis or vengeance. Darling went by Kere or death. Jayne was Shinikuri, the spirit of death, and Hauk had chosen Akuma.

Because all of his family was dead, Syn had refused a moniker claiming he didn't care if they hunted him down and killed him. But now in order to protect Caillen's sister, he went by Shinikami—death wolf.

But only a tiny handful of people knew those names and who they belonged to. Divulging their real identities wasn't something any of the Sentella did lightly which was why Chayden was crying foul. Caillen only knew them because he didn't believe in betrayal in any way and they trusted him implicitly.

When Hauk spoke, his tone was that deadly tight one that effectively conveyed his ire. "Trust me, pirate. No unauthorized being would ever dare use my name." He glared at Caillen who'd actually done that on the colony— oops. Good thing the Andarion loved him or they'd be locked in a death match over it.

"Sanctum Sentella, Aniwaya. On that you have my

word and that is sacred." With those two phrases, Hauk offered Aniwaya safe passage.

Aniwaya hesitated before he responded. "Thanks, Akuma. I'm trusting you with the safety of my men. If you back out on your word, take my life, not theirs."

Hauk arched a brow at Caillen. "You're right. He's not real trusting is he?"

"He's Tavali," Fain said. "We're no more trusting than the Sentella is. The price on our heads is every bit as staggering as yours and like you guys we tend to make more enemies than friends."

Hauk nodded. "I get it."

And that was why Caillen flew unfettered. While there was some safety that came from being aligned to a specific group such as the Tavali or Sentella, there was also a lot of crap and internal politics that could easily drag a smuggler or pirate into a mess faster than sleeping with an aristos's wife. As a free agent, he could be "friend" to anyone without politics intervening.

The bridge door pulsed open.

Desideria finally rejoined them—wearing Caillen's one clean shirt that he'd left out for her. For some reason he couldn't name, he liked seeing her in it even though it swallowed her whole. It sent a strange surge of possessiveness through him.

Yeah, she could definitely borrow his shirts anytime she wanted and he hoped her scent stayed in the fabric . . .

Pausing by his chair, she yawned. "What's going on? I heard a strange voice over the intercom, but I couldn't understand what you were saying."

Hauk grumbled a humorless laugh. "Nothing much. You just missed another near-death experience."

Her eyes widened. "Excuse me?"

Fain indicated Caillen with a jerk of his chin. "Luckily your boy knows people who carry a lot of guns. As long as he doesn't sleep with anyone's girlfriend again, we should be fine."

Oh yeah, if they could freeze the smoldering look on her face as she glared at him, it could be sold as a lethal weapon on the black market and make them all rich. "Pardon?"

Caillen let out an annoyed breath. "Fain has a mental disorder that causes him to spout random stupidity for no apparent reason. It's been a source of constant embarrassment for his brother since they were kids. Ignore him."

Fain snorted in response. "I'll remember that next time you need help, food."

"Good thing I have Hauk's number on speed dial then, huh, pun'kin?"

Hauk laughed.

Fain appeared to want to say something, but then seemed to change his mind.

Good, he was learning . . .

Desideria took a seat beside Caillen as they handled the landing. True to their words, she saw the familiar black fighter that appeared to be held by a brigade of pirates. "Are those what I think they are?"

Caillen winked at her. "Aye, Princess. They be pirates indeed."

"And I take it they're on our side."

"Yes."

Okay . . . She didn't understand it, but if the men were good with it, who was she to argue?

How long did I sleep? Obviously, she'd missed something important. Turning her thoughts back to the renegade at hand, she watched Caillen with a new awareness of him. It wasn't just that his scent was branded into her memory or the way his eyes lit up with that childlike spirit. She felt connected to him in a way she'd never been connected to anyone.

What was it about him that had made her love him when she'd never loved anyone else? Of all the men in all the universe, why Caillen Dagan?

It didn't make sense and yet she knew she'd die to keep him safe. What a shocking realization. She'd never really thought to feel this way about anyone and she knew her mother had never loved her consorts. Not like this. Yes, she was fond of them, but when Desideria's father had died, her mother hadn't even reacted. She'd taken the news with the same degree of stoicism as she did the morning news from her advisors. Cold. Calculating. Distant.

If something were to happen to Caillen, she had no doubt it would devastate her entire being. The mere thought of losing him was enough to drive her to her knees.

A swell of emotions she couldn't even identify choked her.

I love you.

Three simple words that seemed so inadequate for what she felt for him. How could anyone convey so much emotion with mere words? And yet she knew they could never be together. Especially not if they cleared their names. He was the prince and heir of his empire and she was the heiress to hers.

Their countries and politics would never allow them to unite. Two rulers couldn't marry. It was a conflict of interest. One of them would have to step down and she knew it couldn't be her. There was no one else to take her mother's place. Gwen would never be able to handle the responsibility.

And Caillen wasn't the kind of man who would willingly subjugate himself to the role he'd have to play on her world. Nor could she ask that of him.

Maybe he could beat me...

The truth was, she didn't want to fight him for it. The thought of taking arms against him and bruising him...

She couldn't do it.

There was no future for them. None. That reality cut through her as she realized just how hopeless all of this was. It wasn't fair. No matter what, she would lose him.

Caillen turned in his seat to flash that familiar devilish grin at her. "You all right back there? You're being awfully quiet."

Fain snorted. "It's okay to admit you're sick from his lack of skill at the helm. No one here would think less of you for it."

Caillen shot Fain a lethal glare. "You're just jealous I'm a better pilot than you are."

"Yeah, that's so it. I live in fear of the comparison." The dryness of that tone would rival a dust bowl.

Desideria smiled at their banter as she tried not to think about the fact that she'd have to leave him soon. "I'm fine, and Caillen is a fabulous pilot."

All three of the men appeared shocked by her compliment. Honestly, it shocked her too. Since she'd grown up with nothing but criticism, any kind of compliment was hard for her to give to someone else. Yet she couldn't help it. She wanted Caillen to feel good.

Girl, don't feed that *ego. The gods know, it's the last thing you should do.*

Yeah, okay, that was probably true.

Heat stung her cheeks as Caillen carefully guided them into a well-secured space station. A calm, smooth approach that was a nice change from their frenetic launch.

As they entered the bay and continued forward, guided by a tractor beam, Desideria's eyes widened at the impressive display of artillery that followed them all the way to the landing pad. If there was any doubt about how serious the occupants were when it came to their safety, the red targeting dots put it away. If those cannons went off, there would be no escape.

She let out a low whistle. "Wow, they're not playing around with that, are they?"

Hauk shook his head. "The Sentella can't afford to. The League has too big a price on the head of anyone associated with them. You put one of us down, we're taking you with us."

Obviously.

Hauk took over the communications from Caillen as the controller gave him explicit orders to safety lock all of his weaponry. "This is XN-8-2-1 requesting clearance."

There was a moment's hesitation. "Voice analysis match. Welcome, drey," said the smooth computer voice.

Drey? That word confused her as she moved to stand closer to Hauk. "What does drey mean?"

"Brother," they answered in unison.

"What language?"

Hauk's fangs flashed as he spoke. "Syn's. It's a corruption of Ritadarion and Andarion."

Syn...Caillen's handsome brother-in-law she'd seen in his vidframe. Desideria tucked that knowledge away as

Caillen ordered her to strap herself in. She quickly took a seat and did as he asked.

Caillen made a smooth landing on the back pad while the pirates and fighter followed suit nearby.

It only took a few minutes to lock the ship down and open the hatch. Before Caillen could do more than unbuckle himself from his chair and stand, three women ran on board and practically tackled him to the ground. Desideria would have been jealous had she not recognized them as his sisters.

They each took turns scolding and adoring him in a variety of pitches. Their words came so fast and furious that it actually made her dizzy trying to follow them.

"How could you be so reckless?"

"Have you any idea how much trouble you're in?"

"What brain were you attempting to use?"

"How dare you put us through this, you selfish little worm."

"We've been so worried about you!"

"Thank the gods you're all right."

"When was the last time you ate? You look thinner."

"What happened to your face? Do you need a doctor?"

"I swear, you're such an idiot! How do you get yourself into these things?"

A loud whistle split the air and silenced them.

Desideria cringed at the shrillness and plugged her ears. She looked to the source to find the infamous Syn. Dressed all in black, he was dark and deadly. His long black hair was secured with a band at the nape of his neck. With at least a day's growth of whiskers, his face was roguishly handsome and finely boned. Those black eyes took in every detail of the situation with an eerie astuteness that only Caillen's could rival. One corner of his long coat was pulled back, out of the way of his holstered blaster so that he could get to it if he had to.

But there was no need. A person would have to be an absolute imbecile to confront someone with an aura this lethal. Syn's sternness made her appreciate the fact that Caillen's fierce aura was tempered by his humor and good nature. It would have to be hard to live with someone as grim as Syn.

He strode forward with a predator's lope as his gaze went to each of Caillen's sisters in turn. "Dagan women, down. The poor man can't even breathe with all of you stifling him so badly."

Kasen curled her lip as she raked Syn with a less than kind smirk. Oh yeah, Caillen was right. His sister was insane to confront Syn with anything except devout respect. "The imbecile's lucky I'm not choking the breath out of him right now."

Caillen snorted. "Love you too, sis."

Kasen sneered at him. "Don't you dare get lippy with me after the week you've put us through, you little worm."

Desideria's temper flared at the insults and the way Kasen treated him. How dare she! Especially given all the messes she'd gotten Caillen into over the years ... such as the stunt that had almost resulted in his execution.

Before she realized what she was doing, she stepped forward to confront her. "Excuse me, but in case you haven't noticed this really isn't about you, cupcake. For all the misery you think you've suffered, I assure you it pales in comparison to what we've been through over the last few days. So before you continue to jump on him, you might want to steer down and step back. In the mood I'm in right now, I *will* do damage and unlike your brother, I don't mind hitting women. Live for it, point of fact."

Shahara gaped, her expression astonished, then she laughed as Tessa and Kasen glared at her for it. "Oh, Cai, I *really* like her. You done good, little brother."

Kasen's nostrils flared before she started toward Desideria.

Caillen caught her by the arm and held her back. "Girl, don't even. Trust me when I say the little dumpling can take you down. Remember, it's not the size of the dog in the fight, it's the size of the fight in the dog and Desideria has more fire in her than any I've encountered. She *will* hurt you."

The light in Kasen's eyes said she was willing to test them both.

"Kase," Shahara said with a sharp, commanding note. "Be nice for once. It's not often we find a woman who can tolerate your brother, never mind actually defend him."

Hatred flared deep in Kasen's eyes as she shrugged off Caillen's grip. "Fine. Whatever. She's just a passing fancy for him anyway. Just like all the others. I'll be here long after she's gone and he's moved on to his next lay."

Those words viciously slapped her and brought home the fact that Caillen, for all his tenderness with her, was nothing except a player who changed women more often than she changed her mind. Oh yeah, that reality slammed into her and burned.

Caillen felt his own temper rise at Kasen's cruelty. "You need to shut up. Fast. I've about had it with you."

She shoved him back, then invaded his personal space, daring him with her smug expression to hit her. "What are you going to do?"

He wanted to punch her. Hard. But she was right.

Other than shooting her to protect her from the authorities, he hadn't laid a hand on any of his sisters since his adoptive father had died.

Before anyone could react or he even realized her intent, Desideria pulled Kasen back and slugged her, then flew into a round of what he assumed must be heavy Qillaq insults. Unfortunately or perhaps fortunately, his Qillaq wasn't fluent enough to know them.

Kasen moved in to retaliate.

Caillen scooped Desideria up in his arms and physically removed her from harm's way at the same time Shahara blocked Kasen's path. While he had no doubt Desideria could take his sister, Kasen was by no means unskilled and she not only outweighed, but out-towered Desideria by a full head's height. Last thing he wanted was a knock-down, drag-out bloodbath between the two of them.

"Put me down!" Desideria growled between her clenched teeth.

"Nah, I don't think that's a good idea. Both of you need a time-out."

She glared at him. "You're not funny."

"Really not trying to be at the moment. Just trying to protect two women I care about from a mutual ass beating."

Desideria froze as those words broke through her anger and calmed her substantially. She stopped fighting his hold. "You care about me?"

Caillen felt as if all the air had been sucked completely out of the shuttle as every eye turned to him and a silence fell so loud that it was deafening. Yeah, he was like a Gondarion antler beast stuck under a microscope for some kind of genetic mutation.

Tell her yes. You care about her.

Yes, asshole, yes.

He knew it was the wise thing to do.

The *honest* thing to do.

But everyone from Syn to Fain to Hauk and his sisters were watching. Not the ideal place to make a first declaration of affection. Those were for private time between a man and a woman.

His vocal cords seized up so that all he could get out was a very weak "Um…"

That had the same effect as setting fire to a foul mood feline. Desideria literally jumped out of his arms and turned loose more Qillaq that was probably questioning not only his paternal status, but his species and manhood. Even though she'd never been here before and had no idea where anything was, she stormed off the shuttle.

Caillen let out an audible groan as his stomach tightened enough to form a diamond. *I'm so screwed.*

Putting her hands on her hips, Shahara sighed heavily and rolled her eyes so far back in her head it was a miracle they didn't stay there. "I swear I raised you smarter than this." She looked helplessly at Syn. "I swear I did."

Hauk slapped Fain in the stomach. "Gah and I thought *you* were inept with female feelings." He shook his head at Caillen. "Damn, boy, you might as well have told her those pants made her ass look fat."

He was right and Caillen felt like crap over what he'd done. There was only one thing to do…

Desideria stalked through the hangar as her temper boiled. She wanted to beat Caillen until he bled. She wanted…

"You all right?"

That had to be the deepest male voice and the most exotic accent she'd ever heard before. She paused to turn and see a man so perfectly formed he'd rival Caillen in looks. With a mask similar to Fain's pulled down to cover his Adam's apple, he wore his dark brown hair cut short, but long enough to form a beautiful mess of curls around his face. With hazel brown eyes that were tinged with a haunting ferocity, he was devastating. At the same time, there was something eerily familiar about him. Yet she'd never seen him before.

"Who are you?"

A set of perfect dimples flashed in his cheeks as he answered. "Chayden Aniwaya."

Her gaze fell to the patch on his black flight jacket that matched the symbol Fain had on his mask. In the back of her mind, she was trying to think of how she knew this man and why he seemed to be a familiar stranger.

Before she could ask him about it, Caillen came running up behind her.

And with that, her anger overrode everything else. "I'm not speaking to you."

Caillen let out a tired sigh while Chayden laughed.

"Damn, Dagan, what is it with you and women?"

"Don't ask. In the mood I'm in, I might actually tell you."

Chayden shook his head as he laughed again. "As an FYI, we surrendered the assassin to the Sentella who took him to a holding room for you when you're ready. But I should warn you . . . getting any information is going to be damn near impossible."

He figured as much. Bad thing about assassins, even paid ones, they seldom gave info or intel, even under torture. But Caillen had a way for getting what he wanted. "Did you check for a suicide cap?"

There was no missing the offended expression on Chayden's face. "Do I look like an infant?"

"You're still a little wet behind the ears."

Desideria waited for the pirate to slug Caillen for that. The expression on his face said he really wanted to.

Instead, Chayden's verbal response was in a language she couldn't understand, but she was pretty sure it was an insult even though Caillen grinned in response.

"So are you heading out now?" Caillen asked him.

Chayden's gaze went to her and something strange flickered in the depths of his eyes.

What was that look? He was hiding something, but she didn't know what. "I sent my men on before the Sentella changed their mind and decided to arrest them. But I think I'll hang around for a bit."

A tic started in Caillen's jaw as he looked at her, then locked a glare on Chayden. "You're not planning on a payback, are you?"

Chayden held his hands up in surrender. "Absolutely not. I promise you."

Desideria wasn't sure what their vague conversation was about, but she had a bad suspicion that she was the subject at hand and that Chayden might have just insulted her. Great. That was all she needed to feel worse.

Chayden gestured over his shoulder with his thumb. "I'm going to go find the head. I'll catch you two later. Buzz me when you interrogate the assassin."

Desideria watched him leave. Still that nagging sensation was there. She knew him from somewhere. "Is he famous?"

"Only if you travel with a lot of outlaws or hound the bounty posts. He's extremely notorious there. But all in all, he keeps a low profile. Why?"

"There's something about him that's so familiar... I can't place it. It's like I know him somehow." Her gaze sharpened as she pierced him with a malevolent glare. "And I'm still not speaking to you."

Caillen squelched his smile before he made her any angrier. He adored the fact that she was incapable of giving someone the cold shoulder. Unlike Kasen who could freeze a star. "I wanted to apologize about what happened."

She held her hand up in a sharp gesture. "Oh don't even go there. I'm done. Okay? I didn't expect you to like me. That's fine. But did you have to embarrass me in front of everyone?" It was something her mother or sisters would have done and she was tired of being publicly humiliated and ridiculed. She'd expected better from him and the fact that he'd disappointed her cut so deep that she couldn't stand it. "Especially after—"

He interrupted her words with a fierce kiss.

She kneed him in the groin. Not hard, but enough to make him pull back and cup himself. "Next time, I won't be so gentle."

Caillen cursed under his breath as she stalked away. "You don't know where you're going," he called after her, wanting her to come back so that he could explain.

She didn't even pause her gait. "Don't care."

I told you what to say. Did you listen? No. Idiot. Why couldn't you say you cared about her?

Because it would have been an admission of weakness.

No, that wasn't the truth and he knew it. He wasn't

ready to be with one woman forever. Especially not someone so hardheaded and irritating.

And yet as he watched her head out of his sight, all he could remember was how good she'd felt in his arms. How much he wanted to go to her right now, strip her naked and make her beg him for mercy.

He took a step toward her, intending to apologize.

One heartbeat later, an explosion ripped through the bay. The force of the blast literally picked him up and slammed him into the wall. Pain tore through his entire being as he looked down and saw the nasty piece of twisted shrapnel embedded in his thigh. He tried to pull it out, but the gushing blood made it too slippery.

Chaos erupted as techs and Sentella members rushed to put out the fire and prepare for the possibility that there might be another blast coming.

Caillen didn't care about that. No more than he cared about his injuries. He had to find Desideria and make sure she was all right. *That* was his only concern.

But as he tried to walk forward to find her through the flames, something hit him from behind. His legs went numb. His vision dimmed.

An instant later, everything turned black.

20

Desideria saw Caillen go down. Everything moved in slow motion as her world came to an end. He hit the wall with such force, there was no way he could live through it.

None.

Unable to breathe, she ran for him with everything she had while images of his death tore through her. *Don't you dare die. Don't you dare.*

She couldn't stand the thought of it. Not after they'd fought.

Why had she fought with him?

Suddenly, nothing mattered to her. Not her mother's death. Not her standing.

Nothing.

All of that paled in comparison to losing him. She slowed as she drew near. Caillen lay on the ground, covered in blood, completely unmoving. This wasn't like he'd been on the outpost. His features were so pale...

Tears blinded her.

Qillaqs don't cry. Yet, she couldn't stop herself.

"Caillen?" She sobbed, falling to her knees. She pulled him into her arms and held him close. "Don't you leave me." Not after he'd taught her to depend on him. Not after he'd made her want something she knew she couldn't have.

"Caillen, please open your eyes."

He didn't.

"Desideria?"

She heard his sister's voice, but didn't respond. She couldn't. Images of Caillen's teasing smile haunted her. The way he'd felt when he made love to her earlier. The sound of his voice.

I need you. Please, please don't die. Not like this. Not with the last words I said to you…

Shahara pulled her back. "You have to let him go."

She started to argue until she saw the medics. Her entire body quaking in fear, she released him to their care. Syn and Shahara were saying something to her, but she couldn't understand them. Not through the painful haze that shredded everything.

"We'll meet you at the hospital."

She inclined her head to them, knowing that wasn't where she was headed.

First, she had someone to kill.

Caillen came awake to the sound of whispering voices nearby. He opened his eyes to find himself lying on a sterile hospital bed, hooked to monitors in a small room. It took a full minute before he remembered everything that had happened.

The explosion. His leg.

Desideria!

She'd been ahead of him. Right in the line of fire...

Fear seized his heart as he sat up and started to leave the bed to find her.

Shahara stepped out of the shadows to catch him. She refused to allow him to put his feet on the floor. "Don't you dare." She hadn't used that tone with him in a long time.

A tic started in his jaw as he locked gazes with his tiny sister. If she honestly thought she could keep him here, she'd need a lot more backup than Syn who stood behind her. "Where's Desideria?"

She exchanged a nervous glance with Syn over her shoulder that did nothing to help his terror. Oh God... Desideria was hurt.

Maybe dead. Why else wouldn't she answer the question?

Unimaginable pain slammed into him as he struggled to breathe. Their last words had been a fight. Of all people, he knew better than to let someone leave angry.

Why hadn't I been faster?

Why hadn't he apologized?

"Where is she?" he demanded.

Shahara cringed.

He felt tears sting his eyes as unimaginable grief tore through him. How could he have failed to protect her? How? "She's dead, isn't she?"

All the color drained from her face before her cheeks turned bright red. "Good Lord, child, no! I swear you get the most bizarre ideas sometimes."

Relief poured through him. Desideria was alive. He could finally breathe again.

At least a little bit. "Then where is she?"

Syn grinned evilly as he moved closer. "Locked up at present."

Caillen scowled in confusion. "What? How? Why?"

Syn let out a low laugh. "You remember the explosion?"

How could he forget it? His ears were still ringing.

Caillen sat back on the bed as he tried to figure out how that related to Desideria being locked up. Surely they didn't think she had any part in the explosion...

Did they?

"Of course I do. Was she caught in the blast?"

Syn shook his head. "No. She was clear, but she ran back to you when you hit the wall."

"She was hysterical," Shahara interjected. "And worried sick about you. Just like us. She barely beat us to you and she threatened our lives if *we* hurt you."

Syn snorted. "Yeah, she was impressive in her rage and she didn't budge from protecting you until the medtechs arrived. Once you were stabilized and ready for transport, we thought she'd follow us to the med center. She didn't."

Caillen's frown deepened. "Where'd she go?"

Shahara let out an annoyed breath. "Your little bunny headed over to lockup, forced her way in and then damn near killed the assassin who's been following you."

That didn't make sense to him. "Why would she do that?"

Shahara picked at the lint on his hospital gown before she smoothed over a wrinkle. "He was the one who'd set a trap on his ship that the techsperts accidentally set off while trying to see if the ship was wired to detonate. Since you were hurt by the blast, she wanted his head in the worst sort of way."

"And she got it too," Syn said with a hint of laughter

in his voice. "Damn, boy, I thought your sister had a temper on her. I do believe you've found the only woman alive with one worse than—hey!" he snapped as Shahara popped him on the stomach. Grimacing, he rubbed the area where she'd hit him. "See what I mean? She's brutal to live with."

"Anyway," Shahara continued after she passed one last malevolent glare at Syn, "she got information out of the assassin, but not before she almost killed him during the interrogation. And she wasn't beating him for answers. I swear, she hit him twice as hard when he answered her correctly as she did when he didn't. I take it the Qills don't instruct their people on the fine art of interviewing prisoners."

Syn laughed again. "Yeah, it looked like she went to the School of Nykyrian for that."

Caillen wasn't sure if he should be amused or appalled by what they described. In the end, he was flattered that he meant enough to Desideria that she'd come back to check on him and then had decided he was worth breaking someone's ass over. On the other hand, he definitely didn't want her questioning *him*. Especially after their fight. "And you locked her up?"

Syn shrugged. "Had no choice. She was planning on heading to Exeter to beat the crap out of your uncle's advisor. We thought it best to confine her until her sanity returned... or they died of natural causes. Whichever comes first."

Caillen shook his head. "Good call. So what did she find out?"

Shahara's gaze turned grim and deadly. "The assassin was hired by your uncle's primary advisor to kill you and your father. Then after you escaped, he was to make sure you didn't return alive."

He winced at the confirmation of his worst suspicions. "So it's true. Talian purchased the contract on my father's life."

She nodded. "That's what it looks like."

"What about Desideria's mother?"

Syn passed a sympathetic glance to Shahara. "He claims he knows nothing about that at all. He was only after you and your father."

But that didn't go with what Caillen had heard... "The two are tied together. I know they are."

Syn continued to contradict him. "I've searched through every League database and every contract server I could find." Which was impressive since information was what Syn excelled at. "Nothing has the two related. I think it's just damn bad luck that the two of them were together at the time they died."

Maybe Syn was right. Coincidences happened, but...

Something just didn't seem right. It was too pat and too ironic. Caillen refused to believe that it was all happenstance.

He glanced to Shahara. "Can I get up now?"

"You're not supposed to, but there's really no way to stop you, is there?"

"Depends on how much fire power you're carrying."

She rolled her eyes. "I worry about you, Cai. All the time. But you know, I saw the look in your eyes just now when you thought Desideria was dead and I saw how insane she went when you were hurt and the anger she broke on the one who'd harmed you. I don't know what's between the two of you, but from the outside it looks pretty real and pretty fierce. I just want you to always remember that feeling you had a minute ago whenever you think of her. That desperate choking sensation you had when you thought you'd never see her again and that she was gone forever."

She cut Syn a gimlet stare. "Relationships aren't easy. Some days they don't even seem tolerable. Especially when a Dagan's involved. There will be times when she'll make you mad enough to murder her and it's usually over something truly stupid."

"Like leaving the seat up at night or forgetting to tighten the cap on bottled water," Syn muttered.

Shahara ignored him. "But don't ever let yourself forget that the person you care about fills an emptiness no one else ever has and that while life with them can seriously suck at times, those moments when it doesn't are worth all the aggravation of falling into the toilet and getting soaked when you're half asleep."

"What about the water?" Syn asked hopefully.

Shahara glared at him. "You ruined my computer and lost my data. Don't even go there, Syn. I'm still mad enough to choke you for that one."

"I bought you a new one and I got most of the data restored . . . just a few things I couldn't salvage." Now that was a new tone from Syn that Caillen had never heard before. Petulant like a kid, it would have amused Caillen except he'd lived with his sister enough to feel pity for Syn for having incurred her wrath.

She flung her hand up to silence him.

Caillen laughed. "You two have a twisted marriage."

"And I'm grateful every minute of my life for it and for Syn." There was no mistaking the conviction in her golden eyes. "I couldn't live without him."

And he knew she was right, especially given their pasts. The ghosts that lived inside the best of childhoods could be fierce to fight. The demons that stalked them from theirs...

Those were debilitating.

To have someone who would brave those demons and stand beside him was a miracle he wouldn't forget.

Shahara stood back so that he could leave the bed.

As he reached the door, Syn's voice gave him pause. "Just FYI, bud, you might want to put on some pants before you go see her. Hard to sweep a woman off her feet and look badass in a hospital gown when your bare ass is hanging out."

Caillen slowed his steps as he neared the holding cell where they'd locked up Desideria. Hauk, Fain and Chayden sat in front of the monitors, watching as she paced back and forth in her room like a caged predator.

Chayden laughed nervously. "You know, one of you is going to have to let her out of there eventually."

Fain scoffed. "For the record, it ain't going to be me. My parents killed the dumb ones."

"Yeah, well, you don't see stupid stapled on my forehead either. I think *you* should do it." Hauk gave his brother a pointed stare.

Fain's expression was one of abject horror. "Why?"

"You didn't put her in there. She might still like you." He gestured to himself and Chayden. "Dumbass there is the one who threw her in head first and I'm the idiot who locked the door."

Caillen's eyes widened as a wave of anger went through him. "What did you do?" If they'd manhandled her, he was going to make them limp their way to old age.

Chayden stood up and braced himself as if expecting a fight. "I didn't do nothing. I just picked her up and carried her inside over my shoulder before the Sentella sentries tackled and cuffed her. Believe me, I saved her that horror. And by the way, I do not envy you that relationship. She is hell in high heels and she fights like an eight-armed Prostig."

That wasn't good enough for him. "You better not have hurt her."

"Relax." Chayden gestured toward the cell. "Go see for yourself. She's pissed, but fine and unbruised."

"Yeah," Hauk added. "And let her out of there while you're at it. I like having my balls attached to my body so I don't intend to go near her for a while. At least a century or two. Maybe five...dozen."

Caillen disregarded Hauk as he headed for the door. Maybe he should guard his boys too...

With his little Qill, one could never be too careful.

As soon as he entered the tiny bare, steel-walled room, Desideria spun around and by the look on her face he fully expected a kick to the groin like Hauk had feared. But the moment her gaze focused on his face and she realized it was him, a beautiful smile curved her lips and added fire to her eyes.

Two heartbeats later, she ran to him so fast that he staggered back from her assault. She kissed him desperately.

The taste of her combined with the sweet scent of her hair and breath drove all thoughts out of his mind for several seconds as his body roared to life and craved her so badly that it was all he could do to remember they were being watched. Even so, he couldn't focus on anything other than how good she felt in his arms.

She pulled back to stare up at him with a look of such concern that it made his stomach clench. Now this was something he could definitely get used to. "Are you all right?" There was a note of desperation in her voice.

"Am I not supposed to be?" he teased her.

She cupped his face in her hands. "Not the way you hit that wall. I've never seen anything more terrifying. I thought I'd lost you."

"Just damaged my leg. Probably rattled my brains. It hurts, but I'll limp. As for the brains...never used them enough to miss them anyway."

Letting out a frustrated breath, she shook her head at him. "I swear I'm wrapping you in a padded, blaster-proof suit and locking you inside a shielded bomb shelter."

He didn't know why, but that threat made him smile. Gods, how glad he was to see her alive and well. He kissed the tip of her nose. "Am I forgiven then?"

"For what?"

He started to remind her of the "um" mistake, but luckily his errant common sense finally tackled him to the ground and told him to shut his mouth before he ruined this moment. He quickly searched for something a little more intelligent to say.

"For scaring you."

She fisted her hands in his shirt and pulled his head down to hers. "No. Don't ever do that to me again."

He smiled at her angry tone. "I heard you put a major ass whipping on our assassin friend."

"He'll be feeling it for a while. I would have ripped his heart out had Fain not stopped me."

"Why?"

Desideria barely caught the answer before it rushed past her lips. Maybe she should tell him she loved him. But fear of his reaction kept those words locked tight. He might be happy about it or it could make him run for the door. Caillen was a complicated man and this was definitely not the time or place.

Especially after his "um" comment earlier. He might think she'd forgotten about it, but she hadn't. At the end of the day, he was a player and what little she knew about such people was that they were phobic when it came to any kind of commitment or emotions.

Never be the first to lay your heart on the table...

First man in was always slaughtered at the door and she didn't want to be hurt or rejected.

She cleared her throat before she answered. "He had information and I needed it."

There was a light in those beautiful dark eyes that said Caillen didn't believe her. But at least he didn't call her on the lie.

This time.

Instead, he gave her that cocky grin. "Shall we go see an advisor then and give him a concussion or two?"

She laughed at his overexuberant tone. "Absolutely." She gestured with her thumb toward the surveillance camera that was mounted high on the wall over her head. "Provided the crew of lackwits allow us to leave that is."

"I heard that," Hauk said over the intercom. "Didn't anyone ever tell you to be respectful of the man who holds the key to the lock on your cage?"

She scoffed. "Qillaq, Hauk. I was taught to kick him in the groin or the teeth until he handed it over."

Caillen laughed as the door lock buzzed open.

Fain and Chayden were waiting for them just outside the door. "By the way, we're going with you."

What the ... ?

Those words seriously offended his ego. Mostly because it was something his sisters would say and he was not helpless by any means. "I don't need help."

Hauk scoffed as he joined them. "Yeah right. Every time we leave the two of you alone something bad happens. You get lost or blown up or some other shit. I'm tired of cleaning up the bloodstains. So we're taking up a post at your back."

"Great," Fain muttered. "Now the blood will splatter us."

Caillen would argue with Hauk, but he knew better. Hauk was as stubborn and crazy as they came. Any attempt to discuss this would only delay them.

Not to mention the small fact that Hauk happened to be right. Things hadn't exactly gone right since he'd met Desideria. Another pair of blasters, or in this case, three, might come in handy.

"Fine. Your funerals."

Chayden snorted. "Not so loud. The gods might oblige." He led the way down the hallway.

In no time, they were rounded up in Chayden's ship and headed for Exeter to make an unannounced meeting with Talian's head advisor. If ever there was hope of getting to the bottom of this, the advisor should be able to give testimony about who'd ordered him to hire the assassin and why Caillen and his father had been targeted. That would be enough to get the League involved and allow Caillen to clear his name.

Yeah, payback was coming and it was going to be bloody.

Caillen left everyone on the bridge and went to the head so that he could check the wound on his leg. He could feel it bleeding again, but he didn't want the others to know. Better to camouflage it now before it became obvious.

As soon as he was finished and had left the room, he met Desideria in the hallway. Concern lined her brow as she scanned his body with an interest that made him go instantly hard. An image of her naked flashed through his mind and did nothing to help his sanity.

Yeah, that sucked the pain right out of him.

She paused her gaze on his thigh as if she somehow knew what he'd been about. "How's your leg holding up?"

Currently better than his groin...

But he didn't want her to worry about him. "It's throbbing, but I'll live."

She appeared less than convinced. "How do you manage your pain so well?"

"I focus on other things."

"Such as?"

He dipped his gaze to her breasts that he was dying to sample again.

Heat stung her cheeks. "You're awful."

Like he regretted telling her the truth. "You're the one who asked."

She growled at him in the back of her throat. "Why is it I don't think it's quite so simple?

Shrugging, he decided to give her a reprieve from his lecherous tendencies. "Because it's not. You want the truth?"

"Always."

Caillen swallowed as old memories haunted him.

He wasn't much into sharing with anyone, but for some reason he never minded allowing Desideria inside him. Not even something as personal as the unspoken past that always hovered right on the edges of his conscious thought. "What keeps me going is this image I have in my head of my adoptive father dying alone in the gutter. I was there that day, hiding and watching him through a small crack as his enemy rolled him over and ended his life with one cold, brutal shot. It was the second worst day of my life." Shahara's rape had the designation of being in first place.

Desideria choked on the sympathetic grief that swelled up inside her. She heard the pain in his voice as he spoke of something she knew had to give him nightmares to this day. "Caillen, I'm so sorry. Why were you there?"

There was no missing the agony and torment in his eyes as he looked down at the ground. "It was Kasen's birthday and my father had sold his wedding ring so that we could buy her something special since she'd been really sick that year. We'd just picked up her present when my father noticed we were being followed. I'd never in my life seen him afraid until then. He forced me to rush ahead and then he ordered me to run home. I hid instead, thinking...I don't even remember. I was too terrified to think straight. But what haunts me every night when I close my eyes is the image of my father on the street, bleeding and hurt. The sound of the final blast that killed him and the faces of the people who did that to him. I wish to the gods, just once, to be able to give to them what they gave to him."

She wished he could too. It was what they deserved. "Maybe you will one day."

He shook his head. "No. Even if I kill them, nothing will ever make amends for me staying there in that hole, scared and traumatized, and then having to tell my sisters that we were orphans."

She covered his hand with hers. "I wish I could take that memory from you."

"Yeah...it blows, right? And now you know why I hate birthdays so much. Nothing good has ever happened on one. They always end up just a big kick in my teeth. And that's my secret. Whenever I feel physical pain, I remember the day the life drained out of my father and I hold on to that. So long as I feel pain, I know I'm alive and life, even when it sucks sideways, is so much better than death, that I embrace even the agony of it."

How different his view was from what she'd been taught. Her people embraced death. There was nothing more glorious than to die in battle. "Do you not believe in an afterlife?"

"I do. But I'm a pragmatist. This life I know is real. The other...I'm gambling on. So for the time being, I'll take what I know even when it hurts."

How was it that he always surprised and amazed her? Just when she thought she knew him, he exposed a depth and strength that she hadn't even guessed existed. At first glance, Caillen seemed like a simple hedonist. But there was nothing simple about him.

And while he was definitely hedonistic, he wasn't selfish or sociopathic.

She squeezed his hand. "I like your logic."

"Hey, Dagan," Chayden's voice came through the intercom, interrupting them. "We're approaching the Exeterian port in Mykonia. Stay low and we'll let you know when we're scanned and docked. So long as you stay put, they won't be able to pick up any residuals from you."

That was the beauty about pirates she was learning. Their ships had all manner of interesting jammers and devices that helped them to elude authorities and their equipment.

For once, they landed without incident.

Chayden and Fain came to collect them while Hauk stayed on board as a guard for their ship.

Both men had their Tavali pirate garb on, including the mask over their faces so that all anyone could see was their eyes. It gave them a feral, intimidating appearance, especially Chayden's mask which was made of a brushed silver-colored metal. No wonder they wore them. Well that and it kept people from seeing their faces and identifying them on wanted posters.

Chayden passed them both masks that included eye shields. "So long as we're together, they'll think we're here for a shipment and that you two are part of my crew."

"You're not wanted here, are you?" Caillen asked before he pulled the mask over his face.

Chayden snorted. "Like that would be a concern given the fact that the two of you are plastered all over the media right now? Please. Don't insult me." Then his eyes turned a bit sheepish. "But to answer your question, there is a reason I'm wearing the mask." And he quickly lifted his cowl to cover his head.

Caillen laughed. "Looking real brave there, pun'kin."

Chayden made an obscene gesture at him before he led the way off the ship. Desideria kept her head covered as she traveled behind Caillen and in front of Fain. The men walked with that predatorial grace that was unique to soldiers and assassins. The gait of someone who had no doubt they could win any battle or fight.

The collective power sent a shiver over her.

Since it was well after dark, the street traffic was relatively light. Still, every transport gave her pause as she waited for the authorities to be notified and for someone to try and arrest them.

Their luck held as they approached the royal palace. Caillen pulled them to a stop in an alley across the street. Keeping to the shadows, he made sure they were out of sight for the cameras and guards.

"There's a back way in through the servant entrance."

Fain arched a brow at Caillen's words. "You know this how?"

"I crawled through their security while I lived there. I had my father plug most of it, but his head asshole thought he knew better than me, so he left a few holes intact. That one happens to be large enough for me to sneak through."

Desideria shook her head. "Not without me."

Caillen paused at her determined tone. "It'll be faster if I go in alone."

"You're wounded and I've got as much at stake in this as you do. There's—"

"Children, rest it," Chayden snapped. "All of our necks are in the gallows on this one. Caillen, lead. We follow."

"Yeah, but don't get used to it," Fain muttered.

Caillen started to argue, but realized every delay was costing them. "Fine. But keep up and follow exactly in my steps. Otherwise we'll be seen and I really don't feel like running away right now."

He crept along the wall, into the back gardens. There were several dark zones in the surveillance. Part of him was disgusted that they were there after the attempt had been made in this very place on his father's life, but the other part was grateful since it allowed them to slip inside and make their way to his father's office.

Caillen paused at the door he'd entered dozens of times to meet with his father.

Not wanting to think about it, he cracked it open and slipped inside. Completely dark and empty, it looked just as it had when they'd left for the *Arimanda*. Any minute, he expected to see his dad walk in.

Clenching his teeth against the agony of that thought, he went to the monitors and pulled up the surveillance for the palace. His father had everything wired to this room so that he could monitor it and see what was going on.

It only took a few seconds to locate his father's advisor. Ironically, he was in the war room and appeared to be reading over some reports. Good. There was very little surveillance there since it was where his father met with military commanders.

Without a word, he led his small group through the servant halls that were hidden. These should be monitored too, but Bogimir and the others had thought it rude and unnecessary.

We have never in our history monitored them. Why should we start doing so now?

Yeah...

Caillen paused outside the hidden war room door to meet Desideria's gaze. He had no plan on what he was going to say or do once he confronted the advisor. *Oh hell, just wing it.* That was how he flew through his life and he was too old to change his ways now.

He opened the door and snuck inside. His anger rising,

he crossed the room silently and nudged the chair. The instant he touched it, the advisor fell out of it and went sprawling onto the floor where he landed with a thud.

What the...?

"He's dead," Desideria breathed.

Caillen's gaze narrowed on the trail of blood near the chair. A trail that led to the next room. Instinctively, he moved his hand to his blaster as he followed it.

On the other side he found his uncle.

Equally dead.

Shit. *It's a setup.* No sooner had that thought gone through his mind than an alarm blared.

Fain cursed as he pulled his own weapon out to cover them. "Move it!"

They could hear guards coming from every direction. Caillen pulled out a blaster for each hand, preparing to make them regret their decision to come after them.

"Meet up back at my ship," Chayden said before he ran down the hallway alone.

Caillen inclined his head before he grabbed Desideria by the arm and dragged her behind him.

She frowned. "This isn't splitting up."

"Yeah, but you don't know where you are or how to speak or read the language. Do you really want me to leave you to your own means?"

He did have a point. "Fine."

Caillen led her to the guard station where there were several transports parked. Bypassing the guards who were patrolling the area, he quickly commandeered one, then wired it so that he could "borrow" it to get them back to the hangar. The moment he started the engine, the guards scrambled, shooting at them.

Desideria held her breath as Caillen careened out of the lot and then eluded them. A few minutes later, they were the first ones to reach Chayden's ship.

Notifying Hauk who was manning the guns about what was happening, Caillen rushed to fire the engines and do the prelim checks as he waited for Fain and Chayden to join them.

She went to eye the hatch so that she could allow Fain and Chayden inside. Glancing back at Caillen, she saw he'd frozen in place as he stared at the small monitor in front of him.

"Desideria?"

"Yes?"

He enhanced what he was looking at and put it up on the main display. "Any idea why Chayden has an entire file on you and your mother? One that dates back decades?"

21

Desideria was so stunned that she didn't move even to blink until Chayden and Fain had run onto the bridge.

Chayden came to a hesitant stop as he saw what had her transfixed. Even with the mask in place, it was obvious the color drained from his face and panic filled his dark eyes.

Rising to his feet, Caillen drew his blaster and aimed it straight at Chayden's head.

Fain skidded to a halt as he scowled at them both. "What's going on?"

Ignoring the question, Chayden held his hands up. "Whoa, buddy. It's not what you think."

Caillen moved the setting on his blaster from stun to kill with his thumb. The targeting laser never wavered from Chayden's forehead.

Never in her life had she seen anyone with a steadier hand. Caillen cut a sexy, fearsome pose as he glared in angry retribution over Chayden's invasion of her privacy. "It better not be."

Desideria dragged her gaze away from the screen that held every tiny detail of her life and her mother's as well as her sisters' to Chayden. "Why do you have all of that?"

Chayden lowered his cowl and the mask over his face so that she could see the sincerity in his expression. "You're not going to believe me, I know you won't, but I swear to the gods I worship that it's the truth. She's my mother too." He gestured toward the files. "Obviously, I've been collecting all of—"

"Why?" she asked, interrupting him. "Why would you spy on us like this?"

He didn't answer until Caillen tightened his grip on the trigger, pulling it back to let him know that he had no qualms about taking his friend's life if Chayden had betrayed her. "You need to answer, Chay. Now. No lies."

A tic started in Chayden's jaw. "I wanted to feel connected to my family even if it was only from a distance. It was stupid, I know. But when you're alone in the universe, you reach out even when it doesn't make sense to do it."

Turmoil filled his eyes as he stared at her. "You have no idea how isolated you feel when your own mother hates you for something you couldn't help and wants nothing to do with you. You don't want to crave her or the rest of your family because you know they'll never accept you, so you stay at a distance and imagine what it would be like if your family could just be normal, even for one nanosecond." He glanced up at the photo of her mother. "Once I heard she was dead and I realized you weren't the one who killed her, I pulled the files I had so that I could put together a suspect list. Unfortunately, it's long—no one should have that many enemies. But knowing our mother, I'm really not surprised."

Desideria couldn't breathe as all of those unexpected words slammed into her like fists. That was the absolute last thing she'd expected to hear from him.

There was no way he was her brother...

Was there?

"Bullshit," Caillen blurted out. "I don't believe a word of it."

Chayden inclined his head toward the monitor. "My father's photo is in there too. Flip through the files and Desideria will know the instant she sees him."

With his blaster still on Chayden, Caillen stepped away from the con so that she could take his place and scan through the files. The moment she began opening them, she grew even more suspicious. Chayden had every single thing about her family catalogued. Honestly, it was creepy and disconcerting...it definitely reminded her of the dossier an assassin would put together to use against a target. He even had her old test scores from school and her recent promotion. Articles about her mother and private transmissions between her mother and some of her advisors. Everything he'd need to kill them all.

It took several minutes to find a male photograph buried in the multitude of others of her, her mother and sisters. But just as he'd predicted, she knew the minute she'd found his father. There was no doubt whatsoever.

How had she not noticed the similarity before? But the most heartbreaking one was the photo after it...

Chayden had manipulated a picture of her and her sisters so that he was in it too. Pain for him swelled inside her that he'd had to go to such a degree to have a family. She didn't mention it to Caillen or the others. There was no need to embarrass him. She closed the file.

Her heart pounded as she turned toward Chayden and the reality of his identity slammed into her so hard it was all she could do to breathe. She reached out and lowered Caillen's arm so that his blaster wasn't centered on Chayden's head any longer.

Chayden dropped his hands.

She stared at him in disbelief.

He was her *full* brother.

Her mind whirled as she struggled to put all these new pieces together and the reality of who he was sank in with a force that was dizzying. "I don't understand."

"Yes, you do. I'm a male heir. Firstborn and only half Qill. Mom couldn't afford to have me hanging around lest I bring her legitimacy into question or confuse the chain of inheritance."

But that wouldn't make him an heir. Only his daughter would be eligible to rule.

Suddenly she felt stupid. His daughter, should he ever have one, would be able to petition and fight for the throne. Another "non" Qillaq to embarrass her mother and one who would have even less Qillaq blood than she did...

Yeah, it made sense. Her mother would never want the daughter of her son to rule. Her mother wasn't exactly tolerant of men. Especially those as strong as Chayden. If he'd exhibited any of the predator aura that bled from him now as a child, she could easily see her mother banishing him over it.

Still, she didn't understand how her brother could end up as a renegade pirate. "How did you become Tavali?"

Sadness tinged his eyes. "I ran away as a kid and was taken in by one of their order. He was the closest thing to a parent I'd ever known. I learned the business from him and carried it on after he died."

"But why would you run away?"

He gave a bitter laugh that said he thought her question was ridiculous. "If you'd ever seen how they treat the males who're banished, you wouldn't ask that question. Suffice it to say, it was easier living on the streets than in the camp where Mom had me dumped."

That she could definitely believe. Given what they'd done to her and her sisters, she could only imagine how much worse his hole had been. But that still didn't explain why he was here and his actions these last few hours. "Why are you helping me?"

He shrugged. "You're my sister."

Like that meant anything. "You don't even know me."

"No, and when I first realized who you were, I was ready to let the League have you and then some. I'll be honest. I've hated all of you for most of my life. But you're not like the others and that's a compliment." He jerked his chin toward the monitors. "However, right now isn't really the time to hash all of this. We need to get out of here while all of our body parts are still attached, especially our heads."

Caillen stepped back more to allow him to take the controls as she moved out of his way.

Desideria didn't speak as this new knowledge chased itself around in her head. She'd known about her brother, but she'd never expected to meet him. Especially not like this.

There were so many questions. So many things she wanted to know about him and his life. What he'd done. How he'd survived...

He really is my brother.

One who bore a striking resemblance to her father.

It boggled her mind.

Caillen scowled at Desideria's continued silence. She appeared shell-shocked and pale. "You all right?"

"I'm not sure."

"I know the feeling. You have the same sick look on your face that I'm pretty sure I had when they told me I was a prince. Nauseating, isn't it?"

Yes. Definitely.

And she didn't know what to think of her brother who was risking his life to save hers. Narcissa would never do such. Most days she hated her guts and Gwen wasn't that much better. But now that she knew the truth, she understood why Chayden had seemed so familiar to her. He had their mother's eyes and their father's build. There was also something about his movements and mannerisms that reminded her of her father.

The cadence of his voice.

Their accents were different, but the inflections and tones were similar.

He's my brother. That one fact kept echoing in her head.

Fain gently brushed past them to take his seat while Hauk stayed topside, near the guns—just in case—something that was becoming their new mantra.

"Strap in," Fain warned.

She and Caillen complied while Chayden engaged the engines then launched and flew between volleys of fire as the Exeterian Enforcers caught up to them. She groaned while he spun the ship to make it through the narrow opening of the bay's doors. "You know, I used to enjoy flying until I met all of you. Now, I'm not sure I'll ever want to do it again."

Caillen laughed. "Think of it like a carnival ride."

"I would, but those make me sick too."

Fain pitched a small bag at her. "Make sure it all goes in. If you miss, nail Caillen and not me. Otherwise I'll be joining you."

"And I'll be launching all of you out an air lock," Chayden muttered as he arced the ship up. "Big bunch of pansies."

She shook her head at his earnest tone.

Hauk returned the fire while Chayden dipped between their pursuers and shot them into hyperspace. Her head spinning from their wild ride and her recent shock, she saw the expression on Caillen's face that said he was trying to digest this newest twist as much as she was. Forget about Chayden for the moment, they had a larger problem with his uncle dead.

No one would ever believe they hadn't done this too. Who could clear their names now?

"What do we do?" she asked Caillen.

"I honestly have no idea. That was my best thought. Right now...I'm empty."

Chayden snorted. "Normally, I'd take that opening. Good thing for you, I'm preoccupied with the near-death experience in front of me."

Fain cursed as he sat back in his chair. He pulled up a news segment and flashed it on the main screen so that all of them could watch it. "I was scanning for our arrest or assassination warrants to be issued and look what I found." He opened the channel.

The female commentator was brunette, petite and held

a wicked gleam in her eye that said she was enjoying her job a little too much. "This is streaming in live, right this very second...All of you are the first to hear it, just as it's happening on Exeter. Prince Caillen was spotted only moments ago leaving his father's palace where his uncle, the acting emperor, was found slain along with his head advisor. Apparently His Highness is on a major killing spree with the League scrambling to identify who his next target might be and to stop him before he kills again."

Desideria gaped. "How could they have that so fast?"

"Nothing moves faster than the media." Fain changed the screen over to another report on a different frequency. "I swear, they hired a publicist to convict you both. I couldn't get this much coverage if I painted myself pink and ran naked through the League's main hall with a bomb strapped on my back, screaming 'death to syco-phantic pawns.'"

Desideria would have laughed if the situation had been a little less dire. She frowned as a woman around her age who was dressed in royal Exeterian robes stood in front of the media with a dour expression. Behind her were several of Desideria's mother's Guard, but the most shocking was Kara's presence...

Why would her aunt be there? And dressed so strangely? Kara looked more like one of Caillen's people than hers. The younger woman's expression was bitter while she addressed the gathered reporters. The stripe under her face identified the woman as Leran de Orczy.

"It is with a sad heart that I report my cousin's actions. My father was a good man and didn't deserve this any more than my uncle Evzen did. If it's the last thing I do, I swear I shall see justice met and I won't rest until I hold

Prince Caillen's heart in my fist. The League is issuing the bounty on his head and we've already backed it with Exeterian funds. Whoever ends his killing spree and his life will be rich indeed and I will owe them my eternal gratitude."

Stunned, she looked at Caillen whose face was as pale as hers had to be.

Had she heard that correctly?

He met her gaze and she saw the anger smoldering in the dark depths of his eyes. That fury made the hair on the back of her neck stand up. It was the look the angel of death had to wear whenever he went to take someone's soul.

Without a word, Caillen unbuckled himself to take over the con where Fain sat. He isolated Kara out of the crowd and enlarged her photo.

"Anyone know who this is?" he asked in a tone so cold it was a wonder it didn't give them freezer burn.

Baffled by his fury, she frowned. "My aunt. Why?"

Before he could answer, Chayden spoke up. "She's the woman who hired me as a tirador against the Qills."

Caillen felt his heart stop as that unexpected bomb smacked him in the face. "What?"

Chayden pointed to her image. "She came to the North Tavali a year ago and gave a hefty payment for us to make runs against the Qills using a Trimutian flag."

Desideria was aghast. "Why would you do such a thing?"

"'Cause it was a lot of money and I'm a mercenary bastard. Not to mention, I took a lot of pleasure raiding Qill lands and ships. Payback's hell and I was her willing bitch for it."

Caillen gave him a droll glare. "Did you not ask her why she wanted you to do that?"

"Didn't really care. I recognized her as my aunt, but didn't say anything since she didn't recognize me. I assumed her payout was authorized by my mother to start a war so they could raid Trimutian resources with the League's backing."

The same thing Caillen had thought, but now . . .

There was a whole lot going on here. He turned back to the face that had haunted his nightmares for years. "For the record, that's the bitch who murdered my father when I was a kid."

All four pairs of eyes turned to him.

Fain gaped. "What?"

Caillen stared at the cold face of the woman from his childhood. Yes, she was older, but those features were emblazoned on his memory. How could he forget the woman who'd torn his childhood apart and had ruined his sister and murdered the only father he'd known as a child? "She was in the alley when my father was killed. She and the assassin went off together."

"Are you sure?" Chayden asked.

He gave a slow nod.

"It can't be." Desideria scowled. "Kara wouldn't have . . ." Her voice trailed off as the young woman took her aunt's hand and pulled her closer before she answered a reporter's question.

Leran's next words made all of them suck their breaths in sharply. "My mother and I are committed to honoring my father's work. I've already spoken to my cousin Narcissa who is acting regent for the moment until a new Qillaq queen can be crowned and she's put her best people on helping us to track down our parents' killers and to bring them to justice as swiftly as possible. Blood or no blood, Desideria and Caillen will pay for their crimes."

Desideria went cold as she realized who the woman really was. "That's not Kara. It's her twin sister, Karissa." The one who'd married an offworlder...

"Your aunt married my uncle?" Caillen's tone was low and sinister.

"Yes, she did," Chayden confirmed. "I had no photo of her, and never thought much about it, but I remember it now."

Hauk's voice spoke through the intercom. "Are you thinking what I'm thinking?"

"Yeah," Fain said wryly. "We're screwed."

It took Caillen a full minute before he could answer that question. His thoughts whirled through his mind with a dizzying effect. "Karissa paid to have me killed as a kid."

Hauk cleared his throat. "Yeah, we're thinking alike."

Desideria's scowl deepened. "Why?"

Pausing at her question, Caillen rubbed his brow as everything came together and he finally understood a lifetime of weirdness. Things that had seemed like coincidences now made total sense to him. "Don't you see? With me out of the way, her daughter would be in line to inherit my father's empire."

Desideria shook her head in denial. "Look at her. She's younger than I am. Her daughter wouldn't have even been born at the time you were kidnapped."

Chayden cursed. "Not this one, but..." He pulled up an obituary and put it on the screen beside Karissa's photo. He turned his attention to Caillen. "She had another daughter. An older one who, as a teenager, died in an accident about the time you would have been three."

"Not long after I was kidnapped."

Chayden gave a curt nod. "I never realized Kara had a twin sister. All I'd ever seen was that the queen had another sister who was married off. There was no record of their birth or of them being twins because the Qills don't think of births as significant. They don't register them the way we do. They only register when someone becomes an adult which the two of them didn't do simultaneously because of Qillaq law." He smacked himself on the forehead. "I can't believe I never thought to double-check the identities of the women in the pictures."

But who could blame him? As he said, if you didn't know they were twins, there was no record.

Desideria let out a long sigh. "It wouldn't have mattered if you had checked. Karissa's entire history, like yours, would have been erased the moment she left Qilla for Exeter. Likewise, no one ever told us what planet she'd gone to. To our people, it's irrelevant."

Chayden's expression said he thought he was an absolute imbecile for not seeing through it. "Since I didn't know they were twins, I assumed Kara was the one who'd hired me on my mother's behalf to start the war. But now I'm going to bet it was Karissa trying to wage war on them. Frame the Trimutians and then strike while the queen is preoccupied with a war. What an effing idiot I am…" his voice trailed off as his brows came together into a fierce frown. "Unless…"

"Unless what?" she asked.

"We're assuming Karissa was working alone with her daughter. What if she wasn't?"

Desideria went cold as she realized the full extent of this nightmare and her overheard conversation came back to haunt her. Chayden was right. The more she thought it over, the more it made sense. Why would Karissa be working alone? "She and Kara could have been plotting this coup for years." Her mind raced with implications as she replayed a lifetime of abuse at her aunt's hands.

What if Kara hadn't volunteered to train them out of the goodness of her heart? What if she'd volunteered to murder them and shred their egos so that they wouldn't be fit to take their mother's place? Yes, it was Narcissa who'd been there, but Kara had set the scene for those deaths. Maybe Cissy was just her instrument.

"What if Karissa is working with my aunt Kara too?"

Why hadn't she thought of this before?

Fain made a low whistle. "Twins to rule dual empires. Together, they'd be one hell of a force to be reckoned with. No one would be able to fight them. Not even the League."

Chayden shook his head. "Especially with Trimutian resources to call on if they'd taken over their empire too. They'd own the entire Frezis sector."

Desideria raked a tired hand through her hair as reality tore through her. "But how do we prove this? No one will ever believe us."

Before anyone could answer, a blast rocked the ship.

Caillen went flying as Chayden straightened in his chair to engage the new ship that was firing on them. "How the hell do they keep finding us?"

Fain's gaze went to Desideria. "Are you tagged?"

"Pardon?"

"Do you have a tracing chip in your body?" he asked again.

Caillen let out a foul curse. The fact she didn't know what it was said it all.

She wasn't the carrier. The Qills didn't use that technology. His people on the other hand...

"Not her. Wanna bet I do?"

Fain's eyes widened as he got it. "When you were arrested."

Caillen nodded. "You know they tagged me." It was standard operating procedure. "I didn't even think about it." Damn it, he should have. But then he'd never been arrested before and he'd had a lot of other things on his mind the last couple of weeks.

His father. The assassination attempts. And then Desideria's finer and extremely attractive attributes. All of those had combined to keep his thoughts on anything other than the possibility he was tagged.

Chayden shook his head in denial. "Yeah, but my jammers should still keep it blocked so that they couldn't find us."

Caillen wasn't so sure about that. "What are you running?"

"X-Qs. Why?"

They were the best, Caillen admitted. But they weren't perfect. "If my chip's on a TR frequency..."

Chayden growled. "That's it. That's how they keep locating us."

It was how the assassin on the Andarion outpost had kept track of them too. Gah, how stupid for not seeing it sooner. That was how the assassin had been able to get a location for them in the field. But for the frequency his mirrors ran on, they'd have been dead.

And all because he was a moron.

"Is there a medical scanner on board?" Caillen asked.

Chayden indicated the wall with a jerk of his chin. "Med panel behind you. There's a bag in it that should have one."

Caillen moved to it while Chayden did his best to out-maneuver their newest addition and Hauk tried to blow their enemies out of space.

Desideria came forward to help Caillen locate the right bag and to find the scanner inside it so that they could escape this latest nuisance and hopefully prevent any more. How wonderful it would be to have five minutes of peace from the people trying to kill them.

Caillen paused as he caught the traumatized look in her gaze. How could any woman be so beautiful and vul-nerable at the same time? It made him want to protect her. To take her away from all of this and just hold her and make love to her until she smiled again. "I'm sorry."

"For what?"

"Getting you into this mess."

She offered him a kind smile that made his cock come alive in spite of the danger they were in. "It was my aunt who did it. Not you. She'd have been after both of us any-way. Honestly, I'm glad I threw you into that pod and jumped on top of you."

Smiling, Caillen leaned in and inhaled the sweet scent of her hair as an image of her naked beneath him tor-mented him with the most precious memory of his life. Even in the middle of all this chaos, and in spite of the fact that they could die any second, he found comfort in her presence.

She was his breath.

His world.

And he didn't want to lose her. She'd come to mean

so much to him in such a short period of time. He didn't understand it, but there was no denying the fact that he couldn't even think about her leaving without a vicious pain stabbing him in the chest.

You know she can't stay with you.

Refusing to think about that, he handed her the scanner he'd finally found underneath and not *inside* the bag Chayden had mentioned. Figured Chayden would be wrong. "Find the chip, my lady."

She took the scanner and hovered it over his body. Caillen waited for the signal to tell them where it was located, but he didn't hear it.

After a few seconds of scanning all the way down his legs, Desideria straightened. "It's not registering anything."

Caillen frowned. "It has to."

"See for yourself." She handed him the scanner.

He looked through the readings, trying to find anything that she might have missed. But in the end, he had to admit the truth.

She was right.

There must be one inside her after all. He cleared the reading and then scanned her body.

She was also negative.

No way...

"This can't be right." He looked over at Chayden. "Your scanner's broken."

Chayden bristled. "My scanner's *not* broken."

"Obviously it is since neither of us is registering anything at all."

Chayden gave him a droll stare. "Nothing's wrong with the scanner. I had it calibrated a few days ago."

"Wow, you really have no life, do you?"

Chayden made an obscene gesture over his shoulder at Caillen before he dipped the ship to avoid fire. "Did you check your ass?"

He rolled his eyes at the mere suggestion. "It wouldn't be there."

"Yeah it would." Chayden laughed in an evil tone. "Think about it. Where's the one place a prisoner on the run couldn't dig it out and the one place you could put it without them knowing it? Fat of the ass, my friend. Fat. Of. The. Ass."

Caillen groaned in pain as he realized Chayden was right. What better place to put one?

His ass. In fact, the fat there would actually help strengthen the signal.

Yeah, that made sense.

Cursing his luck, he returned the scanner to Desideria and turned around for her to scan his back. There was nothing as she hovered it over his shoulders and spine.

A second later as she neared his buttocks, he heard the sound of it locating the chip.

Unbelievable. It was right in the fleshy part of his left cheek. Of course. Where else would it be? And now that he thought about it, he remembered waking up with his ass sore the day after they'd arrested him. At the time he'd assumed they'd kicked him or dumped him hard on the ground.

He should have known better.

A krikkin tag.

"Will the degradations never end?"

Fain snorted. "Hey, just be glad you have your woman here. Otherwise we'd throw your carcass out the air lock before we went digging on your cheek for it."

Sad thing was, he believed they would.

He handed Desideria a small laser scalpel from the medical pack and inwardly cringed at the thought of what she was about to do to him. "Can you do this?"

"So long as we don't get hit by a blast."

He cut a meaningful glare to their pilot. "Hold it steady, Chay."

"I make no promises and bear no liability for your lunacy, her clumsiness or any injury my unfortunate luck, uncharacteristic ineptitude or continual stupidity may cause."

Nice legal disclosure. Rotten bastard. He should have been a lawyer instead of a pirate. "I'm still going to take it out of your sorry hide if you screw me up for life. And if I die, I'm going to haunt you and shatter all power circuits whenever you need them most."

Then he returned his gaze to Desideria whose brow was lined with worried concern. Damn, she was the most beautiful woman he'd ever seen. Never before had he trusted anyone the way he was trusting her right now. With his life. "For God's sake, please don't sneeze and if you're holding a grudge against me for anything I did, real or imagined, I apologize profusely and swear I'll never do it again."

"Don't worry, Caillen, I'll be careful."

He definitely hoped so. But the wicked gleam in her eye and slight smile on her lips made him wonder if he'd lie down as a rooster and get up as a hen.

Stop being paranoid. You can trust her.

After lying on the floor, he opened his fly and slid his pants down to his hips. Desideria held the scalpel so tight, her knuckles whitened. She was terrified and he hoped that meant she felt at least a little bit for him what he felt for her.

He winked at her to give her encouragement. "Just kiss it later and make it better, baby, and I'll be all good with whatever you do."

Desideria let out a low annoyed sound at his teasing. Would he never take anything seriously? But all things considered, she adored that about him. Her heart pounding over the task to come, she slid his pants down far enough that she could reach the area where the chip was embedded and yet still keep him dressed enough not to be embarrassed in front of the others. "So how big is this thing anyway?"

Chayden made a sound of irritation. "You know, that's not really a question I want to hear my younger sister ask a man, especially not one I consider a friend, while he's lying bare-assed on my floor."

Hauk and Fain laughed.

Desideria was less than amused. "Remember, brother, I'm currently the only one holding a weapon."

Caillen glared at him. "Really, Chay, why don't you concentrate on the people trying to kill us right now? 'Preciate it, pun'kin." He turned his attention to her. "About the size of your smallest fingernail."

Fain laughed again. "Damn, I should have been taping that response and using it for playback at every party from here until I die."

Desideria couldn't believe how awful they were being given how dire this was.

Caillen glared at him before he finished his instructions. "It shouldn't be more than a few centimeters in. Anything deeper and it wouldn't transmit a strong enough signal to trace."

She moved to make a small incision in his flesh. Just as she neared his skin with the scalpel, the ship spun sideways from a blast. She let out a small squeak as she narrowly missed slicing into Caillen. She'd barely pulled back in time. A second more and she could have really hurt him.

I could kill him by doing this…

That thought made her hands shake.

How could she do this? One slip and…

Caillen reached out and covered her hand with his. Those dark eyes seared her with the one thing she knew he didn't give easily.

His trust.

"You can do it, baby. I have all faith in you."

Those words choked her because she knew how rare and sincere they were. It was a trust she had no intention of betraying. Nodding, she moved closer again. If she didn't get the chip out, they'd be a moving target from now on. All of them.

They'd be able to find Caillen and kill him whenever they wanted to.

I have to do this.

Steeling herself for it, she made the incision.

Caillen went rigid, but he didn't make a sound as she very carefully extracted the chip from his body. Ew. It looked like a bloodied silver bean. Just as Caillen had said, it was about the size of her smallest fingernail and held a tiny wire sticking out of the top.

Fain tossed her a small packet of sterilized coagulant for the wound. She applied it, then gently patted Caillen on his undamaged right cheek so that she wouldn't hurt him. "All done, sweetie."

He screwed his face up in distaste as he pulled his pants up and fastened them. "Well after that testosterone-shattering experience, I have no more dignity to worry about. Ever. Anyone have a cushion I can sit on? A really big fluffy one? Hell, let's even make it pale pink with bows on it just for good measure." He took the chip from her and crushed it under his boot heel while she went to wash her hands.

Fain gave him a cocky grin. "Look on the bright side, drey. You've never had much dignity anyway. I know. I've seen the P.O.S. ship you pilot."

"Thanks, Fain. Your personal support means so much to me. Glad I can rely on it."

"Hang tight," Chayden said an instant before he banked sharp left and slung Caillen into a control panel.

Cursing, Caillen banged his injured leg and butt cheek. Pain exploded through him with such ferocity that for a moment he thought he might pass out. But as soon as he caught his breath and glanced to the right, his heart stopped beating.

Desideria.

She was lying sprawled on the ground, half in and half out of the head.

Please be all right. Please be all right.

He ran with a limping gait to where she lay on the floor. Terrified, he turned her over as gently as he could. Her features were pale, but she was still breathing. To his instant relief, she opened her eyes and frowned up at him.

"You okay?"

She nodded slowly before she pressed her hand against her forehead.

Caillen held her tight until his rage took hold of him. "Good, 'cause I'm going to kill that bastard brother of yours." Rising from the floor, he reversed course so that he could reach Chayden and beat him down until he whimpered for death.

That was the plan that went to hell when he saw what Chayden was flying through. All in all, the man was doing a phenomenal job on the horde that had descended while Desideria had tended him. There were League ships everywhere. All of them armed and loaded for pirate.

Crap.

Without conscious thought, he tried to take the controls.

Chayden slapped at his hands. "Sit your ass down. I can handle this," he said between clenched teeth. "Both of you strap in."

Angry at the bitch-slap, Caillen wanted to hurt the man. Normally he would. But now wasn't the time.

Desideria sat in her chair and called out to him. "C'mon, Caillen. Let's not distract the pilot while he's fighting for our lives."

Galled to the center of his soul that he was having to trust his life to someone else's piloting abilities, he followed suit. "I don't like being a passenger."

"Yeah, now you know how I feel," Fain muttered. "Sucks to be back here. However it could be worse."

"How so?"

"You could be the pilot."

Caillen rolled his eyes at the Andarion. But honestly, he had to give Chayden credit. The man twisted through the gauntlet and came out between two cruisers with the narrowest of margins—it was a miracle they didn't scrape metal. Chayden pulled back and they shot up at the steepest of angles. Just as the alarm sounded that they were target-locked and about to be blown apart, Chayden maneuvered into a wormhole.

The ship went dark, then exploded in speed as the natural opening propelled them across the universe.

For the moment, they were safe again.

Caillen let out a long breath. "I think we're probably running out of luck at this point and I know my underwear can't take any more abuse—not that I wear underwear, but if I did it would be soiled. How many more near misses do you think we have in us?"

Hauk laughed over the intercom. "Collectively or individually?"

Chayden leaned back slightly in his chair. "I don't know about the rest of you, but I always run at an extreme deficit."

Hauk came through the door and joined them on the bridge. "So what's the plan now?"

Desideria answered before he could even part his lips. "We need to get to my sisters."

Caillen widened his eyes at her insanity. Heading into her palace was as crazy as breaking into his, the only difference, he knew the security where he'd lived. He was going to bet she had no idea about hers. "Okay, why?"

"My aunts will be after them. Even though they're minors under our laws, they can still petition for the crown, especially since Narcissa is acting as empress. My sisters will be the next obstacle and target. I'm sure it's why Kara hasn't seized the throne. She's waiting for the assassin to take them out, then come after us with all justification. And trust me. A Qillaq tribunal is not something you want to go through."

Chayden backed her stupidity. "She's right about all of

that, especially our sisters. If it is a combined plot between Karissa and Kara, they're unprotected victims waiting to happen—just like your uncle. We have to get to them as soon as possible." He laid in the course for Qilla. "Once they're safe, we can sort this out."

"I don't know," Hauk said. "We're extremely high profile right now. The best course might be to get some of the Sentella in there to secure them and for us to lie low and let some of this die down before we're spotted again."

Desideria gave him a withering glare. "The Sentella didn't keep my mother or Caillen's father or uncle safe, so you'll have to excuse me if I'm lacking a bit of faith in them. Besides that doesn't matter. My sisters wouldn't go with them anyway. They trust no offworlders and would fight to the death if one tried to take them from their dormitory."

Hauk raked a sneer over her. "What makes you think they'll go with *you?* Especially since they think you killed your mother?"

Desideria backed down as he brought up something she hadn't considered. There was no reason for either of her sisters to trust her right now.

None whatsoever.

But that didn't matter to her.

Keeping them safe did.

"I'm hoping they'll listen to reason." She did her best to make Hauk understand. "Either way, I have to try. I'm the best shot at getting them out of this alive. Without me, they're dead."

Fain scoffed. "Oh I don't know. I think I could knock them unconscious and carry them out pretty quick."

She was horrified by his suggestion. "I don't want

my sisters beaten." She passed a probing stare to Hauk. "Would you be able to lie low if your family was in the line of fire?"

Hauk glanced over to his brother. "Depends on the day of the week and the mood I'm in."

She knew better.

And he confirmed it a few seconds later after he let out an aggravated breath. "All right, the name of stupidity right now is us. Let's go fly into certain death to help people who will most likely try to kill us and claw out our eyes."

Fain laughed. "Sounds like a typical assignment to me."

"Yeah, well, there is that."

Caillen sat back as he ran through all the new information they now had and tried to come up with a reasonable plan of action.

Save the sisters. Clear their names.

Don't die.

Simple list. Impossible odds. What the hell was he thinking? They were screwed. Every government was out to capture or kill them...

C'mon, don't give up. You've lived through worse odds than this.

Yeah, right.

His gaze drifted to Desideria, who sat lost in her own thoughts. There was a smudge of dirt across her left cheek. Her clothes were crumpled and she looked completely exhausted. Still, she carried on with a warrior's persistence and her presence gave him strength. Most of all, it gave him a reason to fight to the bitter end. He wouldn't let her die. Not over something she was innocent in.

Even though there was no chance now of his clearing his

own name, he would see her through this no matter what and make sure that when this was done, she was queen.

The one thing she wanted most. He would do everything in his power to give her that dream.

"We're going to make it," he promised her.

She smiled at him. "I can almost believe that when you say it."

"Oh well, paint my ass pink," Fain groused. "'Cause I don't believe it. I think we're going to prison or graves. But hey? What do I know?"

Hauk shoved playfully at his brother. "Stop being an asshole."

"Impossible task. Besides, I enjoy it." Fain turned back around so that he could continue scanning the news reports for anything else they needed to know.

The rest of them didn't speak much over the next few hours. They were too tired and too worried. They knew what they were up against and it was debilitating.

Caillen tried to stay focused, but over and over his gaze went to Desideria. He wanted to pull her into a back room and make love to her so badly he could taste it. But she wasn't the type of woman to welcome that. One thing he'd learned about women, their sex drives were radically different.

They didn't respond well when they had dire matters pressing on them. Women liked to be wooed and romanced. Something that was a little impossible at present.

Gah, to have her lay her hand on his skin right now…

But he was used to putting other people's needs before his own. So instead, he savored the memory of her. And wished for a better ending than the one he saw coming.

As they neared Qilla, Chayden kept the ship back, out of the atmosphere. One of the advantages they'd learned while en route about Desideria's planet was that they didn't monitor anything outside their upper stratosphere. It was only when something broke their official air space that their forces were notified and they pursued the invaders.

Let's hear it for an isolationist planet...

Chayden set the autopilot and prepared the Verkehr to transport them to her palace. "I'll send you guys down and be on standby to get you back."

Caillen arched one brow. "Whatever you do, don't fall asleep on the job."

Chayden yawned. "Now that you mention it, I am a little tired."

Caillen glared at him. "You're not funny."

"Oh please. I'm a riot. You're just incapable of appreciating me."

Ignoring his joke, Caillen took Desideria's hand as he faced Hauk and Fain. "You two really have gone above and beyond."

"Trust me," Fain snorted, "we know."

"Thanks." Caillen's tone was thick with sincerity. "For everything."

That sincerity seemed to embarrass Fain, who inclined his head before he covered his face with his mask. "All right, Princess Pain. Lead us into suicide."

Desideria took comfort from the warmth of Caillen's hand holding hers as Chayden teleported them from the ship down to the back courtyard of the palace where the high brick walls would protect them from cameras and guards. She wasn't far from the training ring where she'd spent most of her life.

How weird to be back now. So much had happened to her since she'd left with her mother's Guard that she felt like a stranger in her own home. Unwelcomed. Unwanted.

Foreign.

She wasn't the same person who'd left here. Everything was different now. Her faith in her mother and her aunt shattered. More than that, she had a newfound strength and confidence in herself that hadn't been there before.

All because of Caillen. He'd shown her that she could survive even in an alien environment where she knew nothing about the people or customs and that she was capable of taking care of herself no matter what her aunt or mother thought. She was a woman, not a child.

For the first time in her life, she actually believed that.

But she didn't have time to focus on that right now. She had her sisters to save and the lives of the three men she'd learned to trust and care for were in her hands. She had to get them in and out of there before they were attacked.

Releasing Caillen, she led them into the east wing where her sisters should be. This time of day, they were normally in their room resting for the next training session that would start after dinner. With any luck, that wouldn't have changed.

Yet.

As she led them through the back palace rooms, she shivered. The hallway had always been cold, but never as frigid as it seemed today. It was like the palace knew her mother was dead and in its own way, it, too, was grieving.

Her heart pounded in her ears as she strained to listen for any sound that could denote detection for them.

Luckily it didn't take long to reach their apartments

and yet it seemed like eternity had passed before she made it to Gwen's room. There was a light beneath the dark wood door and inside, she could hear someone violently throwing things around. It sounded like a war was going on in there.

They're killing her!

Her vision dimming, Desideria swung open the door, prepared for battle.

But there was no army inside.

She froze at the sight of Narcissa who'd also stopped midtantrum at her intrusion. For a moment, everything appeared like someone had pushed pause as they stared at one another in mutual shock. While she stood in the open doorway, Narcissa held one of the clay pots Gwen had collected since early childhood in her hands. One of the few that hadn't been shattered during Narcissa's apparent fit.

Terror replaced the shock on Narcissa's face as she took in the sight of Desideria and the three armed men standing behind her, ready to kill if necessary. "What are you doing here?"

Holstering her blaster, Desideria stepped into the room. She held her hands up so that her sister wouldn't panic any worse and to let Narcissa know that she meant her no harm. "I've come to save you and Gwen. Kara's trying to kill you."

Narcissa scowled. "What?"

"It's true," Caillen said. "She's framed all of us. We're here to help and protect you."

Stunned disbelief hung heavy in Narcissa's dark brown eyes. It was obvious she was struggling with what to believe. "Are you sure about Kara?"

Desideria nodded. "Think about it, Cissy. She's always

pushed us to fight, even to the death. She pushed us all beyond our abilities and then never wept when one of us died. She never thought Mom should have been in power. You know that. I overheard her talking to one of her conspirators. She and Karissa have teamed up so that they can rule the two empires jointly...after all of us are dead."

Narcissa swallowed. "You think she's killed Gwen?"

That question sent a chill over her. "Why do you say that?"

"I came in here to talk to her and she's gone." She gestured to the shards of pottery on the floor. "I was so angry at her for being stupid that I let my control slip."

That was what happened when anger was the only emotion their people sanctioned. Violence erupted over the smallest of offenses.

Now Desideria remembered why Caillen and company were such a welcome relief to her. It was so nice to be around people who had a variety of emotions, most of them pleasant and amusing. People who could tease each other and not go to war over it. People who didn't answer every insult with a punch.

Caillen moved forward. "Have you any idea where she is?"

Narcissa shook her head. She locked gazes with Desideria. "If what you've said is true, we have to find her. Fast. There's no telling what could happen to her."

She was right, but Desideria had a bad suspicion about her sister's whereabouts. "Where's Kara?"

"I haven't seen her since the press conference. She vanished while I was talking to the reporters...you don't think she's harmed Gwen, do you?"

It would make sense, but she didn't want to panic her

sister. "We'll find her." With a calmness she really didn't feel, Desideria ran through her mind where her sister might be. It was dizzying really. The palace was huge with more rooms than their small group could search through before being caught.

But if Gwen had felt threatened...

There was only one place she'd go for safety.

"The crypt."

Narcissa screwed her face up. "What?"

Since Gwen was eight, she'd been drawn to the crypts, claiming the old tombs made her feel safe. For some reason Gwen had refused to share, she'd always believed that the spirits of their ancestors would watch over and protect her any time she was there. While Desideria had thought the dark, dismal tunnels were creepy and damp, Gwen had considered them her solitary haven. Probably because it was the one place Kara would never go. She thought the crypts were haunted and they weirded her out even more than they did Desideria.

"I know it sounds peculiar, but it's where Gwen always goes when she's upset." Not that Narcissa had ever cared whenever Gwen had sought refuge.

"That's idiotic."

Desideria had to force herself to remain patient with her sister's ire.

Caillen ignored Narcissa. "Lead the way, Princess."

Inclining her head to him, Desideria went to the bookcase to her left. Like most rooms in the palace, there was a secret passage behind it that allowed the royal family to escape in the highly unlikely event that they should ever be overrun by enemies. All of them had been forced to learn the access points as children—a task Narcissa had balked at, but it was something Desideria and Gwen had enjoyed learning. More to the point, they'd enjoyed exploring down there too.

The one in Gwen's room was the quickest way to the crypt which lay on the outermost corner of the palace lands. That was the main reason Gwen had chosen this room to be hers. At night, she'd often left the passage door open, wanting the spirits to come visit her.

Yeah, and they all thought I *was the strange one...*

Not wanting to think about that either, she used one of Caillen's light sticks to lead them into the winding darkness. While dank and depressing, at least there were no animals in the tunnels. The exterior access portals were airtight and undetectable to even the smallest creatures.

Closing her eyes, she forced herself to remember where Gwen preferred to hide. The northern crypt that was their great-grandmother's tomb. Since Gwen had favored her most out of their family, she'd chosen that as her special place.

It didn't take long to reach it.

Desideria opened the iron door to the room that had been carved from stone to provide an eternal resting place for the marble sarcophagus. Most of the women buried in the crypt were in wall tombs. Only war heroes such as her great-grandmother who had kept them independent during the Ascardian Revolt were allowed to have rooms dedicated to them. It was an honor all queens aspired to.

On the far wall set in a recess that was decorated with the royal insignia and coat of arms was an eternal flame that paid homage to Eleria's life and reign.

That light cast a dancing shadow through the room. One that highlighted a sight that made her freeze as her gaze fell to Kara who was kneeling beside an unmoving Gwen. Blood pooled around her sister whose features were so pale she was sure Gwen was dead. Horrified, she couldn't breathe.

Someone shoved her from behind, forcing her into the room. She turned to see Narcissa slamming the door in the face of the men before she locked it tight.

"What are you doing?" Desideria demanded angrily.

Narcissa tapped the communications band on her wrist. "There are intruders in the north crypt led by Desideria. I think they're trying to kill Gwen and me. Rally all guards immediately. Help!"

Desideria scowled at her sister while Kara rose to her feet. Her aunt started to attack, but Narcissa leveled her blaster at her and fired. It struck Kara and knocked her back against the wall.

Gasping at the attack, Gwen rolled over and tried to crawl under the sarcophagus.

Dodging the blast Narcissa directed toward her, Desideria moved to shield Gwen with her own body. Even though there was no denying what was happening, a part of her still couldn't believe it. Surely something else was going on here.

Please, don't be the killer...

"Narcissa?"

Her sister sneered at her. "You didn't really think Kara was bright enough to pull this off, did you? Stupid cow. Both of you. The throne is mine, you bitch, and I'm not going to share or fight for it. But I will kill you both to get it." She fired again.

Using a move she'd learned from Caillen, Desideria dropped to the floor, allowing the shot to narrowly miss her. She pulled her own blaster out and returned the blast.

Narcissa dove under a statue of their high goddess and continued to spray fire at them.

Desideria covered Gwen. She knelt by her side to check on her injuries. Her shoulder and side were bleeding and there was a big bruise forming on her right cheek. "Are you all right?"

Her sister was tucked up tight against the stone base as if she was trying to merge with the sarcophagus. "Wounded, but Kara tended most of it."

Desideria glanced over to where her aunt lay unmoving. There was no help there. "Are you armed?"

"No. Narcissa disarmed me before she wounded me. I barely escaped her."

Desideria clenched her teeth as she realized by trying to save her sister, she'd endangered her all the more. Fine. She could handle this alone.

"It's over, Narcissa. Lay down your weapon."

As expected, Narcissa fired more shots. "My Guard will be here any moment and your friends will be dead or captured. Once I kill the two of you, *I* will be queen."

Desideria would ask why, but then, she knew. It was the Qillaq way. *Take what you want.* If someone was in your way, kill them. If they weren't strong enough to fight you off, they deserved to die.

Even family.

Nauseated, she wanted to weep over her sister's psychosis. Later, she definitely would. But right now, she had to keep Gwen safe.

A low moan sounded from Kara. It wasn't much. Just enough to make Narcissa pause and glance in her direction.

Desideria seized the moment to leap out and throw herself against Narcissa. Entangled, they rolled across the cold stone floor, punching at each other. She managed to knock the blaster from Narcissa's hand, but not before she lost her own grip on her weapon.

Krik!

She heard more blasts coming from the other side of the door, out in the hallway.

Narcissa laughed in triumph. "Told you my Guard wouldn't let me down."

Rage, dark and deadly, settled over her as a newfound strength welled up inside her at the thought of her friends being attacked. "They're not your Guard, bitch. They're mine." With a bellow of rage, she kicked Narcissa into the wall with everything she had. It was enough to stun her sister who slid to the floor.

As she went for the blasters, Narcissa launched herself at her back.

Desideria rolled to the floor, away from her, grabbed the weapons and landed in a crouch, both blasters drawn and aimed right at the area of Narcissa's body that should hold her heart. "Don't."

Narcissa froze.

Keeping her gaze on her traitorous sibling, she moved to the door and opened it.

The men stood on the other side like they'd been in the middle of trying to open it. She started to ask about the Guard, but they lay sprawled on the ground, scattered throughout the hallway.

"Are they dead?"

Caillen flashed her that familiar shit-eating grin.

"Stunned. But don't think we didn't consider killing them. What about you?"

"Definitely not dead." She indicated Narcissa with a jerk of her chin. "It was my sister behind this like I originally thought, not my aunt."

Hauk tsked as he moved forward to cover Narcissa with his own weapon. For an instant, Narcissa looked like she was about to try and fight him, but since he literally towered over her, she thought better of it. He cuffed her hands behind her back while Caillen and Desideria went to check on Gwen and Kara.

To her complete amazement, Gwen pulled her into a tight hug. Until she went ramrod stiff. "You didn't kill Mom, right?"

"You heard Narcissa. I had nothing to do with it."

"Just checking." She pulled her back into her arms and held her. "Thank you, Des. Thank you!"

Caillen helped Kara to her feet. "Are you sure we shouldn't be taking this one into custody too?"

Desideria looked at Gwen. "Well?"

"Kara saved my life. Had she not pulled me out of Narcissa's line of fire, I'd be dead now."

Her aunt lifted her chin as if she was mortally insulted. "Unlike Narcissa, I take my oaths seriously. I am Qillaq and I would never kill someone in cold blood. Only in fair combat."

Narcissa curled her lip. "Oh shut up, you sanctimonious whore. I'm sick of all your—"

Hauk stunned her with his blaster.

Narcissa cried out before she slumped to the floor.

Hauk made no moves to break her fall. Instead, he holstered his weapon and met Desideria's gaze unabashedly.

"My mother always said that if you can't improve the silence, you shouldn't be speaking."

Fain let out a low whistle. "You stunned a girl, bro. Then let her hit the floor. Damn, and I thought I was callous."

Ignoring Fain, Caillen left Kara's side to stand by Desideria's. She could tell by his expression that he'd been worried about her. Without a word, he pulled her into his arms and kissed her with a passion that ignited that part of her that craved him most. And it made her hungry for so much more. Closing her eyes, she inhaled the warm scent of his skin and just savored this one moment of peace.

It was over.

Her sister and aunt knew she had nothing to do with her mother's murder.

I'm free...

Caillen tensed ever so slightly before he pulled back and turned her to face her sister and aunt who were kneeling reverently on the floor.

"My Queen," Kara said. "I will serve you every bit as faithfully as I did your predecessor."

Gwen looked up and actually smiled at her. "As will I. Long live Queen Desideria."

Strange how those words weren't as important to her now as they'd been before. Indeed, unlike Caillen, they left her completely cold.

Caillen draped his arm around her shoulders. Leaning down, he whispered in her ear. "You're back where you belong."

Why didn't it feel that way?

She looked up at him. "But you're still not off the hook. Karissa and her daughter are after your throat."

"Karissa?" Kara scowled at them. "My sister, Karissa?"

Desideria nodded. "She's the one who killed Caillen's father and blamed him for it. It appears she and Leran have been behind all of this madness."

Kara winced. "I should have known this would happen."

"How so?" Desideria asked.

"I knew Karissa hated us for the fact that she was forced into a political marriage. To her, it was beneath her and she resented the fact that your mother had won the throne. She swore to me that she'd live to see her daughter as our queen." Kara glanced to Narcissa and sighed. "Stupid child. They would have killed her too and Karissa would have been the one to rule here. Never would they have allowed Narcissa to keep this throne."

Because Karissa's offworlder husband was now dead...

That would clear the line of succession. She could easily return to Qilla and claim her former rank. The plan hadn't been to divide and share rulership. Karissa had wanted it all for herself and her daughter. And since Kara couldn't fight for the throne, with Desideria and her sisters out of the way, no one would have been able to stop her. Cold, but clever.

Caillen sighed. "It was a brilliant plan."

Kara let out a long sigh. "When you spend years plotting and executing it, it usually is."

Gwen shook her head in denial as she stared at Narcissa's unconscious form. "I still don't understand how they seduced Narcissa to help them. Why would she betray us?"

"Remember five years ago when I went to visit Karissa?" Kara asked her.

"You took Cissy with you."

She nodded. "They must have started their plans with her then and kept in touch with her after that."

And that explained why Narcissa's attitude had turned so cold at that time. Why she'd been so vicious toward her and Gwen. Not that she'd ever been particularly kind. But after that visit she had returned very different.

How tragic for all of them.

Gwen passed a pleased smile toward Caillen before she looked back at Desideria. "You'll be able to take a consort now, My Queen."

Yes, but inside she knew Caillen would never submit himself to her as a pet. It wasn't in him and she loved him too much to even ask it.

You could fight him. He would win and be her equal.

But she knew better. She would never take the chance of hurting him and if she didn't fight him with all her strength, the fight would be nullified by their laws.

All she wanted was to protect him. "If you stay here, Caillen, I can offer you political asylum."

He stroked her cheek with his thumb before he dropped his hand away from her face. "Appreciate it, but the League and her assassins would always be after me to finish this. They'd be in your affairs and could hurt any one of you in the crossfire. I have to clear my name and make Karissa pay for killing both my fathers and uncle. I owe them that much."

And once he did that, he'd be a ruler. Then they could never be together.

Her heart shattered with the cold reality.

"How are you going to do that?" Kara asked.

He shrugged with a nonchalance that made her want to beat him. "No idea whatsoever."

Forever by the seat of his pants. Her smuggler would never change.

"When do we leave?" she asked him.

He looked over at Kara and Gwen. "You're a queen, Desideria. Your place is here and your people need you. I finally understand that."

She hated the fact that he was right. She had to stay.

He had to go.

Pain hit her so hard, it was crippling. But she was Qillaq and they didn't show emotion. Especially not a broken heart. "I guess this is good-bye then."

He nodded. "You can always call me when you need someone to yell at."

"You're not good at taking that abuse."

"True, but I've learned to accept it from you."

Her throat tightened at his teasing tone. She'd miss that most of all.

Don't leave me, Caillen. Not here in this cold place with people who don't know how to laugh.

How to love.

She couldn't stand the thought of not seeing his smile every day. Of not listening to him banter with her and his friends.

I can't make it without you.

Those words hung on her lips. She wanted so desperately to say them. To beg him to stay with her and not leave.

But she couldn't. He belonged to a world she didn't understand. One where he needed freedom and independence.

Him and that backpack...

"Take care of yourself, Caillen." She was proud of herself for keeping the pain out of her voice.

"You too." He took her hand in his and placed a tender

kiss across her knuckles. But she wanted so much more from him than that...

Tears gathered to choke her as she savored the warmth of his hand on hers. The softness of those lips that had soothed and pleased her. She would never know that warmth again.

And when he let go of her, she felt her world shatter. The loss of his touch was more than she could bear.

Only the knowledge of Kara watching her...judging her, kept her from running after him and begging him to stay with her no matter the laws or the consequences.

She watched him leave with the others. He paused at the door to look back at her. She saw the agony in those dark eyes. The tangled emotions that said he wasn't any happier about this than she was.

With one last gentle smile, he left her and the agony she felt inside was enough to drive her to her knees.

You could abdicate. The words hung on her tongue as she met Kara's stern expression.

But that wasn't what a Qillaq did either. Her mother would be so disappointed in her.

So would her father. As queen, she'd be able to pardon her father at long last. Salvage his name for their records.

I want Caillen.

But life wasn't about wanting. It was about surviving and following your duty. When those things conflicted, obligation always won out.

Children followed their wants.

Duty commanded adults.

Funny, she'd spent her entire life wanting to be an adult and yet right now, in this moment, all she wanted was to be a kid again. To be able to follow her heart.

And the name of that heart was Caillen Dagan. Renegade. Smuggler. Pirate. Prince.

Hero.

Kara stepped forward. "So tell me, My Queen. What is your first command?"

With every step Caillen took that carried him farther away from Desideria, he felt a part of himself die.

Go back.

The call was so strong that it was almost impossible to resist. But he couldn't. He had to avenge his fathers and make sure the bitch who'd killed them paid for her crimes. No matter what his heart wanted, he had other obligations that took precedence right now.

Besides, they didn't belong together. Desideria was queen in a world that would never accept him and he was...

Outlaw. Scoundrel.

Worthless.

Your problem, Cai, is that you lack all ambition. Really, is this all you want out of your life? Yeah, Kasen's voice rang out loud and clear in his head. *"I don't know how you can be content smuggling hand to mouth all the time.*

"You're just such a waste, little brother."

He was everything a queen was told to avoid. Everything that would taint her reign. Yet his heart belonged to Desideria and there was no denying that one single truth. The only time in his life when he'd felt worth something had been in her arms.

If only he could go back...

Don't.

He had a mission to complete and once it was done, he'd be an emperor.

That thought made him shudder. But the one thing his real father and Desideria had taught him—noblesse oblige.

Chayden slowed as they neared the opening of the crypt. "Are you sure about leaving? Sanctuary's a hard thing to give up."

Caillen scoffed. "You turning craven?"

He narrowed his gaze at Caillen's emotionless question. "You know better." Sighing, he shook his head. "You are an idiot, Dagan. But far be it from me to point that out since going back to her means you'd be with my sister and that mere thought disgusts me. All I'll say is that if I had someone who would fight by my side, I wouldn't let her go. But that's just me and I've never had anyone worth fighting for. Damned if I'd turn my back on her if I did."

Caillen was about to go for his throat when all of a sudden his link buzzed. He started to ignore it and engage Chayden more. Until he caught the ID listed.

It was Darling.

Part of him was angry that Darling had lied to him about his father, but the other was still loyal to his friend no matter the aggravation. So he put the link in his ear and activated it. "Dagan here."

"Hey, drey. We have a little problem."

His gut knotted. What catastrophe now? "Does the League have our CL?"

"No." Darling's tone was completely dry. "That would probably be better."

Dread consumed him even more. "What then?"

"While your father was about to call a press conference, Desideria's mother took advantage of the distraction to escape my custody."

Caillen scowled as he tried to understand what Darling was saying. "My father's dead."

Darling sucked his breath in sharply. "Um...Not exactly."

"What is 'not exactly' dead, Darling?"

"Don't get mad. It's why I sent Hauk to you instead of coming myself. We wanted to flush out the traitors, so I talked your parents into pretending to be dead long enough for the real traitors to expose themselves. The footage you saw of their supposed assassinations was something I had Syn fake. It was all digital animation."

He would call him a liar, but he knew exactly how skilled Syn was on a computer. There was nothing that man couldn't do.

Darling cleared his throat before he continued speaking. "I convinced both of them that if their enemies thought they were dead, you two could stay ahead of them long enough for us to find out who's behind all of this. Her mother caved before your father did, by the way. Said she'd love to test her daughter's mettle even if it meant throwing her to the wolves. Your dad took a lot of convincing. The last thing he wanted was to see you hunted or hurt."

Yeah, that sounded like his father.

"Both of them have been with me the entire time. However, I had to stand hard on your father to keep him hidden and safe while you've been under fire. Believe me, it was no small feat. That man is wicked insane when it comes to you."

Caillen glared at Hauk. "Did you know my father was alive?"

Hauk actually blushed.

Damn them for that. "You lied to me?"

Darling let out an irritated breath. "Let's not argue semantics right now. That's not important."

The hell it wasn't...

"What you need to focus on is that we achieved our objective," Darling continued—it was a good thing the little bastard was nowhere near him right now or he'd make him limp. "The traitors revealed themselves. The problem is your father found out about your uncle's murder—"

"Not my fault. I didn't know he had news access," Maris said over Darling.

Darling took a second to shush him before he continued. "Your father wanted to call for the press so that he could clear your name before someone killed you for something you didn't do. While I was locking him in his room, Desideria's mother took off on her own. She wants the blood of her sister and niece over this treachery, and she won't stop until she has it."

Caillen's concern for his father's safety far outweighed his anger and irritation over their deceit. That familiar battle calm settled over him. "Where's my father?"

"Nykyrian's palace, surrounded by security. I couldn't think of anywhere safer."

He was right about that. Since Nykyrian's wife and children were there, that place was without a doubt the most secured building in existence.

"And Desideria's mother?"

"Commandeered a ship out of the hangar. Since she was leaving and not coming in, security didn't realize they'd screwed up until after she was gone. I hacked her flight plan and she's headed straight to Exeter, no doubt to execute her sister and niece."

Oh yeah, this was bad. And he had no doubt that Darling's speculation was right. Sarra wasn't exactly known for her calm rationale.

She'd be out for blood.

Caillen growled as his thoughts kept coming back to one truth. "They'll kill her if she comes out of hiding."

"Yes, they will."

And if she wasn't Desideria's mother, he'd say good riddance. That kind of stupid needed to be strained out of the gene pool. But in spite of everything, she was Desideria's mother and he couldn't let her die.

"Where are you?" he asked Darling.

"In my fighter, heading after her. I'm hoping I make it in time to stop her from committing suicide. If not, I plan to go down fighting beside her stupid ass."

Saddest part? He knew Darling would stay true to those words.

Which meant they were all heading to the gallows.

22

"You should tell Desideria our mother is still alive."

Caillen arched a brow at Chayden's comment. "You need to pilot and not worry about it. We need to tel ass as fast as possible."

"Yeah, but—"

"Chay, what good will it do to tell her her mother's alive if her mother gets herself killed in the next hour? Really? Call me provincial, but to me it seems cruel to say, guess what? Your mom's alive. Oh wait. She *was* alive. Now she's dead again 'cause our worthless asses couldn't save her. Sorry, hon. Hope you're okay with me jerking your emotions around and stomping on them. And while I'm at it, you got a newborn puppy I can kick too?"

"He has a point."

Chayden glared at Fain for that last comment. "Stow it, Hauk." Then he glanced at Caillen. "Fine, but when she wants your head over the fact you neglected to tell her about this, remember *I'm* the one who tried to save your hide."

"And here I thought I screwed up metaphors." Caillen focused all of his attention on catching up to Darling. Honestly, he didn't want to give Desideria any more bad news. He wanted to be able to tell her that her mother was alive and well. To see the joy and relief on her face, not the sadness.

I can't believe I'm out to save the life of a woman I detest. It would be a public service to let the bitch die.

But Desideria's happiness meant more to him than that.

Fain cursed, drawing their attention to him.

"What is it?" Chayden asked.

"A hornet's nest." He pushed his images up to the main monitor for all of them to see what he was looking at.

Caillen winced as he saw a sizable army heading straight for them. "League fighters?"

"Can't make the markings. But I don't think so. They're not shooting at us."

Chayden hailed the newcomers.

No one spoke or even breathed while they waited for the response. At first all they had was static.

Until a soft voice broke through the stillness. "We're here to assist."

Caillen gaped at the last thing he'd expected to hear.

Desideria's face showed on their com screen.

Amazed, he gave her an arch stare. "What are you doing, sweetie?"

Her smile warmed him. "I'm saving you. You can't go in there alone. I mean, you can. But I don't want to see you hurt. After you left, it dawned on me that I have an army at my disposal. So here we are, assisting you until your name's cleared."

He shook his head at her. "Don't you have a government to run?"

"It'll be okay for a few hours. With Narcissa arrested, there's no immediate threat."

Chayden muted them. "You better tell her."

He was right.

This time.

"Feed the transmission into the bunk room." Caillen unstrapped himself and headed off the bridge to talk to her alone. There was actually a lot of stuff he wanted to talk to her about. But this wasn't the time or place.

The one thing though was the tenderness in his heart for a woman who put everything on hold to come to his aid. She didn't know about her mother or the fact that his name was cleared because his father was still alive.

She had no reason to be here.

Except to keep him safe like she'd said.

And this time he knew what name to give the confusing feelings he had inside him where she was concerned. He loved her. Loved her in a way he would never have thought possible. He trusted her and he would give his life to keep her safe.

Those thoughts hung heavy in his mind as he turned on the link in the bunk room and saw Desideria's beautiful face again. Oh yeah, that was what he needed.

No, what you really need is her naked in your bed.

There was that...

"Hey, beautiful. I have some news for you. Are you alone?"

She gave him a droll look. "Fighter only sits one."

He arched a brow at her dry tone. "I didn't know you could fly. You've been holding out on me."

She smiled. "Only Qillaq fighters. I know nothing about other craft."

Yes and no. Flying was flying. But he could understand her reservation, especially if she couldn't read the language for the gauges and controls. That was a one-way trip to the hospital.

Or morgue.

And as he stared at her, he realized how much he liked being around her. Even when she made him crazy.

"Are you just going to stare at me?"

He grinned at her question. "I might."

"Not really productive."

"But highly entertaining. At least from my perspective."

She shook her head that was covered by a flight helmet. He had to admit he much preferred her open-face style to the League and Sentella's closed helmets. This way he was able to enjoy seeing her.

"Okay," she stretched the word out. "If I cut you off, it's because I need to lead my people and—"

"That's what I wanted to talk to you about."

She frowned at him. "Not sure I like your tone of voice."

"That's because I'm not sure how you're going to take this news."

She screwed her face up in distaste. "More bad news?"

"From my perspective, definitely. From yours, probably not so much."

Fury darkened her eyes. "Stop playing this game with me, Caillen. Spit out what I need to know."

"Your mother's alive."

Both of her brows shot up this time. "Pardon?"

"She was in hiding to draw out the traitors. Now that

she knows who they are, she's headed for them to kill them."

"Is she insane?"

He laughed, grateful she saw it the same way he did. "I'm not touching that one since she's your mother."

"Is she alone?"

"Darling should reach her . . . hopefully in time."

She cursed with a word that shocked him. "There's no way to teleport there, is there?"

"Not if you want to be intact when you arrive. The distance is too great and there's too much interference."

"Can Darling fight?"

"Oh yeah. Don't let his diplomatic demeanor fool you. He's as skilled and fierce a fighter as any assassin the League ever trained. More skilled than most. Something I tend to forget too until I see him in action. He might be shorter than most of us, but he can kick ass with the best of them."

"If he reaches her in time."

"Yeah."

The sudden sadness in her eyes was like a punch to his gut.

"When did you find out she was alive?" she asked.

"A few minutes ago. We were heading to intercept her and Darling when you showed up."

Disbelief etched itself into her features. "You were going to protect my mother even though you hate her?"

"Only for you, baby. Nothing and no one else could motivate me for this suicide venture I promise you."

Desideria swallowed at those words that tightened her chest. She'd never loved him more than she did right now. "Thank you."

He kissed his fingertips, then held them out to her in a sign of respect and caring. "Do me one favor."

"Sure."

"When the fighting starts, hang back. I know it flies in the face of your entire being. But for me, hang back."

Right... he was out of his mind if he thought she was going to send him in and then stay back while he put himself in harm's way. "What if I asked the same thing of you?"

"Yeah, but—"

"No buts, Cai. I can't stand the thought of you being hurt and you're already wounded. It's not fair of you to ask me to abstain from the fight when you're not willing to do the same for me."

"I really hate it when you make sense."

She smiled. "I know. I feel the same way about you."

"So should we blow this whole thing off and go grab coffee? Or preferably a bed?"

She rolled her eyes at him. "You're terrible."

"True." He took a deep breath. "Okay so we go with Plan B. Both of us get our asses kicked. Then we limp to a bed where I kiss your boo-boos and you kiss mine. Yeah. That still works."

She laughed. "What am I going to do with you?"

"As long as it involves our mutual nakedness, I'm up for it."

"Cai—"

"Really," he said, interrupting her. He looked down at the bulge in his pants. "I'm definitely up for it."

Yes, he was adorable in a completely irritating way. "I'm cutting the transmission now."

"Don't."

Desideria hesitated at the grave tone of his voice as he said that single word. "Give me one reason why I shouldn't."

"Because when I look at you, I can see into infinity."

Frowning, she wanted to understand what he was saying. "What does that mean?"

"I love you, Desideria."

Now he said that? She sucked her breath in sharply at words she'd never expected to hear.

"That was why I said 'um' earlier. I couldn't get the words out in front of other people."

"Why are you telling me this now?"

"I have no idea. I know we can't be together. Your destiny is completely different from mine. But should something happen to one of us, I wanted you to know how I feel. I never thought I'd find someone who makes me as crazy as you do. Someone who could mean so much to me."

She knew exactly what he meant since he did the same thing to her. "I love you, too."

Caillen froze at those precious words. "Really?"

She nodded. "Why else would I be here?"

"You live to fight."

"Not really. I hate fighting. But don't tell anyone."

"I would never betray you."

She placed her hand against the camera. "I hate you for not telling me this when we were together."

"Yeah, I suck that way."

"You don't suck...much."

He flashed a grin at her. "Fly safe."

"You too. I'll see you on Exeter." She cut the transmission.

Caillen stood there for several minutes as the reality of what he'd done slammed into him.

He'd made a commitment. A declaration. Never in his life had he ever professed love to anyone not related to him. Not even his own father. It wasn't what he did and yet he wanted to tell her again and again.

I'm such a sappy dumb ass. Too many years with his sisters had corrupted him. All his life he'd prided himself on being able to manipulate any woman in the universe.

Until Desideria.

She controlled him completely. There was nothing he wouldn't do for her. He'd sell his soul just to make her smile.

So why did their relationship have to be impossible?

Not wanting to think about it, he returned to the bridge where Chayden and Fain were arguing over the best course of action. Normally, he'd join in but right now his thoughts were on the army following them and the woman who'd brought them to him.

If I could only have one more day alone with her . . .

By the time they reached Exeter, Caillen was mentally pacing the floor. They'd tried several times to reach Darling, but he hadn't answered. That could be good.

Or *really* bad.

Caillen was the first one off the ship. He didn't wait for Desideria, Hauk, Fain or Chayden. He went straight for the Exeterian palace. With any luck, they might be able to end this before Desideria landed. Something that would keep her safe and him sane.

But as soon as he left the hangar closest to his father's palace, he knew it wouldn't be that simple. There were flames spiraling from the remnants of the front gate. Soldiers were mobilized, yet no one seemed to be in charge. Plain and simple, it was a chaotic war zone where the soldiers wandered around as if looking for someone to tell them what to do. So much so that no one even recognized him.

His heart hit his stomach.

What the hell had happened? There were bleeding soldiers in the street, firefighters trying to control the flames on the north quadrant of the palace and civilians crying and rushing around while medics tried to tend the wounded.

Caillen flipped on his wrist link and ran the locator for Darling. "C'mon, buddy, be in Sentella gear." Each of their suits was equipped with a chip that would allow them to find a fallen comrade. Only the Sentella and those approved by Nykyrian were allowed to know the tracing frequency.

Luckily, Caillen was one of the trusted few.

For a handful of seconds, nothing showed up. But as he rounded a corner, he saw the small, faint dot that indicated Darling's location. Caillen followed it quickly toward his father's office in the palace.

As he neared the main hallway, he saw a familiar form on a stretcher.

Maris.

His heart pounded as he made his way toward him. Covered in blood, Maris had an oxygen mask over his face. His eyes widened the instant he recognized Caillen.

"What happened?"

Maris pulled the mask down. "We got here right behind the queen. She came in with her Guard and... it was a bloodbath. Not long after the fighting began, Darling shoved me out the door and before I could move, something exploded and shattered it all over."

"Where's Darling?"

"He was fighting beside the queen's Guard. Then I lost consciousness and when I came to, he was gone. I haven't seen him since."

Caillen bit back a curse as he put the mask back in place on his friend's face. "You better be all right, Maris. Don't make me buy a suit for your funeral."

He laughed, then winced in pain. "Find Darling. Tell me he's okay."

Caillen inclined his head to him, then went back to following his tracer. As he got closer to the study, the damage was more profound. The alabaster had black blast mark scars. All the furniture was shattered and he could see where the fire had licked and scorched the walls and ceiling. A dozen investigators were in the office, taking notes and conferring.

He followed the locator past them, out into the courtyard where bodies lay all around. This was where they were identifying and storing the dead until they could be transported to a morgue.

Pain and guilt rose up to choke him. Darling was his best friend. The one person he could always rely on whenever he needed anything. They'd been through hell together more times than he could even begin to count.

How could Darling be dead?

The dot started moving. For a second, hope flared. *They're just moving his body to a new spot*. It was the most likely explanation.

Heartsick, he closed the distance to where the largest

groups of bodies were piled. The sight sickened him. Darling was here somewhere.

"'Bout time you got off your lazy ass and made it."

For two seconds he couldn't breathe as he heard that refined accent that spoke his language and syntax. A dichotomy fitting only one aristocrat he knew.

Darling.

He saw the dark shadow leaning against the wall. In full Sentella gear, there was nothing on the outside to betray Darling's identity.

"Your voice distorter's broken."

"I know. It's why I haven't said anything while the Enforcers have hovered near me. I doubt they'd ID me, but not worth the risk."

Caillen scanned the bodies around them. "What happened?"

"The Qill queen is a fucking idiot."

He gaped at a word he'd never heard Darling use before. "Someone's a little pissed."

"Someone's a lot pissed and bleeding all over himself." That was the good and the bad about Sentella uniforms. They were designed to hide injuries. The only person who knew the wearer was wounded was the wearer. It was also what led to the rumor that the Sentella members were immortal and invincible.

"You need a doctor?"

"Yeah. Know one who can treat me without removing my helmet?"

There was that. Since they were wanted outlaws, exposing their real identities was a moron's move. "Hauk's with me."

"Too bad Syn isn't." Syn had once been a doctor. But

while Hauk had no official training, he was as good as most of the medics Caillen had dealt with.

Caillen urged him toward a bench. "You need to sit."

Darling balked and moved away from him. "Hell no. I don't want any of the yahoos to think I'm injured. They'd be all over me." To collect the massive bounty on his head.

That was something Caillen could definitely understand. "C'mon, I'll walk you out to him."

Darling scoffed. "You've got nerve being here uncovered. They still think you killed your father."

"Yeah, but they're not paying attention to me."

"All it takes is one and you're screwed. No offense, I'm over my stupid quota for the day and I really can't take another battle right now, so I'll just stand here bleeding until Hauk makes it to me."

"Your call." Caillen's gaze paused on the number of soldiers who'd gone down with obvious human wounds. "How much of this was you?"

"Most of it. The Enforcers have no idea what happened. Yet. The bomb Karissa set off took out about half the palace staff, hence the bodies around us. The moment she heard Sarra was coming for her, she had her daughter declare war on the Qills and they called in every trooper they could get. I give Sarra credit, she and her people cut through them in a way a League assassin team would envy."

"How many did you take out?"

"Not enough, hence my wounds."

He let out a "heh" sound at Darling's droll tone. "Where are the women now?"

"That's where it gets interesting."

"Interesting how?"

"I was side by side with four members of the queen's Guard when the bitches turned on me."

Caillen scowled, not sure he'd heard that correctly. "What?"

He nodded. "They killed the three members who were on the queen's side, then captured Sarra before she realized what was happening. As they were making their way out the back and scrambling for cover, I knew exactly what Karissa had planned—to kill all of us and buy herself time to escape. I tossed Maris out the doors and tried to save the men who were wounded."

"Of all people, you know how explosives work. You don't run toward them, buddy."

"Yeah and I knew your father's office would be shielded. The same thing that keeps a bomb from blowing it up on the outside also works for containing a blast when it occurs inside."

True, but Caillen didn't like his friend committing suicide either. "Why didn't you get out before the blast?"

"He pulled out six men and saved their lives."

Caillen turned to see Hauk joining them.

"I found one of the rescuees on my way here and he told me he owed his life to the Sentella." Hauk shook his head at Darling. "How wounded are you?"

"Enough that it hurts to breathe. But I've had worse." Darling turned his attention back to their conversation. "I have no idea where the women went. But I give them an A+ on Chaos Theory. They covered their tracks well. No one's going to be hunting them for a while."

Caillen let out a tired breath. Was this ever going to end?

"Hauk, get him out of here and patched up," Darling breathed.

Hauk hesitated before he complied. "What are you going to do?" he asked Caillen.

"Track them."

"I would laugh at your arrogance, but aside from your sister, you're the one person I know who could pluck the right particle out of dark energy." And given the fact that dark energy made up 70 percent of the universe, that was saying something. "Good luck, Cai."

"You too."

Darling wouldn't let Hauk help him so long as there were Enforcers around, but his slow methodical movements confirmed the fact that he was in some serious pain. Caillen admired him for carrying on in spite of it all.

"It's total chaos still. They're trying to sort through bodies."

Caillen froze at a deep, gravelly voice that had haunted his nightmares. A chill went over him as he scanned the people around him, trying to locate its source.

That bastard was here somewhere.

"I will see it done and call you back as soon as I can."

His gaze narrowed on a thin, balding man a few feet to his right. Though he was much older, the features were the same. Even now, he could see the man kicking his father over and shooting him dead.

A dark cloud of rage seized him. Before he even realized what he was doing, he'd crossed the distance in the yard and pinned the bastard to the wall by his neck.

Recognition widened the man's eyes as he struggled to breathe while Caillen held him in place with his forearm over his throat.

"You're only alive because I know you know where my aunt is. If you don't give me her location right now,

I'm going to yield to the need I have to carve you into pieces."

There was no missing the fear in his eyes. "I don't know what you're talking about."

Caillen pressed even harder against his neck. "I was there, hiding, when you killed my father in a back alley."

His face went pale. "What?"

"I saw and heard everything said between you and my aunt. And you were wrong. The garbage didn't burn. It grew into one seriously pissed-off man who's about to kill you."

The man started wheezing from his pressure.

Caillen backed off only a degree. He couldn't kill him yet. Not until he had the intel he needed. "Tell me where she is."

"They're waiting for me in the east bay."

"And the Qillaq queen?"

"She's with them as a hostage."

"Cai?"

He looked sideways as Fain joined him. "Perfect timing."

"For what?"

Caillen slung the man toward Fain. "Hold him. Watch him. Don't let him make a call or a text."

"Why?"

"Because if he's lying to me, I'll be back in a few minutes to kill him."

Before Fain could speak another word, he left them to head to the hangar. It didn't take long to reach it, mostly because he ran the entire way.

Until he reached the north bay where they'd landed. It was virtually empty. There were several large cargo ships and a dozen shuttles docked. But it was the craft with diplomatic markings that drew his interest.

All in all, a dumb choice. However, it fit his aunt's ego nicely.

Blood surged through his body as he headed for it. But after two steps, he rethought the sanity of charging straight in there and confronting them. *Don't let your temper lead you.* Because when it did, it always led to the grave.

He needed to let his battle calm take control. Yet for some reason, it had abandoned him. All he could see was his father dying. See his family struggling to survive with no parents. And why? Because of needless greed.

Let it go.

Something much easier said than done. Closing his eyes, he thought of Desideria. The moment he did, his anger dissipated. He found the peace he needed.

This time, he approached the ship from the back, through the shadows that had birthed and succored him. Even if they were scanning, they wouldn't pick him up. The main hatch was up which would stop most people from getting on board without notifying them. But the beautiful part about being a smuggler was that he knew ships inside and out. Best of all, he knew access points where cargo could be loaded or removed even under the nose of the best-trained Enforcers.

While this was a diplomatic ship, it still had a small hatch that allowed food to be brought on board so as not to disturb the aristocratic passengers. Located in the rear, under the left wing, it was a perfect place to sneak on board.

Making sure they couldn't see him, he quickly made

his way to it and pried it open. It didn't take long to crawl through it and into the galley. He slid into the ship, then closed the hatch. Pulling his blaster out, he went to the door and listened. The ship was so quiet that all he could hear was the beating of his heart.

But as he crept further down the corridor, he started picking up on a conversation.

"We should leave him."

"Don't you dare start this ship. He'll be here in a minute."

"Gah, what is wrong with you, Mother? You're supposed to be Qillaq. Why would you risk our safety for a man?"

"Sit down, you little ingrate. But for me, your father would have married you off years ago for political gain. Just like *you* did me."

Obviously that last comment was directed at Desideria's mother, which meant she was still alive.

That was always a good sign.

For Desideria anyway.

"Mother, you're impossible. We need to leave. Now!"

Caillen veered into the bunk room. As quietly as possible, he went to the crew station and hacked into the onboard computer so that he could use the video system to scout out the bridge.

His aunt sat in the captain's chair while her daughter was to her left. Two pilots were in the forward seats and Desideria's mother was bound and gagged in the seat behind his aunt.

The odds were definitely in his favor. But he had a better idea rather than barging in there and knocking their heads together.

Sealing and locking the bunk door, he opened an audio channel. "Nice move, ladies. But it won't help you."

Gasping, his aunt and cousin shot to their feet and drew weapons. "Where are you?"

"Close enough to be your innermost hemorrhoid."

His aunt motioned for the two pilots to get up and go search for him. Caillen locked down the bridge access doors tightly so that all they could do was pound on the unresponsive portal. The sight of their anger amused him.

Leran ran to the con to fire the engines only to learn that he had complete control of the ship. Not them. There was nothing they could do to retake it.

Not unless they were Syn. Which, luckily, they weren't.

Take that, you bitches.

His aunt cleared her throat. "Look, we don't have to be enemies. If you want we could split—"

"The only thing I'll split with you is your skull. I'm not dumb enough to fall for any lie out of your mouth."

She held her blaster at the queen's head. "Surrender to us or we'll kill her."

"Then kill her. I really don't care. You're the only one I want and I don't care how many bodies I have to crawl over to get to you."

His aunt looked around in disbelief. "Am I really the only one you want?"

"Yes."

She lowered the blaster. "Then you won't care if I kill my niece, Desideria?"

His heart stopped. He didn't dare say anything that might betray him.

She held a remote up in her right hand. "All I have to

do is press this button and Desideria's throat will be cut. Stupid chit is surrounded with my people who are more than willing to kill her on my command. Did you really think I planned all of this alone?"

Caillen scrambled to isolate the trigger's frequency. But he couldn't. Whoever had designed it had skills and it made his temper snap.

There was nothing he could do.

His aunt curled her lip in smug satisfaction. "If you're trying to jam my signal, don't bother. You'll never find it. Now be a good boy and surrender yourself or I'll see Desideria dead within the next minute . . . maybe two."

Caillen knew she would too. She'd already killed off her family. What was one more niece to her?

But that niece was everything to him.

What am I going to do?

In the end, he knew he had no choice. He couldn't let Desideria die.

"All right. Don't press it."

She laughed. "Just like a man. Weak to the end."

Yeah, he'd like to show her just how weak he was. But he wouldn't kill Desideria for his ego.

"Unlock the ship, then you'll have ten seconds to get up here. One second more and my niece will be nothing other than a bad memory."

Even though it galled him, he did exactly what she said. As soon as he'd reprogrammed the computer, he ran to the bridge where his aunt waited with a blaster aimed straight for his head. "Can't you *ever* die? You have been a pain in my ass since the moment you were born."

He raked a cold glare over her. "Yeah, well, you haven't exactly been the light of my solar system either, bitch."

"You pathetic lovesick fool. But that's all right. We can go ahead with our original plan. You killed the Qillaq queen and then we killed you as you were fleeing from the murder scene."

"No one will ever believe that."

"Sure they will. People are sheep. They believe whatever lies they're told, especially when it comes from the media. After all, the news never lies."

Sad thing was, he agreed with her. Most of the time they did.

"Get on your knees."

Caillen refused. "I kneel for no one. I'll die exactly how I've lived. On my feet." Defiant to the end.

"Fine." She flipped the switch from stun to kill an instant before the targeting dot centered on his forehead.

Caillen glared at her as he waited for the sound that would end his life.

A second later, another dot appeared over her heart. Frowning, his aunt looked down as puzzled by its appearance as he was.

"Only *I* get to shoot him."

His jaw went slack as he recognized Desideria's voice coming out of the pilot's mouth…

No, it couldn't be.

Could it?

It was obvious the pilot was female, but the suit gave no indication as to the wearer's identity.

Stunned, his aunt stepped back and aimed for Desideria. Leran started forward to attack her, but the other pilot engaged her.

His aunt went to shoot, but Caillen rushed her before she could kill Desideria. Something not too bright since the blast hit him hard in his chest. Even so, he refused to go down. He wasn't about to let her hurt Desideria.

Desideria rushed forward as she saw Caillen fighting her aunt for the blaster. The moment she reached them, she realized her aunt's shot hadn't missed him. Blood covered his chest and abdomen as he fought her with everything he had.

Anger and terror mingled inside her to form a deadly combination. All the rage of her lifetime built up—the betrayal her aunt had given them both. The fear that Caillen would die as a result of it.

Before she even knew what she'd done, she grabbed her aunt by the neck and snapped it with a sound that went through her like glycerin on glass.

For a full minute after Karissa slid to the floor, no one moved.

Horrified by her actions, Desideria felt dizzy—like something had snatched her out of her body.

I killed someone.

No, she'd killed her own aunt...

"Mom!" Leran's shriek finally broke through their shock as she ran to her mother's side and sank down on the floor. "Mom...please speak to me." She pulled her mother against her as she cried and begged her to be alive.

Caillen staggered back.

"Cai?" Desideria went to him while Kara crossed the bridge to release her mother from her ties.

His handsome features were pale and drawn tight by the pain. "I swore I'd never risk my life for any woman other than my sisters. What is it about you, pun'kin, that makes me stupid whenever someone threatens you?" His legs buckled.

Desideria grabbed him and helped him sink to the floor so as not to injure him more. She tore open his shirt, then gasped as she saw the damage done. The blast had torn through his left side and left it raw and gaping.

"You fucking whore!" Leran let her mother go and rushed for Desideria.

Without a second thought, Desideria was on her feet. She caught her cousin and slammed her down so hard on the ground that it shook the entire vessel. "You killed your own father, you piece of shit. Next time you come at me, you better bring a body bag. You *will* need it."

Both her mother's and Kara's eyes widened at her words.

Desideria cuffed her, then returned to Caillen. "Stay with me, baby."

He swallowed against his pain while she called for a medic evac.

She cut the link, then pulled him against her while her cousin screamed for vengeance.

"Oh shut up, you whiny child." Sarra snatched the blaster from Kara's hand, then switched the setting from kill to stun and shot her.

Kara looked surprised. "You didn't kill her?"

"Oh no. I want the pleasure of seeing her in prison, of torturing her until she begs for a mercy I have no intention of giving her."

Desideria ignored them while she focused on what mattered most. Caillen's blood was all over her as she tried to slow his bleeding. "Where's your backpack?"

"I was so busy trying to end this before you got here that I forgot it."

She felt the tears sting her eyes. "I should have told you

our plan. But I didn't know who among our troops could be trusted and I was afraid a traitor would warn Karissa." Now she wished she'd chanced it. She'd much rather be the one on the floor. "If I'd only known you were going to do something so stupid…"

He smiled, then grimaced. "I'm only stupid for you."

And he'd traded his life to keep her safe. "I love you, Caillen. Don't you dare die on me. So help me, I will chase you to hell to beat you if you do."

"Only a worthless bastard like me would find that endearing."

"You're not a bastard and you're not worthless. You are *everything* to me." She grabbed the link again. "Where the hell are the medics?"

Caillen cherished the sound of concern in her voice. If he had to die, he was glad it was in her arms. He could think of no better way to go into eternity than staring into the beautiful eyes that had given him his soul back.

For her, he fought for his life harder than he ever had before. He'd waited too long to find someone like her to give up now.

She didn't let go of him until the medics arrived. Only then did she pull back and allow them to work on him.

His gaze never wavered from hers. Not even when they put the oxygen mask over his face.

Desideria choked on a hidden sob at the sight of Caillen lying on the gurney. He looked so weak and pale.

Even so, he winked at her. When he spoke his words were muffled by the mask, but still discernible. "I'm not going to die on you, cupcake. I've got too many boo-boos for you to kiss and you owe me a big one for the hole in my chest."

She laughed through the tears that tightened her throat. "I don't find you amusing." She stepped back to give them more room. "I'll follow you to the hospital and let your sisters and father know."

The medics took him out. She started forward only to find her way blocked by her mother.

Some emotion she couldn't name darkened her mother's eyes as she locked gazes. It was like her mother was looking at a stranger and she didn't know what to think of her. "What happened to you?"

Desideria wasn't sure how to answer that. She'd been chased, beaten, shot at.

And she'd learned to love in a way she'd never thought possible.

"I don't have time for this." She brushed past her mother and headed for the door.

"You don't have my permission to leave."

Those words and that hostile tone of voice went over her like an acid bomb. Her days of cowering were over. She'd blame it on her hour as queen, but she knew the truth.

Caillen had given her this gift.

She turned to meet her mother's glare with one of her own. "I'm no longer a member of your Guard, Mother. Remember? You dismissed me."

"Let her go, Sarra," Kara said. "She's only half Qillaq anyway."

Desideria lifted her chin as Kara's words angered her more. "And proud of it." She narrowed her gaze on her aunt. "My father wasn't a traitor. He was a damn good man and I'll cut the throat of anyone who says differently. You should also remember, Kara, that I spared your life once and saved it another. I'm not a child anymore and I will not be treated as one by any of you ever again. You don't run my life. *I* do."

Her mother pulled on the gold chain that she always wore around her neck, a chain she kept tucked right over her heart. As it came free of her body, Desideria saw that a ring dangled from it. The deep purple stone carved with a coat of arms gleamed in the light. Her mother paused to look at it before she held it out to her.

Frowning, Desideria wasn't sure she should take it. "What is that?"

Her mother grabbed her hand, placed the ring in her palm and closed her fingers over it. "That was your father's insignia ring. He was a prince on his world and yet he chose to stay with me even though he knew he'd never be respected again. Even though he knew he'd never see his family." To her complete shock, her mother's eyes teared. "You're right, Desideria, he didn't betray our people, but he did betray me. He swore he'd come back and instead he was killed in a ridiculous accident when the fuel line in his ship ruptured."

Desideria couldn't breathe as she realized her mother had lied to her about his death. "He wasn't fighting?"

She shook her head. "My son ran away from his training facility. He was all alone and I was terrified of what would happen to him. Your father went to bring him home to me. He swore he could find him and he was the only one I knew who could, so I let him go."

"Why did you lie to me all this time?"

"You were too young to understand and I didn't want you or anyone else asking me questions when the mere thought of his death was more than I could bear. You were the only one who loved him as much as I did and I didn't want you to hate him for leaving us. I'd rather you hate me and cherish his memory. He deserves that much more than I do."

She was appalled by her mother's twisted logic. "You allowed everyone to call him a coward. How is that love?"

Her mother winced as if the question hit her like a blow. "I'm not perfect and I hated him for years afterward. I kept thinking if he'd been stronger he would have lived. I know it doesn't make sense, but I thought if other people insulted him, it would keep me strong."

That had to be the most screwed-up thing she'd ever heard. And to think, they allowed her mother to lead their planet...

Part of her felt sorry for her mother, but the other part wanted to slap her for what she'd done to her father, her brother and her.

"I don't understand why you're telling me this now."

Her mother glanced at Kara before she spoke. "I was stupid when I was young. I put duty ahead of family. And what did I get for it? One daughter who tried to kill me. A son I'll never see again. Two sisters who despise me, one so much she was planning on blowing my head off, and the only person who ever really loved me died because I lacked the temerity to stand up to a law I knew was stupid and keep my son where he belonged. At my side. Chayden should have never been in harm's way and your father should have been allowed to be the king he was born to be."

She reached out and cupped Desideria's cheek in her hand. "I've done a lot of thinking since you left and I've worried about you every step of the way. I wanted to see how you would fare on your own and you more than surpassed my expectations. Never have I been prouder of you."

Her mother sighed heavily. "All my mother ever gave me was the mantle of responsibility. What I want to give you is the freedom you need to not make my mistakes. You are your father's daughter. Only he ever stood up to me. And now you." She dropped her hand. "Go to your prince, daughter. Be with him."

"She'll be abdicating her place in our line if she does."

Her mother curled her lip. "So what if she does? Being queen has never brought me anything except misery." She turned back to Desideria. "You stood up for him when I tried to stop you a few minutes ago. Never stop doing that." She stepped away to let her pass. "Consider yourself disinherited."

Desideria felt the tears start to fall. For the first time in her life, she didn't try to hide them. "I love you, Mother." She took her hand and pulled her toward the door.

Her mother frowned. "What are you doing?"

"I have a surprise for you."

Her mother dragged her feet. "I don't know if I can take any more surprises today."

Desideria smiled. "Trust me, you're going to like this one." She looked past her mother to Kara. "I trust you can take care of Leran and Karissa's body?"

"Don't insult me with such an insipid question."

Desideria would have answered with an insult of her own, but it wasn't worth it and she didn't want to waste another moment when she could be with Caillen.

She took her mother out of the hangar and hailed a transport while she called Caillen's family and let them know what was happening.

It didn't take long to reach the hospital. But with the explosion her aunt had caused, it was total chaos. Fain and Hauk were in the bustling waiting room. At least they didn't appear to be wounded.

The moment they saw her, they got up and allowed her and her mother to have their seats. She skimmed the bloody areas of their clothes, but none of it seemed to be theirs. "Were you hurt?"

Hauk shook his head. "No, we're fine."

"So how did you know about Caillen?" She hadn't had a chance to call them.

They exchanged a confused frown. "What about Caillen?" Fain asked.

"He was seriously wounded. Aren't you here for him?"

Hauk cursed. "No. We're here for Darling. He was wounded protecting her." He gestured angrily at her mother. "Because she couldn't listen to anyone."

Her mother glared at him. "How dare you take that tone with me."

"Lady, if either of my friends die because of you I'm going to take a lot more to you than my tone. That you can bank on."

Desideria stepped between them. "Let's not kill each other right now."

With a regal lift to her chin, her mother took a seat while she continued to give both Hauks a snarled lip that said she didn't think much of them.

Before she could say anything else, Chayden came into their area with a drink carrier. Her heart pounded as she feared what reaction he might have.

You should have thought of that before now.

Yeah, she should have.

"They were out of dairy, so you guys'll have to man-up and drink it…" His voice trailed off as he saw her. A slow smile curled his lips. "Hey, sis. Where's Dagan?"

Her vocal cords froze as her mind debated what to do. How to tell him.

With no real idea and no better thought, she stepped aside so that he could see their mother. As she did so, Fain took the drink carrier from Chayden's hands so that he wouldn't spill the hot drinks on them or himself.

Silence rang out as her mother rose slowly to her feet.

The expression on Chayden's face said he was torn between wanting to hug her and kill her. Her mother's face was completely stoic. Desideria had no idea what she was thinking or how she would react.

Until her mother crossed the small distance and drew him into a tight hug.

Chayden stood there with his arms out, still not touching her. His confused gaze went to the Hauks and then to her.

Still their mother held him and rocked slowly back and forth. "You look so much like your father. For a minute, I thought I was seeing him again."

That was the wrong thing to say. Chayden all but shoved her away from him. "Don't even come at me with that shit." He turned his angry glare at Desideria. "You had no right bringing her here without clearing it through me first."

"I thought you'd be excited."

"Like having my fingernails peeled back…which I had done a couple of times when I was on Qilla."

The color drained from her mother's face. "What?"

"Oh don't give me that. You didn't think I left because it was warm and toasty. Surely you're not that stupid."

He took another step back. "I'm out of here. Hauk, call me later with a report on Darling." He turned around and headed for the door.

Her mother ran after him.

Desideria started to follow, but Fain caught her by the arm.

"Let them settle this on their own."

"Yeah, but—"

"No buts, Princess. Take it from someone who was disowned by his family, Chayden has to come to terms with this. It's hard to let someone back in your life after they've kicked you in the teeth."

Since she had no experience with what Chayden was going through, she deferred to Fain. But after her mother was gone for more than twenty minutes, she began to get worried again. "You don't think he's killed her, do you?"

Hauk tossed his cup into the wastebasket. "I was beginning to have that same thought. C'mon. Let's go check on them."

He led her across the room and back out the electronic doors. At first she didn't see them. But as one of the transports moved, she saw them standing together by the side of the building. Her mother appeared to be doing all the talking while Chayden listened with an unreadable expression. The only clue to his mood was the tic in his jaw.

Her mother turned and looked at her, then said something more to Chayden.

He nodded before he walked away.

Crossing her arms over her chest, her mother headed back to them.

"Is everything all right?" Desideria asked when she rejoined them.

"All right would be a stretch. But he is willing to talk to me in a few days, so maybe it's not all bad. How did you find him?"

She shrugged. "He's a friend of Caillen's."

Her mother shook her head. "So I owe him for keeping my daughter alive, saving my throne and now for giving me a second chance with my son...What other miracles is he capable of?"

Hauk rumbled a deep laugh. "Trust me, Dagan's no saint."

That was most certainly true. "No, but he is a war hero. He saved two thrones..."

Fain came running up to them. "Dagan's out of surgery and he's asking for you."

Desideria wasted no time heading back inside and finding a nurse to take her to Caillen's room. Sterile and cold, the room wasn't any bigger than her small bedroom. Caillen lay on the bed, hooked to more monitors than she'd ever seen before. A white blanket covered him.

"Don't get him excited," the nurse warned. "We need to keep his blood pressure down."

She inclined her head to the nurse before she crossed the room.

Even though his face was covered with a clear mask, he smiled at her. "Hey, sunshine."

Relieved that he was alive and alert, she took his hand into hers. "How are you feeling?"

"Like I got one leg shredded, sliced in the ass and then shot in the chest." He frowned as he saw the ring on her hand. "You get married while I was out of it?"

"It's my father's. My mother gave it to me."

"Really?"

She nodded. "I think she's coming around to things."

"Ah God, I'm dead, aren't I?"

She let out an irritated breath. "Stop being so melodramatic, you big baby."

"I'll stop if you promise you won't."

"Won't what?"

"Stop loving me." The tone of his voice brought tears to her eyes. She heard the deep vulnerability and fear.

"Don't worry, Cai. There's no way I could live without you."

He pulled his mask off and kissed her hand. "I'm going to hold you to that."

"Is that the only thing you're going to hold me to?"

He laughed evilly. "No. I still have boo-boos to be kissed."

"Well in that case...I better start with your lips."

Caillen's head spun the moment she kissed him. In all the misadventures of his life, he'd never expected to find someone like her. Never expected to feel this alive while he lay one step from death. But as he tasted her, for the first time in his life he looked forward to the future.

He now had a goal. To keep her with him to the day Death separated them. No one would ever come between them again. "Marry me, Desideria."

She nuzzled her cheek against him before she whispered in his ear. "Absolutely."

EPILOGUE

Six Months Later

Bogimir danced around Caillen's desk in silent aggravation as he screwed up the paperwork he was supposed to be filling out. "Boggi, I swear to the gods if you don't stop doing that, I will shoot you where you prance."

Huffing and puffing in indignation, Bogimir made a hasty retreat to the safety of Evzen's office. Whatever. Caillen had actually learned to enjoy his father's lectures. Better to be yelled out than to stand over the man's grave.

Sometimes you just had to suffer for your family.

Like right now. He wanted to burn all the crap on his desk. He felt like he was drowning in it.

Or worse, going snow blind.

Yes, he still had a small itch to climb into his ship and return to his old life. But all he had to do was think of Desideria in harm's way and it quelled his desire immediately. Nothing was worth risking even a hair on her head.

Kasen still wasn't happy with the arrangement.

However, Desideria's sister Gwen was more than grateful that Desideria had decided to live on Exeter as his wife.

He glanced to the wedding band on his hand and smiled. It still felt weird to have it there, but it served as a reminder of all she'd brought into his world. Every day they had together was better than the one before it.

A knock sounded on his door.

No doubt it was his father to bitch at him. "Come in."

To his delight, it was Desideria. Dressed in a cream gown that highlighted her dark complexion, she had a lovely blush on her cheeks that made him instantly hard.

Yesterday when she'd disturbed him, they'd had a hot interlude on his desk that had sent papers flying everywhere. It'd taken him hours to resort them, but he was more than ready for it again.

"What's up?"

She frowned. "I have a strange question."

"No, I'm not the one who ate your candy. It was Darling. I swear."

Laughing, she rolled her eyes at him. "It was both of you. I saw it on playback from the security monitors."

"Damn. I should have erased that." He pulled her down to sit in his lap so that he could feel her warmth.

"But that wasn't my question." She looked at the door and scowled. "Are you sure Darling's gay?"

"Yeah, why?"

She bit her lip before she answered. "I swear I just caught him ogling Maris's new female secretary."

Caillen scoffed at the mere thought. "You must have been mistaken. He's my best bud in the universe. I'd know if he wasn't."

"If you say so, but I know what I saw. Maybe he's bisexual."

"Again, I'd know."

She held her hands up in surrender as she straddled his waist. Oh yeah, this was what he needed.

"Fine. That wasn't what I wanted to talk to you about anyway."

His blood heating at the thought of tasting her, he slid his hand under the hem of her dress and skimmed it over her soft skin so that he could cup her bare bottom. "No?"

She slid closer to him until she pressed against his hard cock in a way that drove him insane. "No. Do you know what was six weeks ago?"

He searched his memory, but couldn't place it. "Baby, I barely remember what I had for dinner last night. Was it important?"

She leaned down to whisper words in his ear that hit him like ice water. "My birthday."

Caillen cursed at his stupidity. He'd wanted to remember it so that he could make it extra special for her.

How could he have forgotten?

I'm such an asshole.

"I am so sorry, Desideria. I can't believe I forgot. I swear I'll make it up to you. Tell me what you want and I'll get it. Anything."

She placed her soft hand over his lips to stop him from speaking. "It's all right. I promise I won't hold it against you. Besides you did give me the best present of all time."

Again, he tried to think of what he'd done six weeks ago. "What?"

She reached out and took his hand into hers, then led it to her stomach. "A baby."

His breath caught in his throat as those two words hung in the air between them.

A baby.

"Are you serious?"

Biting her lip, she nodded.

Caillen pulled her against him and held her close. Sheer ecstasy pounded through him. He was going to be a father. And the de Orczys would have a new heir.

Desideria smiled at the happiness she saw mirrored in his eyes. Strange, she'd always known she'd be queen one day. She just hadn't thought it would be on a world not her own. Caillen had given her everything she'd ever wanted.

But never the way she'd envisioned it.

That was his gift. He was unpredictable and wonderful... at least most of the time.

Still that was all right by her. As her father had so often said... Laugh as much as you breathe and love as long as you live. So long as she had Caillen and their baby, she knew she'd be laughing constantly.

And loving, and, most importantly, being loved forever.

Darling Cruel is the most highly
regarded co-conspirator of
Resistance leader Zarya Starska.
Together they're working to
overthrow the brutal government.
But when Zarya betrays Darling . . .
the hero becomes
the monster.

Please turn this page for a preview of

Please turn this page for a preview of

Born of silence

PROLOGUE

"You have to be the biggest manwhore in the entire universe. What are you trying to do? Tie Caillen for the record of how many people you can sleep with in a single month? And just so you know, his is twenty-two."

Maris Sulle, Darling's oldest and dearest friend, laughed at his dry tone. "You're only jealous *you* didn't get the waiter's digis."

Leaning back in his ornately padded chair, Darling snorted in response. He swirled the wine in his crystal glass while they finished eating lunch in one of the most exclusive restaurants in Perona—the capital city of the southern part of the Caronese Empire, where Darling's family had ruthlessly ruled for more than three thousand years.

After the brutal suck-ass morning he'd already had, he really wanted something much stronger than this weak shit to drink, but his public persona kept him from ordering the hard liquor he craved.

He could only drink that whenever he was alone. Even then, he had to be careful no one found out.

"I thought you were still involved with…" Darling paused as he tried to sort through all the men his best friend had been with over the last year. "I can't even remember his name now."

"Gregor?"

Darling snorted as he finally flashed on the last boyfriend's name, and it wasn't Gregor. He'd fear senility had already set in, but it was more he had a lot of other things on his mind. Besides, no one could keep up with Maris's ever revolving list of boy-toys. "I'm behind apparently. The last one I remember was named Destin."

"Drustan," Maris corrected. "And yes, you are. You really should try to keep up. That was a good two months ago, and I've had three since then." He looked down at the number on his mobile and smiled as he stored it. "Soon to be four."

"So does Gregor know he's being replaced?"

"Oh don't get me started on that repulsive slut. I caught him in flagrante delicto with his personal secretary. His secretary…really? If you're going to be a whore, the least you could do is not be a common, cliched one. Right?"

Darling laughed, then took a deep drink of wine before he spoke again. "I'll keep that in mind for future reference."

"Oh please. You're such a monk. I'm not even sure you've lost your virginity." With a deep, horrified expression, Maris looked up from his mobile and slapped his hand over his mouth as he realized what he'd said and the land mine of pain he'd unintentionally exploded all over Darling. "I'm so incredibly sorry, Dar. That was so insensitive of me. I didn't mean it. Gah, I can't believe I said that to *you*. I wasn't thinking. You know I would never, ever

hurt you . . . You can punch me if it'll make you feel better."
He clenched his eyes shut and tensed as if waiting to be hit.

It took Darling several more seconds before he could
club the monster from his past back into the closet, slam
the door on it, and then speak over the surge of harsh
emotions that gutted him.

"It's all right, Mari," he said finally, his voice decep-
tively calm. "I know you didn't mean anything by it."

But that didn't stop it from cutting him all the way to
the marrow of his bones.

He set the glass on the table and wished he could
rip some of his memories straight out of his skull. Most
pathetic part? As horrifying as *that* had been, it wasn't at
the top of the list of things he'd kill to forget.

Opening his eyes, Maris reached out and covered his
hand. "You're the strongest person I've ever known. You
know that, right?"

Strange, he didn't feel that way. Most days he felt
even more battered inside than he was outside. And here
lately those feelings of rage and resentment, of hatred and
vengeance, were forcing him into a place of darkness he
wasn't sure he'd make it back from.

Before he could stop himself, he brushed his hand over
the latest bruise on his cheek. Luckily the long hair he
wore covering the left side of his face concealed it and the
deep, rancid scar that no matter amount of plastic surgery
could get rid of.

Another pugnacious memory he could do without,
and a perpetual reminder that he really was in this world
alone.

His mobile alarm chimed.

Maris scowled. "What's that for?"

Darling cut the alarm off, then slid his mobile back into his pocket. "My uncle's activated my UNPS chip." A lovely nano tracking device that was so microscopic it couldn't be located, removed or jammed. But the one thing his uncle Arturo hadn't counted on was Darling's ingenuity in writing a program that would intercept Arturo's access to the chip. "I set the alarm to notify me whenever he sends his goons out to drag me home." A constant in his life that always fire-bombed his temper.

How the hell could he still be deemed a minor at twenty-eight years old?

Only by something as backwards as Caronese law...

A law originally designed to protect him and his people. Instead, it'd proven to be a jail sentence that had hung around his neck like a perpetual noose.

And honestly, he was getting really sick of all this shit. Kere, the feral warrior in him, wanted blood. Any day now, he expected that darkest part of himself to take over, forget all consequences, and lash out against the world. May the gods help whomever was in the line of fire when that happened.

In the past, he'd been able to quell his anger and outrage with cold rationale, but every day they were getting harder and harder to harness. No amount of logic soothed him anymore. If anything, the attempt to rationalize his situation and the injustice of his life made him even more furious.

He felt like he was starting to go insane from it all.

Daintily, Maris wiped his mouth with his linen napkin. "We should get going, then. I don't want you in trouble."

It didn't matter. The fact he breathed got him into trouble.

I can't take this much longer…

But he had to. It wasn't just his life on the line. It was his mother's, brother's, and sister's. And unlike his older brother Ryn, he wasn't about to turn his back on his family. Ever. Even if he hated his mother more than he loved her, he couldn't sacrifice her to his uncle.

He would never spit on his father's memory that way.

But he was getting really tired of holding that line. Sixteen years of utter bullshit had taken its toll on him. Not just physically, but mentally.

C'mon, Dar. Just eighteen more months. You can do it. Then he'd inherit his father's empire and finally be in control of his own destiny.

You don't really think that'll happen, do you?

He had to. Even though his gut told him that he'd most likely be murdered between then and now, it was all that kept him sane these days.

That and the one person he couldn't talk about to anyone.

Not even Maris.

Darling lifted his hand to signal the waiter they were ready for the check. If his uncle followed his usual routine, he only had about fifteen minutes before he was dragged out of here by royal guards.

That was the last humiliation he needed, especially after this morning's round of Humiliate Darling in Front of the Ruling Gerents.

Don't think about it. He would be governor soon, and then they'd all learn just how not weak he was.

He pulled his card out and laid it on the table. He didn't need to look at their bill. It didn't matter to him if it was right or wrong. Time meant more to him than money did.

The waiter came by, flashed a dimpled smile at Maris, and took the check and card.

He was back in record time...with a small container of the cake Maris had started to order, then changed his mind about. There was something to be said for Maris's outrageous flirting. They always received the best service in the United Systems.

Darling pressed his thumb against the scanner, then signed his name on the electronic ledger. As soon as the payment was accepted, he got up and followed Maris toward the entrance.

"Where are you heading after this?" Maris asked as he held the door open for him.

What Maris really meant was where would Darling try to hide to keep from being dragged home like a felon, and beaten because he'd dared to have five minutes of peace out of his uncle's sight.

"I'll grab my fighter and head over to Caillen's for a while. I haven't had a chance to see my goddaughter since she started walking. What about you?"

Maris glanced back into the restaurant. "I want to grab something, all right. But it's not a fighter."

In spite of his disgust at having to leave so abruptly, Darling laughed. It was what he loved most about Maris. No matter how bad he felt, Maris could always amuse him. "Seriously, you want to come with?"

"Sure. I can always stare at Caillen. That man..." Maris bit his knuckle with lustful glee.

Darling shook his head as they joined the huge crowd on the street and had to push their way through the sea of shuffling bodies. "Better be careful, his wife might get jealous."

"True. And I'm not dumb enough to upset a woman who knows how to use a blaster and a blade. I like my body parts attached."

Darling didn't respond. Damn, the crowd was always thick this time of day, but this was ridiculous. He could barely get through them.

Then again, he should be grateful. It would slow down his uncle's men and help conceal him from them.

His alarm buzzed again.

"Bastard." He snarled under his breath before he looked down and reached to silence it.

"Dar! Forward front!"

With reflexes honed by the best assassins in the business, who'd taught him to protect his vital areas, Darling turned around at Maris's warning. The instant he did, he felt the sting of a knife sliding into his flesh, just below his shoulder blade.

A knife that had been aimed at his heart.

Cursing, he reached around to catch the assassin's wrist. For several seconds, Darling's blue eyes glared into those deadly gray ones that were too stupid to realize their owner had just made a fatal mistake.

The assassin yanked the knife out.

Grinding his teeth against the pain, Darling let him. But the moment it was clear of his flesh, he tightened his grip on the man's wrist and head-butted him. Wrenching the assassin's arm, he heard the bone snap before the knife fell from his broken hand. The assassin came at him with another knife he'd pulled from a sheath on his leg.

Bring it...

Darling jumped back, out of his reach. Stomping his left heel on the pavement, he ejected the blade in the toe of his boot and used it to catapult the knife on the street up so that he could catch it with his hand. People realized what was going on and began to scatter, screaming in fear of being accidentally injured or killed in the fight.

The assassin lunged again.

The demon inside Darling salivated for blood. He gave the assassin an insidious smile as he twirled out of the assassin's reach. He rolled around the man's back, then turned and stabbed him in the shoulder.

His attacker screamed out and whirled to lunge at Darling again. Laughing, Darling motioned at him with both hands, daring him to come closer. The assassin scowled at the knife Darling had cradled in his palm—the way he held it let the bastard know that he was as proficient with a blade as the assassin was.

For the first time, fear darkened the assassin's gray eyes. He dropped his knife and reached for his blaster.

His mistake.

Wanting to protect the innocent who'd be shot down with him, Darling grabbed the assassin's arm and twisted until he was at the assassin's back. Before the assassin could recover, Darling grabbed his chin, lifted it up, and made one hard slash across his throat.

Darling shoved him forward.

Choking, the assassin fell to his knees on the sidewalk. He clutched at the gaping wound, trying to block the blood that flowed between his fingers.

His anger boiling, Darling stood back to watch. The decent part of him wanted to finish the assassin off and end his suffering. But the part of himself that was slowly devouring his conscience enjoyed seeing his struggle to live.

Let him die in utter agony. It was what he deserved.

Better him than me.

Darling quickly glanced around to make sure there was no other threat coming for him. His gaze met Maris's and he saw the horror in his friend's eyes. He thought it was over what he'd done, until Maris stepped forward.

"You're bleeding really badly on your back. Are you okay?"

Only then did Darling feel the pain again. "Yeah. It hurts like hell, but I'll live." He'd had far worse wounds than this. And those given to him by people who supposedly loved him.

The assassin continued to writhe on the ground, begging for mercy in a black jacket that held over three dozen hash marks on its sleeve—a sick accounting that bragged about how many people he'd murdered. And he'd intended to add one for Darling's life.

He curled his lip at the bastard who'd tried to kill him.

His friends had dubbed him "Kere" as a joke. The Caronese god of the death, Kere was said to pull all of his sustenance from the blood of his enemies. He lived to fight and drew strength from those who begged him for clemency. Since Darling was normally so even keeled and easy-going, they'd thought it funny to call him that.

But now...

There was no pity as he stared at the man who was dying from the vicious wound he'd given him. In fact, he only felt one thing...

Would you die already, and shut the fuck up while you do it?

Before he even realized what he was doing, Darling grabbed the man's blaster from his holster and shot him with it.

A single shot through the back of his head.

Darling stood there on the street with the blaster smoking and his hand as steady as it could be. Worst of all, he felt nothing about his actions. No regret. No remorse.

Total emptiness.

He wasn't sure when it'd happened, but he'd become as callous and numb as any assassin he'd ever known. His emotions were now strangers to him.

There was only one person who could still reach past it and make him feel something other than his own bitter pain and rage.

Please, God, help me...

This time, he knew the horror in Maris's dark eyes was definitely over his actions.

"You're really beginning to scare me, Dar."

Yeah... I'm beginning to scare me, too.